I0738278

A novel by Daryl Leonardo

Palm trees, beaches, and rolling seas
The waters will carry both you and me
Though a storm brews upon the horizon
When our boat sinks, please, don't you be frightened

I'll gather you, we won't sink below
The surface, we'll reach, so don't you let go
You will not drown with me at your side
I'll hold you until the weather subsides

This story was meant to be my way out. I was feeling really stuck, and I had no idea what to do with my life. I wanted to be an actor since I got into Theatre during my sophomore year of high school, but I wasn't aware of any opportunities for me where I was living at the time. I was also under the impression that, being who I am — an LGBTQ person of color — roles were likely to be limited. So, I decided to write my own and set off to write a screenplay. I pulled a lot of inspiration and even directly lifted a few aspects and events from my own life to put this story together. Once it was finished, I sent it out to different script agents whose contacts were listed in a reference book I picked up at a local bookstore. I got one rejection letter, which I pinned to my bedroom wall to serve as proof that I was actually reaching someone.

The screenplay eventually got shelved. I had all but forgotten about it until years later when I dug it up with the idea of adapting it into a musical, and then a comic series that I'd post on Instagram, and finally a novel. These characters and this story were meant to be my way out when I was feeling stuck, and I keep coming back to them as if they are. So, in a way, I guess they *are*. My hope is that I'm able to share that with people. As someone who likes to tell stories, I think my ultimate goal is really to be heard and to reach people. The fact that you're reading this is proof — just like that one rejection letter I had posted on my bedroom wall — that I am. So, thank you and enjoy.

drown

chapter one

erik

I'm standing outside of Andrew Logan's house. Yes, Andrew Logan, the football guy. I don't know what position he plays and even if I did, I wouldn't know what that means. Sports are confusing for me because I never learned the basics of them. Also, I'm not at all competitive when it comes to those types of things, but that's beside the point. Andrew invited me over to work on our science presentation. We got stuck as lab partners earlier this week and I can't say I was all that excited about it. I mean, he's not a bad student really; I just don't have very much in common with him. I don't know what we'd talk about outside of our project, or if we'd even talk at all.

"Hey, buddy," he says when he finally answers the door. He's wearing a half-smile that makes him seem more boyish than his chiseled features would suggest. He looks like a model with his perfectly quaffed golden hair, his sapphire blue eyes, and his strong jawline with a dimple in his chin. Normally, the kids at school would make fun of someone for having a "booty chin," but Andrew's was carved out with such perfection, it almost makes the rest of us look like we were God's mistakes. It's intimidating to be around him. I feel like a teapot standing next to him, short and stout. Though I feel like that around most people, seeing as I'm a vertically challenged Korean-Filipino mix, standing at only five foot four inches tall. "Do you need anything? Water? Soda?"

"I'm fine, thanks," I say. His house is one of those houses that doesn't quite live up to the person. Don't get me wrong, it's a nice enough house, but Andrew Logan is high school royalty. I expected him to live in a mansion or something. The fact that he lives in a single-story ranch style home that's decorated with things stolen right out of a seventies sitcom is... comforting. He's human.

"My room's this way," he says, leading me down the one narrow hallway in his house. I follow him, taking in my weirdly painted surroundings. The walls are an odd mixture of pink with a sponged on layer of tan. It makes everything look super old. And not in, like, that chic rustic way. "Excuse the mess," Andrew says apologetically, as he opens the door to his bedroom. It's smaller than I would've imagined. There's a pile of clothes strewn about in one corner. His bed is a twin that has yet to be made. There's just enough space to fit a small desk — which is covered in loose leaf papers — a wooden drawer chest, and an old non-HD TV. At least the walls in here are a solid blue color, as opposed to that strange off-brand Tuscan Villa motif his family's got going on in the rest of the house.

"Cute," I say. What? I'm trying to be polite.

"Make yourself at home," he offers. I go over to the bed and take a seat, setting down my backpack and pulling out my science textbook and binder. I've got all of our handouts hole punched and organized to make this project easier for us. We were assigned a chapter and we're supposed to put together a presentation to teach the material to the rest of the class. It feels like an unfairly tall order for the first quarter of our junior year, but what can you do?

"So, do you have any thoughts?" I ask. I'm not sure how to initiate a conversation with him. He doesn't seem at all prepared for me to be here. I gathered that much just looking at his desk.

"Um, honestly, I haven't even read the chapter yet," he confesses. What am I even doing here? "I thought maybe we could read it together. You know, so that we're both on the same page. Is that cool?"

"Uh… I guess that's fine." It's not fine, but I don't wanna be mean. I was just hoping that if I had to spend my Saturday in an unknown environment, it wouldn't be for too long. But now, I have to reread nearly forty pages of stuff about the Golgi Complex. That stuff is complex. Just look at the name!

"You seem upset," Andrew says. I shake my head quickly in denial.

"Not upset," I lie. "I'm just… weird. I don't really go to other people's houses that often. It's really out of my comfort zone. Especially since, you know, you and I don't really hang out at all."

"Well, why don't we put the project on hold and get to know each other?"

"What do you mean?"

"This thing's not due for another week. Why don't we just hang?" He picks up his football from atop the drawer chest and sits down on the bed next to me. "Do you like football?" I shake my head.

"I don't really know anything about it."

"It's not hard, really." He starts to explain things like the different positions of the game and how to score goals and whatnot, but I don't really get it. In fact, as soon as he started talking about the subject, I started doing this thing where I nod my head and go, "uh huh," but I'm not actually listening to a word he's saying.

"That's really fascinating," I say, eventually cutting him off. "You know, if we're gonna get through this project, we should probably just read the chapter and call it a day." At this point, I want to leave. We're not doing anything productive and it makes me really uncomfortable being in someone else's space. The only other person whose house I've been to is my best friend, Mackenzie's, and even that was a long while into our friendship before I made that move. I don't know. When I'm out of my element, I just feel like the world is judging me or something, and so I have to be extra careful about what I say or do and how I behave. I suppose that's why I'm kind of a homebody.

You see, I'm the type of person who likes to be at home, where I know the rules and I can be comfortable and safe. But I'm also the type of person who gets depressed when I don't get invited to parties I would never show up to to begin with. I'm a living breathing conundrum. But then again, so are most sixteen-year olds, so I don't really feel that special.

"You don't wanna just chill?" Andrew asks. He's staring at me with his sapphire-y eyes and I can't help but get lost in how pretty they are. Typically, when my eyes meet Andrew's it's because I've noticed that he's looking at me and then I get super self-conscious and start acting all stiff and wonky. I don't know why he looks at me, but I usually just chalk it up to a popular jock being judge-y. That's how high school is. That's how life is. I think?

My perception of high school has been greatly influenced by Hollywood, but there are some aspects of our school that don't quite fit that. For one.) being in the marching band is considered kinda cool almost, and two.) most of the cheerleaders — the ones I know anyway — are actually pretty nice. Knowing that, maybe I should give Andrew more credit. Maybe he's not just a judge-y jock. Maybe we can actually "just chill."

I take in a deep breath.

"You know what, sure," I say. "Let's just chill." The words feel incredibly awkward coming out of my mouth. Andrew smiles and then looks away. His expression is pensive and I'm starting to worry. Me saying, "just chill," couldn't have been *that* off-putting, could it? I watch as Andrew sits there, pondering whatever might be on his mind. I don't know if I should say anything, or do anything, or what, so I just keep watching him. Eventually, he takes a deep breath and then turns to me. I can tell he's nervous now, but about what? What would Andrew Logan have to be nervous about?

"Erik, can I ask you something?" he asks. There's a strange fear visible in his eyes and it's making me nervous now too. More so than I normally am.

"Sure," I answer.

"Promise you won't freak out or anything?" My heart starts thumping with anticipation.

"I guess." Say it. What is it? What is it, Andrew? He takes in another deep breath and I'm starting to freak out a little. Whatever he's gonna ask me feels like it's gonna be big. Mic drop at the end of a rap battle big. They do that at rap battles, right? It's not really my thing.

"Can I suck your dick?"

...

...

...

I'm not really sure if I heard him correctly. What did he say? What did he just say to me? Did I hear him straight? Did he just ask me if he could suck my... WHAT IS GOING ON!?

"Um... can you repeat that?" I finally manage. There's no way. There's no way I heard him correctly. It must've been that I was doing that nodding and "uh huh-ing" without really listening thing. This time I'll hear him straight.

"I said, 'can I suck your dick?'" he repeats. Ehhhhhhhhhhhhhhhhhhhhhhhhhhhhhhhhhhh...

Something must be wrong with my hearing. That, or he's playing a really strange and sexual practical joke on me. Maybe he's just trying to be funny and wants to see how uncomfortable he can make me. I mean, it's no secret that I'm Catholic. Like, VERY Catholic. My mom makes me carry around a pocket Bible and I'm always wearing a scapular under my shirt and a cross around my neck.

"Can you say that one more time?" I repeat after a long pause.

"Erik, are you messing with me?" Andrew says with a mixture of disappointment and confusion.

"No! I'm just… I… I'm… uh… I'm not sure what you're asking me." I can hear myself stuttering and jumbling my words all together.

"What, 'can I suck your dick?' isn't clear enough?"

"Oh… so that… *that*… that is what you said."

Andrew shakes his head and smiles, though it's a defeated disingenuous one.

"Look, just forget I said anything," he says.

"Why did you ask me that?" I question, still completely unsure of his motive.

"I dunno. I thought I'd give it a shot. Why do you think I invited you over on a Saturday when my parents aren't home? I mean, it's kinda obvious that you've had a little crush on me. I can tell you've been sorta in-fatuous."

"That's... not a word."

"You know what I mean. So, you wanna do this or what?"

"I… I don't know how to respond to that," I say. I'm still trying to figure out what exactly is happening at this moment because I'm not only confused by his question, I'm also a little insulted by it. "What... makes you think I'm gay?"

"I'm sorry if you're not," he replies. The look in his eyes tells me that he means it. "It's just that's how it seems. The way you look at me like you do."

"I only look at you because I always notice you looking at me."

"Yeah, because I'm trying to figure you out."

"You wanna figure me out?" For some reason, him wanting to figure me out hits me pretty hard. I've never known anyone, aside from Mackenzie, who's shown any interest in figuring me out. I'm usually the guy that no one pays attention to. I'm the guy that people forget is there when I'm standing right there. I'm that short, kinda chubby kid in the glasses who the other kids see in the hallway but don't know his name. I'm Mr. Might-As-Well-Be-Invisible. To hear that a guy like Andrew Logan — golden boy sports guy — wants to figure me out, that makes me feel… visible.

We sit in silence for a moment. There's an uncomfortable tension between us, but it's different than the uncomfortable tension I walked in with. Something in my gut is pushing me towards him. A part of me wants to get closer to him. And that scares me. It scares me because to let that happen would be a sin. An abomination.

Andrew looks over at me. I can feel his gaze on me and I turn to him. He's biting his lower lip. Suddenly, but slowly, he leans in toward me.

Shit.

I feel his lips press against mine and mine pressing against his.

Shit.

A slip of the tongue.

Shit.

Andrew begins pushing his weight forward. If I don't do something, he'll soon be on top of me, and then where will we be? I need to stop this, but I really don't want to. It feels too good, even my glasses are fogging up. But how? Why? I don't understand. I'm drunk off of him — not that I've ever been drunk, but I imagine — and I'm feeling myself drifting away into the moment. There's a pressure on my groin. And then I feel a squeeze.

"No! I can't," I say breathlessly pulling away. I throw his hand off of me. His mouth hangs open with the shortness of his breath. There's a little bit of moisture around the side of his lip, where either his spit or mine — there's no way to know — escaped from us. My heart is pounding as quickly as a hummingbird can flap its wings and all I want to do is achieve what that little bit of spit on Andrew's face did, escape from us. "I have to go," my voice cracks, having jumped up a whole octave. My hands scurry around to gather my things. Andrew just watches me while I shove my textbook and binder back into my backpack. I don't even bother putting it on before I make for the door.

"Erik, wait!" Andrew says, grabbing me by my wrist.

"I can't. I really have to go," I feel hysterical saying this, but he doesn't let go.

"Please, Erik, just wait. You don't know how much I need this."

"You don't know how much I need to leave."

I yank my hand away and race out of his bedroom, through his hideous off-brand Tuscany Villa hall, and out his front door. I run so fast I don't even check to see if he's chasing after me. I keep running, even once I'm outside, and I don't stop running until I'm at least a quarter mile away. I'm in pain, literally, because I don't run. I'm not a runner and it's not something I can see ever enjoying. People who run for recreation are aliens. The only reason to ever run, in my opinion, is if you're being chased by a slow-moving serial killer in a generic Halloween mask, or if you're running away from a boy who just destroyed your whole world and cursed you into eternal damnation with a single satisfying — oh, so satisfying — kiss.

What am I to do now? I can't simply deny it. That would be a lie. A sin. Because the truth is... I liked feeling Andrew's mouth exploring mine, and I want to do it again, and again, and again. But when I look over in the direction of his house, which is long out of view, all I see is... nothing. There's nothing there. No future. No possibility. No happiness. There's nothing there to be had. That's why I can't.

I feel the pressure inside of me building, and the tears coming up fast from my heart. It's not long before I'm sobbing out there on the curb, on a sunny Saturday afternoon, powerless to stop myself. Luckily, it seems hardly anyone goes outside in this neighborhood — I mean, why would you? — so there are no witnesses around to see me. I cry, and cry, and cry until I can't cry anymore. Then, I pull out my phone and call my dad to pick me up. But how do I explain to him why I look so haggard, or why I'm not at Andrew's house working on our presentation? I can't just be like, "Well, Dad, it's a Golgi Complex issue that I can't talk about." Can you imagine if clever puns like that actually worked? You could get away with murder! But then, God's watching. God is always watching. I bet that's why he instilled in us Catholic Guilt, so that we would know he's watching even if he decided to take a day off from watching. I mean, there are seven bajillion of us in the world. He can't always take care of all our problems, can he? Because I would say that this is a pretty big one.

nicholas

Today is the day. Brenda and I have been dating since the end of sophomore year. We agreed that we'd take it slow and we lasted throughout the entire summer without succumbing to any temptations. We've worked for this. We've earned it. Trust me, keeping our hands off each other was not easy. We live, maybe, a twenty minute drive from the beach when there's no traffic — which is almost never, since the 405 is always packed, so really it's more like a forty minute drive from the beach, but that's not important. My point is, I spent most of the summer watching this girl prance around in little more than a pair of denim booty shorts and a bikini top. And she's had to suffer having to behave herself around me. Now, I don't mean to brag, but I try to keep myself tight. Gotta make sure I'm well defined for the ladies. You know how it goes.

Brenda and I spent all week planning this, so I was basically counting down the days till Sunday. We would've done it last night, but Bren got stuck babysitting, and she couldn't exactly get out of it for reasons of planned virginity loss. Plus, her parents have plans to take her little sister to a local children's theatre show today, so it actually works out better. We'll have the whole place all to ourselves for a few hours.

Now, I've got a whole list of things I need to do before I head over:

> 1. "Rehearse" with myself. I've heard that if you do this before you get into the act, you'll last longer when it comes time to actually perform.

I don't really need to go into detail about this, do I? I've done it millions of times before — sometimes multiple times a day — and I'm not ashamed at all to admit it. Any guy who responds to this with an, "Ew, that's gross," needs to grow a pair. We're not children anymore. Let's behave like the young adults that we are.

2. Properly groom Nick Jr. That doesn't need explanation. Nobody likes a bushy man. Unless, you know, you're into the lumberjack vibe. Personally, I don't get it.

Hmm… I'm debating if I should shave my chest. I've got a little bit of baby stubble right between my pecs and I can't decide if Bren will think it's hot or not? I think I'll leave it. She's seen me shirtless before and I think it'd be weird to show up without it when she already knows it's there.

3. Shower and dress. Mental note: Brenda once said she really likes me in a form fitting henley. I didn't even know what a henley was until she told me it's basically like a polo but without the collar. As it turns out, I already own a couple.

Shower done. I made sure the water was warm before I got in to promote healthy blood flow, if you know what I mean. Right now, I've got an issue though. I can't find my henley. It's not in my closet. Is it in the laundry? Fuck! It's in the laundry. I sniff it and it smells fine. Would that be, like, super gross if I wore it despite that? I mean, I don't foresee myself having it on for too long. Whatever, I'll just wear it. It'll be fine.

4. Double check to make sure I've got condoms and lube available.

Already done. I've got a shoebox stashed under my bed for just this occasion. I made sure to hit up the local free clinic for the supplies during the week, because I wasn't sure they'd be open on the weekends. Man, if those places ever get defunded, I'm totally screwed. Or rather, I'm totally *not* screwed. I mean, I'm not about to ask my parents for this stuff.

> 5. Stop by the grocery store for some chocolates and a single rose. I'd get a bouquet, but my allowance will only get me so much, since my stupid self decided to spend the bulk of it on hair wax. I'm not made of money.

Alright, I'm at the grocery store now and I can't seem to find any single roses. The only thing they have in stock are these potted plant arrangements that I can only picture old ladies buying to "spruce up" their kitchens. Maybe I'll get some other cute thing? I take a walk around, looking down every aisle, but nothing seems to pop out at me the way a rose would. Let's see, there's a whole section of one aisle dedicated to just stuffed toys and what not, but they're way out of my price range. I'm ready to go. I grab the cheapest box of chocolates I can find and make my way to the checkout lanes. That's when I notice them: a small bunch of foil balloons that read: "Happy Birthday." You know, the last minute gift balloons on sticks. I take a quick look at each one and, damn, they all say, "Happy Birthday." You know what? I can make this work. It's better than nothing, right? I pay the cashier, who smiles at me and asks, "Is this for someone special?"

"Yup," I say. I don't need to fill her in on all the details.

I pull onto Brenda's street and park a few houses down. If we're not done by the time her parents come home, I don't want my car — well, technically, it's my mom's car — to be sitting in their driveway. That would be a dead giveaway. I'm playing it smart today.

I grab the stuff I picked up at the grocery store and my shoebox of condoms, then walk the distance from my car to her front door and ring the bell. While I wait for her to answer, I pull out my phone and open up the camera app to make sure my hair's holding up. It took some trying, but I got it to shape into a fluffy faux hawk. It kinda makes me look like one of those video game characters from, like, Final Fantasy or something, and I'm not mad at it. The door swings open and Brenda's standing in front of me wearing an incredibly short pair of cotton shorts and a tank top.

"Hey there, Latin lover," she greets me in a light and breathy tone. Freakin' Sopranos. You gotta love them.

"Mi amor," I say in my whitest of white accent. It's not intentional. I just never learned to speak Spanish. My mom is Colombian while my dad is Puerto Rican, and for whatever stupid reason, they didn't bother to teach me any Spanish. My mom claims it's because learning two languages would confuse me, and she didn't want me getting discriminated against by the other kids for being Latino. I don't buy that excuse one bit. Why? Because most people can't tell I'm Latino to begin with. I'm about two shades lighter than most of my Latino peers and my hair is naturally brown, as opposed to black. When people find out I'm Latino, I'm always met with, "Oh, my God! I had no idea. You don't look it at all," and I'm never quite sure if I should thank them or punch them in the face. It's annoying, because most people don't bother to ask. They just assume one thing or another about a person without the care to actually get to know them. They immediately go from "Hi" to "Hola," which is actually super off-putting, especially if they themselves don't speak Spanish. But I digress.

"What's all this?" Brenda asks. I hand her the chocolate and the balloon as I step through her doorway.

"It's nothing. Just trying to be romantical," I explain. I'm pretty proud of myself at the moment.

"Happy Birthday?"

"Yeah… to you and to me… being born as adults." God, I'm so full of shit, it's no wonder why my hair is brown. But the girl seems to like it so I'm all about it.

We head into Brenda's room and it's a picture of girlishness. The walls are pink. There's makeup all over her vanity. Clothes, including, but not limited to, bras and panties, are strewn about everywhere. What's not to love?

Brenda shuts her bedroom door and turns to me wearing a mischievous smile. She takes my hand and presses it against her boob. I can feel she's not wearing anything underneath her tank and, mentally, I'm ready to go. Within seconds, our tongues are entangled, and our mouths are caught in an intense wrestling match. This is happening. Today, I'm turning in my V Card. We fall onto the bed. She's on top, straddling me. She quickly pulls off my henley top and buries her face in it. I feel bad now. Maybe I should've left that piece in the laundry. She doesn't seem to mind though, seeing as she inhales it again before tossing it aside. She dives in to kiss me some more. Her movements are crazy and erratic. She's like some sort of feral housecat or a dog that's never been neutered. I unzip my pants and slide them off. I feel her pelvis brushing back and forth against mine through my boxers and I'm suddenly struck with this terrible feeling of… concern.

I'm *soft*.

I'm starting to panic a little bit. Bren's grinding and twerking on top of me and… nothing. She looks so freakin' delicious bouncing on me, so I reach my hands up and grab both of her little B cups and squeeze. Still nothing. She's moaning and groaning and yelling out things like, "Yes, Papi!" and "Your hands are so strong. Oh! It feels so good!" and still nothing. Her eyes are locked into mine, piercing with desire. I feel her reaching down and before she can even touch it, I grab her hand.

"Wait," I say. It sounds almost harsh when it comes out. "Just wait."

"What's wrong, Papi?" she asks. Her voice is quiet, but still flirty.

"You know, you don't have to call me that."

"Okay, Daddy."

"You don't have to call me that either." She knows something's up. I can see it in her face.

"Nick, is something wrong?" Now I'm regretting having "rehearsed" earlier. Obviously, I can't tell her that.

So I lie.

"No, Babe. Nothing's wrong. I just… I want this to be special for you," I explain, getting up from her bed. "Why don't we just take it slow and easy?"

"Okay." She leans back and spreads her legs. I can see her itty bitty through the leg hole of her shorts. God, she wanted this just as much as I did. Maybe even more. I mean, *I* still bothered to put on some underwear. Now I really need this to work. I reach down and — FUCK! Still soft. Maybe if I jiggle it around in my boxers a few times, that'll get it to wake up? Brenda's looking at me funny now and I'm feeling like I'm losing my damn mind. What is wrong with me?!

"Nick, are you alright?" Brenda asks, her look of concern's growing way more than I am. "You're acting really funny."

"I… don't know what's wrong. My thingy isn't doing what it's supposed to."

"Well, here. Let me try."

"No! No! No!" I back away, raising my voice at her. "You can't see him when he's in his baby form! Do you know how embarrassing that is for a guy?" Probably not as embarrassing as me saying my penis has a baby form.

"What do you want me to do, Nick?" Hmm... What do you want her to do, Nick? Think. Think. Think. I'm totally in panic mode at this point. I don't know if there's anything she *can* do. Her boobs aren't doing it for me. Her naughty bits aren't doing it for me. I really don't know. I start racking my brain for some kind of solution. Anything that might increase my blood flow. As crazy as it is, I start doing jumping jacks. Brenda's staring at me like I'm a total psycho, but I'm desperate.

Fifteen.

Sixteen.

Seventeen.

Eighteen.

Nothing.

"Nick," she says, but I'm stuck in my head counting.

Nineteen.

Twenty.

Twenty-one.

Still, nothing.

"Nick, stop."

"I can't," I insist, still doing these jumping jacks, though I've lost count with her distracting me. "I have to make it work."

"Nick, just sit down." I do just that. There's no point in tiring myself out when it's clearly not doing anything for me. She's looking at me with so much sympathy. Or maybe it's pity. I really can't tell. She leans in to kiss me. It feels nice. One kiss. Two kisses. Wet tongue. Moist lips. We're making out again, but this time, I'm so hyper focused on what she's doing that I'm actually saying all of it in my head and it's sounding like some perverted nursery rhyme. I reach down and feel myself in hopes that I'll find even a little bit of growth, but still... nothing. We roll around in her bed and continue to make out. I'm doing everything I can to wake myself up down there. I'm squeezing her boobs. I'm groping her butt. I'm letting her explore whatever she wants from the waist up. It's fun, yeah, but none of it is working. No matter what she or I do, I'm completely flaccid. I'm starting to give up hope on the whole thing. Maybe today *isn't* the day. It's looking like my V Card is gonna remain valid and that sucks, but not in the fun way.

We're lying side by side now. The making out's gotten stale. Neither one of us seems to be up to fooling around anymore. I'm staring up at her white popcorn ceiling, totally pissed off at myself. Why did this have to happen? All that planning we did. All the preparation. This should've gone on without any problem. What gives?

"Nick, can I ask you something?" Brenda says, after a really long stretch of awkward silence.

"Hmm?"

"Do you even find me attractive?" The question takes me by surprise.

"What? Of course I do! Why would you ask that?"

"Because you obviously don't wanna have sex with me." What is she talking about? How is it that that's what she took away from this? If I didn't want to have sex with her, I wouldn't have gone through all this trouble. Is she freakin' kidding?!

"Of course I want to have sex with you!" I say, way louder than I intended.

"Then why can't you get it up?"

"I DON'T FUCKING KNOW!" All of my frustrations are pouring out through my voice. I'm screaming. I can hear that I am, and it's the absolute worst. Brenda glares at me for a moment before she says anything. And when she does, she hits me where it hurts.

"I think this is over between us." To be honest, part of me was thinking the same thing, but hearing it out loud pisses me off. I'm angry. I know I'm mostly mad at myself, but the fact that she's breaking it off *right now*, seems almost… malicious. If she's going to break up with me, I'd rather I be clothed and have a little bit of dignity. Not in my underwear, after failure to perform.

"Look, I'm sorry I yelled. I shouldn't have." God, this whole situation is pathetic.

"Whatever, Nick. It's over."

"No! No, you don't get to make that call. It's not over until I say it's over."

"You're being a pig."

"Yeah? Well, you're being a COLD BITCH!"

"GET OUT OF MY HOUSE!" I grab my clothes and make for the door. But before I leave, I swipe the box of chocolates I brought, as well as the stupid birthday balloon, and my shoebox of condoms.

"I paid for this. I'm taking it!" I stumble out of her room and head for the front door, which starts to open as I approach. Perfect. Just perfect. Brenda's mom, dad, and little sister enter. I don't even bother trying to hide. Brenda's family stands at the threshold with wide eyes and shocked expressions. "Hi, Mr. and Mrs. Lee."

"Nick, what's going on?" Mr. Lee questions. At this point, I see no reason to hide anything. If Brenda wants to be heartless and break up with a guy over his faulty manhood, then I think she deserves some instant karma.

"Brenda invited me over to have sex, but she couldn't get me hard, so she broke up with me," I explain, my words coming out quick and pointed. "Have a nice life." I pat Mr. Lee on his shoulder before squeezing past him, his wife, and his younger daughter, Bebe.

I make my way down the street to my car, still in my underwear, and climb in, tossing everything into the passenger seat. I feel terrible. I probably shouldn't have said anything to Brenda's parents because, really, they would've figured it out on their own. Whatever, she hurt my pride. I know that's an ugly excuse, but I actually really liked her. I liked Brenda, like, a lot. I wanted this to work. I abided by our agreement to take things slow and I waited patiently for her for months. Why couldn't she wait just a little bit longer for me? Aren't I worth waiting for?

chapter three
erik

I'm not gay.

I'm *not* gay. I keep repeating these words in my head during Sunday Mass. You can imagine how uncomfortable I felt coming to church today, knowing what I had done yesterday with Andrew. One curious occurrence doesn't make me gay, right? That question kept me tossing and turning all last night, because the more I thought about it, the more it all started to make sense. I remembered things from when I was really young and every time something remotely homosexual crossed my mind, I'd be hit with a sudden, "Oh… that would explain it," moment. And it happened over and over again, with each long forgotten memory that came back to me.

For instance, back in elementary school, we had this Life Skills program, which was run by this teacher. Let's call him Mr. Jansen. That's probably not his name, but I can't for the life of me remember his real name. Anyway, Mr. Jansen would come to our class every other Thursday with a two hour lesson that focused on a different Life Skill like Initiative, or Integrity, or Patience, or whatever. I remember having this gross fantasy that he'd come visit me at home, and we'd get naked, and sit in my blanket fort that I made, and cuddle for days. I don't even recall Mr. Jansen being attractive. In fact, the picture I get of him is that of a dorky thirty something year old white man with a bowl cut, so I don't really understand why my mind went to that place.

Then, there was the time when I was watching an R rated movie on TV after my parents started letting me stay home alone without a babysitter. I think I was about eleven. The movie was essentially about a group of middle-aged men who wanted to get their sexy back, so they formed a band together and started a male strip show. It wasn't even explicit. It only showed butts, but that was enough to get me to watch the whole movie over again the next time it came on. It was a two hour movie and the stripping scene happens at the very end of the film. God, I was a repressed kid.

The one past experience that really drove the point home about this gay thing was the first time I searched for porn on the internet. I was, maybe, thirteen. I typed the words "cartoon sex" into the search bar. I was a pubescent little boy; those were the two things I wanted to see. One of the things that came up was a webcomic series, featuring a cartoon space captain, who would spend his time fighting galactic monsters and going to bed with alien women of various colors of the rainbow. I didn't read the comics. I just stared at the pictures and had a natural tendency to linger on the ones of the space captain. I was so enamored with the cartoon, I actually printed a couple of pictures and took them into the shower with me, so that I could touch myself while looking at them. That didn't work out the way I had wanted since I was a stupid kid who didn't realize that ink runs in water. The pictures were ruined before I got anywhere with myself.

All of these things happened to me while growing up, and I never once considered that, maybe, it was because I was attracted to men. That thought never crossed my mind. Why would it? I was brought up to think that being straight wasn't just the default, but the only option, so growing up, I liked girls. Or, at least, I thought I liked girls. There were a few that I was attracted to and a few that I had actual crushes on. But looking back, I'm not sure if it was that I liked the girls or just the *idea* of them. Being gay would explain everything about myself and that scares the crap out of me, because I'm not gay. I can't be gay.

"Do not be deceived," I hear an older Filipino woman with a very heavy accent begin from the podium. I'd been so lost in my own thoughts this whole time I'd nearly forgotten I was supposed to be paying attention to mass. "Neither the sexually immoral nor idolaters nor male prostitutes nor homosexual offenders—" You've gotta be kidding me. Of all the readings they could've used from the Bible today, this is the one they went with?! You may as well tuck me into a handbasket and send me to Hell via one of those many readily available courier apps. I mean, what are the odds? "Nor thieves nor the greedy nor drunkards nor slanders nor swindlers will inherit the kingdom of God." This feels like my own personal divine punishment. "And that is where some of you were." Just say it, lady. That's where you, Erik Park, are. "The word of the Lord."

"Praise be to God," the entire congregation responds in unison.

The Knights of Columbus are holding a barbecue buffet after mass. My mother insists that we attend and socialize instead of doing our normal after mass ritual of trying out a new local pho place. There are so many in our area that there's always a place that we haven't tried.

My dad doesn't argue. He simply agrees and delivers his now infamous catchphrase, "It's whatever you want." Actually, this works out perfectly for me. All this pondering about my sexuality has me itching to go to confession. I tell Mom that I want to go, and she doesn't question it. She just nods with a proud smile.

Between my parents, it's my mom who's the religious one. She's the kind of woman who prays the Rosary every single night without fail. In fact, she gets pretty violent if you interrupt her during her prayer session, which is a bit ironic if you think about it. It's that Filipino fire that she possesses from having grown up in the ghettos of Manila. It's passionate, out of control, and totally unhinged if you piss her off. That's why everything has to be perfect. That's why *I* have to be perfect. Or, at the very least... normal.

My dad on the other hand is super relaxed. Nothing bothers him at all. He doesn't seem to worry about anything. If my mom's like fire, then my dad's water: easy, cool, and flexible. Maybe that's why they work well together.

"Meet us in the rectory when you're done," Mom says to me. She and my dad exit the church, blessing themselves with holy water on their way out.

I head over to the pews near the confessionals and take a seat. I'm nervous. I don't enjoy going to confession. The idea of sitting in a dark enclosed space and speaking with the disembodied voice of a priest always made me uneasy. It was the part that I dreaded most when I was going through Catechism growing up. I need a few minutes to talk myself into it. I don't know what's so scary about it. It should be a comfort to know that there's a way to be absolved of your sins. It should be a comfort to know that you can talk to God through a priest and be forgiven. I think it's the judgement that scares me. They do say that God's the only one who can do that, you know?

I take a deep breath.

I'm not gay.

I'm not gay.

I'm *not*. I repeat this in my head a few times as a way to, maybe, psych myself up. There's nothing to be scared of. I've done this many times before and nothing bad has ever come out of it. But all those times before, I wasn't gay… What am I saying? I'm *not* gay. I'm not!

I gather up the little bit of courage I've managed to summon and fall in line for confession. There's only one other person in front of me, an older Asian woman who reeks of menthol and roses. Her hair is dyed a sort of reddish brown — which she clearly did at home out of a box — and she's wearing a knee length dress with a flowery print that she's accessorized with a string of pearls and a pair of simple black heels. Her sense of fashion is intriguing. It's gaudy, but still tasteful, in a sort of demure way… I'm not gay. I'm NOT.

The confessional door opens and a woman, who's styled just like the Asian woman in line, steps out. She smiles and nods to us as she passes by. The Asian woman in front of me enters, and now I'm standing here alone, resting against the white walls of the church and staring out at a sea of empty pews. You know, this might be bad of me to say, but churches are pretty creepy when they're empty. I'm looking around at all the holy statues watching over me with stoic expressions, and the framed pictures on the walls depicting the Stations of the Cross. There's blood, whips, and torture involved in nearly all of the pictures, and it's really unsettling to look at for too long. Maybe that was the intention. I don't know. I hear the confessional door open and the rosy menthol Asian woman emerges. Like the woman before her, she smiles and nods as she passes silently by. That was quick. I'm not ready. The little bit of courage I had mustered up leaves me, but it's my turn. I've got to go in, whether I'm ready or not. I inhale a deep breath and step into the confessional, closing the door behind me.

Inside the confessional, it's nearly pitch black. The only source of light comes from a small window that looks into the adjacent booth where the priest is, but you can't see into there because of a paper thin screen. I feel around with my feet. I know from past visits that there's a kneeler in here, so that you can be level with the window. I kneel down and fold my hands together, assuming the position.

"Bless me, Father, for I have sinned," I can hear my voice quivering, and I can feel my shortness of breath. At this point, I know I'm supposed to say when my last confession was, but I don't remember because I've been avoiding it for so long. "My last confession was…" I trail off.

"That's alright," a gentle baritone voice comes through the screen. "Go ahead." I stop. A part of me wonders if confession was a good idea. But I suppose I'm already here.

"Yesterday, I went over to my classmate's house to work on a project for school. It was meant to be a homework session, you know? Nothing funny. But then, out of nowhere he…" My heart's pounding so hard I'm afraid it's gonna fly out of my chest.

"Relax, son. You can speak freely here. Now, what did he do?"

"He… kissed me. And… groped me, and…" The priest doesn't say anything and I'm losing my nerve, so I decide to steer my confession to where I really need it to go. "I was wondering, do thoughts count as sins?"

"I suppose it depends."

"I just… I can't stop thinking about it. It's like deep down, there's a part of me that… liked it. Is that bad?"

"Well, it's not good."

"I don't know. I sorta thought I had everything figured out. I thought, one day, I'd get married, you know, to a girl and have kids or, at least, a dog or something. And now, I'm not sure about anything anymore. I'm confused. I feel guilty. I'm worried about what my parents are going to think, especially my mom, and I'm just… I'm scared."

"What are you scared of?"

"Everything." Saying it out loud gets me to thinking. I think about my parents and what this might mean for them. I can only imagine how this might affect my mother. I can't be gay. I can't. Because if I am, I'm ruining everything. I think about the things my parents might want for me: a wife, a family of my own, grandkids. I'm their only child. All of that starts and ends with me. "You see, Father, my family is really religious, and I don't want to break their hearts. Actually, I don't want them to break mine. I suppose I could just forget about it. Go through life playing as if these feelings aren't real, but wouldn't that be a sin? And isn't it a sin to lie? I just don't know what to do. I keep telling myself I'm not gay. I'm not, but then I don't believe myself when I say it. And I really, really want to believe myself." I can feel tears streaming down my face. I hear the priest take a breath and I wait eagerly for his answer. I know he can fix this. I know that he can fix *me*. I know that. At first, he doesn't say anything and it's absolutely killing me having to wait for the remedy.

"Listen," he says finally. I perk up and I'm ready to take in everything he's about to say to me. "Why don't you go home and clear your head? Relax and just try to forget about it, alright? Feelings are feelings. That's all they are. You can have feelings, but the trick is to never act upon them. Continue to fight the temptation."

That's it? That's all he's gonna say? "Fight the temptation?" I don't understand. He is God's vessel. At least, he's *supposed* to be. He was supposed to fix me, and now he's telling me that all I have to do is continue to fight temptation?

"Now, for your penance," he says. "Let's have you do the Apostle's Creed, and why don't we throw in a Prayer to the Holy Spirit as well, St. Augustine, alright? Now, go forth, my son."

"That's it?" The question gets away from me. I'm panicking, because I'm finding nothing useful in what he's saying. He's about to send me away with more questions than I came in with. "But father—"

"No, no. God has spoken," he says, dismissing me. "Go forth, my son."

I want to scream. I want to cry, but I know I can't without causing a huge disturbance. I get up and leave the confessional, and immediately exit the church.

"Continue to fight temptation." That's what he said. It doesn't make sense. He just presented me with a huge conundrum. I mean, am I not supposed to love anyone? Am I supposed to go on living a regular heteronormative life, pretending any feelings I might have for someone of the same sex don't exist? If that's the case, am I supposed to lie to myself, like I have been, and just keep telling myself I'm not gay?

I'm gay!

. . .

I'm gay... and I don't believe that I'm not.

Based on what the priest said, it's sounding like I have a decision to make. Do I sacrifice my own happiness for the sake of everything else? Or, do I sacrifice everything else for my own sake? It's gotta be the former, because how could anybody be so selfish and choose the latter? You'd burn in Hell for that.

chapter four
nicholas

Erectile Dysfunction.

I type the words into the search bar and skim through all of the links that come up on my phone. Ads for Urology Specialists come up first, followed by sites that list symptoms and causes. I click on one of the links and am greeted by a colorful diagram depicting a sad flaccid penis, and a happy ready one. The artist even took the time to make sure the color scheme of the illustrations matched the mood. The sad and flaccid penis is blue. Literally. I read through the accompanying article and one of the first things that pop up is the question: "When should you see a doctor?" I didn't realize having a soft one was that serious. Then, I see the list of causes and words like high cholesterol and blood pressure pop up. They also list a bunch of diseases, some of which I can't even pronounce. I'm probably gonna die.

When the first link is a bust, I find my way to another one. This link looks more official, because it's got more than one page of information — for starters — and far fewer random ads. Again, color coded penis diagrams, symptoms and causes, diseases, yada-yada. I click through the pages and land on the last one, where I read: "If the problem persists, contact your trusted medical professional." Isn't that what this site is for? It's useless. None of the information is very helpful. It's just blurbs of basic general information, enough for someone to self-diagnose. Someone like myself. And I have come to the conclusion that it's probably Peyronie's disease, caused by my chronic masturbation problem, and my dick's probably gonna fall off. And yes, I *did* have to look up what Peyronie's disease was, and if my dick does fall off, I'd rather just die.

I'm bored of the research. It's getting me nowhere. I exit out of the browser and click on my text messages. Nothing. I was thinking Brenda might text with an apology at some point or another. At least, I was hoping she would. A couple hours pass and nothing. I'm thinking now maybe *I* should apologize, but I don't really want to. She's the one that did me wrong. I mean, who breaks up with a guy when he's practically naked and can't get a hard on? That's rude.

Thinking about the whole situation pisses me off. I really liked Brenda, like, a lot. I went above and beyond for that girl. I started blow drying my hair because she liked how it looked fluffy. I started wearing slim fit jeans — which I had to beg my mom for money for — because she said that men should wear clothes that accentuate their body instead of hiding it. Thinking about how I dressed before, she wasn't wrong. I used to just pomade the crap out of my hair, and I would favor baggy pants because they were comfortable. That girl, with all her opinions, changed me, and I like it. I like who I've become, because I actually look like what I think I am: a romantic. All summer, I would write her notes and leave them in her mailbox when I'd go to visit, just so she'd know I was thinking about her. I would sit through all the girly movies with her and watch all the shows that she liked, just so we'd always have something to talk about. I set aside every penny of my allowance just so I could afford to take her to her favorite fancy restaurant, the Olive Garden, on her birthday. I never would've imagined we'd break up over… God, I can't even say it. I'm just mad at myself. Why didn't it work? Why didn't *I* work? I've never had a problem when I'm by myself.

My room's growing darker now. It's already sunset. Still, no messages from Bren. I open up Instagram and navigate my way to her page. She's posted a new selfie. It's her holding up the peace sign while making a kissy face, and she's posted it with the hashtag #livingmybestlife. It's as if she didn't just break up with me. I guess that isn't something that people typically post about, so it's whatever. But then, I scroll down to see what else she's got on here and I see another selfie: it's her taking a picture of herself in her bathroom mirror and doing that kissy face. There's another selfie: her in the passenger seat of my mom's car wearing sunglasses and a kissy face. Another selfie: her with an ice cream cone and that kissy face. I'm starting to notice a theme here. All of her pics are selfies of *just* her, making a kissy face. Kissy face with a dog. Kissy face with a coffee cup. Kissy face while applying lip gloss. God, I never realized how freakin' basic Brenda was. It's just selfie, after selfie, after selfie. There's never anyone else in her pictures. Every now and then, I run into a picture that I know I was there for, and it's just her and my shoulder, or her with me blurred out in the background. What the hell, Bren? I scroll all the way down to the day that we decided that we were boyfriend and girlfriend. Finally, there's a picture of me and her. I'm dressed in a backwards hat and wearing what is clearly an oversized polo, and she's pointing at me and making that damn kissy face. I scroll to the comment section just below and see that it's hashtagged #thisguy.

This guy? Are you freakin' kidding me?! What the hell does that even mean? There's no heart emoji, no mention of us getting together, no nothing. My whole relationship with Brenda was a lie. I'm over here with my stupid self thinking we're gonna be Romeo and Juliet, but our families don't hate each other and nobody dies for no reason, but no. Judging by her feed, I wasn't in a relationship with her, because *she* was in a relationship with *herself*. I feel like my phone just smacked me in the face. Then, I lose my grip, and my phone *actually* smacks me in my face. Perfect. Just perfect. Stupid gravity. I decide — pretty easily, I'd like to add — to unfollow and block her across all social media platforms. I won't see her, and she won't see me. It'll be like we were never a thing. Just how she wanted it, apparently.

I'm ready to knock out when there's a knock on my door.

"Nicky, you in there?" my mom asks.

"Yeah, Ma. Come in," I say, though I'm not in the mood to chat.

"God, Nicky, it's a mess in here." I've got clothes scattered about and a couple of half-empty cups of water sitting around, but it's nothing crazy. I mean, the trash bin in the corner is overflowing with used tissues, but that's to be expected. It's a typical guy's room. "What did I tell you about leaving cups in your room?"

"I get thirsty, Ma. Sorry." She pulls the swivel chair out from under my desk and takes a seat. That's when I notice that I left the chocolates, birthday balloon, and my shoebox of condoms sitting on the desk just out in the open. I want to go and grab the shoebox, but that would look super suspicious if I did, so I resist the urge. I can't take my eyes off it though. Ma sees that I'm staring at it.

"Oh, did you get new shoes?" Ma asks. She reaches for the box, and I make a sudden lunge forward, snatching it away from her.

"No, no, no! You don't need to see that," I say, my voice jumping way higher than what's natural for me. Ma eyes me suspiciously.

"Is that a box of condoms, Nicky?" How does she always know?!

"What? No. No, they're just… really expensive shoes. I don't want to expose them… to sunlight, because it might damage the, um, colors. You know, colors fade when they're exposed to light."

"You're exposing yourself right now with that terrible excuse, mijo," she quips, as if what she said was the cleverest thing in the world. "Now, put your condom box away. I need to talk to you."

"It's not a condom box, Ma," I insist, defiant. "There's lube in it too." What? I'm panicked! Whatever.

She chuckles. Good. She finds this amusing. It means I'm likely not in trouble.

My mom and I have always been close. She and I spent all our time together when I was growing up. Dad was hardly ever around. He was always busy striving to provide us a better life. See, my parents had me just as they were both starting college. Between the two of them, my dad had better prospects, and my mom knew this. So, she gave up on her plans to go to school, while my dad focused on his pursuits full-time. My mom gave up everything to live with her then soon to be in-laws and raise a child, all in the hopes that one day, life would be better. I can't imagine she was happy during that time, but she believed it was for the best. And as it turned out, she was right. My dad got a job offer for an entry level position in the field of investment banking, right out of college, and moved us from New York to LA before I even became aware of the concept of money. Dad worked his fancy day job, and Ma became a stay-at-home housewife, and by the time I was ten, I was a bonafide mama's boy. I'm not one bit ashamed to admit that either. My mom's basically my best friend. Though talking about sex with her is still super uncomfortable. I mean, come on, she's still my mom.

I stash my box of condoms under my bed and sit down for whatever she came in here to talk about.

"What's up?" I ask when she fails to start the conversation.

"Um…" she begins. She's visibly nervous, which makes me nervous. "How are things with you and Brenda?" This isn't what she came in to talk about, I can tell. But I know my mom, and I know that when she's avoiding a subject, it means that I'm gonna have to do some work if I wanna know what it is.

"Not so good," I say, responding to her question. "Brenda and I broke up. Well, she broke up with me."

"Oh, no. What happened?"

"We got in a fight."

"You lost your temper, didn't you?"

"No! I mean, I did, but that's not what the fight was about."

"No?"

"No, it's really… embarrassing."

"I'm assuming it has to do with the box of condoms?"

"You know, you saying that actually makes it worse." No way in hell am I about to talk to my mother about my penis. I may be a mama's boy, but that is where I draw the line. She chuckles and it's right at my expense.

"Aw, mijo," she says, offering up a hug. I move into her arms and we fall into an embrace. I can feel her shaking against me. It's slight, but noticeable. Something's up, but what? "Lo siento mucho, hijo. Mi corazón está rompiendo." Her voice comes out like a croak. She's choking on her words, which I — unfortunately — don't understand. This is one of those moments where I wish she had taught me her language.

"Ma, are you crying?" I pull out of our embrace. She's got tears rolling down her cheeks and she's biting her bottom lip, avoiding eye contact. "What is it?"

"Your father and I…" Ma trails off. Her voice is small and sad. I look at her intently, waiting for more. She hesitates at first, but then, "we're getting a divorce." The news hits me like a ton of bricks. The impact is so hard, I don't even believe it.

"You're joking. Tell me you're joking," I demand. She shakes her head.

"We were planning on telling you together. Your father… I suppose he wanted to defend himself," Ma pauses. My mind is racing. Defend himself? Defend himself from what? "He's been having an affair, Nicky. For a long time. I was hoping it would blow over, that he'd get bored of her and just come home because 'men never leave their wives.' Everything could go back to normal then, but here we are." I'm in shock. I don't know what to say, if there even is anything to say. It doesn't feel real yet. It's one of those surreal moments that you go through where something devastating happens, but the effects haven't quite arrived, so a part of you feels like nothing's changed.

"What's gonna happen to us?" I manage.

"I don't know. I was thinking to stay with your Tio Roger," Ma explains. Tio Roger is my mom's older brother. He was the golden child of their bunch. He got good grades growing up, which led to him going to a really good school and getting a job as an architect in San Francisco. According to my mom, he never had any hiccups. Everything Tio Roger did seemed to go to plan. The only thing is that he never married, which is actually kind of a huge thing, being Latin and all. No one knows why he never got married. He's had girlfriends in the past. Pretty ones at that. He just never popped the question.

"Tio Roger," I start to say. I'm thinking it's a solid plan, but then it hits me. "Ma, that's across the state!"

"I know," she says. She takes in a breath and lets out a sigh. "Nicky, you're gonna be seventeen this year. You're old enough to make your own decisions. Just promise me you'll make good ones." With that, my mom gets up and makes for the door.

"Ma," I say. She stops and turns to me. "You know I'm going with you, right?" The decision comes easily to me. I don't even have to think about it. She offers me a weak smile. I know she's happy with what I chose, but this situation isn't one that you can be happy in. Regardless of my choice, we both lose.

chapter five
erik

I find myself in the middle of the ocean, sitting on a tiny island, small enough for me to see the boundless waters extending in all directions. There's nothing here but a single palm tree, which has sprouted from the center of the island, and a wooden rowboat resting on the sandy shore. Where am I? What am I doing here? I sit for a while, gazing up at the billowy clouds above as they travel aimlessly across the azure sky. It's peaceful. Every problem that I have floats away with the gently humming sea breeze, but I still don't know why I'm here. For a long while, nothing happens. The tide never climbs, the sun never moves, there's nothing but stillness. It's strange and unnatural. Something in my gut is telling me that I can't stay here. It's not because of a lack of food, or company, or anything like that. It's just the stillness. I eye the rowboat and decide to leave.

I'm out on the water now. I think I've made a mistake. There are no oars in the rowboat and no way for me to move or steer the vessel. Only about thirty feet from shore and I'm at the mercy of the sea. I can't exactly jump out because I never learned to swim. If I jump out, I'll drown, so I have no choice but to hold fast onto the boat, and hope the waters carry me to where I need to go. In the distance, I hear the rumbling of thunder. I look up to see the skies ahead of me darkening, and angry clouds of black and gray begin to obscure the once vibrantly colored sky. I feel the splashes of the waves pushing against the boat, rocking me back and forth. Rain plummets down and pummels against me as me and the boat are thrown in all directions. I hear the roar of the sky and the crash of the sea. There's a spark of lightning, and everything flashes to white. Suddenly, I find myself underwater, far below the surface. Pieces of my vessel float around me, just out of my reach.

I never learned to swim.

My lungs start to tighten, and my body starts to convulse. My vision goes black, and I can feel my consciousness leaving me, floating away into an endless abyss.

I'm drowning.

I'm going to die.

My eyes shoot open and I'm lying safely in my bed. I'm covered in a cold sweat. My room is dark, and there's an air of unease and loneliness looming all around me. I've just escaped possibly the most vivid dream I've ever had. And the worst one at that. I sit up and, gathering myself, fight against my shortness of breath. The clock on my nightstand reads 3:16am. I don't have to be awake for another three hours, but the dream I'd just awoken from has left me shaken. I'm afraid to go back to sleep. I think I'll just lay here till sunrise.

At around 6:30am, I get up out of bed and hop into the shower. I can't stop thinking about that dream and being pelted by this water only reminds me of it. My heart's racing and all I'm doing is standing here. Is this what it's like to have PTSD? I make a mental note, a reminder to look up symptoms of PTSD. Must evaluate and self-diagnose. God, I'm so lost in my own head that I can't even remember if I've washed my hair or not. Wait… did I even soap myself? All I'm thinking about is broken rowboats and the ocean. What is wrong with me?

I think I must've washed myself at least four times, because I kept going back to that dream and then forgetting about what I was doing. I'm certain that one armpit got cleaner than the other, but I'm not worried about it. I'm a hairless Asian; I don't generate body odor.

I get dressed and slip into my favorite hoodie — it's a teal zip up with white trim — despite the day's forecast for warm weather. You see, I'm all about the layered look. It's not necessarily because I like how it looks. It's because it's the only style I've figured out for myself that hides my little man boobs. I wouldn't say I'm, like, fat, but I'm also too chunky to be considered thin. Basically, the problem I have with my body is that I'm jiggly in very specific places, including, but not limited to, my breasts, my underarms, the sides of my stomach, and my calves. This is why I favor hoodies and avoid slim fit pants and all forms of shorts. I know what you're thinking: "Aren't you hot?" *No, I'm not.* That's why I cover up.

I head downstairs into the kitchen, where my mom is in her PJs, frying up breakfast. The TV is alive and buzzing with the harsh rapid-fire sounds of Tagalog. It looks like there's another flood in Manila. I'd say that with a little more concern if the people over there didn't treat it as an opportunity to dress up as mermaids so they can take selfies in the flooded streets of the ghetto. Crazy, right? But I can't make this up. I've seen the memes. I guess they're just used to it.

"Morning," Mom welcomes me without looking up. "Come eat."

"Do we have any coffee?" I ask, exhausted from my lack of sleep.

"You drink that stuff and you won't get any taller," my dad jokes as he enters. I sit down at the table and Mom sets a plate of garlic rice, fried eggs, and pork tocino in front of me. I'm not hungry, but I eat it anyway, because if I don't, my mom will ask questions and I really don't have the energy to explain myself. I need coffee, but we have none. Mom doesn't drink it, claiming it gives her "high blood," and my dad takes hot chocolate in the morning.

"Slow down, Erik," Mom says, practically scolding me. "You eat so fast, that's why you're getting fat." Didn't she just put this plate in front of me like two minutes ago? She practically insisted I eat. See, this is why I'm so confused about everything. Because I have a Filipino mother who tells me to do one thing, and then insults me when I do it. I wish I was more Korean, but my dad was super whitewashed growing up, he has trouble remembering his Korean birth name.

I make a conscious effort to eat slower to appease my mother. The whole time, I'm watching the TV and cringing internally, because now, one of the many, many terrible game shows that exploit poor people for prizes is on. These game shows always start off with a poor person telling a really dramatic sob story — I can follow along with them for the most part — before the hosts ask them to perform their special talent. Ninety-nine percent of people sing, and their voices are usually nice, but they never seem to be able to get on the right key.

"You know, if they really wanted to help those people, they could just give them the money without making them go through all this," I say.

"I thought that was part of the charm?" Dad replies. I shrug.

"Ay! Did you two remember to pray before you eat?" I stop with a piece of tocino hanging from my mouth. I'm already halfway through with my food. Mom's glaring at me, knowingly. Dad and I both swallow our last bites and then set our utensils down for prayer. Dad leads.

"Bless us, Oh Lord, and these, thy gifts, which we are about to receive from thy bounty through Christ, our Lord. Amen."

"Amen."

My dad drives me to school every morning on his way to the BART station. We don't really talk about much besides how school is going and stuff like that. The conversation stays casual. Sometimes, I feel like I don't know anything about my parents. To be honest, I don't even know what my dad does for a living. I think he works in HR for some bank with computers, maybe? I never asked. And that's how my relationship with my parents has always been. We only ever talk about surface level things. We don't talk about our feelings, or our hopes, or our fears, or anything. Most of our communication is done through context clues and, on my mom's part, mild invasions of privacy. That's why I can't keep a diary. This is gonna sound harsh because I do love my parents, but sometimes I wonder if they weren't my parents, would we have been friends if they were close to my age?

"Alrighty, have a good day," Dad says, as we pull into the neighborhood across from school. Dropping me off here is easier than braving the garbage fire that is my high school parking lot, and Dad is all about keeping things easy. "Study hard." Dad flips a u-ey and I make my way over to the crosswalk. My head feels light and my body feels heavy. I'm so tired. I have no idea how I'm gonna make it through today.

My high school is comprised of three separate buildings, each one featuring a different style of architecture. Originally, each building had a different purpose. They weren't all built together, and a lot of this place wasn't intended to be a high school, not from the start. It just turned into one. The English building used to be an old elementary school, with long hallways jutting out from one main hall. The annex, where most of the Senior and Advanced Placement classes are held, is a two-story brick building that, I believe, was meant to be a university way back in the olden days of black and white television and babies named Ethel and Herb. The main campus building, where the Science and Math classes are held, is the newest and most high school-y building of the three, because it was the part that was *actually* meant to be a high school. I spend most of my time around main campus because that's where the lockers are, and I hang out at my locker because I'm a loner. Well, except for Mackenzie. Speaking of...

"Give me your lunch money, kid, or I'm totally pants-ing you," a gravelly alto threatens from behind my open locker door.

"Hi, Mackenzie," I say, weary and monotone. I move my locker door so that I can see her. Mackenzie is a really, really pretty girl with dark wavy hair and fair skin. She's like if Snow White had a sarcastic cousin, who had an affinity for pairing leather straps and harnesses with baby doll dresses.

"How'd you know it was me?" she asks.

"You're the only bully I know outside of grade school who gets a thrill from seeing other people's underwear."

"What can I say? I find unmentionables mentionable."

"You're a pervert."

"So spank me." This whole time, I'd been thumbing through my pocket bible just skimming, not looking for anything in particular. Mackenzie notices and, though her eyes narrow judging-ly, she wears a slightly amused grin. "What are you doing thumping your Bible at school? You're not usually so evangelical."

"Yeah… about that," I begin, shutting my pocket bible and shoving it into my bag. "Do you happen to know if there are any books about becoming a homosexual and, um… preventing it?"

I felt okay bringing the subject up to Mackenzie. She is the one person I can talk to about anything. We've been friends ever since the sixth grade, when we got put into the same class together. A bigger dude was openly bullying me in class, always threatening me and demanding my lunch money because I was nerdy and wore glasses — not much has changed — and our teacher never did anything about it. Honestly, I don't think she even noticed. Half the time, she was falling asleep in her chair, and the other half of the time, she was too busy eating something to pay attention, much less do her job. Mackenzie noticed though, and she pulled the kid's hair until he started crying. "If that guy ever picks on you again, tell me and I'll make sure he gets a big ol' bald spot," she said. After that, I followed her around until she started acknowledging my presence. She was so fearless and confident, and I was so wimpy and scared of everything that I just wanted to be around her so she could keep the bullies away. We formed a sort of pact that she'd hang out with me at school, so long as we didn't *only* hang out at school.

In the eighth grade, Mackenzie and I even tried dating each other. She stole my first kiss by daring me to kiss her and then teased me endlessly until I did. That relationship lasted for approximately two weeks before she broke up with me, claiming that she was "too woman" for me, and that we were better off as friends. And we've been the best of friends ever since.

"Come again?" Mackenzie asks, in response to my question.

"I was wondering if there was, like, a guidebook for homosexual prevention," I say, without an ounce of humor. This is a serious thing.

"I'm hitting the rewind button, Erik, and we're gonna restart this conversation with a little more context. Now, what's going on?"

"I think I might be gay."

"Well, that's obvious."

"Don't joke."

"I'm not. I've known since the eighth grade. That's why I dumped you." Huh… That's funny. This whole time I thought she dumped me because, maybe, I was a bad kisser. That's a relief, as far as my kissing skills are concerned. But about this… am I really *that* obvious?

How is that possible? I didn't even know myself. "Anyway, go on," she says.

"Andrew Logan and I made out," I say, almost at a whisper.

"WHAT!?" she yells. A bunch of people in the hallway look over at us, and Mackenzie and I wait until they go on about their business before continuing our conversation. "Andrew Logan, star of the... sports ball team... with the jerseys?"

"Football. Yes. He asked me if he could go down on me, and then he tongue raped me in my mouth and grabbed my junk."

"Erik, oh, my God! He is like sex on legs. He's like a gay porn star or the front man of a 90s boy band before people knew better." Mackenzie is getting a little too excited about this. I look around to make sure no one is still staring.

"Can we keep this down? I don't want people finding out about this. Also, a *gay* porn star? Wouldn't he just be, like, a regular porn star?"

"Ha! Not anymore," she cackles, prompting me to look around once again. "Besides, have you seen the men in regular porn? Yikes."

"I don't look at porn."

"Lies."

"Okay, I do. But I always feel super gross about it. It's just so shameful."

"Separate church and state, Erik. Right now, we are talking about some, hopefully, very *big* things," she says, holding up her hands as if to measure something.

"I think you're missing the point," I say. I'm not finding her hysterical excitement the least bit amusing.

"So you're gay. So what? Like, one in every ten people are gay. And frankly, I don't think anyone would be surprised."

"I'm not gay. Not for sure. And what do you mean no one would be surprised?" A lot of the things she's saying to me are really insulting. I don't know why I put up with it. Then again, she *is* the only person I know personally, who can call me a bitch and make it feel like a kiss on the cheek. She's looking at me sideways, as if to say, "Do I really have to explain?"

"Well, Erik, you *do* have a couple of tendencies," she begins with a sigh. "When you talk, your hands dance at the wrist, you always speak with an upward inflection, and whenever you answer a phone call, you're always greeted with a, 'Good afternoon, Ma'am.'"

"You're the only person that does that to me, Mackenzie."

"Well, it's always really confusing when I hear a woman answer your phone." I hate her. I hate her so much.

We're about to head over to our first period classes — me, to English with Ms. Maple, and Mackenzie, to Calculus — when I spot Andrew down the hall. The six foot tall, golden haired adonis is laughing with a group of equally tall, yet not nearly as attractive "bros," all dressed similarly, in different colored versions of the same plaid shirt. They're like if Andrew had been cloned, but the experiment went wrong. This is why people should never attempt to play God. Andrew notices me and breaks away from his pack. He walks over. It takes him, like, five steps because his legs are so freakin' long. Man, I wish I was taller.

"Erik, hey," he says, the corners of his eyes crinkling in his smile. I look over at Mackenzie, who looks completely dumbfounded that this guy is standing in front of us.

"Will you two excuse me? It's not my time of the month, but I'm feeling very moist," Mackenzie says, like that's a normal thing to say to people. "I have to go put in a tampon." She backs away from us slowly, and then walks off, disappearing around the corner.

"Wow, she's disgusting," I say.

"I dunno. She's kinda funny," Andrew replies. "What's her name again?"

"Mackenzie — Um, look Andrew. I, uh… I've been thinking about the other day."

"Yeah, that's what I wanted to talk to you about… You didn't tell anyone, did you?"

"Just her, but she won't say anything."

"Good. Let's keep it that way, yeah? I don't want this getting out, alright?"

"Yeah, of course." Wow, we're actually on the same page here.

"Cool, thanks," he smiles, and then goes back to rejoin his friends. I wonder what it must feel like to be him; cool, popular, good looking, and surrounded by people who insist on looking like discounted versions of him. Huh, it sounds like a nice life.

"So, are you guys, like, dating now, or what?" I jump. Mackenzie's standing next to me. I didn't even notice her come back. God, she's got such quiet footsteps.

"No, he just wanted to make sure I keep quiet," I tell her.

"You okay?"

"Yeah, in fact, this is exactly what I wanted," I smile feebly. Mackenzie seems concerned, but I'm not in any mood to dive deeper into it. I'm happy. Keeping this a secret is a good thing. It means that I can deal with it without ever being judged. I'll figure out a way to purge this sin that blights me, and everything will go back to normal. None will be the wiser. The priest, yesterday, told me to continue to fight temptation, and that's exactly what I'm going to do. It's gonna be difficult though, because every time I think about Andrew kissing me and putting his hands on my junk, I feel my blood start to rush to places it should not be rushing to. I already know fighting temptation is gonna be a lot harder than it sounds.

Like, literally.

chapter six
nicholas

It's about a five to six hour drive from LA to the Bay Area depending on how fast you're going. In this case, it's looking closer to a four hour drive with my mom speeding along Highway 5, trying to get as far away from my dad as fast as she possibly can.

Ma and I started packing up our things yesterday. There was no fight or resistance because Dad wasn't home. Apparently, he left the house the night Ma came and told me about their divorce, which was why Ma came and told me about their divorce. He left thinking she wouldn't say anything, because they were supposed to talk to me together. I guess Ma couldn't take it anymore.

Then today, a little after noon, we left. Ma wanted to tell dad to his face that she and I were going away, but because he hadn't come home in the last couple of days, she resorted to leaving him a text and voicemail. She sent those messages around 9:00am. We waited to see if he'd come home to try to sort things out, but he never did. We got no response. I mean, yeah, he could've been busy at work, but the text message my mom sent indicated that it had been read. It's already 3:30pm. Still no word from him.

"You hungry, Nicky?" Ma asks.

"I could eat," I respond. Ma takes the next exit off the highway and we pull into the drive thru of the first fast food place we see. I order a twenty piece of chicken nuggets, two double bacon cheeseburgers, and a large order of fries. I know it sounds like a lot, but I haven't eaten all day. We've been driving for hours and the anxiety I was feeling about leaving suppressed any appetite I might've had earlier. Ma orders a breakfast burrito and an iced coffee. We pick up our food from the drive thru window and Ma parks the car in an empty space in the corner of the lot. I pull out my phone so I can put on some random videos to watch while I eat, but I stop when I see I've received two text messages from my dad. My heart's racing now. I wonder what he's gonna say. I'm hoping it's some sort of apology, or explanation, or *something* that's gonna make us turn the car around and go back home. I tap the notification and read the first text. It says literally one word: "Sorry." That's it. Nothing else. Sorry? Sorry for what? That we left? That he's allegedly been cheating on my mom? Is he not gonna own up to anything? I scroll down to the next message and it reads: "Come visit sometime." What? What does that even mean? It's like he's completely cool with the fact that we're gone. It's like he's not even affected at all by their pending divorce. The fact that he said next to nothing practically confirms my mom's claims.

"Did your dad text back?" Ma asks. I quickly hit the power button so that my screen goes black and shove my phone back into my pocket.

"No. Nothing," I lie. I don't see what good telling her would do. I don't wanna make her feel any worse than she probably already does. No response from my dad is better than the one I got. I start in on my fries and try to put the whole situation into the back of my mind.

Watching a woman cry while eating a breakfast burrito is one of the most unsettling things I have ever witnessed. I want to comfort my mother, but what do you say in this kind of situation? What she's going through is the end of a lifetime of marriage. I can't just be like, "It's okay. You don't need him. You'll find someone better." It's my freakin' dad! Before this, I couldn't imagine anyone better for her. Or for *us*. He was our provider. She needed him. We needed him. *I* needed him. And he just didn't show up.

About half an hour later, we're back on the road. I offered to drive the rest of the way. I knew my mom needed a break. She has huge bags forming under her eyes and she's sitting silently, listless, as if all of the life in her body has left her. I want to turn on the radio because this silence is deafening, but with the current mood, music seems inappropriate.

It's not long before I start to recognize a few somewhat familiar landmarks. I remember certain signs and geography from the times we visited my Tio Roger over the years, and I know my exit's close. I pull off the highway and follow the long stretches of road that cut through the seemingly endless plains of grassland. We pass through several communities consisting of only a handful of rickety houses and continue to drive for another forty minutes before things start to resemble civilization. By 5:00pm, we've entered suburbia.

We arrive at Tio Roger's and I pull into the driveway next to his SUV. Tio Roger lives in a modest ranch style home in a relatively old neighborhood, one that was around before new developments started popping up with uniform houses that are virtually carbon copies of themselves. Ma and I climb out of the car and

I ring the doorbell. Moments later, Tio Roger opens the door and welcomes us into his home. Tio Roger and my mom look very similar. They're both roughly five feet seven inches tall, with a slightly plump, bottom heavy shape to them. They've both got light beige skin and dark brown hair. Their side's the reason I look white. Aside from that, I don't resemble them very much at all. I look more like my dad, five foot ten, lean and athletic, but painted in my mom's color palette. The one non-color related feature I got from my mom's side are my heavy eyebrows. When I was younger, my mom worried they'd grow into a big bushy unibrow. Fortunately for me, they didn't. Actually, if you were to ask me, I'd say I grew into them quite nicely. In fact, there have been a few girls in the past who've approached me just to ask if I pluck them, but no. These babies are all natural. I got lucky in that department.

"How was the drive?" Tio Roger asks as we step into his living room.

"Not bad," I say.

"Miserable," Ma offers. She goes in for a hug and sniffles into Tio Roger's shoulder. My uncle holds my mom for a bit while I stand here, biting my lip just trying to hold it together. As much as I might feel the need, I refuse to let myself cry. I need to be strong for my mom, so she doesn't get it in her head that I'm unhappy being here in this situation. We're in this together.

"Rosie, you should rest," my uncle says. "Lemme show you to your room." Ma and I follow Tio Roger through the one hallway in his home as he leads us to the guest room at the very end of the hall. "You can have this room," Tio Roger tells my mom.

"Perfect," Ma says. "What about Nicky?"

"The futon in my office pulls out. Nick can stay in there," my uncle explains. He turns to me. "I hope you don't mind me barging in every now and then to do some work."

"Oh, no, Tio Roger," I begin to reply. "I don't want to put you out. I'll just crash in the living room."

"Nonsense, a kid your age needs his own space."

"Yeah, but you need your workspace."

"Mijo, why don't you take the guest room?" Ma suggests, but I'm not about to take a room away from my mom.

"Ma, no."

"Okay, I have an idea," Tio Roger cuts in. "Nick, if you help me move the futon, you can take the garage."

"¿El garaje? ¿Estás loco?" Ma exclaims.

"¡Esperate! Dejame explicar," my uncle replies. All I'm hearing is the start of a potential shouting match. "Just think about it. Nick will have all that space to himself. I can give him the clicker and he'll have his own private entrance. He'll be able to come and go as he pleases."

"Actually, Ma, that doesn't sound too bad," I say. I mean, living in a garage doesn't sound ideal, but people convert garages into living spaces all the time. It can't be that bad.

"I don't know, mijo," Ma worries. "Are you sure?"

"Yeah. I'd feel better if I don't have to put anyone out."

"It's settled then," Tio Roger announces. "Come on, Nick. Let's move that futon." I nod, agreeing, but Ma looks reluctant.

Moving the futon into the garage was way easier said than done. My uncle and I had to push and pull, back and forth, and figure out how to bend several laws of physics just to get the thing out of the office. Then, we had to somehow maneuver the stupid thing around a really tight corner of the hallway. It was bullshit! Once we managed to get it through the hall, it was smooth sailing across the living room and kitchen, before we had to repeat the whole process of removing the futon from the office, except backwards and into the garage. We did it, but it took, like, an hour.

"Alright, if you're both good, I've got some sketches I need to finish up for work," Tio Roger says. He goes back into the main house, leaving me and Ma to evaluate my new living arrangement.

"It's spacious enough, that's for sure," Ma says, though not sounding very excited about it. "You'll probably need an air conditioner and a heater, or something, you know, but it's not terrible."

"I'll make it work," I assure her.

"Yeah, you could do a lot with the space. Maybe we could put some curtains up. Dust everything off and make it look nice."

"Ma, it's a garage."

"I know, Nicky, but we don't know how long we'll be here for. We might as well try to make it comfortable."

"Yeah," I say. I can feel my mood starting to shift and decline. She's right. We don't know how long we'll be here for. Suddenly, I feel the temper I inherited from my dad start to boil in my gut and I have to sit down. It hits me all at once. The cheating. The divorce. The move. Everything. "FUCK!" I scream once I've got myself situated on the futon. The tears finally escape me.

"Ay, mijo."

"No, don't... I didn't want to cry about this."

"It's okay that you're upset. I get it." I'm surprised by how collected she is right now. It seems the tables have turned. Ma's calm and I'm a mess. Maybe I'm just tired. I blame moving the damn futon.

Ma takes a seat next to me.

"You know, I never imagined myself ever getting a divorce. I never imagined I'd be running away from your father, and I certainly never imagined I'd be shoving my kid into a garage so he can have his own space, but that's the situation I have." I watch as my mom lets her head sink into the back of the futon. She's talking normal, meanwhile her eyes are pouring waterfalls. "I don't want to be sad about this. I know I'm going to be, but I don't want to."

"Ma, you know you don't have to be strong right now, right?"

"I just don't want to drown in it, Nicky," she says. Her words kill me.

I hate seeing her like this. She's breaking apart, but still moving forward. She's like a flower trying to survive a drought, or a kid who can't swim who's found themselves in the deep end.

"Promise me something, Nicholas," Ma says, getting up. She never calls me by my full name. So, whatever this promise is, I know it's gotta be serious. "Promise me that you will never commit yourself to someone unless you're going to commit yourself to someone. Do you know what I mean by that?"

"Yeah," I nod. "I do."

And I promise.

chapter seven
erik

Vaginas are weird.

I never thought about it before, but the more that I look at them, the more strange they seem to me. Maybe it's because I'm a boy, but I can't imagine looking down at my groin and seeing nothing there. I've been watching porn for the last couple of days, specifically lesbian porn. You see, I don't want there to be any chance that my eyes will drift and focus on a man. If there's no temptation, there'll be no temptation to fight. But seeing all these artificially engineered women bumping and grinding on each other is doing nothing for me. It's just making me feel gross. When I told Mackenzie about my plan to purge my gayness through lesbian porn — which, now that I think about it, doesn't really make sense since lesbians are also gay — she just laughed at me.

"That's the stupidest thing I've ever heard, Erik," she said, choking through her amusement. "You're gay. Get over it." But I can't just get over it. I can't simply accept that I was made with a built-in deficiency, and I told her that. Her response was, "God makes no mistakes." Okay, I'll give her that, but I also know that God likes to test people. Like how he tested Abraham by asking him to kill his only son before sending an angel down to be like, "Just kidding!" Or how he kicked Adam and Eve out of the Garden of Eden and cast them out into the barren wastelands because they failed his test by eating an apple. The point is, God likes to test people, and maybe this is my test. I could be like Job, who God took everything away from just to see if he would be loyal, and he was... even after God took away his children, health, and home...

He got a bigger house for it!

Now, I've been trying different things that I think might help me set my mind straight, you know, aside from the lesbian porn. Like, every time I picture Andrew and I get excited about it, I slap myself on the wrist. Or, if I'm walking around school and I spot another guy who I think is attractive, I'll whisper to myself, "He's ugly, he's ugly, he's ugly," and I'll just keep repeating it until I start to believe it. So far, I think only one of the guys I did that with heard me and I had to apologize, which was super awkward. I even make it a point to talk to myself about female anatomy while I'm servicing my *own* anatomy, and usually the moment is lost, so then I get to celebrate the fact that I successfully avoid committing *two* sins. I will say though, fighting temptation is hard, and despite my best efforts, I don't know how much longer I can deal with this on my own. I know I told Mackenzie, but she's no help because her goal for this is the complete opposite of mine.

I decide... tonight's gotta be the night.

Mom's dominating the dinner conversation with a long-winded story about this couple who contacted her to tour a home they had no intention of ever purchasing. My mom works as a part time real estate agent. She doesn't have to; it's more like a hobby for her, but it gets her out of the house.

I'm sitting here listening, waiting patiently for the perfect opportunity to talk about what I need to talk about, but every time there's a break for silence, I lose my nerve. I have no appetite, I'm so anxious. Still, I don't want it to be obvious that I've got something big coming, so I take a few bites of my chicken adobo and rice just for show.

"I got an email today from church," Dad says, now steering the conversation. "They sent a newsletter out. They're looking for more altar boys. Erik, you should volunteer. It might be good for you."

"Oh, you should," Mom adds. "You can serve the Eucharist." I can feel my eyes bulging out of my face. This is not the conversation topic I had expected to follow. How am I supposed to go from my parents saying, "Erik, you can serve the body of Christ," to me going, "I think I'd rather *service* the body of Christ." I can't do that! One.) that's sacrilegious as all hell and two.) it's just plain wrong. It's like switching the channel from a children's television show to porn!

And now, I can't stop thinking about porn!

Vaginas!

. . .

Okay, I'm good.

All I have to do now is muster up the courage to tell my parents. They'll still love me, right? They won't, like, disown me or anything, right? I mean, it's not like I decided on a whim that I'm gay. I didn't choose this. Why would anybody choose this? So long as I am committed to fighting against homosexual temptations and living a pure life, then there's no way they could possibly be angry about it. At least, that's what I hope.

"Erik, is something wrong?" Dad asks. "You've hardly touched your food." My heart sinks into my stomach. He knows. He can tell something's up. He and Mom exchange a look — you know, the parental kind, where they seem totally indifferent, but they care just enough to press you about something. There's no turning back now. I've gotta say something or I'm never gonna come out with it. I open up my mouth to speak, but all that comes out is a long uhhhhhhhhhh…

My parents lean in. I'm acting super weird. Suddenly, this dinner's gotten so intense. If I don't say something now, this meal's gonna end on a major cliffhanger, and then my parents will just assume that I've done something insane. I can see the gears in their heads turning in their eyes. What's wrong with Erik? Is he failing a class? Is he doing drugs? Are he and Mackenzie dating again? It should be noted that my mom really dislikes Mackenzie, finding her vulgar and indecent, which isn't wrong.

"Erik, what's wrong?" Mom says, sounding more like a demand than a question.

"It's nothing. Really." I respond. I'm panicking now. My parents exchange another glance, but this time it's the kind that says they don't believe me. I *know* they don't believe me.

"You know, you can talk to us," Dad offers, more sympathetically than my mother ever could. "If something's bothering you, you should talk about it. It's not healthy keeping things bottled up." I really don't give my dad enough credit. I take in a deep breath and let it out slowly. Alright, I'm ready to talk.

"Well…" I begin reluctantly. "I was wondering… what happens to gay people?" Both of them pause, and what immediately follows is the most uncomfortable silence imaginable.

"Um… why do you ask?" My father says, after taking a moment.

"No reason," I smile nervously in response. Mom is staring at me with her Filipino death glare. I don't know if you've ever been stared down by an angry Filipino woman, but it feels like they're reaching deep down inside of you so they can rip out your soul and murder you with their talon-like manicures. It's not so much that they stare daggers, it's more that they stare death itself. In fact, the blood of their victims is probably how they concocted the recipe for dinuguan.

"Erik, what's going on?" Mom asks. Her voice is soft and even, but I know her well enough to know that it's all an act. She's like a hungry jungle cat lying in wait, ready to pounce.

I'm not scared.

I'm freaking terrified.

"Um… I think I might be gay," there, I've said it. I'm so freaked out at this point that I don't even wait for my parents to respond before I launch full speed into a long-winded ramble. "I mean, I don't know for sure, but

I kissed a boy and I liked it. Actually, he kissed me, and I talked to the priest at confession about it and he told me to just fight temptation, so that's what I've been doing. I've been trying to look at girls more and convince myself that I'm not attracted to boys but I am, and I don't know what to do to stop it, because I really don't want to be gay and burn in Hell, and I'm just… I'm scared."

No one says a word.

We sit silently for what feels like eternity, and I keep thinking, "Please, just put me out of my misery." I can't take this. Suddenly, my mother scoots her chair back.

"Will you excuse me?" she says, getting up.

"Chris," my dad says, reaching for her from his seat, but she's too quick for him. She exits the kitchen and moments later, I hear the sound of her bedroom door slam. Dad looks at me with a stern expression. I can't tell if he's sympathetic, or upset, or what, but he gets up and exits without saying another word to me.

I'm alone now.

I had braced myself for what I thought would be the perfect storm of yelling, screaming, and tears. I imagined us arguing about whether or not it was a choice. I imagined them crying hysterically and blaming themselves, as if *my* faults were caused by something *they* had done. I imagined them scolding me for entertaining the idea of homosexuality. But no. None of that came. Instead, what I got was far worse:

They left me alone.

Friday. October 4th.

It's 5:13 am. I wake up in the middle of a coughing fit, covered in a cold sweat. I had that dream again, the one with the island, and the boat, and the drowning. It was worse this time around. I could really feel myself gasping for air. It felt like I was actually gonna die.

I shower, get dressed, and head downstairs to the kitchen. It's still earlier than when my parents usually get up, which is good, because I'll need the extra time to find my nerve again.

As I enter the kitchen, I can see all of last night's dishes in the sink where I left them. This is unusual. My parents never go to bed without cleaning up first. They must not have come out from their room last night. I decide to rummage through the pantry for anything that might have caffeine and find a box of generic brand tea bags. I put a kettle on to boil and take a seat at the table. It's eerily quiet and there's a heaviness in the air left over from the night before. I don't like it. I don't like it one bit.

It's nearing 7:00am and neither one of my parents has come out. I sip on my tea and continue to wait, wondering if I'm gonna end up missing school over this. If they don't come out, I won't have a ride. I'll have no way of getting there. I suppose I could take the bus — I take it after school — but I'm not familiar with the morning schedule, and by the time the bus would get there, I'd already be way late for my first class.

At around 7:30am, I hear footsteps approaching and I tense up.

"You ready to go?" my dad asks as he steps into the kitchen. He's already dressed for work, in khakis and a blue button up. I nod simply in response.

Dad drives me to school without a word. Even though we never talked much before, I can feel the difference in our relationship. It's like we went from white to… I dunno, *off* white. It's subtle. Very subtle. But it's there. I stare out the window, watching as the world passes by. Everything seems to be moving about, business as usual. It's as if nothing in the world has changed, when, in actuality, everything has. We pull into the neighborhood across from my school, as we normally would. I grab my backpack and move to open the door.

"Erik," Dad says. I instantly freeze. I don't know what to expect or how I should behave, so I remain still, my hand resting on the door handle. "Your mother… she's gonna need some time." I don't respond to this. I mean, what am I supposed to say? Dad seems to want to say more. He opens his mouth to start talking, but then bails before anything comes out. I'm ready to leave. I pull on the door handle, and that's when he manages to say, "You're still my son, right?"

I'm speechless. Again, I don't know how to respond, or if I should even respond at all. Dad sighs. I know this must be hard on him.

"Nothing's changed," Dad adds. I want to believe him, but I don't. He can say nothing's changed and that everything's okay, but that doesn't make it true. His struggle just to say it is proof enough. He offers me a tiny pitiful smile. It's almost painful to look at. I appreciate him trying though.

Mackenzie's hanging out by my locker. I'm not quite ready to talk about it just yet, so I'm thinking of keeping the conversation light and casual. We've only just greeted each other and, already, she can see that I'm putting up a front. I guess I don't hide my emotions well.

"Everything okay?" she says.

"Yeah, fine," I answer.

"Your eyes betray you, Erik. Something's up." I shake my head. I'm really not ready to talk about it.

"I'm fine," I insist, though I admit I'm not the least bit convincing. "We'll talk later, yeah?" I start heading to my first period, without waiting for Mackenzie. She doesn't follow me, thankfully. I need some time to rebuild myself and to figure some way to deal without being completely defeatist about everything.

As I'm heading toward English, I get it in my head that maybe I should skip class so that I can mull things over, but I decide against it. Thinking about it hardly seems productive at the moment, and right now, I could use the distraction. We're currently reading through and analyzing *Romeo and Juliet*. It's cute, I think... you know, from what I understand. At least, until they die at the end.

At lunch, I meet up with Mackenzie in the quad and we head into the cafeteria to pick up some food.

"What's going on with you?" Mackenzie starts, wasting no time.

"Can we talk about it somewhere a little more private?" I ask. It's high school. I'd rather we not talk about my personal issues when we're surrounded by our peers. If we did, we might as well just project our conversation over the loudspeakers.

"Football field," she suggests. "Behind the bleachers." We pay for our food and head out, making our way wordlessly toward the football field behind the gym. You can't get behind the bleachers through the stadium, and it's usually locked up anyway, unless there's a class going in. We walk along the fence surrounding the field until we reach the gravelly area behind the bleachers.

It's a largely unmonitored area of the school. It's just so out of the way from everything else on campus that hardly anyone comes here, unless they're planning on getting high or having sex. Luckily, there's no one else here, so we don't have to worry about either of those things. "Alright, spill."

"I told my parents," I explain. "Last night, over dinner."

"What?" Mackenzie asks with genuine concern. "Well, how'd they take it? Like, what did they say?"

I recount the happenings of last night, from Dad suggesting I volunteer to be an altar boy, to the moment I told them what happened between me and Andrew. Saying out loud that my parents just walked away from me gets me choked up, but I make sure to defend my dad's little bit of effort from this morning. I don't want Mackenzie to think my parents are terrible people. I mean, she probably already thinks that, knowing my mom doesn't care for her, but still. No reason to add fuel to the fire.

Mackenzie is silent for a moment. It's unusual for her to not have a response ready. I wait for her to say something catty and sarcastic with her devil-may-care attitude, but she doesn't.

"I'm sorry, Erik," she says finally. It throws me. I have to bite my lip to stop myself from breaking. I would've rather her say something like her usual

Mackenzie self. At least then, this wouldn't feel so serious. There's no avoiding it anymore.

"The thing is, I knew they were gonna be upset, but I thought there'd be more talking," I explain. "I thought we'd have a discussion about it. I was even prepared for them to yell and freak out, but nothing. I just feel so unsure about everything, and it's super awkward. I mean, why did I have to be like this? It's like I'm broken."

"You're not broken, Erik," Mackenzie says gently. "Your life is just in that ugly metamorphosis stage. It'll get better."

"Easy for you to say."

"It *is* easy for me to say. And it'll be easy for you to say too, once you stop acting like it's the end of the world. I mean, I know it's gotta be hard, and scary, and whatever, but you've still got a lot to be thankful for. You just gotta remember to count your blessings."

"Like what?"

"Well, you're healthy. You've still got a roof over your head. And last I checked, you've got a beautiful man lusting for your virginal attention, which is more than I can say for myself." I chuckle, unexpectedly. She really knows how to steer the topic away from self-pity.

"You really gotta stop obsessing over that," I tell her.

"And you need to start," Mackenzie replies, sharp and quick. "Come on, isn't *he* the whole reason you're in this situation to begin with? Any straight girl or gay guy would kill to be in your position."

"No. Andrew Logan… he's out of my league."

"What?"

"You've seen him. We don't exactly look like we go together."

"Erik, what are you talking about?" I don't want to say it out loud because it'll make me feel worse than I already do.

"Can we change the subject?' I say, trying hard not to sound like I'm begging.

"Oh, my god. Erik, do you think you're ugly?" How does she always know?! I turn, trying to avoid her. "Erik!"

"What do you think, Mackenzie!? I don't have the best body, or the coolest clothes. I'm not exactly what you'd call cute, or hot, or whatever. I'm just… nobody. I'm that quiet kid in the back that no one pays attention to. I might as well be invisible. I have no business being attracted to someone like Andrew Logan." Mackenzie rolls her eyes at me.

"Erik, you can be attracted to whoever the hell you want," she says, her voice coming out sounding more like an authority figure than a friend. Sometimes I wonder what Mackenzie would be capable of if she wasn't restricted by the confines of suburbia, but then she adds, "Regardless of how hideous you think you are," and I instantly go from moderately impressed to annoyed. She knows how to drive the conversation topic, sure… right into a deadly pile up.

"You know, that's really not helpful."

"You are fine the way you are, Erik. What? Do you want me to twirl my hair around my fingers and be all, 'Oh-em-gee, Erik, you are so cute!' because I'm not gonna do that."

"I dunno… it might help." Mackenzie narrows her eyes, cocking her head to one side. Then, she reaches up and begins twirling her hair around her perfectly manicured fingers.

"Oh-em-gee, Erik," she says, raising her tone to sound something like a breathless toddler. "You are so cute. I want to have your baby."

"I hate you." Mackenzie just laughs, playfully hitting me on the shoulder. With all this uncertainty, at least there's one person I know who's on my side.

I start to unwrap a foil-wrapped burger I got from the cafeteria when, in the distance, I hear the sound of the school bell ring. We'd spent the whole lunch period talking, neither of us had a chance to eat.

"Crap, already?" I say, starting to rewrap my burger.

"What are you doing?" Mackenzie asks.

"Lunch is over. I gotta go to class."

"Skip it. They won't miss us." For a minute, I second guess the idea, but then I decide there's no point in going to class on an empty stomach, especially considering all I had before school was a sad cup of tea. I'll be useless with my stomach growling the whole time. I start in on my burger while Mackenzie digs into a bag of potato chips while taking selfies of herself eating violently. You'd never think that those pictures would turn out good, and they never do, but she doesn't take them to look good.

"It's my form of societal rebellion," she claims, when she notices me watching her. She's so strange. Just then, through the spaces in the bleachers, I see a group of people enter the stadium, all dressed in their P.E. uniforms of gray tops and red bottoms. They meander onto the field and start running laps. Among them is Andrew. He's super noticeable because he's one of the few boys in their class who's confident enough to go topless and actually has the body to justify it. "Hey, look, it's your boyfriend," Mackenzie says, chomping on a potato chip. Boyfriend, huh? I suppose that would be nice.

I start to imagine Andrew and I together, walking around campus hand-in-hand. I imagine sitting at a table with him and all of his popular friends at lunch. Then, after school we'd walk to the nearby coffee shop and share a java shake, using two straws. It'll be just like in all the movies set during the 1950s, except I won't be running around in a poodle skirt and he won't be going around boasting about how he "conquered" me, because there will be a mutual respect between us. Yup, that's what it'll be like. We'll be — what's that old-timey saying that people used to describe these things? Ah, right. We'll be going steady.

"If only," I mutter to myself.

"Let's make it happen," Mackenzie says. I was so lost in my daydreaming I'd nearly forgotten she was here.

"Please, Mackenzie. You know there's no way."

"Why not? You have Bio with him in sixth period. You could just ask."

"I can't just ask him to be my boyfriend, it's not that simple."

"It is. You're just complicating it because of your insecurities. May I remind you that *he* came on to *you*." She has a point. I just don't know where I'll find the nerve. "Listen, just ask him to meet you after school. Say something like you wanna review your project, or whatever, and then bring him back here so you can talk in private."

"Yeah… I don't think I can do that, Mackenzie. I'm gonna miss the bus."

"Oh, don't give me that excuse. I'll give you a ride. Come on, we'll meet here after sixth. And then, when he comes to meet you, I'll, like, hide out in the bushes or something, so he doesn't see that I'm here."

"I don't know."

"Erik, trust me. It'll be fine." Everything Mackenzie's saying makes it sound so easy. It's as if relationships aren't this big and terrifying thing, and that the only reason they *are* these big and terrifying things is because we allow them to be. Maybe she's right. Maybe it is actually that simple. I haven't decided if this is a good idea or a bad idea yet, but I agree to it anyway. I hope I'm not kicking myself about it later.

I head over to sixth period and take my seat at the back corner table. I'm hoping all that running Andrew did during last period has worn him out and that he doesn't show up. I'm staring up at the clock, waiting for the final bell to ring. Don't show up. Don't show up. But, of course, Andrew comes in just as the final bell sounds. He takes his seat next to me, and I can smell the manly fragrance of the fresh application of deodorant he must've recently put on. He looks over at me and smirks. I'm dead. Seeing him in front of me, and within arm's reach, causes me to tense up. How am I supposed to do this now? His sapphire eyes are like a gun pointed right at my face. Asking him to be my boyfriend would be like handing him a bullet and hoping his response isn't to simply load up and pull the trigger. This is the dumbest thing I could've ever agreed to.

"Sup?" Andrew says. He's so casually cool, it's not fair. My heart is racing, and I can hear the voices in my head screaming at me to bail. There would be no shame in that. There's no shame in trying to spare yourself from an impending heartbreak. I'm about ready to give up on the whole thing, but then I start thinking about Mackenzie. If I don't go through with it, she'll never let me live it down. I can already hear her screaming, "HE WAS RIGHT THERE! WHY DIDN'T YOU FREAKING ASK HIM YOU DUMB BITCH?" Though my imagining of her is undoubtedly the more family friendly iteration. I just have to suck it up.

Deep breath…

And go.

"I wanted to go over some stuff with you about our presentation," I lie. These words coming out of my mouth sound disgusting to me. I know what I'm really asking, and it has nothing to do with the Golgi Complex.

"Yeah, sure," Andrew replies. Great! Step one of my boyfriend inquiry is complete.

"I was thinking we could meet up behind the bleachers after class." Andrew looks at me suspiciously. He's clearly taken aback. What did I just say?

…

Oh no, the bleachers! People only go there for one of two things: marijuana or sex. And there's nothing about me that would indicate that I do or take pot. "This was a bad idea, Mackenzie," I think to myself. "A very bad idea!" It's clear to me now that we didn't exactly think this plan through, and I am freaking out.

Our teacher begins to lecture, and despite my best attempts to focus, I can't. Nothing of what our teacher is saying reaches me. I'm too distracted. Why? Because I'm feeling something, a hand, resting on my inner thigh, but I've got both of my hands on top of the table. I look over at Andrew, who seems to be keeping up with the lecture, and I'm kind of impressed by his ability to multitask. He gives my leg a gentle squeeze. I feel like a slut.

After sixth period, I race out of Bio without saying another word to Andrew. Anything else I say is likely to land me in some deep water and, again, I never learned to swim. I quickly make my way back toward the football field and around to behind the bleachers. I'm the first one here. My heart is pounding. I want to yell. I want to scream. Where is Mackenzie? This is her fault. She talked me into this. She better show up.

About five or so minutes later, I see Mackenzie ambling over, giggling at something on her phone.

"Look, my hideous potato chip picture got a bunch of likes," she says proudly. "It's, like, scarily ironic."

"Mackenzie, we've got a problem!" I exclaim, way louder than I need to. I'm in full panic mode, pacing frantically back and forth over the gravel.

"Whoa, what's wrong? Did Andrew not agree to meet you?"

"Oh, he's gonna meet me. In fact, I'm pretty sure he thinks he's coming over here to fornicate with me."

"Huh, that's an F word you don't hear every day," Mackenzie quips, as if none of this is of any consequence. I guess it's not to *her*. She's not the one who unintentionally lured a hot guy into expecting gravelly behind-the-bleacher sex with her. She just pressured *me* into doing that.

"Mackenzie, people don't come behind the bleachers to talk," I try to explain.

"We do," she replies. She's not getting it.

"Well, other people don't! The only things people come back here to do is have sex and do pot!"

"First of all, Erik, you don't 'do' pot. And second, you're freaking out over nothing. Unless you explicitly said, 'Andrew, meet me behind the bleachers to fornicate,' I highly doubt he's coming here with that expectation."

"He was groping my thigh all period."

"Well... then, yeah, he's definitely expecting something," Mackenzie finally admits. She's no help at all. Before I can get too frustrated with her, however, she points to something behind me. I turn around and see Andrew walking towards us. "Everything will be fine, Erik," Mackenzie says. "You have all the control. Remember, he came here because you asked him to. Not the other way around. Take control."

"Hey," Andrew greets us as he approaches.

"Hi," Mackenzie waves. "I'll wait for you by the gym, Erik." I've never been so disappointed to see her go.

"I have a feeling she's gonna be waiting a while," Andrew says once Mackenzie's out of earshot. He quickly closes the gap between us and moves in for a kiss. I immediately put my hands up against his chest — his solid, *solid* chest — and catch him just in time to hold him back. "Are you playing hard to get?"

"What? No," I say. I'm really uncomfortable standing here with my hands all over his... uh, boobs? No, pecs! Don't get me wrong, they're nice pecs. *Very* nice — wait, what am I saying!? Oh, God! He's staring at me, smiling. He's got perfectly straight teeth, like a spearmint cave of pearls. I can smell the mint on his breath, and I feel myself start to loosen, allowing him to move closer. He kisses me just once, leaving me wanting more. God, I want so much more.

"What are you doing tonight?"

"I dunno. Why?"

"My parents are going on a date night and I have the house to myself for a couple hours. I was thinking you might wanna come over and… you know, do stuff."

"I do," I can't believe what I'm saying. This boy is having such a terrible disarming effect on me. Any doubt I might've had about my sexuality floats away on his minty breath. It's so far gone I can't even deny it. But I'm still me. I still have my morals. "I want to, Andrew, but I can't. Not yet."

"Erik, I don't understand what's going on here," Andrew says, pulling away.

"Well, I just think that if we're gonna start dating, I would like it if we take things slow, you know?" I have the control. Mackenzie was totally right about this. All I have to do is stick to my guns, and things will work out the way that I want them to.

"Dating?" Andrew asks. "Who said anything about dating?" I'm confused now. I don't understand what he's saying. Isn't that what this is about? So we could date and eventually do stuff together?

"I thought…" I'm not even sure what to say.

"Erik, no offense, but if I'm gonna be dating someone, I'm kinda out of your league." I stare at him with widened eyes, completely dumbfounded. What does this mean? What is he saying? Is he saying that I'm good enough to have sketchy behind-the-bleachers sex with, but I'm not good enough to date? I'm the type of guy who only dates! I'm not a… I'm not a… I can't even finish the thought. I simply walk off.

"Erik, wait!" I hear Andrew calling after me, but I don't stop. I refuse. I walk away as quickly as I can without breaking into a full on sprint. I have to get away from this guy. This is a guy who preyed on me. He saw my deficiency from afar and took advantage of it. He turned my whole world upside down for his own pleasure, his own gain. Because of him, I've been questioning everything. I've second guessed a vessel of God, I've potentially ruined my relationship with my parents, particularly my mother, and for what? What do I have to show for it? Not a boyfriend, that's for damn sure.

"How'd it go?" Mackenzie asks when she sees me approaching the gym. I shake my head. Her expectant grin disappears when she sees I'm fighting to hold back tears. "Erik, what happened?" I don't want to say it, because I don't want to relive it. Hearing what Andrew said once was enough. I don't wanna repeat it.

"I just wanna go home," I say. I see Mackenzie looking behind me, and I turn to see Andrew coming this way. I don't want to be anywhere near him. Thankfully, I don't have to. Mackenzie walks over to him, and I see my opportunity to bail.

"WHAT THE FUCK DID YOU SAY TO HIM!?" Mackenzie's voice echoes from behind me. I don't need to be around for what happens next. I don't need to listen to them arguing about me. I don't need any of it. All I need is to get away from here, but since Mackenzie is my ride home from school today, I guess I'm stuck.

God, nothing's going my way today, is it? Nothing ever goes my way.

I was stupid to think otherwise.

nicholas

The day after we arrived at my uncle's house, Ma suggested that we go shopping for furniture. We drove over to a local discount department store and picked up a couple of things like a new dresser, an end table, a bookshelf, and a desk. There wasn't much variety, but even so, I tried to keep my choices on the cheap and more basic side, because I wasn't sure that us spending money was a good idea. Ma doesn't have an income of her own right now and, though I doubt he'd cut us off, I don't think we can rely on my dad forever.

The day after that, I spent much of my time struggling to assemble my new furniture. I know the manufacturers include extra screws and bolts in case you lose one, but each time I'd finish putting a piece together, I'd second guess myself because I'd have all these extra bits lying around. It really messes with your head thinking you've missed something. I'm almost expecting my desk to collapse from under me while I'm using it, all because I forgot to put in a screw… Huh, I wonder if this is how my mom feels about her marriage. Who knows? She hasn't talked much about it and I don't wanna be the one to bring it up, especially since Dad still hasn't reached out. Not since the day we left.

The rest of the week has been pretty uneventful. Mom's been busy doing research, making phone calls, and running around with her head chopped off, all in an effort to transfer me into the local high school before I fall too far behind. Apparently, she ran into a snag when she tried to enroll me because we technically don't live in the school district. That's when she claims to have had a full on Colombian meltdown in the office, which involved her screaming at the school administrators about how she ran away from her cheating husband. Once she released the floodgates and let the tears start rolling, she was able to coerce them into doing whatever she wanted, and now I'm set to start school tomorrow.

That's at least one good thing to come out of their divorce, I guess.

I don't want to go to school.

I really don't.

Don't get me wrong, I'm not *not* into school. In fact, I do pretty good, I think. It's just I don't want to go to a *new* school. See, it feels like if I go to this new school, then everything is final. There's no more going back home. There's no more possibility of my parents getting back together. I'll be starting over. It was one thing to move into my uncle's house, but to *also* be starting school here makes everything feel like this is really our life now, and there's no going back. And I want to go back.

I'm lying in bed, staring up at the exposed wooden beams of my ceiling, and hoping that Ma forgets that today is supposed to be my first day. I'm still in my underwear, putting off getting dressed. It's sort of my own little way of protesting.

"Nicky," Ma's voice comes through the door, accompanied by a sharp knocking sound. "Nicky, are you up?" I close my eyes, hoping she'll just go away. "Nicky." She keeps knocking. Just go away. "Nicky, are you dressed?" The door swings open and Ma steps into my garage. "Nicky, are you kidding me? Get dressed. You're gonna be late." I let out a heavy sigh. I know better than to argue with my mother. She comes from a third world country. There's not a single part of her that would hesitate to backhand me if I even so much as tried to talk back to her. "Dress. Now."

"Okay, okay," I say, getting up. I've got my hands raised in surrender. She shakes her head, annoyed.

"Hurry up." Ma goes back into the house so I can get dressed. I slip into a trusty pair of slim fit jeans and put on a simple red V-neck. I'm going for a no effort look. Once I get my high tops on, I head over to the bathroom and take a quick glance in the mirror to make sure my hair isn't looking totally hideous. I know I said I don't want to go to school — and I don't — but since I'm being forced to, I might as well look semi presentable. I give my hair a quick rinse in the sink and blow dry it into a nice upward swoop before securing it with a touch of hair wax. Semi presentable? Who am I kidding? I'm a freakin' stud.

After I'm ready, I head back into my garage to grab my backpack and class schedule, and then go to meet Ma in the living room.

"Come on, you're gonna be late," she says. "Are you excited?"

"Yay," I answer, with absolutely no excitement or energy whatsoever. The sarcasm is strong with this one. Ma doesn't care.

Ma drives me to school. The whole time she's talking about how great everything is gonna be and how I should be happy that I'm getting a fresh start like this. But I'm just staring out the window all forlornly, pretending to be in a sad music video. The song is a haunting piano ballad sung by a raspy voiced woman, possibly British. I can just imagine the music swelling at the bridge with a generous helping of strings, and the possibly British singer's hair getting swept up in the wind, while she stares at the camera with a look in her eyes that says, "I dare you not to cry."

Also, the video should be in black and white.

Brilliant...

Ma pulls into the school and it's immediately clear that this place is a cluster fuck. The parking lot is backed up with cars that can't seem to go anywhere because kids are too busy staring at their phones to look both ways before they cross. Like, seriously? Do they not realize they could die? See, this is why teenagers get a bad rep. We're all so freakin' stupid.

"Hmm… maybe you should just get out here, Nicky," Ma suggests. We're trapped near the middle of the lot, sandwiched between two cars. We aren't moving and we can't go anywhere.

"I guess," I say. I push open the door and climb out of the car. I then throw my backpack over my shoulder and turn to head towards… I don't even know. I guess I'll figure it out.

"Nicky," Ma calls out of the driver's side window.

"Yeah?"

"Here," she reaches her hand out and hands me a ten dollar bill. "Your lunch money." I don't like that she's handing me money, seeing as though she has yet to start looking for a job — at least as far as I've seen — but I don't want to open up a private conversation right here in the parking lot, so I just take the bill. "I love you, mijo."

"Love you too, Ma." She rolls up her window and inches forward. I turn around to see a pair of dumb neanderthal looking guys snickering at me.

"I love you Mee-ho," the stupid looking one says mockingly.

"Oh, mommy, I wuv my mommy. Fuckin' loser," the even stupider looking one adds. They laugh like they're clever or whatever, but they couldn't be any more basic.

"What are you guys, like, twelve?" I ask them, totally un-phased. "If you're gonna be bullies, don't be fuckin' babies about it. We're in high school. Dicks."

"What'd you call us?" Stupid one says.

"I called you dicks, what are you gonna do about it?"

"Boy, I'll knock you out," Stupider one threatens.

"Ooo, I'm shaking in my high tops," I answer, dripping with sarcasm. They seem genuinely surprised that I stood up to them. I guess they're the kind of bullies that don't get any pushback, so they must be reeling from the shock that someone's not taking it. When they don't offer any sort of comeback, I turn and walk away. Fun times. Here's to hoping Stupid and Stupider aren't a definite precursor of things to come. Otherwise, buckle up.

I'm walking through the hallways of what I think is the main campus building — it was the one building that had a marquee sign in front of it — but the whole layout of this place is confusing as all hell, I don't really know where I'm going. I feel like I'm walking through a funhouse and trying my luck with whatever doors I come across. From what I can tell, I'm in the Math and Science building, which is definitely not where I'm supposed to be. According to my schedule, I've got English with Ms. Maple. Where that is, I have no idea. I see a trio of mildly attractive but totally interchangeable girls standing around an open locker halfway through the hall. I figure one of these girls is bound to know where my English class would be.

"Excuse me," I say. As I approach, I notice they're all dressed in these really form fitting jeans and precariously high heels. I can't imagine they're comfortable, but whatever. It's their business.

"What?" The girl nearest to the open locker says without turning to me. The locker's been turned into a makeshift vanity, complete with a mirror in which I can see her smack her lips together in annoyance after a careful application of lip gloss. I swear, some girls get real mean when you try to talk to them while they're putting on their makeup.

"Hi," one of the other girls greets me, twirling her hair around her finger flirtatiously. The girl in the mirror then turns. I can see her eyes roll in the reflection, but her expression softens as soon as she sees me.

"Oh... I'm sorry. Are you, like, new?" Mirror Girl asks, and I can tell by her smile that she too is flirting with me.

"You're, like, really cute," the final girl says.

"Oh-em-gee, Angela, you can't just say that to people," Mirror Girl scolds her. "That's like sexual hare-ass-ment."

"It's pronounced her-ass-ment," Angela replies. "Boys don't like stupid girls, Becca. It's not cute and it's anti-feminist."

"Oh, go shave your armpits. I call dibs," Becca, the mirror girl, retorts.

"You can't just call dibs, Becca," Angela says. "He's not an object."

"Yeah, Becca," the girl who has yet to be named agrees. "Hashtag feminism."

"Shut up, Jen. You're not even involved," Becca says. "Besides, you're objectifying him just as much as I am." Well, this is awkward. I just wanted directions. I had no idea I was walking into a pack of hungry hyenas when I came over to talk to these girls. Even though they're busy bickering with each other, I'm afraid to move. I know if I do, they'll notice me. Curse these good looks.

Their bickering continues for a few minutes, and I'm just nodding along, waiting for a moment to make my escape. They start throwing insults at one another, tossing out words like "slut," "chicken head," and "fire crotch," despite the fact that none of them are red heads. You'd think that as a dude, having three girls fighting over you would be, like, super hot, but it's just weird and uncomfortable, and I'm just trying to get to class.

"I'm, like, so sorry about this, uh… what was your name?" Becca asks. After watching her and her friends argue, I don't really want to give them my name. I'm afraid to. People these days are tricky. If someone wants you enough, they'll take even just your first name, and find ways to stalk you on all your social medias. I know. I watch a lot of those murder documentaries. Introducing yourself to the wrong person is how you end up becoming ground meat to be fed to a lonely woman's cat, and I'm not about that life. In my mind, I start scrambling. Gotta think fast. How do I get a bunch of ravenous teenaged girls to immediately lose interest in me?

"Uh… I'm gay," I say. It's the first thing that comes out and, actually, it's not a bad thing to say. Either they'll be completely disgusted with me for wasting their time or they'll become my fruit flies, and I'll just have to come out of the closet as straight, once they've gotten over it. I'm hoping it's not the latter, because their energy is really exhausting.

"Ugh, what a waste," Jen says.

"Aw, I'm so sad. You were, like, really cute," Angela whines.

"Whatever. I guess it's true what they say, 'all the good ones are taken or gay,'" Becca adds, along with her signature eye roll. She shuts the locker and the three of them head off down the hall. Thank god. I turn and — HOLY SHIT!

"Hi, the name's Mackenzie," a freakin' gorgeous, porcelain skinned girl with dark, wavy hair introduces herself to me. She scared the crap out of me though, she was standing so close. I had no idea she was even there. "Did I hear you correctly? That you're into dudes? Because I have a gay friend—"

"Oh, I'm not gay," I cut her off, trying to explain. I'm immediately regretting my choice of words earlier. "I just said that so they'd leave me alone."

"Yeah, that's Becky-With-The-Not-So-Good-Hair for you," she quips. "So, I take it you have no shame?"

"What?"

"Erik!" She yells to a short, kinda pudgy, Asian kid with glasses who's apparently been watching us from down the hall. Mackenzie waves him over and he approaches seemingly reluctant. I can tell from his expression that he's nervous. "This is my gay best friend, Erik."

"Can you not introduce me like that?" Erik asks in such a small high-pitched voice I'd almost call it cute.

"Get over yourself," Mackenzie says to him scoldingly.

"Nicholas," I introduce myself. These two seem like an odd pairing, but Mackenzie's hot, so whatever.

"Hey, buddy, you're in front of my locker," someone else says. I turn around and see this buff blonde dude with a butt chin staring at me.

"Sorry," I say and sidestep out of his way.

"Do I know you?" He asks. "Why don't I know you?"

"It's my first day. I'm Nick."

"Andrew."

"Ugh, you're disgusting," Mackenzie interjects.

"Was I talking to you?" Andrew snaps at Mackenzie.

"You know, just 'cause you're on the sports... ball team, that doesn't give you the right to just swing your dick around," she fires back. "Who the hell do you think you are? You can't just go around toying with people's feelings like that. Like, what the hell is wrong with you?" What did I just find myself in the middle of? Erik and I take a step back and watch as Andrew and Mackenzie start arguing. Andrew towers over her, but Mackenzie's feisty, and she's not backing down. It's like watching a Chihuahua barking at a Great Dane. It's kind of amusing, if I'm being honest.

"What's going on?" I ask, leaning into Erik.

"It's complicated," Erik shakes his head. He seems sad now. At first, I thought Mackenzie and Andrew's argument was about them. I thought, maybe, they had been dating and they had just recently broken up, but looking at Erik, I'm wondering if it's actually about him. He's staring at the ground not even watching their barking match, and he looks a little embarrassed.

"Hey, you okay?" I say. Erik nods. I don't believe him though. I decide not to press him. He'll talk about it when he wants to talk about it.

"Do you need help finding your class?" Erik offers. Oh, yeah, class. That's how I got caught up in this business in the first place. I nod and hand Erik my class schedule. He reads over it. "English with Maple. US

History. Algebra II. It looks like we've got our first three classes together."

"Great, so you won't mind if I just follow you around all day then?" I say in my friendliest voice, a bit jokingly. I notice Erik brightens up at this. He smiles. Good. Maybe, if I play my cards right, I won't be stuck eating lunch alone today. Maybe I'll even get the story behind Mackenzie. I kinda can't get over how cute she is, you know, when she's not screaming at dudes like a raging lunatic.

chapter nine
erik

Oh, my god. Oh, my god. Oh, my god!

He smells like an ocean breeze. What an intoxicating scent for a body wash. Or maybe it's the scent of his deodorant. Who knows? His olive skin is smooth and naturally tan. His messily textured hair is the color of chestnuts. His eyes are small and almond shaped, and rest in a seemingly perpetual squint that makes it look like he's constantly deep in thought. And he's got the most perfectly placed beauty mark on the outside of his right eye. He looks like a model you might see in a fashion magazine, and is significantly taller than me, but shorter than Andrew, which is nice. To be honest, I feel really small standing next to Andrew. Standing next to Nicholas, I still feel short, but not *too* much like a hobbit.

As I walk with Nicholas over to the English building, we make small talk. God, everything about him is so cool and effortless. Every now and then he flashes me a crooked half smile and I just about die. He is quite possibly the most beautiful boy I've ever laid my eyes on. To top it all off, when I momentarily fall behind in pace, I catch a glimpse of his butt… I've never seen one so tight and round. Wait. No. Stop it, Erik! Stop it right now! Fighting temptation is definitely going to be hard with this one around. That ass… no!

"So, where are you from?" I ask, trying to keep our conversation going. It's little more than small talk, but I'll take what I can get.

"My mom and I are from LA," he answers, in a velvety baritone.

"What about your dad?"

"Uh… he's not really in the picture right now, but that's not important." As we approach the English building, Nicholas changes the subject to something school oriented. I wonder if he's more studious than his first impression would let on. "What are we working on in English?"

"We're reading through *Romeo And Juliet*," I tell him.

"Oh, great. I actually just read that last year at my old school."

"Well, maybe you could help translate some for me? English is actually one of my better subjects, but Shakespeare is, like, whoa." At this moment, I've become acutely aware of what my hands are doing — waving at the word "whoa" for emphasis. God, I'm a walking embarrassment. And I can't for the life of me stop smiling like an idiot.

"For sure!" He pats me on the shoulder, which sends a tingle through my body. I feel myself spasm a bit. "You okay?"

"Yeah. I just… I felt a chill there for a second." Smooth, Erik. Very smooth.

We enter the English building just as the first bell rings. Nicholas raises his eyebrows with a look of concern. God, even his eyebrows are perfect. It's not fair. They're like two gorgeously shaped caterpillars. I wonder if he plucks them.

"Don't worry," I tell him. "The campus is so spread out most teachers expect us to be late." We walk down the main corridor, through another hallway, and into our first class. We arrive just moments after the second and final bell.

Despite the fact that we don't have assigned seating in English class, most kids have gotten into the habit of sitting in the same place they do every day. The first three rows are filled with the overeager kids, nerds, and honor students, and suck ups, like Tim Martinelli, who's basically a scrawnier buck toothed version of me, but with pimples. The back three rows are filled with kids who are too cool for school, like Becky-With-The-Not-So-Good-Hair, as Mackenzie likes to put it — though I'm not sure what that's in reference to since her hair's pretty flawless — and other kids, who spend most of their class time playing with their phones under their desks. You know, 'cause they're too cool to pay attention. I'm not nerdy enough to sit right up front. Plus, being close to the teacher makes me extremely uncomfortable. But I'm also not cool enough to sit further in the back either. I'm just kinda in the middle, which is where my usual spot is. I manage to find a couple of empty seats next to each other. It's my lucky day — no! Get a grip, Erik!

Nicholas is up front checking in with Ms. Maple. She's a plain looking woman who looks like she's just given up on everything. I suppose she could be considered pretty if she tried, but her messy bun and rubber clogs aren't exactly doing her any favors. That's none of my business though.

I'm sitting here, patiently waiting for Nicholas to take the seat next to me. Once he's finished talking with Ms. Maple, he looks around the room and finds me. He puts on that crooked grin, the one I'm quickly falling in love with, and makes his way over. He sits down next to me and my heart starts pounding like crazy. I look over at him. He's so cool and nonchalant. I wish I could be cool and nonchalant. Instead, I'm dowdy and melancholic.

"Good morning, class!" Ms. Maple starts to speak. "I hope you all had a nice weekend. Before we begin, we have a new student, Nicholas. Please try to make him feel welcome." None of the kids in class react at all to his introduction, but Nicholas doesn't care. I suppose it would be weirder if they did react, but what do I know? Most of my social references come from either movies or Mackenzie, and I'm not sure how reliable either one of those sources are. "Now, who can give me a brief summary of Act Five of *Romeo And Juliet?*" Ms. Maple asks. Several hands toward the front of the class go up. Tim Martinelli's hand waves eagerly, practically begging to be picked. I personally don't have much interest in participating today. I turn to Nicholas and am taken aback. He's staring at me with that pensive squint, like he wants to ask me something. Whatever it is, the answer is yes.

"So, you wanna fill me in?" He says. Yes, of course I do. I just don't know what he's asking me.

"Fill you in on what?" I reply.

"That whole thing with Mackenzie and that blonde dude. What was up with that?"

"Nothing." My answer is short and to the point. As much as I wanna get to know Nicholas, and have Nicholas get to know me, I don't want to relive being told that I'm not good enough for someone. Being told by Andrew that he's "kinda out of my league" was not only insulting, it was confusing. He basically said that he thought I was an ugly slut. He may not have used those words per se, but that's what I got out of it.

"Come on, Erik," Nicholas says my name and it sounds like a song. "If we're gonna be friends, I kinda need to know the basics."

"You wanna be my friend?" I ask. Andrew's words have haunted me all weekend, I'm finding it a little unbelievable that a guy like Nicholas, who's so clearly out of my league, would want to be my friend. Most people just want to be friendly acquaintances.

"Yeah. I'm new, I don't know anybody, and you seem cool."

"You don't think that you're too cool for me?"

"Why would I think that?" It's official, I'm dead. He knows exactly what to say to have me melting into the palm of his hand. My heart is fluttering with a strange excitement that this guy — this beautiful, *beautiful* guy — wants to know me. Nothing could bring me down from this high… except, maybe, Ms. Maple.

"Erik. Nick. Quiet, please," she says. Nicholas smiles innocently, but he keeps looking at me through a side glance. There's no getting out of this, is there? I lean in closer to him and he does the same.

"It's stupid, really," I start to explain in a hushed tone. "Me and that guy, Andrew, were partnered up for a project in science. He made a move on me and I thought it meant something, and I was wrong."

"He just wanted to score?"

"Yup. Mackenzie was defending me."

"Well, that sucks. And not in the fun way."

"Boys," Ms. Maple interjects. "If there's something more interesting than the lecture, would you care to share it with the rest of the class?" I feel my heart stop for a moment. I've never been busted for talking in class. I usually don't have anyone to talk to. What do I do? What do I say?

"We were just discussing the ending to *Romeo And Juliet*," Nicholas says. It's a complete lie, but he's explaining it as if that's actually what we were doing. "And we decided that it was... stupid."

"Would you care to elaborate on how you came to that conclusion?"

What is Nicholas doing? Of course the teacher's gonna ask us a follow up question. He's dug us into a hole. I look on, nervously, when I notice Nicholas nodding at me, urging me to say something. I turn to see Ms. Maple waiting for my defense. It feels like the whole class has their eyes on me, watching with anticipation, expecting me to put my foot in my mouth.

"Well… if Romeo would've had some patience, then they both would've lived?" I answer, my voice wavering with uncertainty. Ms. Maple's eyes narrow.

"Alright then," she says, and I let out a huge sigh of relief. Nicholas is chuckling to himself, and I'm not sure whether I should join him or be upset that he got me into this predicament. Then, a couple minutes later, he tosses a folded up piece of paper onto my desk. I open it and see that he's written down a phone number with the words "Text Me" underneath. I'm a little shocked to see that his handwriting is neat and legible. I dunno. I guess I expected it to look like that of a sugared up grade schooler's, like most other guys'. God, even his handwriting is perfect.

I pull out my phone discreetly and add in his contact. I've never had a friend who I texted during class. Mackenzie and I talk about everything in person, so neither of us has ever felt the need to text each other during class, unless there was an emergency. This, right here with Nicholas, is uncharted territory for me. I'm afraid of getting caught with my phone out, but I'm just as afraid of letting this opportunity to connect with him slip away. I decide to just bite the bullet.

"Hey," I text.

"What up?" He responds almost immediately.

. . .

"How many cats do you think Maple has waiting for her at home? [Cat emoji] [Thinking emoji]." Nicholas follows up, before I can even respond. Huh... He decorates his texts with emoji. How does he find them so fast? It takes me days to find the appropriate ones, so I tend to just save them for very specific things, like "Happy Birthday" [Cake emoji]. I'm impressed he can use them so quickly.

"7?" I text. "Idk. She seems like someone who believes in luck, even though she hasn't had any."

"I'm dead. [Laughing emoji]." Was what I said really that funny? Like, laughing emoji funny? I feel like this is just an obligatory overstatement, like when you add an 'lol' after everything, even when it's not funny at all. He sends another text. "You're stupid. [Winky-kiss emoji]." Ah, cute, a winky-kiss emoji. Wait... A WINKY-KISS EMOJI?! I look over at Nicholas. It takes him a moment to notice me staring, but when he does, he does this thing where he raises his eyebrows, but only for a second, sorta like in those old cartoons when the characters are flirting with one another. Oh, my god, is he flirting with me? I immediately open up my browser and search for "raised eyebrow body language," which leads me to the term "eyebrow flash," which then leads me to an article about unspoken sexual cues, which talks about how when you're attracted to someone, your eyebrows go crazy and start moving all on their own. Does this mean that Nicholas wants me?

. . .

No. No, that can't be right, can it? I see him take a quick glance at his phone. It seems he's waiting for me to respond, but I'm afraid I'm misinterpreting something, and I don't want to freak him out by making naughty assumptions. I have to play this cool. After giving it a moment of thought, I concoct my response — [Shrug emoji]. Question mark. Question mark. Question mark. — and hit send.

Nicholas and I text throughout the better part of our shared three class periods. Most of it is pretty inconsequential, but you can learn a lot about a person through small talk. For instance, I learned that he's into FPS games, enjoys soccer, will always pick cookies and cream over all other ice cream flavors, and that he refuses to watch scary movies because he gets jumpy. One time, he said he went to a theme park on Halloween and got asked to leave because he accidentally punched one of the scare actors while walking through a pop-up maze. I couldn't help but giggle at the story I'd nearly gotten caught by our second period History teacher.

The bell rings, marking the end of Algebra II, my last class of the day with Nicholas. I'm sad to have to separate from him. Even though we barely spoke an actual word, having him sitting next to me and communicating via text message was really nice. I hope he's not one of those out of sight, out of mind kind of guys, because I'm really not looking for any more friendly acquaintances. Then again, I don't really know what I'm looking for.

I'm sitting in Art class, refreshing my messages every five minutes or so. Nothing. He's not texting me now. I mean, maybe he's busy. Maybe he's got one of those strict teachers that's a stickler about phone usage. I refresh my messages again, thinking that maybe my phone's just being dumb and not loading things properly. Nothing.

Nothing. Nothing. Nothing.

What to do now? My Art class is essentially a free period, where we're encouraged to draw something so that the teacher, Mr. Grumpy-McGrumpleson — that's not his name, that's just how he is — doesn't have to bother with actually teaching us anything. I suppose I could work on my perspective drawing, but I really don't want to. Art's not exactly my thing. I'm only in it for the easy credits. That's how electives are for you. I just want Nicholas to text me again. Why isn't he texting me?!

. . .

Oh, a text.

"Omfg. Physics is so boring. I'm gonna pass out here! [Sleeping emoji]." I waited a whole twenty minutes for that? I'll take it.

"Art's no better," I respond.

"What you doing for lunch?" He wants to have lunch with me? Wow, things are moving pretty fast. I know it's not the same, but it feels almost like he's asking me on a date. I mean, we *are* in high school, so maybe we can count this as a date? Possibly?

"Idk. I usually just meet up with Mackenzie."

"Mind if I join?"

"I'd love that. [Heart emoji]." I respond, almost immediately. Wait... I feel like the heart emoji is a little much. Actually, the word love is a little much. Uh oh... I wonder if there's a way to take a text message back. Like, can I just cancel it? I see the ellipsis appear on my screen, so I know he's typing something. It's taking way longer than I expect, and now I'm starting to panic. Stupid emojis! Finally, his reply comes through, but he doesn't say anything. Instead, I'm treated to a single emoji:

Winky face.

What the hell is that supposed to mean?!

I'm standing at my locker scrolling through all of my textual exchanges with Nicholas from earlier. It's got me feeling giddy reading everything back. I'm finding myself obsessing over our entire conversation, which is almost enough to write a novella. I'm especially caught up in the winky-kiss emoji he sent during first period: "You're stupid. [Winky-kiss emoji]." I can't make heads or tails of it. Was it like, "Oh, I jokingly insulted him, so I need to follow it up with some affection, so I don't come off as a douche?" Was that his way of thinking? Or maybe, just maybe, he *was* flirting with me. What am I saying? I don't even know if he's gay. But then, straight guys don't throw out the winky-kiss face all willy nilly to their guy friends like that, do they? It's really hard to tell, because straight guys have a tendency to talk about gay sex, like, a lot.

One time, I tagged along with one of my cousins and his guy friends to the mall to do some Christmas shopping. The whole time, he kept arguing with his friends about what floor the infomercial gift store was on.

"If it's on the second floor, y'all are gonna lick my booty hole," I specifically remember my cousin declaring. As it turned out, the infomercial gift store *was* on the second floor, and my cousin's reaction to that was, and I quote, "Somebody's booty hole is getting licked tonight!" See what I mean? It's not like straight people do that kind of thing… or do they? Anyway, it's really hard to tell, but I shouldn't be obsessing over this.

"Ugh, why are Mondays the worst?" Mackenzie says in her most exaggeratedly tired voice as she approaches. "If I collapse right here, don't call for help.

Just let me lie here and be trampled by all the dirty sneakers and slutty stilettos."

"That's poetic," I reply, tucking my phone into my back pocket. "Bad day?"

"I got detention. I had a pop quiz in second period. Like, why do teachers insist on pretending surprise quizzes are fun? Because they're not, under any circumstance."

"Wait. You got detention?"

"A teacher walked by the moment I introduced Andrew's face to the back of my hand."

"Wow. You really go all in," I shiver at the sound of that familiar baritone. I turn around and find Nicholas standing right in front of me. I don't know why his presence scared me, it's not like I wasn't expecting him. I suppose I'm just not used to having someone other than myself and Mackenzie around. This is new.

I like it.

Nicholas, Mackenzie, and I walk over to the cafeteria and pick up some foil wrapped cafeteria burgers and a couple bags of chips. Nicholas also grabs a hot dog, a corn dog, a small tray of some microwaved chicken tenders, a carton of milk, and a fruit cup. I'm not sure where he plans to put it all, but who am I to judge? I can probably fit him in one of my pant legs.

As I wait for Nicholas to finish checking out of the lunch line, Mackenzie pulls me aside and leans in close.

"What do you think?" She whispers to me. This can't look normal.

"About what?" I say glancing around, afraid we're making a scene of ourselves.

"About Hot Boy. Do you need me to disappear for a minute so you can…" she makes a crude sexual gesture with her fingers, "… because I totally will."

"I mean, he's alright." Lies! He's perfection! "But we don't even know—"

"Know what?" Nicholas says. I jump and let out a high-pitched squeal, which causes a whole bunch of people to stop and stare. If we weren't making a scene before, I definitely am now.

"If these burgers actually have any meat in them," Mackenzie jumps in, coming to my rescue. "You know what? I just remembered I need to get something from my locker, so I'm gonna go do that and I'll meet you guys in the quad in, like, five, yeah?" And just as quickly as she came to my rescue, Mackenzie pushes me into the deep end. She's gone before I can protest, which is fine, I guess. I just need to keep the conversation light and choose my words wisely, so I don't accidentally let something stupid slip out like, "You're beautiful and I'm totally available."

Nicholas and I walk over to the quad and post up at an empty table under a tree. I start to unwrap my cafeteria burger when I'm suddenly stricken with self-consciousness. I'm afraid to eat in front of him. He's this gorgeous, in-shape guy, who looks like he can run a mile without stopping, and I'm this blob who can't stop stopping when I try to run any sort of distance. I don't want him to judge me the way I feel like people do when I go back for a third slice of pizza at a party. I start to rewrap my burger when I catch sight of Nicholas' face. His cheeks are stuffed like a chipmunk. How is he so comfortable with himself? I suppose I'd be more comfortable with myself if I looked like him. I swear, it's not fair.

"So, what's Mackenzie's deal?" Nicholas says, after swallowing down a few bites of his hot dog.

"What do you mean?" I ask.

"Like, is she seeing anyone?" My heart starts to sink a little.

"I... I don't know." I push aside my burger and try to avoid eye contact.

"Come on, you're her best friend. You would know. I mean, do you think she'd be into me? What's her type?" I don't want to answer his questions, but I can't just not answer them. That'd be weird, and rude, and it would totally give away the fact that I'm wishing he was saying my name instead of Mackenzie's.

"I really don't know. Mackenzie doesn't seem to have a pattern when it comes to guys. Usually, she's sold if she thinks they're hot. You could always just ask her. She's pretty direct."

"Huh… well, do you think she'd be into me?"

"Who wouldn't be?" He flashes me that crooked half smile of his and it kills me, but not in the fun way. Honestly, I should've seen this coming. I mean, what are the odds that I get propositioned by one of the hottest guys in school, get dropped like a sad sack of potatoes, and then immediately get introduced to my soul mate? That doesn't happen. Of course it doesn't, because he's straight. I'm starting to wonder if this is a godsend of sorts. It is possible that God sent Nicholas to me to tempt me, but he made Nicholas straight so that I would know that nothing could ever, or *should* ever, be done about it. Nicholas could be my gift from God, to remind me that my attractions to him are wrong. It sure would explain a lot.

"You boys have fun without me?" Mackenzie arrives, cheerfully joining us at the table. I look over at Nicholas and he can't seem to take his eyes off of her. It's not fair, but whatever.

"Hey, Mackenzie," Nicholas says, his pensive squint attempting to burrow into her. "I was wondering if you'd wanna… I dunno… go out with me sometime?"

"With you?" Mackenzie's genuinely taken aback. I, on the other hand, just want to leave. There's not the slightest bit of me that wants to be here to witness the birth of their romance. I know that sounds selfish, but all of this is starting to seem like a big divine slap to my face. "You mean, like, on a date?"

"Yeah." Nicholas offers her that stupid grin he's been abusing me all morning with. This is so messed up. I'm about to excuse myself from the table when suddenly, Mackenzie bursts out laughing. "What's funny?"

"I'm sorry. I thought you were telling a joke."

"Why would you think that?"

"Because I'm not your type. Clearly."

"How could you possibly know that?"

"Trust me. I know." Nicholas is visibly confused, if not a little embarrassed. If I wasn't so distraught about my own feelings, I'd probably feel sorry for him. Mackenzie glances over at me with a look that says, "Is he for real?" I'm glad someone at the table is finding this amusing…

The three of us finish our food silently and then part ways. Only two more periods left in the day, and then I can be done with everything. I just want to go home.

chapter ten
nicholas

"Because I'm not your type. Clearly."

What the hell does that even mean? How would she know what my type is? Mackenzie doesn't know anything about me. And she's obviously wrong, because she's totally my type. What gives?

I'm waiting in the parking lot, trying to make sense of what Mackenzie said. It's gonna bother the crap out of me for, like, ever. Right now, the lot's pretty empty, so I'm able to mull over my thoughts in peace. See, I texted Ma in the minutes between my last two classes and suggested she wait an extra fifteen minutes before she comes to get me. I figured that way, there'd be less of a clusterfuck to deal with. Turns out I was right.

Ma pulls into the lot and stops the car right in front of me so I can hop in.

"How'd it go?" Ma asks as we pull out of the parking lot.

"Not bad," I say. And it's true. The day was pretty good… that is, up until I got majorly rejected. I'm not about to say that to my mom though.

"You make any friends?"

"Actually, yeah, I did. This kid, Erik. We got our first three classes together. He's a pretty cool guy."

"Good, I'm glad." The conversation right now isn't exactly interesting. I know there are so many things I could be asking my mom: "Did you look for a job?" "Did you and Dad talk?" Stuff like that. There are things going on that are far more pressing than the stupid thing on my mind. And trust me, it's stupid.

I pull down the sun visor and examine my partial reflection in the tiny mirror. I'm good looking, right? And yes, that is actually what's on my mind. Like I said, stupid. I just can't help thinking about what Mackenzie said: "Because I'm not your type. Clearly." Did she mean that she's too good for me? I doubt she thinks that she's *not* good enough for me, because a girl that walks around wearing leather straps over a billowy dress is not a girl who's self-conscious about her looks. She must've meant that she's too good for me, and if she did mean that, why? Ever since dating Brenda, I've made nothing but improvements to myself and my appearance. I fucking blow dry my hair! What other teenage guy is that extra?

"Ma, can I ask you a weird question?" I say, having decided to get a grown up's opinion, even if it is only my mom's. I could use the biased validation right about now. "Am I good looking?"

"Of course, Nicky. You're very good looking."

"Okay, but hypothetically speaking, if you weren't my mom, and you were my age, do you think you'd maybe have a crush on me?"

"Ay, mijo, I'm not answering that question." Not the response I was hoping for.

"Why not, Ma? Because I'm ugly?"

"Because it's a loaded question," she replies. "If I say yes, you'll say I'm your mother, but if I say no, then you'll say I think you're ugly. There's no winning here."

"So you *do* think I'm ugly."

"No, you're not ugly. You look like your damn father."

"Well, thanks, Ma, that's even worse given the situation." Ma and I are a lot alike. Neither of us has the patience for this conversation and we're both talking way louder than we should be. We're practically yelling. "I JUST WANNA FEEL PRETTY!"

"WELL, SO DO I, NICHOLAS, BUT IT LOOKS LIKE NEITHER OF US ARE GETTING WHAT WE WANT!" Somehow, I think I must've stumbled onto a heavier topic than I thought, because suddenly the tension in the car is utterly palpable.

We sit in silence for a moment and I stare out the window, debating if I want to press her on the subject. She hasn't mentioned Dad much, or the divorce, and it's starting to worry me because I feel like that's something that she — *we* — should be talking about. My mom is not the type of woman to hold her tongue about anything.

"If you wanna talk about the divorce, we can talk about the divorce," I offer.

"No, Nicky, I don't want to talk about the divorce."

"Okay…"

We get back to my uncle's house and I go straight to my garage. I plop down on the unmade futon bed and stare up at the ceiling. What to do? What to do? This has been my thing since after I got my furniture assembled. There's nothing to do here. I have no TV in my room. I've already read *Romeo And Juliet* and I don't really care to review and translate it right now. I'm just bored. I've got nowhere to go and no one to talk to. Except my mom, but that's like walking through a field of landmines. I guess I could hang out with Tio Roger, but he's, like, really into buildings. Yeah… I have no idea.

. . .

Erik, duh! I should just text him. It was a little awkward at lunch time with the whole getting rejected by Mackenzie situation, but if anyone would have some insight, he's probably my best bet. I pull my phone out of my pocket and navigate to my text messages. To my surprise, there's a message from Dad: "How are you holding up?" he asks. I'm not sure how I should respond to this, or if I should even respond at all. I know I'm his son, but I'm also my mom's son, and I've sorta taken her side in the whole divorce situation. Maybe not in so many words, but he's probably figured as much since I'm here and not there. I stare at the message for a minute, letting my fingers hover over the touch screen. Should I respond? No. To answer my dad without consulting my mom feels like a betrayal. I exit the message and scroll to my conversation with Erik. Huh… his last text message was before lunch when he texted me where to meet him. I wonder if he's one of those out of sight, out of mind kind of people. Well, I don't see any other options at the moment, so I'm about to be on his mind whether he likes it or not.

"Hey," I text. The ellipsis immediately pops up. Seconds later, his response.

"Hi." One word replies. The bane of my existence. You know, I don't really have the patience to sit here and try to carve out a conversation through single syllable pleasantries, so I exit out of the text box and just call. "Hello?" A rather effeminate voice comes through.

"Erik? Wait. Did I hit the wrong number?"

"Nicholas, it's me." Wow, the distortion over the phone doesn't do his voice any favors. It sounds like I'm talking to a straight up woman.

"You sound different over the phone."

"So I've been told," Erik says. This must be a regular thing for him. Now I feel bad for mentioning it. "What are you calling for?"

"Nothing. I just wanted to talk."

"Huh. What do you wanna talk about?" He's coming off cold and distant, very much unlike the guy I met earlier today. What's his deal? I'm almost regretting coming to him, but then I remind myself that he's my only "in" with Mackenzie, so I extinguish the little flame that ignites my temper and dive right in.

"So, you know Mackenzie really well. I was wondering if you could explain something to me. She said that she's not my type, and I don't know what that means, but it's kinda pissing me off."

"Mackenzie likes to make a lot of assumptions," Erik explains. "She thinks she knows the world, and how it works."

"She doesn't know me."

"She thinks she does." There's something really odd about the timbre of his voice when he says this.

Maybe it's just that the phone makes him sound like a girl, but his tone right now seems delicate and vulnerable. A part of me starts to suspect that something's wrong.

"Hey, we should hang out," I suggest. I want to know what's up, and I have doubts that he'll tell me over the phone. If I get him face to face, he can't avoid me. And if I put him in a good enough mood, maybe he'll be more inclined to help me figure things out with Mackenzie. "I was thinking we could get, like, yogurt or, I dunno, boba?"

"You like boba?" He asks, genuinely surprised. "Aren't you, like, El Salvadorian or whatever?"

"Are you saying El Salvadorians can't like boba?" I'm not sure if I should be offended by this or not.

"No. It's just, I'm always surprised when non-Asians like Asian things."

"That's incredibly racist, but okay," I laugh. "Wait, how'd you know I'm Latino?"

"Well, your last name was on your class schedule. I kinda figured as much," he explains. "So, what are you? Your ethnicity I mean."

"Colombian-Puerto Rican."

"Seeeeeeeeeexy," he says as a joke, but it throws me a bit. Does he find me sexy? That's, like, super flattering because aren't gay dudes supposedly really picky? I can feel a stupid smile forming on my face. Earlier, I just wanted to feel pretty.

Well, I fucking do now.

I ask Ma if I can borrow the car and if I can have a few bucks for a snack later. She hands me the shared credit card she has with my dad and tells me to have fun. I feel weird about taking it, but she insists, explaining that it's really important to her that I make friends. It's hard to argue with that. I get Erik to text me his address and then head out.

Erik is waiting for me on the curb when I arrive at his house. He climbs into the passenger seat and directs me to drive us half an hour to the next town. They have the "good" mall there. Apparently, the mall in our town is practically deserted, with the only prevailing offerings being the gym and an overpriced clothing department store. I don't protest. He knows this place better than I do.

As we're driving, I look over at the opposite side of the freeway and thank God that we're not sitting in that traffic. We listen to music on the radio. I find out Erik is partial to current female pop artists. I don't hate it, but, sonically, it's not really my thing. I'm a little more old school with my tastes.

"Is she singing about not being able to walk straight after sex?" I ask when the singer breaks into the chorus, which I admit is actually pretty catchy.

"No," Erik replies, but he's not at all confident. "It's about her being in love and wanting to spend the night with a guy."

"So that they can have sex and she won't be able to walk straight!"

"That's not—"

"That is!" I laugh. Erik's mind is visibly blown.

"Great, I'll never be able to listen to this song the same ever again," he says, all defeated. It only makes me laugh harder.

I scroll through the radio channels until I come across a station that's playing throwback R&B music from the early 2000s. You can thank my mom for my musical tastes. She still hasn't let go of her dream that someday, she'll wake up in Usher's bed. That old song, "U Got It Bad," comes on and I start singing along to the track. I kid you not, I know every word. It's too bad I can't carry a tune to save my life. My pitch is all over the place, but I'm fully committed, hand gestures and all. I glance over at Erik and he's just sitting there awkwardly, his knees together with his hands clasped between his thighs. God, is my voice really that bad?

"I know, I know. I can't sing for shit," I say, trying to lighten the mood. "It's whatever, we're having fun."

"I like your singing," he says rather timidly.

"Quit fucking with me, man," I laugh, nudging him playfully. I swear, he exists only to flatter me.

We arrive at the "good" mall, and as it turns out, the place is huge. Two stories, with each floor stretching a quarter to a half a mile long, or at least that's how it seems. I'm not exaggerating either, this place is *that* big. I can't see the other end of the mall from the end that we entered.

"What are you in the mood for?" Erik asks, walking now with a bit of a pep in his step. He leads me to the food court and I'm a bit overwhelmed by all the selections. There are two burger joints, a pizza place, some Chinese, and even a Mongolian BBQ, where they cook the noodles on a big hot slab of metal right in front of you. "We can get yogurt, or bobas, or both. Whatever you want."

"How about we grab a pretzel and take a walk?" I suggest. I want to have time to talk to him and, maybe, get to the bottom of the Mackenzie deal, without having to worry about possibly the most important decision of the day, by which I mean dinner.

"Alright, which pretzel place do you prefer?" He asks.

"Wait. There's more than one?"

It takes me a minute to decide between two pretzel places — Pretzel Pete's and Mama Alice's — and, honestly, I'm not sure what the difference is between the two. I end up going with Pretzel Pete's, just because they have these bite sized pretzel bits, and I thought they'd be easier to share. I suppose I could just break off a piece of a regular pretzel, but it really doesn't matter. It's not important. With our pretzel bits in hand, Erik and I walk aimlessly down the long stretch toward the other end of the mall. He seems happier now. I guess I must've picked the better pretzel place.

"So, is this what you do when you and Mackenzie hang out?" I ask, popping a pretzel bit into my mouth. "You drive all the way over here and hang around the mall?"

"What else is there?" Erik replies. "We're broke teenagers."

"Eh. You have a point. Anyway, I wanted to talk to you about Mackenzie."

"And here we go." The sarcasm is strong with this one.

"Okay, I need you to clarify something. You said that Mackenzie thinks she knows me and that she makes a lot of assumptions, right?"

"Yeah?"

"Well, what assumptions has she made about me for her to say that she's not my type?" Once I say the question out loud, I start to worry that the answer I'll get is not an answer I'd like to hear.

"Do you want me to be honest with you?" Erik asks. Great. Now I'm definitely sure the answer's not an answer I'd like to hear, but I nod my head anyway. Erik pauses for a moment, thinking about how he's gonna say whatever he's gonna say. "Well, she thinks you're gay."

"WHAT!?" I say, practically screaming in my outrage. My voice echoes throughout the mall, and I have to pull Erik aside so that we're not completely out in the open for all the world to see. "Why would she think I'm gay? Because she overheard me lie and say that to a bunch of girls to get them to leave me alone?" Erik just shrugs. "What about me screams gay to you?" Erik shrugs again. I scoff in disbelief. I guess whatever chance I had with his best friend is out… just like a pride parade.

I'd be lying if I said I wasn't mad or upset about the whole Mackenzie thinking I'm gay thing, but there's no sense in dwelling on it. I'm out — not "out" in *that* way, but, like, physically out — enjoying the mall with Erik, so I'm gonna fuckin' enjoy the mall with Erik. We continue walking around passing various shops, some selling ridiculously expensive stuff, and others selling stuff that likely no one would ever buy. Erik stops for a moment to check his phone.

"Hey, what are we doing for dinner?" He asks. "My parents want to know what my plans are, or if I'm gonna be home by then."

"I dunno, actually," I say. Since I've been snacking on these pretzel bits, I hadn't really thought about it.

"So, what should I tell them?"

"I guess that we're having dinner?"

"But are we really gonna have dinner?"

"Do you want to have dinner with me?" Erik takes a moment before he responds, and within that moment, I start to wonder if I've said something wrong. I hope he also doesn't think I'm gay, because if he does, I've definitely said something wrong. In fact, I've probably been saying all the wrong things this entire time. He avoids the question and with it, eye contact.

"Maybe we should go home? I can't really afford to eat out," he says, switching directions and starting to head back toward the entrance we came in through, though it's still a long way away.

"I mean, we could go home, but then we'd be sitting in, like, an hour of traffic," I try to explain as I jog to catch up to him. "Why don't we just have dinner? I saw a nice seafood buffet. We could pig out."

"I can't afford that."

"It's fine. I got it. Courtesy of my mom." Erik looks at me hesitantly. His eyes are telling me that he wants to say yes, but for some reason he's holding himself back. I'm getting the tiniest inkling that, maybe, he's developing a little bit of a crush on me. If he is, I have no problem with that. I'd be flattered. But nothing's ever gonna happen between us. He knows that, I'm sure he does. He knows I'm straight. And if he didn't, he knows now.

"Alright, let's have dinner," Erik finally says. "But under one condition." My eyebrows go up questioningly. "Let's not talk about Mackenzie." Erik holds out his pinky and I take it with my own. We shake on it.

"Deal."

chapter eleven
erik

He's straight.

He's straight.

I'm sure he's straight.

That's what he says.

He's straight.

He is *straight*.

Nicholas is straight. I know that and I know nothing is ever going to happen, because you can't make someone not straight. It's not like he chose to be straight, just like how I didn't choose to be gay. It just… came out… all inconvenient and stuff. Nicholas is straight.

He's straight. That being said, I can't seem to shake the feeling that this might be a date. I mean, the restaurant is dimly lit, there are candles on every table, and they're blasting classical piano music — the kind they use and abuse in the Korean soap operas my mom watches — over the speakers. It's very romantical... you know, in the way a cheap seafood buffet is romantical. It's starting to make me uncomfortable.

He's straight!

He's straight. And, you know what? He's not even cute, digging into his fourth plate and stuffing his cheeks full of sushi. It's disgusting... and I love it. Ah, who am I kidding? Even with his appetite and lack of restraint, he's beautiful. I thought I could get the idea out of my head if I just kept reminding myself that he doesn't play for my team, but since that isn't working, I thought I'd try to convince myself that he's ugly. Nicholas, ugly? That's such a far stretch, I can't even take myself seriously.

I hate this.

I'm at home now, just lying in bed and staring at the wall all pathetic like. I don't even know him, so why do I want him so bad? Staring at this wall is like staring at a blank canvas, and my mind starts to paint little pictures and scenes of what I wish would happen. I'm imagining Nicholas entering my room. He walks over and climbs into my bed, wrapping his muscular arms around my waist. He leans in and whispers into my ear, "Mi Amor," in the thickest, most exotic accent he can muster, which in my mind, is how he talks. Then, he kisses the nape of my neck and I just melt away into him.

You know, at dinner, I learned his full name: Nicholas Ray Santiago. It sounds like poetry. *Nicholas Ray Santiago.* Maybe, one day, I could be Erik Santiago. Or we could hyphenate it, and I'd be Erik Park-Santiago or Erik Santiago-Park. I'd use my full name, but it's like super long and extra Filipino: Erik Alan Tolentino Santiago-Park… What am I doing? I can't get married to him! Or any boy for that matter. I'm forgetting about my morals and getting lost in this... nonsense. I'm getting so lost that I feel myself fading away into a dark abyss, and when I open my eyes, I find myself lying in an all too familiar setting, on an island in the middle of the sea. There's nothing here but a single palm tree and a small row boat, beckoning me to leave.

Again with this dream? Damn it… I know I shouldn't get into the boat. Everything inside of me is telling me not to, but I do it anyway, because I'm an idiot. Once again, the storms are raging on the rolling seas, and I fall into the water, and sink deeper and deeper below the surface.

Tuesday. October 8th.

I wake up with a start. Morning already? I don't even remember falling asleep. I look over at my alarm clock. It's a quarter past six. At least, this time, I slept through the night. I pull myself out of bed, hop into the shower, then get dressed. I make my way downstairs and hear the boisterous sounds of the Filipino channel echoing throughout the house.

"Morning," Mom says, as I enter the kitchen. She's preparing breakfast in her PJs, as she normally does. For a while, I wasn't sure we'd get back to this level of normalcy. She avoided me all weekend up until Sunday morning when we had to go to church. We went about the rest of the day, doing all the things that we typically would, like our after church Pho luncheon. It was awkward and there wasn't much talking, but at least we were in the same room. It wasn't until yesterday morning that things started to feel like they used to. She came out and made breakfast as usual, and we watched all the awful exploitative game shows while we ate, before my dad drove me to school. It's nice to know there's an effort being made. Because now, it doesn't feel like I'm being blamed for something I can't help. "How was last night?" Mom asks. "Did you get a lot of work done?"

"Uh… yeah," I reply, taking a seat at the table. Last night, when I went out with Nicholas, I lied to them. I told them I was going over to Andrew's house to polish up our presentation, which is due today. As far as I know, they have not figured out that the boy I told them I kissed was Andrew, and if they have, they haven't said anything about it. And because Andrew's my lab partner, thus making him schoolwork related, they didn't protest. "I'm excited to be done with the project."

"Oh? Why is that?"

"You know... public speaking." I hate lying to my parents. I hate lying in general, but what can I do? I can't exactly tell them the truth. They'd never let me go outside again. I'd be like that telepathic girl in that movie where her mother keeps telling her to go to her closet and pray, and when she doesn't, she gets pig's blood poured all over her. Such a shame...

They could've made some perfectly good dinuguan with that.

Dad comes into the kitchen and joins us for breakfast. We eat together as a family and watch as a sad old lady comes on TV to be interviewed by the obnoxiously upbeat game show host.

"Ang aking asawa ay nagpunta sa Dubai para magtrabaho," the lady weeps. "Naiwan akong mag isa kasama ang aming tatlong anak at aso. Matagal na kaming hindi nagkikita at ako ay nangungulila sa kanya."

"What did she say?" Dad leans in to ask.

"Something about a dog," I explain. I can kind of understand Tagalog, but it's pretty fuzzy. They talk so fast, I can only catch a couple of words here and there. My dad, however, even after all these years of marriage, still only knows how to say, "I love you" — "Mahal kita" — and "How are you?" — "Kumusta ka?"

"Did she eat the dog?"

"Ay, bastos! Hindi. Koreano iyan!" Mom interjects.

"Should we be offended?" Dad asks me.

"Very," I reply.

It's nice being on good terms with the family.

I arrive at school and am surprised when I get to my locker. Mackenzie's here, and she's not alone. Nicholas is with her and he's dressed in a gray henley, which hugs the curves of his muscly pecs and his slender waistline. Ugh… why is he so delicious?

"Hey, you," he greets me. My name is "You" now, because his informality feels personalized.

"Hi," I say. I'm worried I look as flushed as he's making me feel.

"Thank God, you're here, Erik," Mackenzie says. "Will you tell your boyfriend to quit flirting with me?"

"He's not my boyfriend."

"Well, I did take you to dinner last night, Erik," Nicholas interjects with a wink. My eyes just about fall out of my face, they're so wide. Why would he say that? It's so cruel.

"I'm going to class. I'll leave you two love birds alone," Mackenzie teases as she saunters off, leaving

Nicholas and I alone together. I can't decide if her leaving makes me happy or upset. All I know is that I feel stupid and awkward standing here with him looking all gorgeous like that.

"God, she's so cute," he mutters, mostly to himself, which brings me right back to reality. He's straight and totally not my boyfriend.

"Too bad she thinks you're gay," I offer, a little more snide than I intend.

"Yeah, I'm gonna have to convince her otherwise."

"Those comments about you taking me to dinner don't help."

"You don't like it when I flirt with you?" He nudges me gently with his fist, while flashing his signature crooked half smile. I want to say, "No, I don't like it when you flirt with me," but I'm afraid to, because what if he actually stops flirting with me? I *need* him to keep flirting with me. It's all I have!

We head over to first period English with Ms. Maple and, aside from receiving a few text messages from Nicholas throughout, the class is wholly uneventful. She does however assign us a homework packet, which directs us to translate a handful of Shakespeare's sonnets, which is super exciting. Not... I mean, don't get me wrong, I actually like English, and I enjoy reading, and Shakespeare — when I can understand it — but I swear, it feels like some teachers just hand out busy work because they have no other hobbies keeping them occupied. I guess they need something to grade. Why can't they just learn to knit or something?

Second period US history is that one obligatory class no one really wants to be in. Even our teacher doesn't care to put in the effort, telling us to read the chapter on the Declaration of Independence and not much else. Nicholas and I spend most of the period giggling over memes he finds on Instagram. I notice he's got a few shirtless pics on his profile, and I'm tempted to ask him to let me have a closer look, but then I resist, reminding myself to fight temptation.

Note to self: must follow his profile for later use.

Third period Algebra is difficult for me for two reasons: one.) despite my being Asian, Math is not my strong suit, and I have to pay extra attention just to earn a passing grade. And two.) Math is something Nicholas doesn't seem to have a problem with, so he offers to help me during the portion of class when we're asked to solve a few problems ourselves. He's sitting really close to me, and I smell the fresh ocean breeze scent on his skin. I have to keep my legs together to keep myself at bay. I know that sounds gross, but being so close to him is making things… hard.

God, I'm so disgusted with myself.

Fourth period is miserable. I'm missing him, and I don't like it. I don't like it at all. He sends me a text every now and then, but it's not the same. I find myself watching the clock intently, because perspective drawing is not keeping my interest. Not one bit.

Lunch time!

Nicholas is already at my locker when I get there. He's leaned up against it, looking like a model right out of a magazine. He looks up and gives me that signature crooked half smile as I approach.

"Long time no see," he says.

"Yeah, feels like forever," I reply.

"Should we wait for Mackenzie?" Oh… right. He hadn't brought her up in any of our text messages throughout the day, I had almost forgotten he had a thing for her. I love Mackenzie and she's my best friend, but I almost hope that she doesn't show up, because I want Nicholas' undivided attention. If she's here, I know he'll go all straight boy and forget all about me. But then again, maybe it's better that she is here, so that I don't let myself get caught up on a guy who can never and will never like me back… Not in the way that I want him to.

"I'm surprised you two waited for me," Mackenzie says as she walks up to us. "I thought, by now, you two would be touching butts behind the bleachers."

"Maybe if you're there," Nicholas responds, raising his eyebrows suggestively.

"Ew," Mackenzie answers. My sentiments exactly. Maybe I'm just a jealous fool, but the sound of Nicholas flirting with Mackenzie feels so icky and predatory to me. I don't know what it is, but with her, he loses all his game. Maybe that's what happens to him when he's flirting with someone he's actually attracted to. Seeing him attempt to flirt with my best friend is, like, the biggest turn off ever.

The three of us head into the cafeteria. Mackenzie grabs a fruit cup and a tuna sandwich, I pick up a PB&J and a carton of chocolate milk, and Nicholas grabs pretty much one of everything, before we sit down at an empty table in the quad.

"What are you guys doing after school?" Nicholas asks, taking a fat bite of his tuna sandwich.

"Nothing," Mackenzie answers. When she says this, I know immediately what Nicholas must be thinking: "Maybe we can go on a date, Mackenzie? Tonight, I'll take you to the cheap seafood buffet." Just the thought of Nicholas possibly saying this makes me mad, and I don't want to be mad, because I would have no right to be. Even though the cheap seafood buffet was *our* thing.

"I've actually got a ton of homework," I say, deciding to take the highroad. He wants her, so let him have her.

"Oh, my God, I know," Nicholas responds. "That fat packet from Ms. Maple, like, what is that?"

"Aren't you guys in, like, all the same classes?" Mackenzie asks.

"Yeah. Why don't we just do our homework together, Erik? We can help each other out. Mackenzie, you should join us." My eyes dart from Nicholas to Mackenzie. I can see Mackenzie's eyes narrowing. I know this look. She's trying to get a read on me.

"Um… actually, I can't. I got detention," Mackenzie claims. "I smacked a kid across his face as a teacher was walking by."

"I thought that happened yesterday?" I ask.

"And it happened again today," Mackenzie answers quickly. "Erik, you don't know my life." She winks at me, proudly, as if she's just solved all of my problems with her obvious lie.

"What was that wink?" Nicholas asks.

"The sun's in my eyes, Jackass," Mackenzie shoots back. "I have sensitive retinas." The look Nicholas gives her is the best. I can see that he's questioning whether or not he still finds her attractive. If I were in his position, I wouldn't.

"Alright then, Erik, you wanna get together after school?" Nicholas asks me, and only me. My heart starts to flutter.

"Sure."

"Hang on, I forgot to grab a drink," Nicholas says, excusing himself from the table. How he forgot a drink is beyond me, since he grabbed everything else. I put on a stupid smile and watch him as he walks away. God, his butt in those pants… He's wearing slim fitted, black pants that hug every single curve of his juicy—

"Are you an idiot?" I hear Mackenzie's voice pierce into my ear.

"What?" I'm so distracted by Nicholas' behind, I'm not fully registering anything else at the moment.

"I am bending over backwards to exclude myself so that you and the walking sexual harassment suit can have some boning time together, and you're here calling out my bluff? What the fuck?"

"You need to learn to lie better."

"And you need to stop being so dense. The guy is clearly in like with you."

"I appreciate the effort, Mackenzie, but stop, okay? He's already flirting with me, and it's very confusing, because he's clearly straight."

"He's clearly not, if he's flirting with you this hard." She has a point. I don't want to believe her, but I do. At least, a little bit. I know there are straight guys out there who are comfortable enough to be able to joke with gay dudes and it not be anything, but to this extent? Maybe I'm reading too far into things, but he asked me to dinner, insinuated I'm his boyfriend, and sent me that stupid winky-kiss emoji, which I still have yet to decipher. It's all so very confusing. Why is he doing this to me? Or a better question: Why am I so affected by this? He's a boy. I'm a boy. The answer's pretty clear. If we were meant to be together, we'd be playing for the same team, but we're not. And here I am getting my hopes up.

I feel Mackenzie rub a gentle hand on my shoulder. She's a good friend, even if her methods are a little overly aggressive.

"Please, don't get my hopes up," I mutter, fighting to hold back the tears I've got welling in my eyes.

"Get your hopes up about what?" I hear Nicholas' voice. Immediately, I rub my eyes like crazy, in the hopes that he'll chalk my dramatics up to allergies.

"Uh… that dodgeball isn't a thing in P.E. anymore," I lie.

"Yeah, because he's actually terrible at dodging balls," Mackenzie adds. She really doesn't know when to quit, does she? "He usually takes them right in the face."

"That's unfortunate," Nicholas says, taking a swig from the bottle of apple juice he just brought back with him.

"Is it though?"

Thanks, Mackenzie. Thanks for that…

"Wait, I thought Juniors and Seniors don't have to take P.E.?" Nicholas asks.

"They don't," I say. "You only need two years of it, but I… uh… am planning to take it next semester…"

"As an elective," Mackenzie adds.

"Yes, as an elective… because I'm… fat." Nicholas looks suspicious. I don't blame him. We're acting so strange and tense.

"Dude, you're not even fat," Nicholas says nonchalantly, and it warms my heart. "A little pudgy, maybe, but not fat." Never mind.

My fifth period class is Choir. It's another one of my throwaway electives. It was either this or Theatre and I'm not a fan of having to be the center of attention. I'd rather just blend in with the crowd. Plus, I imagine you have to work closely with other people in Theatre — like rehearsals and what not — which just sounds uncomfortable and inconvenient. I'd rather not have to work closely with anyone if I can avoid it. I mean, look at how my project with Andrew went down.

Speaking of Andrew…

I arrive at sixth period Bio a little late. I had to stop by my locker to pick up my presentation notes. Andrew's already here. When I take my seat next to him, he leans in towards me and stares, the way people do when they need something, but they don't want to say it. His sapphire eyes are intense, and they pierce into me, so much so that I can only ignore him for so long.

"Can I help you?" I ask uncomfortably. Our teacher's given us a few minutes to prep before we start the presentations, so I don't feel a need to whisper. But Andrew does.

"I saw you in the quad. You've been hanging out with that new guy," he says. This suddenly went from a level five kind of discomfort to, "it's over nine thousand."

"Yeah?"

"I just think he's really cute," his voice drops to near inaudible levels at the word "cute," and I'm completely disgusted. Not to mention offended. "So, is he, like, into dudes?"

"Oh, my God." I want to smack him. As if it wasn't already bad enough that he wanted to use me for sex, and then say that he's "out of my league," now he wants to pump me for information on another guy. I can't believe him. "To be honest with you, Andrew, I don't want to talk to you about this. Or about anything really."

"Why not? What'd I do?" I can't help but scoff at how unbelievable he is.

"You know what? Let's just get through our presentation and call it a day." He looks annoyed, and I really don't care. I may not be pretty or popular, but I still have my self-worth. And I'm worth more than what he was willing to give. A lot more.

Our presentation went off without any major hiccups. I stumbled over my words a few times, when the nerves got to me, but it was definitely a B+ presentation, at least. I'm just happy to be done with the project, and with Andrew. I'm ready to move on, and I'm doing just that.

Nicholas texted me to meet him at my locker. He has his mom's car today and figured that it'd be easiest if he drives me home, we do our homework at my place, and then he just leaves from there. It was a sound plan, so that's what we're doing. Once again, he's a male model waiting for me at my locker. Together, we walk over to the parking lot and hop into his mom's car. It was only last night that I was in this car, but sitting in the passenger side makes me feel like I'm returning after a long time. I already have memories of him in here: him poking fun at my musical tastes, and him singing off key to that old *old* R&B song. What I wouldn't give to have a permanent seat here while he drives.

"So, what are your parents like?" Nicholas asks, as we pull out of the school parking lot.

"What?" I hear the question and my heart stops. I never told my parents he was coming over and I don't know if I can act like he's anything other than a boy I'm in deep *deep* like with. I'm not in Theatre. I can't act. If my mom's home, which is not unlikely, I'm doomed.

"Your parents. What are they like?"

"They're... nice... um... they're religious..." I don't really know what to say about them. I don't know how I can prepare him for the garbage fire I'm potentially going to start by bringing him over. There's no reason for him to come over that isn't personal, unless I can convince my parents that he's another lab partner from a different class. That's believable, right?

"That's cool."

"Um... sure?"

"Okay, you're acting really nervous, so I'm gonna need you to be straight up with me, Erik. What's the deal with your parents?" I suppose I should tell him. The more he knows, the more he'll likely be able to help. At the very least, he'll be less likely to let something crazy slip, like his straight boy flirting.

"I came out recently," I begin to explain. "My dad handled it well enough. My mom, not so much. And now, you're coming over, and you're a boy." Nicholas is nodding his head, absorbing the information. I half expect him to back out and tell me that he's gonna just drop me off and leave, but nope. He only has one thing to say.

"Okay."

We arrive at my house, and I let Nicholas in through the front door, past the fancy seating area with the furniture that my mother bought for display purposes only, and into the living room. I invite him to sit and make himself comfortable while I check the rest of the house for my parents. It's too early for my dad to be home, but my mom works when she feels like working, so I never know.

"Mom, I'm home," I call out.

"In here," she responds. Her voice is coming from the laundry room. I make my way over to greet her, but mostly to let her know that Nicholas is here and that I'm not doing anything sexy with him, as much as I may want to. He's just a friend. "Erik, can you make sure to take your laundry out of the dryer?" she says, practically scolding me when I enter. "You keep leaving your clothes in here, and I need it."

"I can take them now," I offer.

"It's okay. I already put it away."

"Sorry. So, um…" I begin to say, feeling myself tense up a bit. "I brought a friend over, if that's okay."

"Oh?" She's in the middle of sorting and separating the laundry.

"Yeah, he's new. He's in, basically, all my classes and we were thinking we could do some homework together."

"Okay." Mom's expression is blank. It's hard to read. I can't tell if she's angry, annoyed, indifferent or what. I head back into the living room and she follows me. Nicholas stands up when we enter. He seems a bit stiff, slightly more reserved than how I've come to know him. My mom tends to have that effect on people.

"Hi, I'm Nicholas," Nicholas introduces himself, offering his hand. My mom shakes it and smiles, though I can tell it's entirely insincere. "You have a very nice house."

"Thank you. So, you boys are doing homework? For what class?" I open my mouth to answer, but Mom raises her hand, gesturing for me not to speak.

"English. We got a huge packet of sonnets to translate," Nicholas says brilliantly. "I was also helping Erik out with some Algebra. He mentioned that he struggles with it." Nicholas is such a freaking dreamboat. He knows just how to answer to satisfy any mom. The only problem is my mom isn't any mom. She's... *my* mom.

"So, will you be joining us for dinner?" my mom asks, in a way that sounds more like a warning not to, than an invitation.

"Oh, I don't wanna impose."

"It's not a problem." It's worrying me how cordial and inviting my mother is being toward Nicholas. You might chalk it up to Filipino hospitality, but I know my mom, and I know that she can be a sneaky woman. She's probably hoping Nicholas will stay for dinner so she can give him the third degree about our friendship. I look over at Nicholas. He's smiling, sincerely, and doesn't seem pressured at all.

"It's okay. I probably shouldn't be out too late," Nicholas declines, smoothly.

"Right, well, I'm sure your parents would prefer you home for dinner."

"Actually, it's just me and my mom. My parents are in the middle of a divorce. My mom sorta ran away from my dad, which is why we're here." Oh no… He was doing so well. I mean, don't get me wrong, I feel bad about his situation, and I'll try to unpack it sooner than later, but divorce is not one of those things that my mom fully approves of.

"I'm sorry to hear that. What is this world coming to?" Mom says. I can't tell if she's being real or real sarcastic. Regardless, Nicholas seems unfazed by it. "Anyway, I will let you boys get to it. All I ask is that you keep your studies in the living room." My mom then turns to me. "Gwapo naman siya," she says, then heads back to the laundry room.

"What'd she say?" Nicholas asks once we're in the clear.

"She said you're handsome," I translate. And that's actually what she said.

"She didn't seem happy about that."

"She's not."

Nicholas and I start on our homework packet from Ms. Maple. He decides to read the first sonnet out loud to me, pouring a touch of emotion into every word.

"Why didst thou promise such a beauteous day," he reads, allowing his hands to conduct the flow of this passionate prose. "And make me travel forth without my cloak, to let base clouds o'ertake me in my way." I lose myself in the sound of his voice and the gracious way he paces around the room.

Just look at him, I think to myself.

There's a way in which he carries himself that seems so at ease with his entire existence. He doesn't restrain himself at all, allowing his body to express everything that he needs it to, from the way that he talks with his hands, to the way that he laughs so fully and freely when something amuses him.

"Shakespeare's a pervert," Nicholas chuckles to himself. He catches me staring at him, wonderstruck. I know I've been caught, but I can't look away. A tiny crooked smile forms on his lips. "What?"

"I've never met anyone so enchanting to me before," I want to say. "You're perfection." I *want* to say that, I really do. But I don't. Instead, I chicken out and simply say, "Nothing." He replies with a cool smile and continues reading. I keep staring at him, watching as this heavenly creature floats around the living room. I wish I were like him, so confident and seemingly without worry or care. I wish I liked myself as much as I'm finding I like him, and not just in the physical sense. His presence here allows me to see myself in the way that I always imagined I could be.

He reads me sonnet after sonnet, and we attempt to translate them together. Sometimes we argue, albeit playfully, because we don't agree on what a certain line means. Other times, we just giggle because the sonnet sounds so stupid to us after it's been translated. It takes a few hours to get through Ms. Maple's packet, so we decide to call it a day once we've finished.

"I should get going," he says, gathering his things. "Thanks for having me over." Before I can do anything, he's got me wrapped up in his arms in a tight farewell embrace. Underneath his scent of a fresh ocean breeze is the scent of *him*, and it subtly finds its way to me, floating into my nose and caressing my lungs with its warmth. I melt. He smells like what I imagine home is supposed to smell like. Not of meat stews like sinigang, or anything funny like that, but of comfort and safety. It's ironic really, because in his arms is probably the most dangerous place for me to be. Despite this, I let my head fall onto his shoulder, and I inhale in his warmth. As soon as I do, I feel tears start to well in my eyes.

"You okay?" Nicholas asks, when he lets me go.

"Allergies," I lie. "They get really bad this time of year."

"You know there's a pill for that."

I walk Nicholas to the door and see him off with one last wave. I can't hold the tears in anymore. Once the door shuts, the tears fall. I stand there for a moment, trying to steady myself. What is this feeling? Why am I going to pieces? I don't understand.

"Erik," Mom says. I don't even hear her come in. "Nicholas went home?" I nod, wiping my eyes with my fingers. "Why are you crying?" I shake my head.

"It's nothing. I'm just a little confused," I say. I don't want to be scrutinized, and I know my mom well enough to know that that's likely what'll happen if I stay here. I quickly move past her and up the stairs.

"Erik," her voice stops me, midflight. "What's going on between you and that boy? Be honest with me."

"Nothing's going on," I reply.

"It's okay, Erik. Just tell me the truth. I won't get mad."

"He's just a friend, Mom. And that's all he'll ever be." I climb the rest of the stairs and hole myself up in my room. I'm tired and I want to go to bed, but something in the pit of my stomach leaves me feeling incredibly unsettled. I'm starting to think that this isn't just a stupid schoolboy crush, but something more. And the thought of that scares the crap out of me.

What am I supposed to do?

chapter twelve
nicholas

It's just past sundown when I arrive home. I go into Ma's room to return the car keys and find her standing in front of the mirrored sliding doors of her closet. She's wearing a black cocktail dress that looks to be about two sizes too small. Good Lord, is she planning on dating again? I can't even stomach the thought. I mean, the divorce isn't even final yet. What gives?

"Oh, good, Nicky, you're home," she says to my reflection. She then turns and poses. "How does this look?" I let my mouth hang open, but don't give an answer. Honestly, I'm afraid to. I'm almost one hundred percent certain this is a trick question. Ma stands there, waiting for me to respond, and when I don't, she drops her pose. "That's comforting. You might as well tell me I'm hideous."

"You're not hideous, Ma. You're just…" I trail off. I'm not really sure what I can say here that won't earn me a big chancla to the face. I decide to approach it playfully, and hope my charming innocence is enough to win the day. "You're just so beautiful that nobody understands." She narrows her eyes, unamused.

"Where's my chancla?" she threatens.

"Mami, no!"

"You're grounded."

"What do you want me to say, Ma? You're hot? Like, ew!"

"That would be weird, wouldn't it?"

"What are you wearing that for anyway?" I ask. "You're not planning on dating again, are you?"

"God, no!" she answers with disgust. "I pulled this out of my wardrobe to see if it still fits, but I think it makes me look like a streetwalker."

"What's a streetwalker?" Ma and her old-timey slang. I can never keep up with it. I bet it means something super unflattering, like poor old lady with cankles. If that's how my mom sees herself, that's sad, because we're not even poor. Dad's still taking care of us at the moment. I don't know about the cankles though.

"Anyway, your father called," she changes the subject, completely dodging my question. My ears perk up at the word "father." Dad actually called her? Could this be good news? "He wants to see you and have a face to face. Maybe even have you down for a weekend."

"Great, when are we going to see him?" I ask, my heart pounding with the tiniest bit of hope.

"*We* are not. Your father asked to see you," Ma explains. "I bet he wants to try to explain his side of the story. You can make your own decision about it."

No, I really can't.

It's weird being the kid of a couple going through a divorce. Sides get established and lines get drawn, and you want to take a side, but you also don't want to take a side, but then you find out why they're getting divorced, and you end up taking a side. Then, once you've taken a side, you start to feel guilty for not taking the other side, but your side is so mad at the other side, that it makes even talking to the other side feel like you're betraying the side that you sided with. And there's just so many different sides to the whole thing.

Ma, Dad, and I, we used to be a trio, a family. But now the word "father" sounds like an insult. "Your *father* called," is said with such contempt and disdain, my mom could easily say, "Satan called," and it would carry the same connotation. It makes me feel bad because I don't know how my dad is. I don't know what he's feeling. I don't know why he did what he did, or if he even did anything at all. I just trusted my mom's hearsay and followed her blindly because she seemed to be the one that needed me more. Or maybe I followed her because she got to me first. Or worse, maybe I picked a side way before the divorce, which is why I didn't question Ma much when it happened. I mean, I am a mama's boy. Maybe I owe Dad a chance to explain?

"You'd let me drive to LA alone?" I ask.

"Of course not," Ma replies. "But I'm not going to see that man. We can rent a hotel room or something, if you really want to go. I'll find something else to do while you're with him." She says this with so much spite, it makes me think that I really don't have a choice. I can just hear her punishing me with some heavy-handed Catholic guilt if I decide we should drive down to visit. "I hope you had a good day with your *father*. I just sat in the hotel room, by myself, watching infomercials of all the things I'll never be able to have, like a faithful husband," I imagine her saying. In my mind, she's that petty. Actually, in reality, she's pretty petty, so it's not a big stretch.

"I'm sorry, Ma." It pains me to see her like this.

"There's nothing to be sorry about," she says. "Why would you be sorry?" There's a certain tone in her voice that gives it a very "I don't give a fuck" kind of attitude, but I know she does. This is all a front. I don't know if it helps her to keep her feelings about the situation all bottled up or what, but pretty soon that bottle's gonna break, and I'm not sure I'm well equipped enough to keep her together when it does. I mean, it's not just her and Dad going through this divorce. I'm going through it too. And I have the hard job of having to be the one who's stuck in between them.

"I don't know," I mutter. "It's just... I know it's a lot."

"Anyway, how was your friend?" Ma changes the subject again. I don't feel the need to fight her to stay on topic about the divorce. She's gonna talk about it when she wants to talk about it. Or not. Who knows? I can't force her. And maybe it's better this way? Maybe the less I know, the better? I mean, I don't want to hate my dad. But being here with Ma makes me feel like I have to. It's for my own sake and sanity that I don't push the subject.

"Erik? He's good," I answer. I'm just going with the flow.

"You guys get a lot of work done?"

"Yeah. We translated a bunch of sonnets for English class. He's a really cool guy. A bit repressed, I think, but cool." I notice Ma looking at me funny. I don't know why. I don't think I said anything out of the ordinary. "What? Why are you looking at me like that?"

"Nothing. I'm just happy for you," she says. "It's been a while since you've had some real friends. You've always been such a loner."

"What are you talking about? I had friends," I say, all defensive.

"You had *girlfriends*. That doesn't count. And anyone you weren't dating, you never cared enough about to mention them to me. Not that I remember anyway."

"Okay, Ma. What are you getting at?"

"I'm not getting at anything," she says, still staring at me with that funny look on her face. "I don't know. You just seem happier. In fact, you're glowing. I'm just happy for you, that's all."

Way to make things awkward, Ma, I think to myself.

Very awkward.

I head into my garage. I've still got a bunch of homework to get through. I swear the teachers have no sense in how much time all these assignments actually take, but I'm not in the mood to do much of anything. Translating all those sonnets with Erik really took it out of me.

I need to eat. I rifle through my drawer chest to find a pair of basketball shorts and change into them. Before I go out, I make a point to gather the collection of cups that have accumulated in my room. If Ma notices them, I won't hear the end of it. I take all the cups into the kitchen and throw them into the sink before heading over to the fridge.

"Where'd all these cups come from?" I hear Tio Roger say when he comes in. I don't volunteer myself to take the blame and shrug all innocent like. "Would you grab me a beer while you're in there?" He says, taking a seat at the table.

There's so much in my uncle's fridge, but nothing to eat. It's all just raw ingredients and I'm too hungry to try to cook anything. I manage to find some deli sliced turkey and cheese and decide to make a sandwich. I grab the stuff, and a beer for my uncle, and join him at the table. He's pulled out his laptop. I figure he's planning on doing something for work, but when I go to hand him his beer, I see he's got his browser window open to some dating site.

"She's pretty," I offer, commenting on a photo of a thirty something, freckled, red headed woman.

"You think so?" Tio Roger asks.

"Uh huh," I reply, as I take a seat. "Are you looking to finally settle down, or are you dating, or whatever it is people your age do?"

"People my age? Ha! You're funny."

"Well, what are you doing?"

"I don't know, Nick. Just keeping my options open I guess."

"You don't want a girlfriend or anything?" I ask. Tio Roger's relationship status has always been a bit of a hot topic. Why isn't he married? Why doesn't he start a family? Why don't the women he associates with stick around longer than a few weeks? There was even a sneaking suspicion that he might be a closeted gay, because — of course — that's the only reason why a Latin man in his late thirties hasn't settled down.

"I'm not looking for anything serious like that right now, Nick," Tio Roger answers, but offering no further explanation.

"Why?" I begin to prod. "Don't you want to get married?" I'm genuinely curious. Tio Roger looks at me with a look that tells me he's tired of hearing this question, despite it being the first time I've ever asked him. He contemplates something for a moment, then lets out an exasperated sigh.

"Nick, marriage is a big deal," he begins to explain. "I'm not in a place in my life where I can see myself making a commitment like that. I have too many other things going on, and I would never want to make a promise that serious if I wasn't one hundred percent sure that I could keep it. If it happens, it happens, but right now, I'm just keeping things simple. No strings attached. No labels. Just simple."

I finish putting together my sandwich and take a bite. What Tio says makes a lot of sense to me. I start to think about my own parents, and how their marriage is panning out. It's messy, with so many severed strings, and far from simple.

Like I said, it's got a lot of sides.

Maybe Tio Roger, despite what anyone might think about his relationship status, has figured out the secret: making no promises means breaking no promises. I continue to ponder this idea as I take another bite of this sad excuse for a turkey sandwich.

It could really use some mayo.

chapter thirteen
erik

A never-ending hug.

I'm not sure if I heard about it somewhere or if I just made it up, but it's one of those hugs that are so gentle, and soft, and safe, where every point of contact feels like perfection. It's so perfect that the feeling lingers long after you let go, and there's this tingle left there to remind you that what you've just experienced is… *coming home*. That was the kind of hug that Nicholas gave me. That's why I couldn't keep myself together. That's why I'm sitting here, face crusty with dried tears, flipping through my Bible. I'm looking for something, anything, that will tell me that what I'm feeling is okay.

"Because of this, God gave them over to shameful lusts. Even their women exchanged natural relations for unnatural ones. In the same way, the men also abandoned natural relations with women and were inflamed with lust for one another. Men committed shameful acts with other men and received in themselves the due penalty for their error."

Hmm… I wonder what else the Bible has to say about my predicament. I flip through the pages, quickly skimming through the passages until I come across a verse in Leviticus:

"If a man has sexual relations with a man as one does with a woman, both of them have done what is detestable. They are to be put to death; their blood will be on their own heads."

. . .

Well, that's lovely.

I don't understand. If God wanted me to be attracted to boys, why didn't he just make me a girl? If I had been born a girl, I could like Nicholas freely without feeling weird or conflicted about it. In fact, I think I might make a good girl… except bleeding from my naughty bits every month sounds terrible, and I think I'd miss having a penis. Penises are convenient. But nope, I was born a gay boy with an intact penis that's not allowed to ever stand up for anything that it actually wants. Why? Because the Bible says so.

I don't want to go to school tomorrow. I don't wanna run into Nicholas. Hanging out with him has been the definition of "the best," and I don't want to ruin that by having to avoid him because of my religious beliefs. I suppose I could just explain my position to him, but I can already imagine how awkward that conversation would be: "Nicholas, I want you, so we can't be friends. Bye." No. That's stupid. I could never say that. It's moments like these when I wish I didn't care about things like my beliefs or my religion, but I do. I wish I didn't care about God, and I wish I didn't worry or wonder if there's a place for me in Heaven, but I do. Because the alternative is terrifying. It's either eternal damnation in hellfire, or absolutely nothing. I can't decide which of the two is worse.

. . .

Hello, palm tree.

Hello, ocean.

Hello, row boat without the oars.

I must've fallen asleep, because I'm having that dream again.

I'm staring out at the ocean toward my inevitable fate. I don't know why I'm going through this again. Just let me die now. It would save me the trouble of having to drown, just like I always do.

The next morning at school, I decide to make myself unavailable. If I'm gonna play the avoiding game with Nicholas, I want to make it so that he never has a chance to talk to me face to face. And if he texts me, I'll just pretend I didn't see it. Rather than go to my locker, I spend the time I have before class walking aimlessly around campus. I walk down hallways, and up some stairs, and then down some stairs, and then up some hallways. I'm actually surprised with how much ground I'm able to cover, when I'm not standing around, talking about nothing. I'm about to make my way over to Ms. Maple's when I get a text. It's from Nicholas.

"Morning, Sunshine [Sun emoji]." I don't respond. A few minutes later, another text from him comes in. "Where you at???"

Again, I don't respond.

When I get to Ms. Maple's class, the door's still locked, so I can't get in. I set down my backpack and plop myself on the ground. I pull out my phone to check the time and find two messages from Mackenzie. I open them up to see a picture of Nicholas pouting at me and, under it, the words "Your boyfriends missin you" are written alongside a broken heart emoji. They're really playing hardball, aren't they? And they're not even using proper punctuation. Or spelling, for that matter. No! I'm not falling for it! I'm gonna be a good Catholic boy, and I'm not gonna fall for any more temptations. I refuse!

Just before the first bell rings, Ms. Maple opens her door. I gather my things and get up, but don't go in. I have a plan. For now, I just stare at the picture of Nicholas and tell myself that he's just a boy. He's a boy like any other. He shouldn't have such a strong effect on me. It's tough though, trying to convince myself, because I can see what he's wearing. Today, he is dressed in a short sleeved, plaid button up, which he's left unbuttoned, so you can see the practically skintight, white tank underneath.

I hate this so much.

After I see a few of my classmates go in, I enter Ms. Maple's classroom and scout for a desk that has someone sitting next to it on all sides. The closest I can get to that is a seat in the back corner, where all the too-cool-for-schoolers usually park it. I take the seat and wait, trying to keep my head down, in case one of the kids who usually sits back here attempts to glare me out of their spot.

"Hey," a familiar voice greets me. Please don't be him. Please don't be him. I look up, and it's him. It's Nicholas. He's kneeling down so that his face is right next to mine. "You okay?" I don't respond. "Here, I brought you something." He opens his bag and pulls out a small pill bottle, which he then slips into my hand. "They're non-drowsy. For your allergies. I swiped them from my uncle's medicine cabinet." I don't think we're supposed to have meds on campus, but I don't wanna get either of us in trouble, so I quickly shove the allergy pills into my backpack. Nicholas pats me on the shoulder, then leaves to find a seat a few rows up. I'm watching him go, and I feel totally disgusted with myself. Did I really think I could keep this up?

I can't.

I grab my backpack and hop over to the empty seat next to him. He seems happy, but a bit confused. I think I made this seat thing a bigger deal than it had to be, but whatever. I'm a complete failure at this avoiding game, so I guess I'm just gonna have to pretend like everything's cool. I can do that... I think.

At lunchtime, Nicholas and Mackenzie meet me at my locker.

"Look who decided to show his face," Mackenzie says. "Where were you this morning?"

"I was feeling a little off," I tell her. It's not a lie. "I just wanted some alone time before class."

"It's cool. Just don't go disappearing on me," Nicholas adds. God, why does he do that? Why does he show affection so freely? Even with just his words, it's deadly.

We go about our routine of stopping at the cafeteria, then finding a table in the quad. Nicholas and Mackenzie complain about how boring their classes are, and the two of them banter about how they'll likely never use half the stuff that we're all required to take. Advanced Math? That's what calculators are for. I chime in every now and then, but for the most part, I just listen. A part of me feels like I need to restrain myself to keep from getting more invested in a certain person than I already am. Aside from my religious hang ups, things are feeling pretty good. Then Andrew walks up.

"Hey, guys. What's going on?" He greets us, inserting himself between Nicholas and me. It's pretty jarring. Andrew's never hung out with us, like ever. And after the whole lab partner situation, I really don't want him to.

"Do you need something, Andrew?" I ask, in the nicest tone I can muster for him.

"Can't a guy just stop by to say hello to some friends?" He replies. It's so beyond phony, it makes me wanna gag.

"What friends? We were lab partners. The project's over now."

"Wow, Erik, that's really insulting."

"Well, you're a huge dick, so go away," Mackenzie snaps at him, in a tone so icy you could chill a hot bowl of soup in it.

Nicholas sits there awkwardly, his eyes darting between Andrew, Mackenzie, and myself. It occurs to me that I've never explained exactly what happened to Nicholas, at least not in detail. We all sit there in a tense silence until, finally, Nicholas leans in and interjects.

"Listen, Andrew, right?" he begins. "I'm sure you're a cool guy and I don't want this to be awful for you, but from what I've been told, you've sorta been painted as a villain here, and I don't want this to be uncomfortable for anyone."

"Oh… I see," Andrew replies. "I didn't realize I did anything wrong." I can't help but scoff at this. Nicholas shrugs. Mackenzie gives Andrew a death glare. "Alright, well… laters, I guess." Andrew gets up. He's clearly pissed, but I don't care. I feel I gave him the same amount of consideration that he gave me, so... bye.

"Okay, one of you is gonna have to fill me in," Nicholas insists, once Andrew is out of earshot. "I want details."

"I'll tell you later," I say. "Not here." As much as I may despise Andrew, the last thing I need is for someone to overhear about how he kissed me, and fondled me and, essentially, tried to use me as his sex toy. What happened between us affects both of us, which is why I don't want it spreading around just as much as I know he doesn't. Mum's the word.

After my last class gets out, I go to meet Nicholas at my locker. He offered to drive me home in exchange for the details between me and Andrew, which, frankly, I can't wait to unpack for him. Andrew was being all sorts of obnoxious in sixth period today. We were asked to partner up with the person next to us — which, annoyingly, happens a lot in that class — and were given these cell samples to look at in a microscope. Andrew wouldn't let me look through our microscope. In fact, he wouldn't even talk to me, which I'd be totally fine with, if we didn't have to work together.

Every time I tried to assert myself and reach for the microscope, he'd shift around so that he could body block me from it. I came very close to losing my cool and shoving him, but that would've been a terrible move on my part since he's built like the freakin' Statue of David and is probably just as strong. Plus, our teacher, Mr. Reed, would've caught me and I'd get stuck with detention. Sadly, there's not really anything I can do, but hope that Mr. Reed decides to rearrange our seating arrangements sooner rather than later.

"You look upset," Nicholas greets me, as I approach him at my locker.

"Andrew's a butt," I say.

"You wanna get some frozen yogurt and talk about it?" I nod.

Nicholas drives us across town. There's, like, nothing fun to do around where we live, so if we wanna do anything worth doing, we gotta drive, like, half an hour. Nicholas doesn't seem to mind it though. He says it gives us more time to talk.

"So, fill me in," Nicholas says. "I know that Andrew made a move on you and that you thought it meant something, but it turned out he was just trying to score."

"Yeah," I reply. "That's the abridged version of it."

"So give me the unabridged version."

I take a breath, and then begin to recount everything that happened, from the day I went to Andrew's house, to the time he met me behind the bleachers and told me that he was "out of my league."

"He actually said that?" Nicholas asks.

"Uh huh," I nod.

"What a dick!" he exclaims.

"Yeah," I quietly agree.

"I mean, to reject you is one thing. That sucks, but fine, whatever. But then to insult you too? The thing that gets me about the whole thing is that it seems like he doesn't even know, you know? Or maybe he does, but he doesn't care?"

"Who knows?"

"Well, if it makes you feel better, if I were into dudes, I'd totally swoop in on you." Ugh, why does he say such things? He's bothered by the idea that Andrew might not know that he hurts people, yet he's sitting here, saying things like *that* to guys like *me*.

"Don't say that," I say softly, and with a smile, so as not to make it evident that he's killing me with his straight boy flirting.

"Why?" he replies, with a look of genuine concern. "Do you actually believe what he said to you? Do you actually think that you're not good enough?" I don't want to talk about this. I don't want to divulge my insecurities and, more importantly, I don't want it to slip out that I'm stupidly attracted to him. I stare out the window, hoping that he'll take the hint and just drop the subject. But then, he says something that catches me completely off guard. "Erik, my dad had an affair. My family's falling apart, and I feel like a terrible person. I've been avoiding my dad without hearing his side of the story, and I blindly followed my mom in running away from him without giving him a chance to explain." We go silent for a moment. I'm trying to process the information he's giving me, but it's difficult, because I'm so taken aback by how open he is about everything. "There. I showed you mine. Now, you show me yours," he says to me. He's so stern, it almost sounds demanding.

"I… uh…" I'm trying to figure out what I want to say and how much of myself I want to reveal, but my mind and my mouth don't seem to want to meet in the middle. After fumbling my thoughts for a bit, I finally manage, "I'm not allowed to like boys."

"Because your parents?"

"Yeah, that's part of it. But, like, I grew up very Catholic. I go to church every Sunday. I went through Catechism. Got confirmed. This gay thing, it wasn't a thing until Andrew. I never thought about my sexuality because everything was supposed to be a certain way. But then I have this gorgeous guy flirting with me and saying all these nice things, and it's making me feel good." At this point, I'm no longer talking about Andrew. "I'm not really sure how to deal with it, because I don't want to go to Hell, but he just makes me feel so… good." I'm staring at Nicholas, who's listening, but keeping his eyes focused on the road. A part of me is hoping that he's hearing me, like, *really* hearing me, and that he knows I'm not talking about Andrew at all. He has to know that. It's obvious, isn't it?

"Can I be honest with you?" Nicholas asks. This is it. He knows. I brace myself because I'm expecting that he's about to let me down. "I think you can do better than him." He doesn't know, does he? "I mean, if a guy is gonna be the center of why you're so conflicted about everything, I think you can do better than Andrew. You deserve better." He really doesn't know…

Straight boys are so dense.

"Do you wanna just share one?" Nicholas asks, holding the door to the Frozen Yogurt place open for me.

"Umm… sure," I respond with uncertainty. I mean, sharing platonically… that's weird, isn't it? Or is it just me? I dunno. My mind just goes right to a milkshake with two straws.

Nicholas grabs a big tub and goes to fill it with chocolate and vanilla frozen yogurt. He then proceeds to the topping station without so much as consulting me — I mean, if we're sharing, I should have a say — and he fills up our tub with cookie crumbs, a couple cubes of brownies, some yogurt chips, and cheesecake bites. When we go to get our portion weighed, it's a bit shocking. It's the same price it would've been if we had just gotten two tubs and doesn't that, like, defeat the purpose of us sharing? I don't know. When it comes to Nicholas, I know nothing. He's so forward and unpredictable, it's difficult for me to make any sense of him.

We sit at a high top table near the front of the store, right next to the window looking out toward the parking lot. Nicholas hands me a spoon, and then digs into the frozen yogurt mountain he's created. For a while,

I just watch him. I don't really have much of an appetite after all the deep conversation on the way over.

"You're not gonna have any?" He asks when he notices I haven't touched our yogurt.

"I'm not really hungry," I say. I sound depressing, and I hate it.

"Oh, come on. We drove all this way. The least you can do is take a bite," Nicholas says. I don't budge. "Fine. You wanna do this the hard way?" He sticks his spoon into the yogurt mountain, and then brings the scoop right up to my face. "Open your mouth." Good Lord, he's trying to spoon feed me. And aggressively I might add.

"Nicholas, no," I refuse. There are several other patrons around and I don't want any of them to see this. It's embarrassing.

"Open your mouth."

"Nicholas." I try to grab at his wrist so I can move his spoon away, but he's much too fast for me. Every time I reach for him, he dodges and comes back at another angle.

"Open your mouth!"

"Nicholas, stop!" I start to laugh. I'll admit, it is a little fun trying to fight him off, but I'm mostly laughing because the nerves are starting to kick in. I can feel people starting to stare. Finally, Nicholas puts the spoon down, and I let out a sigh of relief. The relief, however, is short lived because a split second later, I feel his fingers moving around my belly. He's tickling me. "No, no tickling! Nicholas!"

"You gonna be a good boy and eat your yogurt?" He asks with a playful sort of authority. I nod, but he continues to tickle me. It's not long before I'm laughing like an insane person, and I have no choice but to surrender.

"I'll eat it! I'll eat it! Stop!" Nicholas stops tickling me, thank God. He gives me a second to breathe, before he goes on to spoon feed me my first bite of our frozen yogurt mountain.

"Gay," I hear someone cough under their breath. Nicholas turns and cocks his head to see who said it. A few tables away from us, I see a couple of boys, roughly around our age — maybe a bit younger — snickering to themselves, while not so discreetly eyeing us through their side glances. Nicholas gets up quickly and approaches them. I can't react fast enough to stop him.

"Nicholas, don't," I plead, but he's not listening. He's already standing over the boys, leaning on their table. The snickering boys look extra small with Nicholas hovering over them, and their once insidious smiles have all but faded.

"What'd you guys say?" I hear Nicholas saying to them. The boys appear to sink into their chairs nervously. "Oh, now that I'm standing here, you don't have nothing to say, huh? You guys are funny." Nicholas turns from them and heads for the exit. "Come on, Erik, let's get out of here." I stick both of our spoons into our yogurt, grab our tub, and follow him out. If I'm honest, I'm a little bit nervous being around Nicholas right now. I had no idea he could be so firm and intimidating. It's kinda hot, but it's also kinda scary. The unpredictability of him worries me, because the part of me that wants to give into temptation — the weaker part of me — finds it almost exciting. And that's anything but a good thing.

nicholas

Erik and I have been hanging out for a couple weeks now and things are going well. He's quickly becoming my new best friend. It's easy. We have this sort of natural connection between us, and nothing ever feels forced. There *is* a little bit of an awkward tension that comes up every now and then, and I think it has a lot to do with Erik having a crush on me. I mean, I don't know that for sure, but there have been times where he's said something a little off or acted a bit suspicious.

Back when Erik and I first started hanging out, we went to pick up some frozen yogurt, and he was talking about a guy flirting with him and making him feel good. I know he was talking about Andrew, but the whole time it felt more like he was talking about me. Of course, I could never say that — it'd be super awkward, regardless of if he was talking about me or not — so I just tried to be encouraging. Then, a few days after that, I invited him over so we could do homework together, and we got to talking about Mackenzie.

"Girls are so freakin' complicated," I complained, after a long-winded venting session.

"Yeah, wouldn't it be great if we could just date each other?" he said. "I mean, if I was a girl, 'cause you're straight and all." It caught me off guard. Hearing him say that was a little jarring, because he's gay. When I say shit like that, it's different, because we both know I don't mean anything by it. But for him to say it… I don't know.

"Too bad the universe doesn't work that way, huh?" I replied, kinda jokingly. But then I took a second to think about it and I decided — you know, if Erik *was* a girl — I wouldn't really be opposed to the idea of going out with him. Like I said, our relationship feels natural. We fit together in a way that I've never felt I've fit with anyone before. There's just one problem…

He's a dude.

If only, right?

If only Erik was a girl, things would be perfect. He'd be, like, the best girlfriend. Not like all the girls I've dated or been attracted to in the past. Speaking of girls from my past, a couple nights ago, I got a message from Brenda, of all freakin' people. She texted me from one of her friend's phones, since I had blocked her.

"Hey. It's Bren. You ok? You haven't been at school," she texted. I almost didn't respond, but then I thought, why the hell not? Whether we're cool or not, it doesn't matter now.

"Yea. Parents are splitting. Me and ma moved. Kinda crazy." I texted back.

"You doing ok?"

I tapped in a thumbs up emoji and proceeded to unblock her on all accounts. I have to admit, it was nice hearing from her. It's only been a couple weeks, but it feels like forever ago since I had my old life.

With Brenda getting in touch with me, I started to think back on my relationship with her and how I changed. She put me in different clothes and changed up my hair, which took a long time for me to adjust to. I mean, admittedly, I like it now, but when we were going through the process, I remember thinking, "Why do I have to change? Am I not good enough the way that I am?" Then I started to think back on my other major relationships that I had prior to her.

There was Melly, who I dated for a few months during freshman year. She was a little punk chick who liked to draw on her eyebrows real angular, so she always looked upset about everything. Melly was a trip, because she was kind of — for lack of a better word — a raging bitch. She was super mean to people for no reason, and claimed that she *had* to be in order to get what she wanted. She sorta had a Chihuahua complex, in the sense that she was short, but walked around like she was above everyone else, when, really, she could barely see over their shoulders. In hindsight, her attitude was probably just her overcompensating, but she did teach me to stand up for myself and to never back down when it comes to things like being disrespected.

There was also my first *real* girlfriend, Hanna, from way back in the seventh grade. She was sweet and a little nerdy even. She wasn't the type of girl you'd think would be bossy, but she was such a perfectionist that she couldn't help but boss me around. She was constantly telling me what to do and would criticize me if I didn't do something or, if I *did* do something, that I didn't do it right. I didn't know how to say no to her because I wanted to have a girlfriend so bad. We were together for most of the school year until about a week before we went on summer break, when she dumped me, because she was — in her words — "tired of dealing." I wasn't perfection for her, I guess.

That's really just the tip of the iceberg.

I've dated an eclectic group of girls and each one had a pretty profound effect on me, from my style, to my attitude, to degrading of my confidence, which I do my best to compensate for on a daily basis. I realize, looking back on all of them, that I'm consistently attracted to girls who are over assertive and domineering. And the outcome was that it never lasted. Not long enough for me to fall in love. I mean, yeah, I might've said, "I love you" to them, but I don't know that I really felt it. And I think that's what I want, because I don't just date to date. I believe in courtship. I believe in romance. How could I not? My favorite movie is based on a Nicholas Sparks novel for crying out loud. And if Erik was a girl, with his same personality, he wouldn't be like the girls I've dated before. He'd listen. He'd be there. He'd... care.

If only, right?

It's lunch time. I'm waiting here at Erik's locker, when Mackenzie approaches. Ah, Mackenzie... I stopped barking up that tree the day after Brenda texted me. I quickly realized that Mackenzie was right. She's not my type. Or rather, she *is* my type — over assertive and domineering — and I don't want that to be my type anymore. Don't get me wrong, she's a cool girl and I love that I'm a part of her crew, but after having reflected on my dating history, I have no interest in repeating my dating history. Plus, every time the subject of me and her as a potential couple has come up, she's shot me down. And hard. Each subsequent time that I made a move on her, she's gotten meaner and meaner in her response. The last time I made an attempt, she gave me the death glare.

"Stop flirting with me, you fucking queer," she said, every word dripping with disdain. I don't care how confident you are, after a while, that level of harsh rejection starts to sting, so I just gave up. Can you blame me?

"Hey," I greet her.

"Hey," she says coolly. "God, can you believe that it's about to be Halloween already? Ugh, I don't even have a costume."

"What were you thinking about being?"

"I don't know. I'm thinking either a sexy rabbit, a sexy doctor, or a sexy nun."

"Huh, you don't strike me as the type to slut it up."

"You know, feminism and showing boobage are not mutually exclusive. Plus, I sorta do it ironically."

"Classic Mackenzie," I chuckle.

"That's me," she sings, rather monotone and with very little humor.

I see Erik walking towards us from down the hall. He smiles when he sees me. I'm almost one hundred percent sure he's crushing on me. It's actually kinda cute. And a total confidence booster.

We head to the cafeteria to pick up some food and find a table out in the quad as per usual.

"So, what are you guys up to this weekend?" I ask, removing the plastic wrap from the tray of chicken tenders I picked up.

"Nothing," Erik says.

"Eh, just figuring out my Halloween costume," Mackenzie adds. "Why? You have something better in mind?"

"I was just wondering," I explain. "Last weekend, all I did was sit at home and watch reruns of old sitcoms from the nineties. I was thinking maybe we could do something fun this weekend?" We all fall silent as the three of us start to think of something to do. After a moment, Erik breaks the silence.

"We could go to the city," he suggests.

"The city?" I ask.

"You know, San Francisco."

"Huh… I've never actually been." Both Erik and Mackenzie pause as if they've just choked on their food.

"Wait! You have family out here and you've never been to the city?" Mackenzie asks in disbelief. I guess "the city" is how Bay Area kids refer to San Francisco.

"No. We've only ever come up for the holidays, so I never had a reason to go."

"You don't really need a reason to go to the city," Erik interjects. "You just go. Walk around. Be a tourist."

"I mean, I guess that could be fun," I say.

"It's settled then. We're going." Mackenzie asserts. "Tomorrow good for you guys?" Erik nods. I shrug and nod as well.

"Ma, I'm home," I call out when I get home after school.

"I'm in Tio Roger's office!" She calls back. I go over to the office and find her sitting at the computer with a notebook spread out beside her. "How was school?"

"Fine. What are you doing?"

"Finally started looking for a job. I'm thinking I might go back to school. What do you think, mijo?"

"School? Really?" She shrugs.

"By the way, your father called. He wants you to come down next weekend for your birthday. He wanted to talk to you about it, but he mentioned you haven't been answering his calls."

"I haven't." The whole situation with my father is still tricky for me. I've been avoiding him for the last couple of weeks, because I don't know how I would face him, or what I would say. I picked my mom and ran away from the man, and that can't exactly feel good for him.

"Why haven't you been answering him?" Ma asks.

"I don't know. I just don't know how I want to deal with it."

"Well, can you start answering his calls? It's not exactly fun for me to be hearing from him when he can't get a hold of you, mijo."

"Why are you answering his calls, Ma?"

"Because you're here. You're his son. I can't deny him that," Ma explains. "If he calls again, you better answer him, or else you're getting the chancla. You know I don't want to deal with him."

"Alright, I'll talk to him," I say, begrudgingly. I obviously don't mean it.

I go into my garage and plop onto my futon. It lives permanently as a bed now, because I can't be bothered to put it in its couch form. I pull out my phone and navigate to my messages. All this talk about my dad has put me in a weird mood. I suppose I would call it… nostalgic? Anyway, I decide to text Brenda.

"Hey," I send. A minute or so passes. Nothing.

When she doesn't reply, I navigate over to her Instagram page, where I'm greeted by Brenda, making a kissy face and holding up the peace sign. Oh… right. As I scroll through her pictures, I'm reminded that she never posted any of me, save for the one that she hashtagged #thisguy. Seeing the lack of pictures of me makes my past with her feel all the more distant, and somehow less real, like it was a dream that I'm just trying to remember.

"Hey you," Brenda finally texts back. The message is accompanied by a heart emoji. I close the notification and continue down the rabbit hole that is Instagram. I find myself scrolling through Mackenzie's page. Most of her pictures are of her eating while making the ugliest faces she can, while somehow still looking hot. There are a couple of pictures of her and Erik and, in every one of them, Erik's been caught off guard. I then click the tag on the picture, which takes me to Erik's page. He's got a bunch of random stuff posted, like pictures of YA novels that he likes, food plated all fancy like, and a couple of selfies. I scroll down until something catches my eye, a picture of an allergy pill bottle with the caption: "These things are magic!" Wait a second… Didn't I give those to him?

"Miss you," another text message from Brenda comes in. I don't even bother clicking on the notification to see if there's more. Instead, I navigate to my text feed with Erik and begin to type.

"I see the pills I gave you are working [Smiley Face emoji]," I message him. I continue to scroll through his pictures. He's got a couple shots of him and Mackenzie hanging out, a video where he talks Mackenzie into tasting a weird purple thing he calls "Ooo-bay," and a picture of his #FreshlyCleanedBedroom. It looks… normal. I dunno. I guess I sorta expected it to be sterile, with religious memorabilia mounted all over the walls, but it looks like a normal teenage boy's bedroom. There's a small collection of books and movies on his bookshelf, a little HD TV — he's even got the latest Nintendo console — and his bed is guarded by a stuffed dog wearing a t-shirt. It occurs to me that I've never actually seen his room in person. I think I'd like to. But then again, having met his mother, I get the feeling that if I did see his room in person, I'd probably be the first person outside his family to do so.

"Yeah! I was surprised!" a text response from Erik comes in.

"No more crying?" I reply.

"Not today, Satan." I laugh out loud at this. I wonder what he's doing. I try to imagine what Erik might do on a Friday night and all I can picture is him lying on his bed, playing video games, all alone. Maybe because that's pretty much all I've been doing on my Friday nights since I got here. You know, sans video games. God, I miss my stuff. I had a whole collection back home… with my dad… ugh! I really don't want to be thinking about him.

"Plans tonight?" I text Erik.

[Shrugging emoji]. That's his response.

"Wanna take a drive? Pretty sure Ma will lemme have the car."

I see the ellipsis pop up. It's a yes or no question. I wonder why he's taking so long to respond. The ellipsis goes away. Huh. A few minutes pass and no response. I guess I'm staying in for the night.

. . .

My phone buzzes. Finally, Erik texts back.

"What do I tell my mom?" he asks. The question catches me off guard. What does he mean by that? Seconds later, I receive another text. "I can't say, 'going on drive.' Need better excuse." I can't recall ever being in a position where I had to tell my parents anything but the truth. At least, not when it came to my plans. I don't really know what to say. I try to think of something, but I'm drawing a huge blank.

"Idk. I'm coming over," I finally respond.

I'm sitting outside of Erik's house without any sort of plan to break him out. When I check my phone, I see five unread text messages. The first is from Brenda. She sent a selfie of her in just a bra, making that stupid kissy face she's plastered all over her social media. It doesn't do anything for me. If I wasn't over her before, I'm definitely over her now. The other four messages are from Erik, which were sent just before I left my uncle's house, and they read:

"Wait! What's the excuse!?"

"Nicholas!"

"Nvm. I can't go."

"Abort!"

He's just as neurotic in texts as he is in person.

"But soft, what light through yonder window breaks," I message him, making sure to type every word out in proper English. Punctuation included. I wait a couple of minutes for his response.

"You're outside, aren't you?" he replies. I chuckle. At this point, I decide to hop out of my mom's car, walk up his driveway, and ring the doorbell. A slightly taller, more Korean version of Erik, with no glasses, but some small wrinkles around the eyes, answers the door. This must be Erik's dad, I assume.

"Hello. Can I help you?" he asks, looking at me with a bit of confusion.

"Hi, is Erik home?" I say. I expect there to be more to this interaction but, to my surprise, there's not. Erik's dad turns away, leaving me at the door.

"Erik!" he calls out. "There's a kid here to see you!" Erik's dad disappears into the house. Moments later, Erik appears. He runs over to me with a look of concern.

"What are you doing here? Didn't you get my texts?" he asks, all intense like.

"Yeah, but I didn't see them till I got here," I explain. "So, we going out or what?"

"Nicholas, you can't just show up here on a whim. We're about to have dinner."

"I don't mind waiting."

"Nicholas, don't take this the wrong way, but why are you here?"

"I want to hang out with you," I shrug. Erik's expression softens. It seems I've flattered him. "And I can tell by the look on your face that you want to hang out with me too. Am I wrong?" Erik considers and bites his bottom lip.

"Give me a minute," he sighs. He then runs off and disappears into the house. I'm left here, standing outside on their doorstep, just waiting. It's a little awkward since he left the front door wide open. I'm not sure if I should keep standing here or if I should shut their door and wait for him in the car. Eventually, Erik comes running out, having thrown on the teal hoodie that he always wears.

"Okie dokie, let's go," he says breathlessly as he steps out, shutting the door behind him. We walk over to my mom's car and hop in.

"So, what was the excuse?" I ask, buckling my seatbelt. "What'd you end up telling your mom?"

"Nothing. My dad got home a little before you got here. I asked him," Erik explains.

"And your mom?"

"My dad told me to just go and not say anything to her. I was actually pretty surprised."

"Maybe you just don't give him enough credit."

"Yeah, maybe. My dad is a little bit more easy going than my mom. But I always thought they would be on the same page about everything."

"Well, parents are two separate people. That I know for sure. So where do you want to go?"

"Anywhere." Erik smiles, and I can't help but smile back.

We drive around town aimlessly, exploring everything from the backroads to the neighborhood streets. We don't have a destination or a plan. All we have is each other's company and our conversations. Erik tells me about his fears about being gay and Catholic, and what he thinks his parents might think about it. I try to get him to look on the bright side of things and remind him that his dad's already surprised him once tonight by letting him go out without having him tell his mom.

Erik and I move from topic to topic almost seamlessly. I tell him about how I've been avoiding my dad, and how the idea of talking to him feels like a betrayal to my mom. I don't know what I want to do about that.

"Why does it feel like a betrayal?" Erik asks. "I mean, yeah, you picked your mom, but it sounds like even your mom would rather you talk to him than not."

"I don't know. It's just weird," I say.

"Do you think maybe the reason you don't want to talk to your dad is because you don't want to see him for what he is? You left with your mom without even hearing his side. Maybe you're holding on to something that isn't there, and talking to your dad would confirm that?"

"Maybe. It's tough, you know? I never thought my parents would separate. That was never something I imagined, and them not being together makes me feel like something's wrong with the world."

We continue to drive and drive while talking about everything and nothing at the same time. I follow a road at an incline through a neighborhood until we find ourselves in a cul-de-sac at the top of a fairly steep hill. The sun's set now and, from this cul-de-sac, I can see the whole of the suburban city, lit up in thousands and thousands of seemingly tiny lights in the distance. It's actually kind of beautiful.

I park the car, get out, and climb onto the hood. Erik follows suit, taking a seat beside me, and we just stare out into the illuminated landscape of suburbia.

"Would you look at that," I mutter in awe. It's always a little surprising when something so mundane is transformed by lights glowing under a darkened sky.

"I've never been up here before. It's pretty," Erik adds. "You can see everything."

"Right? I'm glad we found this place."

There's something about the view and being here right now that's affecting my mood. I feel… content. Relaxed even. Maybe it was all the talking Erik and I did. Maybe that was the release I needed to let go of all the tension I felt about my parents' divorce. I look over at Erik and, though he isn't smiling, he's got a certain glow about him that I can tell means he's happy. Suddenly, I find myself thinking about a time when he was being super awkward with me, and my curiosity wants to pick his brain about it.

"Hey, do you remember when you said, 'wouldn't it be great if we could date each other,' you know, if you were a girl?" I ask him. "What did you mean by that?"

"What do you mean?" he says, his eyes widening with embarrassment.

"I mean, *what did you mean by that?* Did you mean that you think we'd make a good couple, or that you liked me?" I'm terrible. I'm pretty sure I already know the answer and I'm feeling really giddy about it. Am I really so narcissistic that I would use Erik's crush on me to feed my own ego? Yeah. Yeah, I am.

"I'm not answering that," Erik replies.

"So you don't like me?" I ask, jokingly.

"I'm not answering that either."

"So you *do* like me?" I'm pretty sure I'm the only one finding any humor in this, but I can't stop myself. It's too much fun.

"Nicholas."

"Erik."

"Nicholas… look, I'm not gonna say 'yes' and I'm not gonna say 'no.' That's not a fair question." Erik starts to explain. He's seeming really frazzled now. It's freakin' terrible that I'm enjoying this. "I'm not gonna stroke your ego just because you find it amusing."

"I bet you'd like to stroke something else." I laugh. Erik looks at me, dead serious.

"I think you'd better take me home now." The giddy high that I felt immediately dissipates. Why the fuck did I say that? Knowing what I know, that was cruel.

"Shit. I'm sorry," I say. "That was too far. I'm sorry, I'll stop."

There's a long awkward silence that falls between us. Suddenly, I start to feel uneasy. I messed up. It's not right to tease someone about their feelings, even though I don't know for sure if he does have feelings for me. I make to climb down from the hood of the car when Erik mutters something.

"Both," he says. "I think we'd make a good couple and I… um… I—"

"It's okay," I cut him off. "You don't have to say it. I think we'd make a good couple too." He smiles to himself, blushing. "If only, right?"

"If only," he agrees.

"Come on, I'll take you home."

"Wait. Just a little longer? Please?" I'm afraid to say yes, because I know that giving him what he wants is dangerous. The thing is, I also know that giving him what he wants would make him happy. And is it really that bad to play this game with him if it makes him happy?

"Okay," I say, albeit reluctantly.

There are clear lines that are drawn by our respective sexualities, and I hope that he doesn't forget that, because the last thing I want to do is break his heart.

chapter fifteen
erik

The lights are beautiful.

The view is beautiful.

The boy I'm sitting next to is beautiful.

Everything about this scene is beautiful. So why am I waiting for it to end? Maybe I'm just anxious because I'm expecting it to end, since nothing ever goes the way that I hope. Nicholas looks at me with a twinkle in his eye. "If only," he said. Those are two words I'm never going to let go of. "If only." If only I was a girl. If only we could be together. Maybe then, the light reflecting off his lip from the nearby streetlamp would seem like more of an invitation, rather than the glow of the serpent's eye beckoning me to take a bite from the Fruit of Eden.

If only…

Nicholas drives me home and I sit in silence, contemplating my feelings. I have to remind myself that I shouldn't be feeling like this. Why am I feeling like this? It's not like Nicholas means any of what he says when he's straight flirting with me. It's not like he means anything at all. He's just messing around. The more that I think about it, the more I want to cry. Why is he messing with me?

Neither of us say anything the entire way home. I don't know why, since there's so much to be said. There's so much that *needs* to be said. Nicholas pulls into my driveway and I immediately unbuckle my seatbelt.

"Thanks for hanging out tonight," he says finally.

"Uh huh," I nod. I flash him a closed mouth smile and reach for the door handle.

"Hey, you okay?" Damn… Am I really that easy to read? I need a minute. I just need to take a second to collect myself and put on a happy face, so that I don't have to say any more about anything. Lord knows I've already said more than enough. I don't know what I was thinking, admitting to him that I have a crush on him. I guess I thought maybe if I said it out loud and just owned up to it, that it might make me feel better, like I was getting something heavy off my chest, but no. The weight on my chest feels heavier than before.

"Yeah, I'm just really hungry," I lie. I even make a show of it by rubbing my tummy. It's so pathetic.

"You wanna go grab something?"

"Oh, no, thank you. My mom's probably got something set aside for me. I did just duck out of dinner, so..."

Nicholas nods. It appears my lie satisfies him.

"Well, I'll see you tomorrow." I rack my brain quickly and remember that we made plans with Mackenzie to go to the city tomorrow. I'd been so distracted I'd nearly forgotten about it.

"Yeah, see you then," I say, and let myself out of the car. As I make my way to my front door, I turn to see him waving at me through his windshield. He sits there in my driveway until I get the door open before he reverses the car, pulls out of the driveway, and leaves. What a gentleman, I think to myself.

Once inside, I head into the kitchen. It wasn't a complete lie when I told Nicholas I was hungry. I pull open the fridge and have one of those moments where you see your kitchen is fully stocked, but there's absolutely nothing to eat. I rifle around an assortment of raw ingredients, looking for anything that might make a quick snack. Trust me, if it was anyone but Nicholas that showed up to take me on a drive, I'd totally be regretting skipping dinner right now.

"Where did you go?" I hear the voice of my mother say from behind me. I pull my head out of the fridge and turn to face her. She's standing at the kitchen threshold with her arms crossed, looking all sorts of imposing, in the way only a small Filipino woman can.

"Nowhere," I reply innocently. "Just went for a drive with a friend."

"Which friend? The good looking boy that came here to read you poetry the other week?" I'm not really sure how I should respond to this. I feel like no matter what I say, I'm about to get in trouble.

"Dad said I could go." Mom stares at me for a moment. Her look is that of thoughtfulness. I can only imagine what kind of thoughts she must be thinking, given what she knows. "My son just came back from fornicating and now he's hungry for more meat," though, if that is what she's thinking, I feel like the language would be much more eloquent. And probably in Tagalog.

"You know, Erik," Mom begins, "I worry about you. I look at you and I think, you don't know how cruel and difficult the world can be. I don't think you should be spending so much time with him. It's not... it's not right."

It's uncomfortable listening to my mom talk like this, because I know she's right. Everything she believes in, I believe in. And it frustrates me because it feels so unfair. I want to be mad that she's saying this, but what is there to be mad at? She doesn't make the rules, she just wants me to follow them. And as frustrating as it can be, I know that it all comes from a place of love. You see, I was her miracle baby. Before me, she suffered two miscarriages and nearly gave up hope on ever having a family. But then, after a whole lot of prayer — and my mother's the type of woman who prays the Rosary every single night — God blessed her with a child. I know that my mom wants what's best for me. It just saddens me that I'm not turning out to be like the kind of child that she wanted: normal.

"You don't have to worry about that, Mom," I mumble. "There's nothing going on. Like I said, he's just a friend." Mom smiles, warily.

"I left some food for you in the microwave," she says. "Don't forget to wash your dishes when you're done. Oh, and can you please stop leaving your clothes in the dryer? I'm tired of putting them away for you." She disappears around the corner. Suddenly, I'm not feeling so hungry anymore.

Palm tree.
Island.
Ocean.
Drowning.

Lather. Rinse. Repeat. I've been suffering through this same dream over, and over, and over again, I've lost count of how many times it's been. Some nights are better than others. On good nights, I'm able to sleep until morning. On the bad nights, however, I wake up at an ungodly hour, feeling as if I've just been suffocated. The bad nights are the nights when the dream feels real, and there's this looming sense of dread throughout the whole thing, because I know I'm going to make the same mistake again. I'm gonna get in that stupid rowboat, and I'm gonna ride right into that stupid storm, and I'm gonna stupidly drown, like the stupid idiot that I am. It's stupid. It's just stupid.

"Erik," I hear a distant voice echoing through the watery abyss. "Erik, wake up."

"God?" I somehow manage to say while floating underwater.

"No, it's Dad." I open my eyes to find myself lying in my bed. Damn it! I died in the dream again! At least, that's what I assume happens, because I've never managed to get to the end of it. I always wake up in the same place. Ugh… whatever. At least this time wasn't a bad time, since I was able to sleep through the night. Still, it felt just as bad as a bad time. Oh, who am I kidding? They're all bad times. This dream sucks!

"What time is it?" I ask, sitting up. I'm feeling so incredibly groggy, I'm struggling just to keep my eyes open.

"It's a little past ten," my dad says, sitting next to me on my bed. "Get up, you've got visitors." Visitors? Who would come to visit before noon on a Saturday? I'm a little confused and, for a second, I almost get mad that some rando would have the audacity to just show up and wake me on a weekend. Then I remember…

The city! Immediately, I jump out from under the covers, nearly knocking my dad off my bed in the process. I run over to my closet and rustle through all my hideous clothing to find something halfway decent. It's funny how clothes that you thought were cute enough to buy become hideous when you've got somewhere to go with a good looking guy you're trying to impress.

"I've literally got nothing to wear," I complain as I toss nearly half of my entire wardrobe to the ground.

"It's not literal. You've got all of that," Dad chimes in, but I don't care enough to pay him any mind. "Anyway, I'll let them know you'll be down in a minute." Dad gets up and exits. Once he shuts the door behind him, I spring into action. I slip into a fresh pair of boxers and put on some khakis, which I pair with a burgundy polo and a gray hoodie. I race over to the bathroom and apply some deodorant before going to work on my hair.

It's being so fussy. I blow dry it, rub sculpting product into it, I even coat it in hairspray, but nothing will tame this terrible cowlick that's poking up from the back of my head. Normally, I don't pay it any mind and just let it do what it does, but today is different. Today, I'm going to the city with Nicholas. We're going to be in an awe-inspiring setting, and I want to look as awe-inspiring as my pudgy little self will allow. Otherwise, any selfies we take are just gonna look horrendous and I can't have that. I mean, what if he posts it on his Instagram page? He's got a couple thousand followers from all the jailbait, thirst trap, shirtless photos he's got on there. I can't be the one thing that ruins his feed with my hair looking like a place where Betsy grazes. And yes, Betsy is an imaginary cow that I just came up with, because isn't there always at least one cow in the herd named Betsy?

Ugh… the freaking cowlick won't go down! Whatever… It'll have to do. I'll just pretend like it was intentional and none will be the wiser.

"Hey, there he is!" Nicholas proclaims as I come down the stairs. He's dressed in a pair of slim fitted khakis, his red V-neck — the one he was wearing the day we met — and a gray cardigan, which he's left unbuttoned, thus framing his perfect torso. Holy crap… we're matching.

"Oh, my gulay, you guys look like a stock photo couple," Mackenzie says sarcastically as she takes a picture of us with her phone.

"Gulay?" Nicholas asks.

"It means 'vegetable,'" I answer.

"We're in a Half-Filipino household. I'm paying my respects," Mackenzie explains.

"You're culturally appropriating," I say.

"Yes, but you taught me the word, so who's really at fault?" she fires back.

"Alright then, how about we just get going?" Nicholas cuts in. Thank God he does, because otherwise Mackenzie and I would probably go back and forth all day long about it. She never lets me have the last word, even when I'm right.

Nicholas, Mackenzie, and I pile into Mackenzie's car. It's an old hatchback from, like, the seventies, which she inherited from her grandma. Mackenzie's not really a car girl, that much is clear from the clutter collecting on the floor in her backseat. But as long as it gets us from point A to point B, then whatever, right? Nicholas is sitting up front with her, and I'm feeling the slightest bit of jealousy coming on. I want to sit next to Nicholas. At this point, I'd even take sitting on his lap… Wait! What am I saying? Fruit of Eden! Fruit of Eden! God, I feel like I'm going crazy.

"You good back there?" Nicholas asks.

"Yeah," I say, though I'm not even convincing myself. Nicholas leans his chair all the way back, so that his bottom half is up front with Mackenzie, while his top half is right next to me.

"There, now I can sit next to both of you." He smiles. There's something so infectious about Nicholas' aggressively upbeat attitude. Save for the times when he's angry, he's always radiating with positivity, and I love that about him. There's this child-like innocence in the way that he interacts with the world that, if he wasn't so hot and manly, I'd think he was really naive. Or maybe I'm the naive one, and I just haven't figured out how to be happy. That's a thinker…

We pull into the parking lot of the BART station. When I was younger, I had no idea that BART was an acronym for Bay Area Rapid Transit. It didn't occur to me. I just thought that whoever came up with the idea must really like the name Bartholomew, or that that was his name or something. Anyway, Nicholas, Mackenzie, and I climb out of the car and make our way through the massive lot to get to the station. Once there, we fall in line to purchase tickets from the kiosk machine. It takes a little bit of math-ing to figure out just how much it'll cost for a round trip ticket. I do the math twice in my head just to be safe. I always get a little paranoid when it comes to these things.

We ride the escalators down to the platform and figure that we have a good fifteen minutes before the next train arrives. Nicholas pulls out his phone and proceeds to take a selfie with Mackenzie and I standing in the background.

"Erik, come over here," he says excitedly. "Mackenzie, would you take our picture? I wanna get a pic of how extra we are, matching and all that."

"Ugh… you are so basic," Mackenzie rolls her eyes. Nicholas sticks his tongue out at her, winking playfully as he hands her his phone, then comes over and throws his arm around me. Mackenzie takes the picture and looks over it. "Actually, it's really cute. Here." She hands back Nicholas' phone, which suddenly chimes. Nicholas glances at it before immediately shoving it into his back pocket. His brow furrows.

"Something wrong?" I ask. He shakes his head.

"Nah, just my girlfriend texting me," he says. He's so nonchalant about it, I almost don't catch it. Wait… Girlfriend? Girlfriend?! When would he have had time to get a girlfriend? And while he's been flirting with me, no less!

"You have a girlfriend?"

"Ex-girlfriend. Yeah, she's been texting me all this stuff that I don't really want to see."

"Like what?"

"You know, stuff: topless pics, 'I miss yous,' stuff like that."

"Do you think she's trying to get back together with you?" I ask, genuinely curious. This is awful. The green-eyed monster of jealousy is growing inside of me, which is really dumb, because I have no claim here. I know that. Not sure if my heart knows that though…

"Does it matter? She's like three hundred miles away. She's basically taunting me," he explains.

"So, why'd you guys break up? Was it the move?" I continue to pry.

"Not exactly."

"You couldn't get it up, could you?" Mackenzie quips with her signature brand of sarcasm.

"Uhh…" Nicholas begins to say. Mackenzie starts to giggle, realizing she might've stumbled onto something potentially embarrassing. "You know, guys, this probably isn't the best time to talk about this." Oh, my god, he's blushing. It must be true! He must not have been able to get it up. Nicholas goes silent. He takes a seat on a nearby bench, glaring at Mackenzie as she giggles through her amusement.

"Oh, come on, Nick, lighten up," Mackenzie says once her giggling fit passes. "It's not like it's a big deal. Literally." I personally don't find any of it funny. I feel bad for Nicholas. He's looking at Mackenzie through narrowed eyes. "Look, I'm sorry. Can we just go back to having a fun time now?" Mackenzie finally says. "Do you need a hug? Because I will personally find someone to give you one." Nicholas chuckles and it's the cutest thing. "Go on, Erik, give him a hug."

"Me?!" I exclaim.

"What? Now you don't wanna hug me?" Nicholas asks. I can tell by his tone that he's joking, but it's no less uncomfortable being put on the spot like this. "Because I can't get it up for you?" I really don't know how to even begin to respond to this. Thankfully, our train arrives, and I'm let off the hook.

We board the train and make our way toward the end of the compartment. Mackenzie takes the seat against the wall, putting her feet up on the chair next to hers so that neither Nicholas or I — or anyone else for that matter — can sit next to her. Nicholas takes the window seat across from Mackenzie and I sit down next to him. The train begins to move and we're off. It's about an hour on BART to the city for us, so there's a good chunk of time to kill. Mackenzie takes ironic ugly faced selfies, while Nicholas stares out the window, watching the scenery go by.

"Wow, this is really cool," Nicholas mutters to himself, sounding a bit awestruck.

"You don't have a train system in LA?" I ask.

"We have the Metro, but there's really no point in taking it if you've got a car. Plus, you guys got trees."

"You don't have trees in LA?" Mackenzie asks sarcastically.

"We don't even know what trees are," Nicholas jokes. I hear a chime go off. It sounds like Nicholas has got another message.

"You aren't gonna check that?" I ask him.

"Why bother?" he shrugs. "I'm with you." My heart flutters and suddenly my stomach is infested with butterflies.

"Your ex is probably a dumb slut, if you guys ended it over… that," Mackenzie interjects. "No offense."

"Actually, yeah. I didn't realize it until after we ended it, but she's kind of a basic bitch," Nicholas explains. "Just check out her Instagram page."

"Yes, please!" Mackenzie says. I don't exactly feel right scrolling through a girl's social media page to laugh at her expense, but I can't help but giggle when I see that every single one of her pictures is a selfie of her making a hideous duck face. And none of them are ever ironic, not in the way that Mackenzie does it. I'll admit, Nicholas' ex-girlfriend is pretty, but judging by her pictures, she's got no personality whatsoever. She's like a product of basic girl culture, virtually manufactured. I will say though, her cleavage does seem to defy all laws of gravity, which would explain why Nicholas was into her. But if he was so into her, why couldn't he get it up? Hmm… Curious. Curious indeed.

Our train pulls into the Embarcadero station. We ride the escalators up from the platform and find our way to the stairway leading up to the city street. I've always found emerging from the BART station and seeing the buildings towering over you for the first time pretty breathtaking. The sight of the skyscrapers from the ground makes the world feel big and you feel small, as if there's so much out here to find and explore. Despite living relatively close, I don't visit the city very often, so the magic of it was never lost to me. It feels like a whole different world compared to Bay Area suburbia.

"Wow," Nicholas murmurs, whilst taking a near endless amount of pictures on his phone. "That's freaking beautiful."

"You guys don't have buildings in LA?" Mackenzie teases.

"Shut up," Nicholas laughs.

We walk a few blocks until the buildings give way to a large plaza just across the street from the famed Ferry Building. There are pop up stalls and vendors open all around, a sort of souvenir and knickknack market. Nicholas continues to take pictures until one of the vendors scolds him yelling, "No picture! No picture!"

Nicholas apologizes as he, Mackenzie, and I run away laughing. We continue through the plaza and cross the busy street toward the Ferry Building. The place is bustling with locals and tourists alike. To be honest, it's a little claustrophobic. I wasn't expecting it to be so busy today.

"Let's get a selfie," Nicholas suggests. Mackenzie and I huddle up next to him on either side. Nicholas, I notice, throws his free arm around me and extends his other arm out with his phone to take the picture. The three of us separate, and he and Mackenzie look over the shot.

"Tag me in that when you post it," Mackenzie demands. I don't care to look. I'm too hung up on the fact that Nicholas put his arm around me, when he could've easily taken the selfie with his other hand and put his arm around Mackenzie. God, I'm thinking too much about this. He probably took the selfie in the hand that he did because that's his dominant hand. Him putting his arm around me means nothing… right?

Ugh! Get it together, Erik! Get it together!

"So, what should we do?" Nicholas asks.

"I'm thinking we hit Fisherman's Wharf," Mackenzie answers. "We could hang at Pier 39. It's a total tourist trap, but great for selfies. Oh, and we gotta stop for some crepes."

"She has a thing for them," I add, trying to rejoin the conversation.

"I do. They're like my weakness."

"They're just extra thin pancakes," Nicholas says. Mackenzie's expression goes from that of a fair maiden to a wicked queen faster than you can say the word "crepe."

"You shut that fat hole in your face," Mackenzie threatens and then turns dramatically, hitting Nicholas with her hair, before walking off ahead. Nicholas just chuckles. I swear these two live to get each other's goats.

We walk the thirty or so minutes from the Ferry Building to Fisherman's Wharf. Nicholas and Mackenzie bicker for a while about why crepes are or aren't overrated. Their conversation is shallow, but somehow, it seems almost… flirty. I'm starting to get upset, because I can feel the jealousy rising in me. He's not mine. I have no claim. He's not mine, I have to remind myself. It's a fairly long and tiring walk that seems to last forever. I'm starting to feel warm and winded despite the frigid autumn air. We could've taken the MUNI streetcar, but Nicholas and Mackenzie insisted walking was better for photo ops, and I didn't want to pay the extra couple dollars for the fare, which at this point I'm kinda starting to regret. God, I'm out of shape.

I can tell we're getting close when the streets start to get more and more lively. I can see familiar attractions over the growing crowd — the aquarium, the shops, the restaurants. Welcome to Pier 39! There are tourists pouring in and out of the shopping center. It's way overcrowded, which is annoying, but that's what we get for coming here on a weekend. Though it's not like we could come any other time during the week.

"Oh, wow," Nicholas says, sniffing the air as we pass the outdoor section of one of the many overpriced and overcrowded restaurants. "Sensory overload! Good Lord, I'm so hungry. It smells so good."

"God, you're like a dog," Mackenzie quips snidely.

"Woof," Nicholas replies.

Oh, my God…

Oh, my God… is… is this really happening? Seriously?

Are they… are they *actually* flirting?

I can feel the side eyes and eye rolls coming on in my annoyance. I thought he was over her. I thought she had no interest in him. What gives?! Cool it, Erik. Just chill. I have to talk myself down in my mind. This is nothing. Nicholas flirts. He flirts. But, God, he really does flirt with everyone, doesn't he? I want him to just flirt with me. Why isn't he flirting with me today? Is it because we're accidentally matching? Did our synchronized outfit choices freak him out? Was he just putting on a happy face when he got excited about it? I'm thinking too much about this. "Just enjoy the day," I tell myself. This is supposed to be fun. Have fun, damn it!

We pass the famous carousel and stop to "watch" a children's magic show being performed on this tiny, tiny stage in the middle of the shopping center. And I say "watch" with quotations because we're not really watching it. No, I'm watching Mackenzie take selfies while Nicholas photobombs her, practically cuddling her from behind. I'm starting to get upset, because it occurs to me now that I am on a date. I'm on *their* date, and I'm the third wheel.

This is so messed up.

Click.

Click.

Click.

The shutter sound repeats itself as they take selfie, after selfie, after selfie. I may as well not even be here. I'm trying my best to fight the urge to walk away, but I'm getting so unreasonably upset. I mean, it's not like I have any claim on Nicholas. He's not even gay. I keep telling myself to relax. Just relax, Erik. Relax. But I can't help myself. It's too much. It's really too much… so I get up and I walk off.

They probably won't even notice I'm gone.

Sea lions have it so easy. I mean, besides always being eaten by sharks or whatever. They just lie about and lounge all day, without a care in the world. They lie on their rafts, all piled on top of each other, and they just seem so satisfied with themselves. Meanwhile, I'm standing here alone on the viewing deck that overlooks the spot where all these sea lions gather, without anyone — specifically Nicholas — piling on top of me.

I'm staring out at the sea lion colony forlornly when, in the far corner, I notice one sea lion lying about, all alone. He seems so sad and lonely. If I didn't imagine him to be so slimy, I'd totally hug him. Poor sea lion. You're just like me. I pull out my phone, thinking to take a picture, and stop when I see I've got a text from Nicholas.

"Where'd you go?" it says. I don't respond. Instead, I close the message, open up the camera app and take a picture of Sea Lion Erik. Poor Sea Lion Erik.

"There you are!" I hear Nicholas' voice. I don't turn. No, I have to punish him. He made me feel invisible, so now it's his turn to be invisible. "Hey, do you have any idea what all these locks are for? They're all over the fencing." I look down and notice a whole slew of padlocks — all in various shapes, sizes, and colors — hanging from the chain link of the pier fence. Huh, I actually have no idea what they're for. Frankly, I didn't even notice them. It doesn't matter though, I'm not speaking to him, regardless of whatever random thing he might say or ask me. "Why'd you leave?" he questions, when I don't acknowledge him. I'm not responding. Nope, I refuse.

"Erik?"

Not doing it.

"Erik."

I am a fortress.

"You know, Erik, if you're gonna play this game with me, you're gonna lose," he whispers close to my ear. I give him the most irritated side eye I can muster, but I don't say a word. "Alright. Don't say I didn't warn you." He's not gonna do anything, I'm sure of it. Honestly, what can he do? We're in public. And if he *does* do something, if a tourist doesn't stop him, surely Sea Lion Erik will. Then, I feel it.

No…

I feel his fingers caress my sides.

Oh, dear God, no…

No… No! It's not fair! He's tickling me! At first, I fidget, trying hard not to let my stone face crack, but it's too hard. It tickles so much. His hands come at me from every direction, and once I'm tickled once, no matter where it is, everything becomes ticklish. I start laughing uncontrollably and, eventually, get to a point where I might start hyperventilating.

"Stop!" I manage to say through the laughing and heaving. "That's not fair!" Thankfully, he stops.

"You gonna talk to me now?" Nicholas says. "You wanna tell me what's up?"

At first, I think, I don't wanna say too much lest I give myself away, but then I remind myself that he knows I like him — my stupid self admitted it last night — so what harm could it do? I guess it's just scary being honest when it comes to feelings and stuff. I really gotta suck it up. "Come on, what's wrong?"

"I don't know. I… uh… I just… I don't know," is all I can manage to say.

"Tell me," he insists, keeping his voice low and gentle. His pensive eyes pierce into me and I'm completely disarmed by them. How is it that he has such an effect on me? How do I fight him off when the maple of his eyes create a forest I get lost in, one where I can search for days for a way out, only to get lost in them all over again? How do I fight a temptation that I lose myself to with a single glance? How do I even stand a chance against him? I don't.

"Can we… take a selfie?" I ask carefully, after much consideration.

"Yeah, of course," Nicholas responds, as if the answer is obvious.

"Like you and Mackenzie?" Saying this out loud causes my stomach to ache like someone's just taken it and squeezed it as tightly as they possibly could. I'm staring up at Nicholas and I see the exact moment when it clicks for him. He flashes me that irresistible crooked smile of his, and I just about die. I'm really glad this is fun for him. Not.

"You're jealous," he says, his self-satisfied smile growing bigger and bigger with each passing moment. Dear Lord, just kill me now. I can feel my cheeks flushing. "Come here, you." Nicholas throws his arm around me and pulls me close. He whips out his phone and takes our picture. We look over it together, but I'm too distracted to focus on deciding whether the picture is good or not, because his arm is still wrapped around my shoulders. "I like it," he declares, not waiting for my approval.

Nicholas looks out at the sea lions, letting me stand here in his arm. Is he being a good friend or a bad friend? It's so hard for me to tell. I want him so bad right now, and I know he can feel it. He has to. So why does he let me linger here?

"Oh, look at those two in the corner," Nicholas points. He's pointing to Sea Lion Erik and another sea lion that's joined him. They're lounging together with the new sea lion piled on top of Sea Lion Erik. He's found a mate! I wonder if this is the universe sending me some sort of sign.

Nah! It couldn't be, could it?

After the sea lions, Nicholas and I met up with Mackenzie outside the crepe shop. We had crepes of varying flavors for lunch — Nicholas had two to himself, despite his earlier criticisms of crepes. "Shut up, I like food!" He said, when we questioned him about it. Then, we wandered around the pier until it started to feel repetitive. We ended up leaving the pier in the mid afternoon and found ourselves wandering through Chinatown, where we did the whole tourist thing, taking pictures and entering shops where we had no intention of buying anything. We'd just go in to gawk at the jade and porcelain knickknacks and whatever cheaply made items those gift shops had on display, like decorative folding fans and paper parasols. There were even a couple of places that sold cheap Samurai swords, which — come to think of it — I'm not sure have any relation to China whatsoever, and would be totally suspicious to just be carrying around if you actually bought one.

Throughout the rest of the day, Mackenzie and Nicholas kept on with that annoying heterosexual flirting thing they were doing. Every time I caught them in a moment, I had to roll my eyes, it was so obnoxious. Honestly, people always talk about the gays pushing same sex affection in their faces, but I have yet to have that happen to me. Anyway, to Nicholas' credit, when he *did* notice that I wasn't involving myself in their good time, he'd go out of his way to include me, whether it was by asking me how I was, or by pulling me into one of their many, many selfies. Nicholas and Mackenzie took so many pictures that, between the two of them, they had enough to fill up a whole photo album that you'd find in the uppity home furnishings section of a department store. I'm surprised neither of their phones ever ran out of storage space.

We ended up leaving the city a little after sundown. It took a while for us to figure out where the nearest BART station was and how to get there from where we were. Then the actual ride home took another hour, so we didn't arrive back in town until it was nearly 9:00pm. Mackenzie decided to take Nicholas home first, since he lives closest to the station. Apparently, she only picked me up second this morning because I slept in and wasn't answering her calls.

Mackenzie parks at the curb when we pull up to Nicholas' place. She and Nicholas exchange an awkward goodnight hug over the center console before Nicholas climbs out of the car.

"Alright, Erik, get in front," Mackenzie demands. "I'm not playing your chauffeur." I open the door and climb out of the backseat. Nicholas is standing on the curb and I'm a bit surprised. I expected him to be walking towards his house, but here he is just staring at me, expectantly. I look at him, feeling awkward, not sure what he wants.

"Can't a guy get a goodnight hug?" he smiles. Oh, right, duh! He holds out his arms and I fit myself against him, standing snuggly in his embrace. It's funny. He's actually the perfect height for me to rest my head against the crook of his neck. I can smell him. He smells the way he did when he first held me: like an ocean breeze masking the scent of home. It makes me think of the pier, and Sea Lion Erik, and the city, somewhere to go to when life at home gets too monotonous. I want to stay in his arms forever, and I almost think I will, because he doesn't let go. He lets me stay there for as long as I want. For a moment, it feels like we're alone, just the two of us and nothing else matters at all. That's when Mackenzie interrupts.

"Hey, you two, get a room!" she yells out of her passenger window.

"I would, but Erik won't let me," Nicholas answers. I don't really think anything of it. I'm just sad that the hug has to end, though I still feel the lingering tingle of it on my body. A never-ending hug. "I'll see you later," Nicholas smirks at me. "Drive safe," he yells to Mackenzie, and then heads up towards his now open garage bedroom. I climb in the front seat and notice Mackenzie staring at me with wide and excited eyes.

"What was that?" she asks.

"What?" I say.

"That," she nods towards Nicholas, who we can see in his garage room from the car. He hasn't shut the door. "'I would, but Erik won't let me?'"

"That? That was nothing." I'm nearly one hundred percent sure it was nothing. Nicholas is just like that, suggestive and flirtatious. It means nothing, despite my wishing otherwise. "He's been making comments like that for forever."

"What?!"

"Yeah, he's a big flirt. Didn't you notice?"

"Well, yeah, but straight guys don't say shit like that to gay dudes."

"Apparently, they do."

"Not when they know that the gay dude has a crush on them."

"How do you know that he knows I have a crush on him?"

"He told me this morning when I picked him up," she explains. This takes me by surprise. It's not so much that Nicholas talks to Mackenzie about this stuff that surprises me, but rather it's that he talks about me.

"He talks to you about me?" I can't help but ask, my curiosity now piqued.

"Just today. He said that he doesn't know how to deal with you liking him, since he can't give you what you want."

"So he wasn't flirting with me…"

"Oh, he was totally flirting with you."

"Stop saying that! He was not flirting with me. And if he was, it obviously doesn't mean anything, because he doesn't flirt with me the way he flirts with you."

"Of course he flirts with me, Erik. He's in denial."

"Well, you don't have to flirt back," I say, practically yelling at her. I didn't intend for it to come out so aggressive, but this whole conversation has me on edge.

"What are you talking about? I wasn't flirting with him," Mackenzie defends, matching both my tone and volume.

"You were so flirting with him!"

"Well, why aren't *you* flirting with him?!" Mackenzie just about screams. I immediately fall silent. We both pause for a moment to take a breath, then she continues. "I'm sorry that it came off as if I was flirting. I was just going with the flow and trying to keep up the vibe. But you know, Erik, you sit there feeling sorry for yourself because you're not getting what you want, but you don't speak up or say anything. You just expect people to read your mind and when they don't, you run away, get mad, or act like a bitch. And I get that this is a religious thing for you, but don't sit here and be mad at me because that boy wants to pretend to be straight. It's not my fault that you don't have a pussy." Mackenzie's words hit me pretty hard. She's right. She's right about everything.

In my mind, there are only two outcomes: one is that I end up alone, but obedient. The other is that I find a nice boy, like Nicholas, to love and to love me, so that my disobedience doesn't feel like it was for nothing. Right now, I'm stuck in between the two, and I have no idea what I'm doing. I'm just sad and unhappy. I can feel the tears welling in my eyes, and I'm powerless to stop them. As close as we are, I don't think I've ever cried in front of Mackenzie. I turn away from her to try and hide my tears, but I can't cover up my sobs. I feel her rub a hand on my shoulder comfortingly.

"I'm sorry, Erik. I didn't mean to make you cry over it."

"It's not that. It's just… I like him so much," I say, watching Nicholas from inside the car. He still hasn't closed the garage door.

"You know, Erik, I don't think you do," Mackenzie mutters. "I think it might be more than that." Maybe it is. I don't know. I don't know anything anymore. Suddenly, I see Nicholas walking down the driveway towards us and I start to panic. I'm rubbing my eyes dry when I hear him knocking on the window.

Mackenzie's car is so old her windows have to be cranked, so she leans over me and starts cranking.

"Everything alright?" Nicholas asks.

"Uh… yeah. Erik's just having… allergies," Mackenzie says quickly. I nod frantically in agreement. Thank God for her. She's a good friend, you know, when she's not being a complete bitch.

"It's probably all the dust from this old ass car," Nicholas replies snidely and with an amused smirk.

"Oh, ha… ha…" Mackenzie fake laughs. "Go back to your garage." Nicholas laughs and does just that. Mackenzie quickly cranks up my window and starts the ignition. "We should probably go somewhere else to talk this through before your boyfriend comes back and starts asking questions."

"He's not my boyfriend," I say sadly, as Mackenzie maneuvers the car to pull a K-turn.

"Well, we can hope, can't we?" she says, waving to Nicholas as she drives us out of his neighborhood. That we can, Mackenzie. That we can.

nicholas

Friday, November 1st.

I am not looking forward to this weekend. Ma and I are leaving for SoCal after school today. We'll be spending the whole weekend there. My dad's been calling and, while I've done my best to avoid him, I finally caved. We got to talking and he kept insisting that I come visit for my birthday, so I begrudgingly agreed to get him off my back. There are so many other things that I'd rather be doing on my birthday, but maybe it won't be so bad. When I talked to him earlier in the week, once we got past the initial awkwardness of it all, everything felt pretty normal. It was as if I didn't just ditch him and run away with Ma. But I know it'll be different actually being there with him.

Truth be told, my relationship with my dad has always been pretty... I dunno, uneasy? I never felt we connected the way me and Ma do. Maybe it was because he was always working. Maybe it was his traditional outlook on things. For example, he hated the way I started dressing and doing my hair after I got together with Brenda. He said I was letting her take too much control. In his view, I, as the man, should be calling the shots. I shouldn't be wearing form fitting jeans or blow drying my hair because it made me look prissy. He thought that I was losing myself. And maybe he was right. But I didn't care. I was too into Brenda to let him have any say.

My dad is just an old school type of guy. I remember, growing up, he'd always scold me or make fun of me if I cried, or did anything that he didn't consider manly. I guess it's no mystery why I sided with my mom when they split.

"I'm sure it'll be fine," Erik says, while we wait in the parking lot.

"Yeah, and if it's not, just be a total brat and bitch until he gets you a cool birthday present," Mackenzie adds. We're sitting on the curb, mindlessly eating some candy left over from Halloween. Erik and Mackenzie didn't really want to do the whole trick-or-treating thing, despite them both loving Halloween and having costumes already planned out. They kept saying that we were too old for it, but I managed to guilt them into going since it's my birthday this week. They agreed to go on the condition that I join them in their two person horror movie viewing party at Mackenzie's. It was not my favorite thing. I hate horror films. I get so jumpy. Thankfully, the two of them let me sit in between them during the movie, which was just awful. The movie they picked was about this family that was being haunted by the ghost of an old man that died in their house or something. It was okay at first, but then shit hit the fan and scary stuff started popping up left and right, like a smiling man in a top hat, and a demon dressed as a nun. Ugh, I don't even want to think about it. I've got other scary things to worry about, like how I'm gonna get through this weekend with my dad without being completely miserable.

I see Ma pull into the parking lot and I sigh. Time to go. Mackenzie gives me a quick hug and a kiss on the cheek.

"You got this," she says. "And if it's horrible, bitch for the gift. You desperately need a TV in your garage."

"Oh, that would be perfect for horror movies," Erik chimes in. I smile, but it's more of a grimace 'cause I'm biting my back teeth. No way in hell am I gonna get a TV to watch horror movies in my garage. Fuck. That. Shit. Big nope.

"Will do," I chuckle just to humor them. I turn to Erik to say goodbye and notice he's avoiding eye contact. I go in for a hug, which he returns.

"I'll miss you," he whispers. It makes me giddy that I have such an effect on him. God, I'm a terrible person, but I really do like the attention. It feels like he needs me, and I guess I'm just so narcissistic that I get off on that. I hold him a little tighter. I can tell he doesn't wanna let go, and honestly, I'm dreading making this trip so much that I don't want him to let go. The longer he holds on, the longer I can put off getting in the car and having to leave.

"Nicky, let's go!" I hear Ma yell from the car, which she's parked right in front of us. Erik's hold loosens, and he lets go. No more putting off the trip now.

Ma and I drive from the Bay to LA, stopping only to fill up on gas and pick up some chips and energy drinks, road trip style. We're not in a rush at all. I take in the California scenery as we travel down Highway 5. There's not much to see. Most of it is just an expanse of flat land stretching out into the horizon. The one good side to there being very little along the route is that it gives us a pretty gorgeous view of the sunset come dusk. Mom drives most of the way there, but we switch off just before reaching the Grapevine.

We booked a room at a hotel in the Valley, not far from the freeway. Mom sprang for one of the "fancy" hotels, claiming that Dad owed it to us. Since tomorrow is my birthday and all, she said we shouldn't settle for the sake of frugality. Now, when I say fancy, I just mean that the place has a pool and offers a complimentary breakfast. It's not a luxury resort or anything, but the place is pretty nice nonetheless.

"Oh, wow. So fancy!" Ma exclaims, excitedly, when we enter our room for the first time. I'm surprised she's in such a good mood. She's sprawling out on one of the beds like she's on vacation, while I'm here dreading having to see my dad in the morning. I know I shouldn't be worried about it because my parents' divorce is between them. At least, it *should* be. But I just feel like there were clearly defined sides, and I sided with my mom. Plus, I'm still kinda ticked off about the whole reason they split up to begin with. It was *his* fault, as far as I'm concerned. Mom wouldn't lie to me about that, right? Tomorrow, it's likely I'll have to listen to my dad's side of the story, and I don't know that I want to. I like the direction that life has been going now that I've started settling into it. I don't want anything to change that. I don't want to feel any sympathy for him, because I don't want to miss him. "You okay, mijo?" Ma asks.

"Yeah, I'd just rather be home right now," I reply, plopping down on the free bed.

"I know. It's not the way I would've wanted you to spend your birthday, but your father insisted. We'll do something more fun for your birthday next week."

"It's not even that, Ma. It's just… I don't know if I want to be here. I mean, he's been having an affair, you said it yourself. Is there really any more to the story than that? Do I need to hear any of it?"

"You won't hear any of it. I made him promise not to talk about the divorce. Tomorrow's your day, he knows that," Ma explains sympathetically. "Why don't you take the car? That way, if he does bring it up, you can just leave."

"Wait, what about you?" I ask.

"Nicky, I booked a hotel with a jacuzzi. I don't need to go anywhere. As far as I'm concerned, I'm on vacation." That's great, Ma, I think to myself. I'm glad one of us will be enjoying this weekend.

Later, Ma offers to take me out for a late dinner at a nearby diner, but I decline. It's been a long drive over and I'm not really in the mood for celebrating, which I know is surprising because food. She then hands me her credit card and gives me permission to order something in before crawling into bed. I flip through the limited channels on the TV, cycling through a series of infomercials where the people don't know how to pour a glass of milk without knocking it over, and the narrator asks, "Are you tired of being inept?" The narrator doesn't really ask that, but he may as well. Once I'm bored of watching people struggle to exist, I find that there's nothing else worth watching — of course there isn't — and I collapse into my bed, scrolling through my Instagram feed.

Saturday. November 2nd.

As I'm mindlessly double tapping and liking funny animal videos, and pictures of beautiful Instagram models, I get a text message. It's from Erik.

"Midnight!!! Happy Birthday! Your almost an adult," it says. Another text immediately follows, which reads: "You're***" I chuckle, then look over at the clock on the nightstand. Wow, he waited up for it. It *is* actually midnight. I start to type out a generic thank you message, but I stop. Thinking about Erik makes me want to go home to my uncle's house, and to just not have to deal with whatever's coming in the morning. If only he were here...

"I miss you," I type and hit send. I see the little ellipsis bubble pop up in his text box, indicating he's typing his response. Then, the bubble disappears. A moment later, it reappears, only to disappear again. I wonder what he's writing that he's hesitating to send? I mean, at this point, he knows that I know he likes me. He told me himself.

"I should go to bed. Goodnight," his response finally comes in. There's something about his message that feels a little standoffish and, if I'm being honest, it kinda hurts. I shouldn't get upset though. I know that I'm just feeling needy right now, given the situation, but I sorta expected more from him than just that. I wait up for a few minutes, thinking that he might send a follow up text or something, but nope. I guess I'm on my own.

Ma and I have breakfast in the hotel restaurant. It's complimentary, so I was expecting crap, but it's actually pretty decent: eggs, sausage, pancakes. All the breakfast mainstays. Now that I'm well rested and in a better state of mind, my appetite's returned to normal. I think the trip took it out of me yesterday, because I'm feeling pretty good at the moment. I spend the rest of the morning telling myself to look at this weekend in a positive light, reminding myself that I'll be going home to the place I grew up in, so it can't be that terrible, can it? And, if it is, the beach is only like a half-hour drive away, which is great because it's still warm out, despite it being November. You gotta love SoCal weather.

It's a little strange being back here. I know it's only been a month or so since we left, but it doesn't feel like home anymore. I drive through the familiar suburban streets and neighborhoods, taking in the sights. Everything looks the same, but I'm far less at ease here than I was before the split. The hotel isn't far from my house — or rather, Dad's house now — but I'm somehow managing to catch all red lights, so it's taking longer than it should to get there. The tiniest part of me feels like all these red lights are a sign.

When I pull up to my dad's house, I park the car at the curb and take a deep breath. Suddenly, my phone chimes. I've got a text message. It's from Brenda.

"Happy Birthday!" it says, punctuated with a heart emoji. Huh, she remembered. I'm a bit surprised, if I'm being honest. I mean, yeah, we've been in touch, but I just assumed she'd forget that detail since we're not together anymore. I don't give her enough credit, I guess.

"Thanks," I text back, then let myself out of the car. My dad's house looks exactly the same as it did when it was mine. Nothing's changed. Nothing on the outside anyway. I walk up the paved pathway and to the front door. I've still got my old house keys, but I'm not totally sure how appropriate it would be to just let myself in. I'm thinking too hard about this. I sigh, hit the doorbell, and unlock the door, letting myself in.

"Hello?" I call out. "Anybody home? Dad?" I hear footsteps approaching, followed by my dad's voice.

"Yes, I know. I won't!" he says, coming around the corner into the entryway. He's on his cellphone, and dressed in a plain tee and pajama bottoms, though he's clearly showered since his hair's all gelled back. "Rosa, he's here. I gotta go." He hangs up, shoves his phone into his pocket, and stretches his arms out for an embrace. I go ahead and give him a quick hug. "How you been, mijo?"

"Fine. Were you just on the phone with Ma?" I ask.

"Yeah, she wanted to check in on you. Make sure everything was okay." I nod and take a quick look around. Everything seems to be as it was. It almost looks like we never left, like he was waiting for us to come back. The idea makes me feel a bit sad and… conflicted. It's strange, because isn't this what I wanted: my parents to patch things up and for us to be a family again? "Anyway, how are things? Your mom tells me you've been making a lot of friends."

"A couple, yeah." Having a normal conversation with my dad shouldn't be so awkward and uncomfortable, but it is. I don't have much to say to him that doesn't have to do with the divorce, which again, I'm not even sure I want to talk about. He nods. I nod. It seems that neither of us really know what to say.

"I see you're still doing that with your hair," he offers. I roll my eyes and scoff. I know where this is going.

"Yeah, it gets me a lot of attention," I say, trying not to take it so seriously.

"From girls, right?" he asks. I narrow my eyes. Really, Dad? Really? It's both insulting and comical that he'd make a gay joke over my hair when we haven't seen each other in over a month. I'm tempted to say no and tell him about Erik's crush on me, but I decide not to go there. There's such a divide between us right now that I don't want to share with him any part of my new life, no matter how inconsequential it would be to.

"Yeah, all the girls," I answer simply and unenthused.

"Hey, are you hungry at all? I was thinking we could go for lunch and catch up?" He says, after a moment, thankfully changing the subject.

"I could eat."

"Great, let me just change and grab my wallet, then we can head out." He walks down the hall and disappears into his and Ma's old bedroom. After a minute, I decide to wander and take a tour of the place to see how much — if anything at all — has changed. There's something in my gut telling me that something is different here. There has to be. I just haven't spotted it yet.

I casually meander down the hallway, looking over all of the same framed photos my parents had hung up over the years. It's all the same as I remember. Everything checks out. Then something catches my eye. There's a spot on the wall that's darker than the rest. Something's been removed, but what? I close my eyes trying to remember what picture used to hang here, but I can't, for the life of me, imagine it. Maybe it wasn't important.

I move over to the door that leads to what used to be my room and push it open. I stop. Immediately, my heart drops. I can't believe what I'm seeing. My bedroom is... gone. My furniture: my bed, my dresser, my desk, have all been moved out. I take a step inside the virtually empty room. It seems everything that wasn't taken out has been packed away in these boxes that have been stacked up in the corner. I'm standing here, in my old room, frozen in disbelief. It's gone. My bedroom's gone. How? How could he? It's only been a month!

"Alright, you ready?" I hear Dad's voice coming from down the hall, the sound of his footsteps growing louder as he approaches. "Oh, no... Nick, I can explain."

"It's gone," I say. He's standing at the threshold looking completely mortified. Obviously, I wasn't supposed to see this. Maybe this is why he wanted us to go out for lunch. Not to celebrate my birthday and catch up, but to keep me from discovering what was different in our house. I have no place here anymore.

"Nick, listen to me. I can explain."

"What did you do to my room?"

"I tried to get Veronica to hold off but—"

"Veronica? Who the fuck's Veronica?"

"Veronica is my… girlfriend. Alright? She moved in after you and your mom left," Dad explains. I'm watching him, my eyes wide with shock. This is quite possibly the most horrific story I've had to sit through, and it was only a couple days ago that I was watching a movie with smiling demon men and scary nuns. This beats that by a landslide. "Look, I tried to tell her to hold off on making any changes. At least, until after we told you."

"Told me what? That you didn't want me to have a room in your house?" I retort snidely. Dad stops and takes a breath. He's staring at me with a regrettable look, like he's about to deliver a killing blow to something he just ran over with his car. This is a mercy killing.

"You're gonna be an older brother," Dad says. The words come out quick and wooden, as if he'd rehearsed them time and time again.

. . .

"Are you fucking kidding me!?"

I'm about ready to scream my head off, when I hear the sound of the front door slamming and an unfamiliar voice echoing through the house.

"John!" the voice calls out. I assume it belongs to the woman who's replacing my mom, Veronica. "John, where are you?"

"Shit!" Dad exclaims. "Wait here, Nick." He darts out of the room, leaving me here... alone. This must be how Ma felt when she realized about the affair. I take one last look around what used to be my room and it hits me like a ton of bricks. This space isn't mine anymore. It's for him, or her, or whatever comes out of Mom's replacement. I'm realizing now that Dad didn't just leave Mom. He left me too… and he took back what he gave me so he could give it to his new kid. He traded us in for a newer model. There's no reason for me to be here anymore. I suddenly remember what picture used to hang in the hallway: my parents' wedding photo.

I take in a deep breath and hold it while I make my way to the front door. I figure, if I concentrate hard enough on holding my breath, then I'll be able to hold myself together, because I'll be too distracted to fall apart. I can hear my dad bickering with his girlfriend, Veronica. I don't get a good look at her, only a passing glance, but I can see that she looks to be closer to my age than my dad's, and I'm completely disgusted.

"You knew that my son was coming today. Couldn't you have gone somewhere else?"

"Where would I go? The credit card you gave me declined!" I hear them yelling at each other. If this didn't involve my dad, I'd be front and center with a bowl of popcorn, but it does, so I can't be bothered. I don't want to know any more about what he's been doing with himself post-separation. I've learned enough already from the little bit that I heard. I just want to leave. I just want to do what Ma did and get as far away from him as possible. I pull the front door open and let myself out.

As I'm heading down the walkway, I hear my dad coming after me.

"Nick! Nicholas!" He calls out. "Nicholas, mijo, please!" I feel him grab my arm and I forcefully yank it away.

"Don't touch me!" I yell at the top of my lungs.

"Nicholas…" Dad's staring at me with the face of someone who'd just been caught red handed. It's not his fault he committed a crime, is what his eyes are expressing to me. That's bullshit. It's complete bullshit. I do my best to hold back the tears.

"Just answer me this, Dad. Did you even want our family? Did you even want Ma? Or me? Or were we just some accident that you've been paying for for the last seventeen years?"

Dad's response is pretty telling, because he doesn't have one.

"Happy Birthday to me, right?" I say painfully, before hopping into my car and driving off.

Have you ever eaten a cheeseburger while crying? It's actually really depressing. I look like a scene from one of those romantic comedies where the dorky lead gets dumped and copes by eating, all while that classic song, "All By Myself," plays in the background. In hindsight, this would probably be hilarious, but right now it's just really sad. Luckily, I'm in my car, so no one can see me crying and binge eating without looking through the windshield and coming off like a big weirdo themselves.

I pull out my phone. There are no new messages. Nothing from Erik either, who I've gotten used to talking to on an almost daily basis. It's just as well, since I'm still kinda ticked off at him for saying goodnight to me after I texted him that I miss him. Ugh… Whatever.

As I'm scrolling through my contacts, the only people I find worth calling are Erik and Mackenzie. And since I'm sorta mad at Erik — meaning he's gonna have to text me first — I call Mackenzie. Sadly, there's no answer. It's starting to occur to me that I have no other friends. Ma was right. I am kind of a loner. I guess I never realized it before because I was always with somebody. That's just great… What do I do now?

I open up my text messages, thinking to fuck being petty and just message Erik, when I remember that Brenda sent me a message earlier. Brenda… I know reconnecting with her might be a bad idea, but she's here. Erik and Mackenzie are not. As sad as it may be, Brenda's the closest thing I have to a friend out here who isn't my mom. Going back to her's gotta be better than nothing, right?

I took about twenty minutes to collect myself before contacting Brenda. She seemed happy to hear from me, and even happier to know I was back in town for the weekend. I decided not to rope her into any of my personal business and just try to hang with her casually to keep myself distracted. She invited me over, saying that she'd love the company since she was stuck babysitting, so here I am. I ring the doorbell and moments later, I'm greeted by Brenda's little sister.

"Hi, Bebe, is your sister around?" I ask. Bebe stares at me with big bug-like eyes and then screams.

"BRENDA, YOUR OLD BOYFRIEND'S HERE!" She then disappears behind the door before my ex arrives to let me in.

"Hey, stranger," Brenda says, wearing a warm smile. God, she's prettier than I remember her, dressed in an oversized t-shirt and a pair of pajama shorts. Her hair's pulled back into a ponytail and she looks the way I need to feel: relaxed.

Brenda leads me to her room, as she always had when we were alone in her house together. I take a seat on her bed as she shuts the door behind us. A part of me worries that we'll be leaving her sister unattended, but as long as the kid doesn't set the house on fire, everything's good.

"I wish I knew you were coming," Brenda says. "I would've got you a gift."

"It's all good," I reply, shrugging it off.

"So, how you been?"

"Good." Brenda puts on a forced smile and nods awkwardly. I can't help but do the same. She bites on her lower lip and eyes me down. I'm not sure what she's thinking, but it's making me nervous… in a good way.

"Listen, Nick, I've been doing a lot of thinking since we broke up, and I realize that I was wrong for that. You know, the way we broke up and all. I should've been more sensitive. It's just… I wanted our first time to be special, you know? And after all that waiting, I guess I was just disappointed. I hated the idea that my first time would be a total failure." Well, this is unexpected.

"Believe me, it's harder for me than it is for you," I quip. She giggles like a little school girl and it's so infectious, I've got a big stupid grin on my face over it.

"Punny," she says.

"You always did like those."

"Anyway, I wasn't expecting you to be here today. But now that you are, I'm thinking… maybe we could try again?"

"What, like a do-over?" Holy shit, what is happening right now? Is she suggesting what I think she is? And on my birthday no less? She saunters over and climbs onto my lap, as if we had never broken up. Yup, she *is* thinking what I think she is. "Are you sure about this, Bren?" I whisper. When she's this close to me, I feel like I have to be as quiet and gentle with her as possible.

"I missed you," she nods, whispering back before kissing me. Our lips caress one another and it's not long before our tongues come out to play. We're intertwining at the mouth, and I'm suddenly really glad I came. A passion between the two of us ignites. I feel it. She obviously must be feeling it too, because in the midst of our making out, she pulls off her t-shirt, and I find myself staring at her bare breasts. She wasn't wearing a bra… was this for me or do girls just not wear bras when they're babysitting? No, it must be for me. She may not have gotten me a birthday gift, but by the way her body is moving against mine, I know she's more than willing to improvise.

Alright, Nick, you got this, I tell myself. Given what happened the last time I was in this position, I have to talk myself up. I take Brenda, throw her down onto her bed, and climb on top of her. This is happening. We're doing it today. I feel her reaching down, unbuttoning my pants. Yes. Happy birthday to me. She's touching it. Massaging it. Stroking it. I'm so ready. Except I'm not.

"Shit," I exhale. This can't be happening. Not again. Brenda's doing everything she can, but no matter how she fondles it… limp. My member might as well be made of jello, it's so useless. Why!? I guess I'm not feeling this as much as I thought, and Brenda can see that. The passion she had for me fades in her eyes and I feel terrible, as if this is my fault. Like, *actually* my fault.

I lift myself off of her and redo my pants. I feel like complete and utter shit. She gave me another shot at it, on my birthday, and I still can't stand for her. Still couldn't get it up.

"I'm sorry," I say. I'm sounding so pathetic to myself. Brenda shakes her head. She looks just as confused as I feel. I can't blame her.

"I don't know what to do for you, Nick," she explains. She grabs her shirt off the floor and slips it back on. "I thought maybe you just needed some time to get comfortable with yourself, but… you still don't want me."

"That's not true."

"Really?" Brenda lets out something between a scoff and a chuckle, then bites down on her bottom lip.

"I really don't want to be mean to you on your birthday, but this isn't going anywhere. I think you should leave." The first time she did this to me, it really pissed me off. I remember it hurting, and so I left here in a fit of rage. This time though, it's different. The hurt is different. It's deeper… and I want to cry.

"You don't just wanna hang out?" I ask, trying hard to fight back my tears. That's why I came here, to hang out. I didn't ask for this. She sprang it on me. "We don't have to do anything, we could just chill." Brenda considers this for a moment before letting out a small sigh.

"No. I'm feeling really crappy about myself, and it doesn't feel good to be around you right now."

"Okay," I manage. I feel a tear escape me. I can't hold them back anymore. I get up and hobble over to her door, but before I let myself out, I turn to her. "Why don't you want me?"

"Nick, you're the one who—" Brenda starts to say, but I cut her off.

"No, not that. I mean, in general. Why don't you want me? You never posted any pictures of us. You don't want to hang out. You made me change my clothes and my hair. You changed everything about me and yet you don't want me. Why don't you want me?" I don't wait around for her answer. Frankly, I don't know if I can handle being told exactly why I'm not enough for her, so I let myself out.

I have to stop a few times as I drive back to the hotel, I can barely see through all of my crying. I just want to go home. I don't want to be here anymore. When I get to our hotel room, Ma's sprawled out on her bed, wearing a bathrobe and eating a pizza.

"How'd it go?" she asks pleasantly. Then, she sees me and her mom switch flips. "Ay, mijo! What's wrong? What happened?" I shake my head and go to her, collapsing into her embrace. I don't typically cry all that often. Usually, the way I deal with emotions is that I either laugh it off or I get angry, sometimes irrationally so. My mom knows this about me. She knows that when I cry, it's serious, because I don't cry over just anything. "It's okay, mijo. Let it all out." And I do. I cry to the point where I can't breathe anymore, and then the breathlessness knocks me out. It's still fairly early in the day, but that doesn't matter. I'm already done.

Happy birthday to me.

Sunday. November 3rd.

The next morning, Ma and I pack up our things and head out. I just wanna go home and get as far away from this place and these people as I can. My mood's pretty crap and it must be showing, because Ma doesn't even suggest we take advantage of our complimentary breakfast, and she knows how I can get with food. We just grab our things and go. Ma offered to drive first, so I'm sitting in the passenger's seat, staring out at the rolling hills of the California Grapevine. It's pretty, but desolate, which is pretty much how I feel right now. I just keep thinking about everything that happened yesterday, from not feeling wanted, to finding out I'm gonna be an older brother. I wonder…

"Ma, did you know Dad's girlfriend is pregnant?" I ask carefully. She doesn't answer at first, so I press her again. "Ma?"

"Yes. Yes, I know, Nicky," she replies sadly. "That's why I asked for the divorce."

"Wait. You? You asked for the divorce?"

"Yup. I tried to look the other way, I did, but then I found out about the pregnancy and I couldn't do it anymore." God, I felt terrible finding out, I can't even begin to imagine how Ma must've felt when she did.

"Why didn't you tell me?" I ask.

"Because I didn't think it would be fair," she says. Fair to who, I wonder. "He's still your father, Nicky, and, as much as I hate him, I didn't want you to. At least, not because of me." Even though her eyes are focused on the road, I can see that she's struggling to keep it together, so I drop the subject. No sense in diving deeper into this rabbit hole.

After a while, Ma turns on the radio to a station playing old school R&B from the early 2000s, Ma's go-to selection. It's funny, I've always associated this kind of music with my mom, but my mind immediately goes to Erik and the time we went to the mall together, just after we first met. I remember singing along to "U Got It Bad" to him, albeit badly, and him staring at me all awkwardly. God, I miss that guy. I pull out my phone, half-expecting — or rather hoping — he would have texted me back by now, but nothing. Feeling the way that I feel right now, after everything that happened yesterday, I'd much rather he contact me first. Maybe then I won't feel so abandoned.

We get back to my Tio Roger's right around dusk. The place is a sight for sore eyes. I couldn't be happier to be back. This feels like home now. I reach down and push the button on the garage door clicker hanging from the carabiner on my belt loop. I'm relieved to see the place exactly as I left it. Everything's here. Nothing's been touched or moved — not even the half-filled glasses of water that both my mom and uncle scold me about leaving in my room. The sight of it screams to me, "Welcome home!"

Ma and I get out of the car, and I help her bring in our luggage through my room. Tio Roger's in the kitchen prepping his dinner when we enter the house.

"Hey, how was the trip?" Tio Roger asks.

"Don't ask," Ma answers.

"That bad, huh?" Tio then turns to me. "Oh, Nick. I have something for you." He sets down the knife he was using to cut up some vegetables and exits the kitchen. Ma takes her suitcase into her room and I take a seat at the table, scrolling through my phone while I wait for my uncle, who returns a few moments later with a small stack of envelopes. "Your friends came by yesterday and said these were for your birthday. There's one from me in there too."

"Thanks," I say, taking the stack from him. I head back into my garage room and plop on my futon bed so I can go through the envelopes. There's one from Mackenzie, one from Erik, and one from my uncle. I open up the one from Tio Roger first. Inside, there's a generic birthday card, the kind that you'd pick up at any grocery store. I open it to find two hundred dollar bills. He's also written a note, which reads:

Happy Birthday, Nick!

Don't tell your mother I gave you so much cash. She couldn't afford to get you anything and was too proud to use your dad's money. But it's your birthday, so you gotta live it up! You're only seventeen for 365 days. Enjoy it!

Love,
Tio Roger

Thank you, Tio Roger. I set the money and the card aside and open the envelope from Mackenzie next. It's a lot thicker and weightier than the one from my uncle. I wonder what it could be. I open it and a stack of photos, all rubber banded together, falls out. I undo the rubber band and look through them all. These are all the pictures she took of me, her, and Erik in the city. She had them all printed and cut out to look like little polaroids. How cool! I sort through them briefly and find a few that stand out:

- Erik and I on the BART Station platform, in our matching outfits — I know it was a total accident that we were dressed as twins that day, but that makes the photo all the more amusing.

- Me, stuffing my face with a flat pancake — I'll admit that crepes are tasty, but that doesn't change the fact that they're still just glorified flat pancakes.

- A selfie of Mackenzie, with me hugging her from behind.

All of the shots are great. It's like she's given me our memories printed in hardcopy. I'm nearly done looking through the stack when another photo catches my eye. It's a photo of Erik and I on the viewing deck that overlooks the sea lions. We're mostly in silhouette, two shadows painted against a blue sky, but the whole set up of it is really intriguing. Mackenzie's sure got an eye for photography. What strikes me is that I didn't even realize she was there. I wonder why she didn't come up and join us. Anyway, I set the photos aside and rip open Erik's envelope.

Erik's envelope contains a single sheet of paper with a handwritten note. His handwriting is clean and precise, it almost looks like a girl wrote it. There's also a little doodle in the corner of what I think is supposed to be a cartoon version of me and him, but Erik's drawing skills aren't nearly as good as his writing, despite him being in Art class. The note reads:

Happy Birthday, Nicholas!

I really wanted to get you something special, but I didn't have any money. So, I thought I'd give you my sentiments. I know it's not worth anything, but it's all I can afford. I've been thinking a lot about you ever since we became friends, and I've been having this really vivid dream that involves me sailing in the middle of the ocean. I actually wrote a poem about it. And it's kind of about you too. This is really embarrassing for me to share, so I know you'll love it.

Palm trees, beaches, and rolling seas
The waters will carry both you and me
Though a storm brews upon the horizon
When our boat sinks, please, don't you be frightened

I'll gather you, we won't sink below
The surface, we'll reach, so don't you let go
You will not drown with me at your side
I'll hold you until the weather subsides

You're safe with me, so trust my hand
Together we'll manage our way back to land
I'll be your lifeboat throughout the storm
And guide you to safety upon the shore
We'll make it there, so don't be scared anymore.

From Erik
P.S. Promise you won't make fun of me for this.

After opening Mackenzie's gift, I was almost one hundred percent sure nothing would beat it, but… wow. This must've been really hard for Erik to do. And to think, here I was being mad at him for responding to my "I miss you" text with a "goodnight." I chuckle in my amusement over my own pettiness. Forget waiting for him to contact me first. I feel like I should call him. This is really sweet, how could I not?

"Hey!" I say, when he answers his phone. "What's up?"

"Hi," he replies timidly. He must've expected that I'd opened his gift, because he sounds more nervous than usual. Rather than drag it out, I think it best to just put him out of his misery.

"Thank you for the poem. I love it." I hear him breathe a sigh of relief.

"Oh, good. I thought you'd make fun of me for it."

"Oh, I'm totally gonna make fun of you for it."

"That's mean," he whines. It makes me laugh. It feels good to laugh, especially after the last couple of days that I've had.

"Hey, what are you doing tonight?" I ask.

"Just homework."

"Can you get away from it?"

"Depends. Are you asking me to go out?"

"Yeah, I guess I am," I say. "My visit with my dad was a complete bust, and my uncle gave me some money, so I thought maybe you and I could go out and celebrate. What do you say?"

"Well," he begins. "My mom's been on my case all day about me going out so much lately. She's been keeping tabs."

"Oh, geez. That sucks," I reply. Damn. "You can't just sneak out? For me?" He goes silent for a moment and I get one of those nervous knots in my stomach, the kind you get when you feel like you're about to get flat out rejected.

"Alright, come get me, but park down the street." Sweet! I grab a hoodie and ask Ma for the car keys. I tell her I'm going out with Erik and she doesn't question me. She likes Erik. The few times he's come over to do homework, he's always been really polite and well mannered. Ma loves that about him. She said I need to have manners more like him, and that I should stop being so cocky, but I think that's part of my charm.

I drive over to Erik's, but park down the street a few houses down, like he asked. I text him that I'm here and a few minutes later, I see him running down the sidewalk towards my car. He's breathless when he climbs into the passenger's seat.

"You just escape from prison?" I ask jokingly.

"Shut up, I had to move fast in case they heard me leave," he manages through his heaves and sighs.

We drive over to the good mall in the neighboring city, to the seafood buffet, where we had our first dinner together. It's funny. It's only been a month since then, but I already get some nostalgia feels from being here. It's great. We eat our fill — Erik has two plates of sushi, sashimi, and fried rice and I have… a lot more than that. The check comes and I pay, using one of the two bills Tio Roger gave me. I'm feeling really great right now. I'm back home, I'm having dinner with a friend who actually wants to spend time with me, and none of it is attributed to anything or anyone that made me feel bad about myself over this whole weekend. Tonight, this dinner is on my dime. And I don't care that the money was gifted to me, it's mine, so it counts.

After dinner, Erik and I hop back into my car and head home. The mall was closing, so we couldn't exactly wander around, but right now I'm riding a high, and I don't want the night to end. Not just yet. We get back to town and, rather than take Erik back to his house, I drive us over to a local park, not far from my uncle's.

"What are we doing here?" Erik asks, his voice tinged with concern.

"Nothing," I answer. "I just want to hang out." I get out of the car and take a stroll along the paved path that leads to a jungle gym, which sits just outside the gated area of the community pool. The structure is clearly a newer build, complete with slides, monkey bars, and a swing set — not one of those old, junky ones where the seats of the swings are missing, and all that's left of them are the chains. "Ah, hell yeah! Swings!" I jog over and hop on, swinging myself back and forth like a giant kid. No shame. Erik walks up and watches from the cement that surrounds the tanbark where the jungle gym stands. "Come on, Erik! Get on!"

"That's okay," he says. I lower my legs mid swing so I can stop myself. He's being such a square. All I want is for him to join me and have some fun, you know? Make up for the shit birthday that I had on my actual birthday.

"Come on, Erik, have fun with me," I playfully beg. I pout my lips and serve him a big heaping dose of my puppy dog eyes. "Pwease? I want to make up for my terrible actual birthday yesterday." Erik considers it before approaching the swing beside me.

"What happened yesterday?" he asks, taking a seat.

"Eh, I don't really want to talk about it."

"Well, you have me at a disadvantage, because I gave you a poem that you were never supposed to read."

"Wait, you didn't want me to read it?"

"Nope. I let it slip that I'd been writing poems to Mackenzie. She said she was gonna steal my idea of getting our pictures from the city printed, so I didn't know what else to get you. Then, she said I should give you a poem. She wouldn't leave me alone until I agreed."

"The pictures were your idea too?" I say. He nods. I'm a bit surprised. If there was an award for awesome sentimental gifts, Erik would win it, hands down.

"So, are you gonna tell me or what?" he asks, and I feel almost obligated to.

"My dad had his girlfriend move in with him," I sigh. I want to get it out quickly to lessen the hurt. "She's pregnant and he gave her my room to use for the baby."

"Wow… I'm sorry."

"There's more." I'm debating whether telling him this next part is a good idea or not. I know that he likes me, and I don't want to throw anything in his face, but when I see his attentive gaze, I know I'd feel guiltier hiding it. "I met up with my ex… and I tried to hook up with her."

"Oh…" The disappointment in his face kills me, and I panic.

"Nothing happened. I had the same problem. I couldn't… I couldn't get it up."

"It's okay, you don't have to explain yourself." I know he's lying. He wants me, needs me, to explain. I can hear it in the tone of his voice. He's just trying to be strong. Sweet, little Erik is trying to be strong… for me. Now, I feel like a total douchebag.

"No, I do. I do have to explain myself. I made a bad decision, because I was feeling really lonely about my dad. And I thought that Brenda, being my only friend out there, would be able to help me out, but she made me feel just as bad as he did. And I'm so sorry that you have to hear that, but I need you. You're my best friend. I need you so much." Erik stares at me blankly, unsure of what to say. We both go silent for a while. I listen to the rustling of the swaying trees in the breeze. It makes this place feel so vast, and open, and lonely. I don't know what I would do if Erik wasn't here with me.

"You know, the day after we came back from the city, I overslept," Erik finally says. "My mom woke me up to get me to go to church, but these days, I feel like a fraud being there. I asked my mom if I could skip it, just that once. She flipped. Been watching me like a hawk ever since."

"Are you asking me to take you home?" I respond, feeling my heart start to sink.

"No. I'm just trying to level with you about parents. They all have their issues." I breathe a major sigh of relief. Thank God, he's not leaving me. Thank God, he's staying.

"Looks like we're in the same sinking boat," I say, trying to lighten up the mood.

"Funny you should say that," Erik begins. "Lately, I've been having this dream: I'm lying on the beach. It's nice and calm. I notice this boat, just sitting there. The next thing I know, I'm in the middle of the ocean, sailing right into a storm. The waves pick up and I hear this terrible crash of thunder. Suddenly, I'm underwater and I can't breathe. I'm suffocating. That's usually when I wake up. But sometimes, even when I'm awake, I feel it. It's like I'm drowning." I let his words sink in. They're striking a major chord with me, because right now, I'm feeling exactly the same. "It's actually really funny, because I can't swim."

"Wait. Seriously? I thought all Filipinos can swim. You're from an island."

"I'm half. And I didn't grow up there, racist." I laugh, then he laughs. We've come back to us through the storm. It's like we're each other's lifeboats, like in his poem.

"Well, I know what we're doing tonight," I declare. Erik narrows his eyes, nervously trying to read me. I nod my head toward the community pool. When he puts it together, his eyes widen with fear.

"No," he says outright.

"Come on, Erik, let's do something crazy."

"I wouldn't call jumping in a pool crazy."

"So then, why are you so against it?"

"Nicholas, the pool's closed."

"We'll climb the fence."

"But it's cold out."

"Come on, Erik, quit being a little bitch." I get up from the swing and begin to saunter over to the fence. I know he'll follow me. This technique is peer pressure at its finest. I actually learned it from my mom. She used to do this to me as a kid all the time. When I'd be too caught up in something and didn't want to leave somewhere, she'd tell me she was leaving and just start to leave. And, of course, I'd always follow her, in fear of getting left behind. Just like me as a kid, Erik follows.

I climb the fence first. It's your standard chain link fence, and I climb it pretty easily. Erik struggles a little bit and at one point, he starts to complain and says, "I can't do this," but by then he's already near the top, I just have to talk him down. He's about halfway to the ground when he loses his footing and I have to catch him. I give Erik a second to catch his breath, which gives me a moment to pick his phone out of his pocket.

"Hey!"

"I'm keeping it safe, Erik. Don't worry."

I take off my hoodie and fold both of our phones and my wallet into it, then set it aside on a small patch of grass for safe keeping. If I'm gonna get him into this pool to teach him how to swim, he can't have any excuse not to jump in. I kick off my shoes and strip down to my boxers. Erik catches a glimpse of me and turns away, embarrassed. There's not much light out, but from the subtle glow of the lamppost just outside the fence, I can see that he's nervous.

"It's okay, Erik, I don't have nothing you don't have yourself," I tell him.

"Actually, you do," he says coyly. "I don't have abs like that. Or… that happy trail." I laugh, feeling really giddy right now.

"Am I turning you on?" Erik gives a silent response by avoiding eye contact. Ah, it's the best feeling knowing you have this effect on someone. I approach

Erik, playful and flirtatious like, placing my hands on his shoulders. He looks up at me, nervously. I bet he's not expecting me to… throw him into the pool. He falls right in, and I cannonball after him. When I surface, I see him flailing about, crying for help. Holy shit, he really can't swim! "Hold on to me," I say as soon as I reach him. He does so and stops panicking. He's breathless but calms down quick. I mean, he's shivering, but he's calm. "I got you. See? It's not so bad."

"Don't let go of me," he says. His voice is small and trembling.

"I won't." We float here for a little while. As the time passes, I can feel him start to loosen a bit, which is actually pretty surprising, considering the water is cold as balls! I think about the poem he wrote me, and while I don't have it committed to memory, I do remember a couple of lines. "Palm trees, beaches, and rolling seas. The waters will carry both you and me. I'll be your lifeboat through the storm," I recite. Erik smiles. He's staring at me intently, but the water on his glasses obscures his eyes, so I take them off and place them into his hand. "You don't want to lose these." Without his frames, I can see his eyes glistening as he stares. There's something so captivating about the way he's looking at me. I break from his gaze momentarily and take in his features, which are distinctly male, but also possess a certain feminine quality. His face is delicate and symmetrical. His nose is tiny and button-like. His cheeks are full and plump like a little peach. His eyes are shiny and doe-like. His lips are full, with a natural pout. His lips…

His lips…

I don't know what comes over me. I don't know if I'm just getting lost in the moment, or if I'm still feeling that loneliness I felt when I was down in SoCal. But before I can consider anything, I'm kissing him. And holy shit...

It feels like I'm supposed to.

chapter seventeen

erik

Am I dead?

Did I die when I hit the water?

This whole situation is totally unbelievable. I'm in a pool after hours, holding on to Nicholas' bare body, and he's sucking on my upper lip. His breathing is heavy, as is mine. I feel a slip of his tongue and it tastes like a weird mixture of wasabi and ginger. It makes sense though, we did just go to town on a sushi buffet — well, *he* did anyway. His lips caress mine, gently and carefully. It's the most delicate kiss I've ever experienced, not that I've experienced very many. It's unselfish and, dare I say, loving. Despite this, I'm careful not to lose myself. In the back of my mind, there's a voice reminding me, "Erik, there's no way that this is happening. There's no way that this is real." But I desperately want it to be.

The idea of being with Nicholas romantically scares me. Every time I think of that crooked smile and that whole-hearted laugh of his, I melt. He's so caring, and open, and enthusiastic about life. Even when he's sad, there's still a bit of joy in his eyes. The fact that he's built like an underwear model, with the most inviting happy trail leading down to his… you know, is just icing on the cake. Thinking about him makes my heart race, which is why I told myself not to text him while he was gone — his birthday greeting being my one exception — because I think Mackenzie might be right. I think I might like Nicholas more than I initially thought. In fact, I think I might be in love, but that would be a complete waste of my time. At least, I *thought* it would be.

Nicholas pulls his mouth off of mine and licks his lips. He's trembling and he looks confused. Any straight guy would be after making out with a dude.

"I'm sorry," he whispers before stealing another kiss. Why is he doing this? As much as I like it, as much as I want this, I can't help but wonder… why? "You wanna get out of here?" he asks. I nod. He then swims us over to the edge and helps me climb out of the pool. He grabs his clothes and proceeds to dress himself, then picks up his hoodie, takes his phone and wallet from it, and hands it to me, along with my phone. "Here, put this on. You'll catch a cold." I peel off my sweater and put his on before we climb over the fence and make our way back to his car.

Nicholas pulls out of the parking lot and proceeds to drive, not telling me where we're going. A part of me thinks that maybe this is the end of it. Maybe he's planning on taking me home and telling me that this was all a mistake. I don't know how I would feel about that. Now that this is happening with him, no matter how much it might freak me out, I want to see where it leads. No, what am I saying? He should definitely take me home. Take me home now, Nicholas! Of course, he doesn't. He makes a turn at an intersection, and it's very clear that we're not heading back to my house. Nope, we're heading to his. This is happening.

We park by the curb in front of his uncle's house. Nicholas gets out and clicks his garage door open, then gestures for me to follow. I do just that. I'm determined to see how this plays out. Maybe it'll be everything I wanted. Maybe we'll sit down, have a deep and revealing conversation where he'll declare his love for me, and then ask me to be his boyfriend. A guy can only hope, right?

Nicholas closes his garage door, turns on the little heating tower he's got set up near his bed, and goes to rummage through his drawers. He comes over to me and hands me a pair of pajama bottoms, a shirt, and a towel.

"You should get out of those wet clothes," he tells me. "I can give you a minute, if you want." I nod. Nicholas turns and heads for the door leading into the rest of the house.

"Wait," I say. He stops and turns to look at me. His gaze is focused and piercing. I'm hesitant, but I know there's no sense in that. Not now. "Why am I here?" He takes a moment to consider whatever he's about to say.

"How much do you want to be with me tonight, Erik?" He asks. He's nervous. His eyes are glistening. I can see both the fear and the desire within them. I don't even have to think about my response.

"A lot."

Immediately, he comes over to me and puts his lips on mine. His kiss is more aggressive this time. Far more aggressive than it was at the community pool. There's more passion flowing through him now. He reaches down and begins to pull his hoodie off of me. He leads me over to his futon bed, tonguing my mouth all the way. I want him. I want him so bad. I feel the back of my legs pushing against the futon and I fall down onto it in a seated position. Nicholas takes a step back and pulls his shirt off in one quick and easy motion. Now that there's light, I can see that he's even more sculpted than I initially thought. If I wasn't so caught up in the fact that he's throwing himself at me, I'd feel really self-conscious about my own body right now. That's the funny thing about intimacy. When you're in the midst of it, it can make everything you worry about when it comes to your appearance seem inconsequential. It's just you and that other person experiencing one another, getting lost in each other... together.

Nicholas climbs on top of me and I lay myself down to accept his weight. His lips go from my lips, to my cheek, to my ear, to my neck. It tickles, but in a pleasurable way. It doesn't make me laugh. Instead, it makes me breathe harder. He seems to really know what he's doing here. I figured he was a virgin, given that he couldn't get it up for his ex, but he certainly doesn't act like he doesn't know what he's doing. I can feel myself surrendering to him and to this experience. When he peels off my wet shirt, I'm so far gone into it that I don't feel any sort of reluctance or hesitation.

"We can stop this at any time, you know," Nicholas says, breathlessly. I have no words. I can't speak, so I just nod. He kisses me again, and again, and again. Then he sits up and undoes the button on his pants, pulling them off, one leg at a time. I follow his lead and take off mine as well. It's only fair that we're on the same playing field here, right? I mean, I don't really know what I'm doing. I've never gotten this far with anybody before, so I'm sorta just playing a game of Monkey See, Monkey Do.

Nicholas is on top of me again. He's pressing his waist against mine and I can feel him rubbing against me through his boxers. He's… hard. He looks surprised by this too. I know what comes next. Either we stop this now or we go all the way. Truth be told, I'm afraid to lose my virginity, but I also know I don't want to keep it. Not right now. Not at this moment.

"You sure?" He asks. I nod. Still, I have no words. My heart beats faster and I go breathless with anticipation as he reaches down to slip off his boxers. I've never seen another guy before, not in real life, so I have nothing to compare it to but my own. I mean, I've seen guys in porn, but I know that's not exactly a realistic portrayal of the average male anatomy. That being said, Nicholas *is* bigger than me. And by a pretty generous margin. I swallow the little lump in my throat nervously.

What did I get myself into?

Monday. November 4th.

The whole experience felt like it lasted forever. We made out a little while longer, I guess to make sure that neither of us would back out. Having sex was something we both had to have wanted. It had to be consensual on all fronts. Nicholas asked me several times if I was sure and not once did my answer ever change. I never even second guessed it.

At one point, he reached down and brought out a shoebox he kept stashed under his bed. It was full of condoms and a phallic shaped bottle full of clear gooey liquid. Once he was wrapped and we were both lathered up in the goo, he slipped himself in.

It hurt like the wrath of God…

And it was only the tip.

We took it slow from then on. He pushed in slowly, proceeding half an inch at a time, if that much. He could only move in me in between my heavy inhalations of breath. Everything had to be perfectly timed and choreographed if it was gonna work.

"Is this okay? Is this?" he asked repeatedly between each motion. "More?"

"There's more?" I replied at one point, my jaw clenched in disbelief. There was no way this was healthy. The whole process of us coming together for the first time was painful, and not at all like the many young adult novels I've read or the teen romances I've watched, where the sexual encounters seem easy and, like, actually romantic. Maybe it was because my sex was gay that it was so complicated. My experience was strange, and uncomfortable, and sweaty, to say the least. And I don't understand why gay men would subject themselves to this on a regular basis.

Eventually, Nicholas was able to give me all of him. I didn't let him move at first, because I needed some time to let my body get used to him. When I did let him move, it felt… weird. I wouldn't say it felt bad, but I wouldn't say it felt good either. This is gonna sound really disgusting, but it sorta felt like I was having a backwards bowel movement, which was worrying.

There came a point where Nicholas' movements got harder and faster, and it was then that I started to feel a small semblance of pleasure. At least, I *think* it was pleasure. I'm not really sure. I just know that I struggled to keep my breathing whilst he did whatever he had to do to reach completion. It was all very intense and physically exhausting, like doing a pushup. At one point, I think I might've overstretched my hamstring. I screamed. I think it freaked him out because he kept asking, "Are you okay? Did I hurt you?" I just shook my head and collapsed into his pillows. He chuckled, placing a finger on my lip.

"Shh… my mom and uncle will hear."

Once the state of our euphoria was gone, that's when things started to become uncomfortable between us. The high we were riding was gone, and we had to come back to earth to deal with what we'd just done. Questions like "What does this mean for our friendship?" and "Will everything be different after this?" came into my mind.

"We should get in the shower," Nicholas suggested, handing me a shirt and a clean pair of his boxer shorts. I agreed. I threw on the clothes he gave me, then we snuck into the bathroom and climbed into the tub together. Now, I'm sitting here with him. The water from the shower is beating down on us, and neither one of us has a thing to say. Nicholas seems to be lost in his own thoughts, and I… I dunno, I feel like a slut.

What we did goes against every moral that I've held for myself. I never thought I would lose my virginity in a garage to someone I wasn't even dating. I mean, yes, it's Nicholas, and I love him. The problem is, as far as I know, he doesn't love me. That's what makes me feel nothing but regret about this whole situation.

Nicholas offers to drive me home. It's funny. It almost feels like a slap to my face. I know it might sound naive and idealistic, but when I pictured making love for the first time, I always imagined that I would stay with the person throughout the night. I never imagined we would part ways before dawn, but here we are.

We drive through town. Nicholas takes the most direct route from his uncle's house to mine, and we don't talk, not a single word. I wish he would talk to me. I need him to clarify; I have so many questions: Are we okay? Aren't you straight? And for how long is it cool that I borrow your clothes and underwear? I need him to answer all of this, but he doesn't. He just drives. And even though he takes the shortest route possible, it feels like the longest ride of my life. Why do boys go silent when you need them to say something? Anything would satisfy me at this point.

Nicholas drives right up to my house and pulls into the driveway, despite my having him park down the street earlier in the night. It doesn't matter though. I look at the clock and it reads 3:16am. We've been out almost all night. Regardless of how obsessively my mom might be keeping tabs on me, I highly doubt she'd wait up this late just to scold me. She's not *that* crazy, I don't think.

I'm not sure if I should just let myself out or what. Nicholas still isn't saying anything to me, and I feel like this wouldn't be a great place to leave it. We sit in silence for a few minutes. I'm starting to worry about having to go to school in the morning, knowing I'll get very little sleep, if any at all. I look over at Nicholas and it seems like he's in shock. He looks so confused. I wonder if I looked that confused after my encounter with Andrew. Then again, I had a little while before I went all the way to actually deal with my feelings. Nicholas went through it — the fear, the excitement, the guilt, the coping, the remorse — all in one night. I could barely deal with it in the time that I had, I can't imagine having to take it all at once. Suddenly, Nicholas unbuckles his seatbelt and gets out of the car. I watch him through the windshield as he walks around the front and over to my side. It's a little scary, if I'm being honest. He pulls my door open, and I quickly undo my seatbelt and climb out. His movements are fast and decisive. It makes me feel like he wants to get rid of me as soon as possible.

Nicholas walks me to my door, and we stand here awkwardly. Neither of us know how we should say goodnight. Do we hug? Do we shake hands or high five? What do we do? I hate not knowing, because in a way, it sorta undoes the entire relationship that we've built over this last month or so as friends. We were comfortable with each other. We were so comfortable that we were willing and able to share our most embarrassing thoughts and our saddest feelings. Why did the sex have to set everything back? Isn't sex supposed to be a step forward? Isn't it supposed to be another layer of intimacy reached? Is it because the sex was gay? I don't understand.

"Hey… uh… thank you," Nicholas finally says. "For being there tonight. I really appreciate it." His words come out wooden and forced. I can tell by his delivery there's so much more he wants to say. Say it, Nicholas. Say it. He stretches out his hand to me, offering me — of all things — a handshake. The gesture is so cold and distant. It's so weirdly formal, especially for him. It's a gesture I imagine a stuffy high powered businessman would offer to the woman he was cheating on his wife with. It's gross and really insulting. Regardless, I take it.

"Anytime," I say, shaking his hand. After, his hands immediately go into his pockets. He stands there, swaying a bit, forward and back, as if he's not sure whether he should leave or not. If he's not gonna offer anything more than a stupid handshake, I would insist he just get out of here and not drag this on. It would be better for both of us. Leave, Nicholas. Just leave, I think to myself. I meet his gaze and our eyes lock together. He's staring into me through his maple brown eyes, his natural squint giving him a sort of smoldering, passionate expression that melts me in his focus. The next thing I know, he's lunging forward. His mouth presses against mine and his tongue pushes so deep, I swear I can feel him tickling the top of my throat. So… this is happening. Just seconds ago, we felt worlds apart, and now we're practically swallowing each other whole. What gives? I don't understand Nicholas. I don't get him.

When we pull apart, Nicholas rests his forehead against mine, and I take in the warmth of his breath. I love it so much I can't resist stealing one more kiss.

"Stay with me," I plead, whispering in a small voice.

"Okay," he agrees, then kisses me again and again. While he's got the two of us tangled together, I reach into my pocket for my keys. I release myself from his hold and move to unlock my door. "Wait, your parents. I can't." I was so caught up I didn't even bother to think about my parents. But, right now, I don't care.

"Please, stay. Please?"

"I can't. We can't." He looks just as sad as I feel. I kiss him once more, this time slowly and gently. I linger there for as long as I can. He doesn't move, or slip me any tongue, or anything. He lets me set the pace and follows my lead. While every touch of his lips before took my breath away, this is the kiss that claims my heart. It shakes me to my very core, sending a crazy shiver through my entire body. From this moment on, I'm his. And while it's within my better judgement and moral obligation to resist, and to continue to fight against this temptation, I know that there's no denying it.

I'm in love.

I'm in love with Nicholas Ray Santiago. And at this moment, as ridiculous as it may sound, I'm convinced that he's in love with me too.

chapter eighteen
nicholas

What have I done?

What did I just do?

It's nearly seven o'clock in the morning. I'm lying frozen in bed. I have not slept and yet I feel like I'm just now returning to my body, as if what happened between me and Erik last night was some sort of weird, crazy dream. It had to have been a dream, right? I mean, I'm not… gay. I don't look at boys like that. I'm trying to convince myself that it was all in my head, but then I look over and see his clothes scattered around the cement floor of my room. I had sex with Erik…

Holy shit, I actually had sex with Erik…

I hear a knock on my door, and Ma lets herself in before I even have a chance to respond.

"Nicky, are you decent?" she asks, covering her eyes as she enters.

"Yeah," I answer, though I don't get up.

"You're still in bed? Ay, dios mio! You're gonna be late for school. Hurry up and get dressed. I made breakfast. And bring all those cups into the kitchen. Your tio's complaining all the cups are disappearing." Ma turns and exits. I let out an exasperated sigh, then get up and proceed to collect all the empty cups I have stashed around my room. Truth be told, they came in handy last night. A few of them were filled with water, and after Erik and I did it, I was in desperate need of hydration. It just goes to show sometimes clutter can be useful.

I head into the kitchen and dump all of the cups into the sink.

"So that's where all the cups went," Tio Roger remarks with a sort of Ah-ha! type of tone. He makes it seem like I just hoarded every drinking glass, but I only had like five or six, and they were all being used. Whatever, I don't have the energy to argue. Ma serves me a plate of eggs, sausage, and a couple of homemade arepas, and I take a seat next to Tio Roger at the table. "You feeling alright, Nick? You're looking really drained."

"I am really drained."

"When did you get back last night?" Ma asks, now joining us at the table.

"Pretty early. I just didn't get much sleep," I explain. It's the truth, though I am leaving out the bit where I left again around 3:00am to drive Erik home.

"Hey, did you happen to hear something weird last night?" Tio Roger asks. My heart drops and my ears perk up. "I thought I heard screaming, but I could've been imagining things. It was pretty late." He knows. Shit. Shit. Shit! He knows! He heard us! My Tio Roger heard the wild and crazy sex I was giving to Erik last night that made him scream, and now I'm backed into a corner! Should I just tell them? Should I just come clean and admit to everything?

"I didn't hear anything," Ma says. Good, at least *she* didn't hear us.

"Huh," Tio adds. "Maybe I was dreaming." I can feel the guilt building in my stomach. I don't want to say anything, because coming out about having sex with a dude is totally not breakfast appropriate conversation, but the longer I hold on to this, the more I know it's gonna eat me up. I want to talk to someone about it, but I don't have anyone I can talk to besides Ma and my uncle. I mean, I *could* talk to Mackenzie, but I know her well enough to know that she'll talk to Erik. And the last thing I need is someone saying anything that might give Erik any sort of encouragement about this. I can feel the words making their way up. I'm just gonna say it. I'm just gonna tell them, and whatever happens, happens.

"I had sex with Erik!" The words leave my mouth like bullets fired from a pistol. Ma and Tio Roger look over at me and cock their heads as if they aren't quite sure they heard me correctly. I know by the looks on their faces that I'm gonna have to repeat myself and explain… a lot. I take a breath. I know this one is gonna be an interesting conversation to say the least. "I brought Erik here last night and we had sex." At first, neither of them say anything. They just stare at me, trying to figure out what they want to say, and when they can't figure it out, they look at each other, and then back at me, and then back at each other, and then back at me again. The whole thing is super awkward.

"Well, that explains the screaming," Tio Roger quips lightheartedly, finally breaking the uncomfortable silence.

"Roger, déjanos solos por favor," Ma says. Her tone is stern and stoic.

"Bueno," Tio Roger replies. I don't have to know what they're saying to know I'm probably in serious trouble. It was nice knowing you, world. Tio gets up and gives me a hug from behind. It's awkward because I'm sitting and he's standing, but I can appreciate the gesture. "Know that I love you, no matter what, Nick." He then exits, leaving me and Ma alone. She's staring at me with a blank expression. It makes me uneasy, because I can't really read her. I can't tell if she's mad, disappointed, or indifferent. Maybe she's just as confused as I am. Anyway, I brace myself for impact.

"Why did you tell me that, Nicky?" Ma asks. I'm not sure how to approach this question. Since I can't really gauge her reaction, I don't know how to proceed.

"I… I don't know," I say.

"Would you have told me this if Erik was a girl?"

"I dunno. Probably not."

"Well, did you use protection?"

"Yeah."

"Then I don't need to hear about it," Ma explains. "I don't really need to know what goes on in my son's sex life. In fact, I think I'd rather not know. As long as you're being careful and you're being safe, and you're not hurting anyone else or doing anything illegal, then… okay."

If I'm being honest, Ma's reaction surprises me. Given her familial values, our family's Catholic background, and the fact that I'm her one and only son, I was worried that she'd be disappointed. I figured she would be let down by the idea that I had sex with a boy, and she would conclude that I was gay, and that I wouldn't have a family, not in the traditional sense. I worried that she wouldn't love me anymore. But then I think about it again, and I think that I projected what I thought my dad's reaction would be onto my mom, because there's no doubt in my mind that my dad would've disowned me. It's a good thing I beat him to the punch.

"Nicky, I want you to feel like you can come to me about anything," Ma says. Her expression has lightened, and she looks so okay with everything. It almost makes me want to cry, it's such a relief. "I mean, there are some details you can keep, but I don't ever want you to feel ashamed of who you choose to be with. You know, unless they're a lying, cheating, psychopath, in which case, I will put my foot down."

"Ma," I laugh. It really is a huge relief, because even though I don't know that I'm gay, it's nice to know that, if I am, I don't have to worry about losing anything.

"So, how long have you and Erik been going on?"

"Last night was actually the first time, and I'm really confused."

"Why?" She asks.

"What do you mean?" I reply.

"Why are you confused?" I'm not sure I really understand her question. Isn't it obvious why I would be confused? I'm straight, and I just had sex with a dude. I don't want to say that though, because I don't want to come off as being sarcastic when she's being so supportive, but it does seem like a dumb question, doesn't it? I think my thoughts are reading on my face, because Ma's eyes narrow, as if she knows I think her question is a little stupid. "Listen, Nicky. Todo no es blanco y negro. Not everything is black and white. Just keep that in mind, yeah?" Ma gets up, comes over to me, and puts a kiss on top of my head.

"That's it? You're not gonna ground me or anything?" I joke.

"Oh, you're grounded," Ma replies. It's a bit of a shock to hear. If I had been drinking something, I probably would've done a spit take right in her face.

"What? Why?" I ask.

"Well, you had your friend over late without permission, you had sex in your uncle's garage, and then you told me about it. And you've been hoarding all the cups in your room, even though you've already been asked not to. Now get your little teenage butt to school. Okay? Love you, mijo." School? I can't go to school. No way, I have too much on my mind to focus on anything else. Ma makes to leave.

"Ma, wait!" I say, sounding almost like I'm begging. "Would it be alright if I stayed home today? I have a lot to think about, and I didn't get any sleep last night. Please?" Ma stops to consider.

"Fine, but if they ask, mijo, you have terrible diarrhea," she answers so deadpan that I can't stop myself from smiling. Ma exits.

"Love you," I call after her. My mom is fucking amazing. Knowing that I've got my family on my side makes the whole mulling things over process so much easier. I mean, there's a lot to stress about, sure, but at least I don't have to stress about that.

I head back into my room, nursing a cup of coffee. I don't know if you'd even count it as coffee since I've spruced it up with a boat load of milk and sugar. It's more like I'm nursing a cup of warm, sugary milk, with just a splash of caffeine, which is just how I like it. Anyway, I pull out my phone and tap open Erik's text box. I'm debating whether I should text him or not. We left things sorta up in the air when I dropped him off, I just want to make sure we're on the same page. I think on it for a moment and decide against it. I don't want to do anything rash or put myself in a position where I'm gonna have to commit to something I'm not sure I'm ready to. I made a promise to my mom that I would never commit to someone unless I was going to commit to someone. I'm not about to break that promise. There's so much about myself that I have to think about, I decide to go off the grid for the day. I switch my phone to airplane mode and just sit down. Let myself meditate for a while.

Sexuality is such a weird thing. People always want to define each other. We want to put everything and everyone into a box and label it, as if it were that simple.

It's not that simple. Not for me. I like girls. I like how they smell. I like how they sound when they laugh, when they talk. I like their long hair and their delicate features. I like that I'm bigger and taller than most of them. I like their breasts, and the shapes and curves that their bodies make. I like that being with one makes me feel like a man — maybe not in the sexual sense, because I haven't gotten that to successfully work yet, but you know. I like that being with one makes me feel like I'm needed. I like girls… but then, there's Erik.

I like Erik. I like that he has a squeaky, high pitched voice, he almost sounds like a cartoon character. I find his stubborn cowlick on the back of his head endearing, and his features, particularly his eyes, are beautiful, especially when they're not being covered up by his nerdy, thick rimmed glasses. I wonder if he wears contacts at all. I also like that he's small and stubby, and even just a little bit pudgy. He always seems so self-conscious about his body, but I've seen his body and I enjoyed it. I wouldn't say he's fat, but he does have these little man boobs, which in a weird way made it slightly less weird for me… I dunno. I guess there are parts of him that read more feminine to me, it's easy to forget he's not a girl.

The thing that I like most about Erik though, is that he shows up. He cares and you can tell. And I think, despite everything else, that might be the most important thing. You see, I like girls, but they don't seem to like me, not really. I like Erik, and he does. I know that might sound shallow and vain, but is it so bad to want to feel wanted? That's all I really want. After Brenda, after my dad, I just want to feel wanted. If Erik wants me, I can't come up with too many reasons — aside from my own stubbornness — not to give myself to him. It's just weird, because this isn't how I pictured my life going. I pictured myself with a woman. I pictured myself having a traditional courtship, that would evolve into a traditional relationship, that would evolve into marriage, and then a family, and then…

Fuck, I sound like my dad! What am I even talking about? Why am I thinking that far ahead? I'm still a kid. I'm still in high school. Why is this on my mind? I have absolutely no idea if I'm gay, straight, bi, or whatever else is in between. I have no idea what I want, or what I'm gonna do, or how I even feel…

God, why does love have to be so complicated?

I need a nap.

chapter nineteen
erik

A crash of thunder.

A violent sea.

I'm sinking.

My arms flail wildly, but I can't, despite my efforts, reach the surface. I'm running low on air. I feel my chest tightening. My lungs are struggling to hold on to their last bit of breath. I'm drowning.

"Erik," I hear a familiar voice echo through the abyss. "Erik, wake up."

Everywhere I look, all I can see is blue. It's dark, and cold, and still. This is the end. No way I can survive this.

"Erik," the voice calls again, cutting through the darkness like a light at the end of a tunnel. "Erik, wake up. You're gonna be late." I open my eyes, and everything is a blur. I got, maybe, two or three hours of sleep at most, so waking up feels almost painful. I furrow my brow, hoping it might help me keep my eyes open long enough to actually wake up. When everything comes into focus, I see my dad sitting on my bed beside me. He's already dressed for work, and looking a bit concerned.

"What?" I manage, still groggy.

"You're gonna be late for school. Get up."

"What time is it?"

"Almost 7:30. Come on, we gotta go. I'll wait for you downstairs." Dad gets up and leaves the room. I try to rub the sleep from my eyes, but I'm just so tired. I want to lay down and go back to sleep, regardless of how terrible my dreams might've been. I would ask my parents if I could skip school, but I know if I do, they'll start asking questions about why I'm so tired, and I'm not exactly a good liar. My mom would expect something's up and she'd never leave me alone about it. Really, it's best for me to just suck it up and power through the day. I figure I can always take a nap when I get home. I pull myself out of bed, albeit slowly, and get dressed. Fortunately, I showered only a few hours before, otherwise I would feel really dirty, all things considered.

Dad's driving me to school now, and I can barely keep myself from nodding off in the passenger seat. I'm regretting my decision to not try to lie my way out of school today, because I keep drifting off and, every time I do, my head hits the window and I get so confused when I'm jolted back awake by it. It's like, "Where am I? Why am I putting myself through this?"

"Are you alright, Erik?" Dad asks.

"Yeah, I just had a hard time falling asleep last night," I reply, which is true. The fact that I'm leaving out major details, such as having sex with Nicholas, doesn't necessarily mean I'm lying, right? "Will you wake me up when we get there? I just want to sleep a bit more."

"Sure." Thank God for my dad.

It feels like I've only just closed my eyes when my dad wakes me up.

"We're here," he says. The time flew by so fast I almost can't believe it. If I were a more suspicious person, I would suspect that he drove a little faster just to spite me. My dad's not like that though, I don't think.

I open the car door and let myself out. The cool air hits my face and it's enough to sort of shock me out of my sleepiness. Still, I can't help but wish I would've stayed home today. I cross the street and make my way across campus to my locker, where I'm greeted by Mackenzie, who's sitting on the hallway floor and reading a sleazy romance novel. It's the kind of novel that has a cover displaying a muscular shirtless man embracing a scantily clad woman from behind, whilst breathing into her mouth. The muscular man is positioned so that his abs are on full display. And he's got a happy trail, which makes me think of Nicholas, and that makes me walk a little funny because now I've got a hard on. Not good. Not good at all. Mackenzie's gonna notice how uncomfortable I am and — because she's insanely intuitive about sexual stuff, which she probably learned from the sleazy romance novels — she'll assume that something happened. Then, I'll respond with a lie, which she'll immediately see through and she'll figure out that I had sex with Nicholas. I should just tell her, so we can save ourselves a few steps.

"Hey Mackenzie," I say as I approach, having readied myself with a deep breath.

"Hey," she says, looking up. "Whoa, you look like shit."

"Yeah, about that…" I let my voice trail off. Sex still isn't a subject that I'm comfortable discussing openly despite who I surround myself with. Mackenzie bookmarks her sleazy novel, grabs her bag, and gets up. She's staring at me through narrowed eyes.

"Something about you is different. You seem more nervous than you usually are," she says. Oh, God, she knows. I knew she would know. There's really no point in trying to hide anything from her, but I do anyway, out of habit.

"I dunno. It's probably coffee. Jitters, you know? I couldn't fall asleep last night."

"No, you don't smell like coffee. You smell like…" Mackenzie stops mid-sentence to lean in and take a whiff of me. It's incredibly awkward. Suddenly, her eyes widen, and I bear witness to the exact moment when she comes to the realization that... "You had sex, didn't you?" A smile quickly forms on her face. She's so happy and amused by this whole thing, and I haven't even confirmed it yet. Meanwhile, I'm here totally freaking out.

"No, I did not have sex." I'm not lying to Mackenzie because I think there's any point in hiding it from her. She obviously already knows. It's more that I'm lying to everyone around us. Regardless of how comfortable *she* may be about it, I don't know how the kids at school will react. I've already noticed people giving us side glances as they walk by. I wish they'd just mind their own business.

"Do not lie to me you little altar boy. I can smell Nick's scent on you and it is delicious," Mackenzie demands, exaggerating.

"You can *not*. We showered right after."

"I knew it! I'd recognize that ocean breeze scent anywhere! There's only one reason why you would be so tired, walking around with that gross little boner of yours." I cross my legs and pull the bottom of my sweater down in response.

"Will you keep your voice down!?" It's freaking me out how loudly we're talking about this, because that's when I notice Andrew passing by with a couple of his friends — I think their names are Ryan and Jacob. I'm not entirely sure. I know them by face. I mean, I've seen them around school, and I know they're on the football team, but I've actually never formally met them. I might've even pulled those names out of thin air. Anyway, they seem to be consumed in their own conversation, chatting and laughing it up like hyenas. For a split second, Andrew's eyes meet mine and his sapphire blues pierce right through me, but then he pulls his gaze away and keeps walking. It happens so fast I don't even think he noticed me. Not really.

"So, what now? Are you and Nick, like, a couple?" Mackenzie asks, as if this were a casual thing. And to be honest, I have no idea. I don't know if we're a couple. I don't even know if he likes me or if he's even gay. For all I know, Nicholas might've just needed to feel some sort of human connection from… anyone. I mean, he *did* mention he tried to hook up with his ex-girlfriend while he was in LA visiting his dad. Maybe what happened between us wasn't so special.

"I don't know," I tell Mackenzie, sadly. "I'm really confused about everything now. I don't know what we are. I don't even know how I feel."

"Sore?" she quips.

"Mackenzie, be serious. I'm freaking out!"

"Erik, you're fine."

"No. What if I get…" I begin to say in whispered tones. I look around for a second to make sure no one's eavesdropping, and then lean in close to Mackenzie. "What if I get AIDS?"

"Does Nick have AIDS?" she replies, wearing a look that tells me she thinks I'm an idiot.

"I have no idea."

"Oh, shit, Erik, you're gonna get AIDS."

"Mackenzie!" I scold her. I have to restrain myself a bit, because my voice comes out way louder than I intended. I'm glad this is fun for her, because it's really not fun for me. She's frolicking in her own little hilarious place in Heaven. Meanwhile, I'm stuck in Limbo, completely unsure of my fate. Where do I go from here?

"Chill out. I'm sure you're fine," Mackenzie says, finally adopting a more serious tone. "You'll stress yourself out being a hypochondriac. Relax." The first bell rings, and it occurs to me that Nicholas isn't here. Maybe he decided to skip school today, like I should have. Either way, it's good for me, because I'm not sure I'm ready to face him yet. It was so awkward and confusing between the two of us after the sex. One moment, we were sitting in the shower avoiding eye contact, and the next moment, we were on my doorstep making out and talking about spending the rest of the night together. It was so hot, and cold, and hot again, I have no idea where we stand at the moment.

"Huh, he's not here," I say, more to myself than to Mackenzie. I can hear the disappointment in my voice. It's weird. Thinking about Nicholas gives me all these mixed emotions. Yeah, I'm not ready to see him, but I still *want* to. It's complicated.

"If he's in the same state as you, he's probably either gonna show up late or not at all," Mackenzie offers. "Should we text him?"

"No. If he doesn't show, it'll give me time to get my thoughts together."

"Ah, who would've thought that my best friend would be having sex with a hot guy?" She says this with such pride, you'd think that *she* was the one sleeping with a hot guy and not me. If only I could enjoy this as much as she is. I mean, I *should* be able to enjoy it. Nicholas is a very sex-able person to have sex with, and if I'm being completely honest, I think he was good at it. I don't really know what good sex would feel like, but judging by the way he moved in me, he was very giving, and I feel like that's a sign of good sex. At least, I would think it is. I need to get this off my mind. I cannot be thinking about this, especially not at school. I just don't know how to stop thinking about it. And trying to hide my boner is definitely not helping.

Nicholas doesn't show up to first or second period. When he doesn't show up to third period, I resign myself to the fact that I'm probably not gonna see him today, which is both a disappointment and a relief. I debate texting him but decide against it. I don't wanna seem desperate or anything. But this is Nicholas, of course he'd want to hear from me, right? Then again, if he wanted to hear from me, wouldn't he text me first? He was the one who initiated everything. I just went along with it, albeit willingly, but still.

Should I text him?

Should I not text him?

Should I text him?

Ugh, I don't know.

What do I do? I ask myself this repeatedly throughout the entirety of fourth period. I'm thinking way too hard about it. Nicholas is one of my best friends. It shouldn't be this hard deciding whether or not I should reach out, so when fourth period lets out, I send him a text.

"Hi," I message him. It's tempting to say more, something like, "Missing you today," but I'm afraid I'll end up putting my foot in my mouth if I do. Or worse,

I'm afraid of scaring him away. They say that sex complicates things, but for me, it's the feelings that I have that are complicating things. I want to be with Nicholas, I really do. I just can't be sure that he wants to be with me. Not for anything more than sex. That seems to be a recurring thing with me. Always the hook up, but never the catch.

I head over to the quad and meet up with Mackenzie for lunch. We make a stop at the cafeteria to pick up some food, and then walk around the football field to behind the bleachers. Mackenzie wants all the dirty details on what happened between me and Nicholas. How was it? What did it feel like? Is he big? All that kind of stuff. No better place to discuss this than the place where people go to take pot and get laid.

"So, how did it happen?" Mackenzie asks excitedly, taking a bite out of her cafeteria burger. She's so invested, she doesn't even stop her questioning to swallow first. "Actually, first, how big was he? Put me out of my misery. Was he, like, half a ruler or closer to, like, a full-length ruler?"

"I don't know," I reply uncomfortably. "I didn't stop to measure it."

"Okay, well, was it like a corn dog, a soda can, or a water bottle?"

"Mackenzie, I'm not gonna give you the details about his penis. That's private."

"But it was big, right? I mean, he's Colombian-Puerto Rican, so it had to be, right?" I stare at her with a blank expression. I know she's not gonna stop asking until she gets something out of me, so I nod in affirmation, biting my lower lip. I can't help that it's true. She squeals the highest pitched squeal I've ever heard come out of a person. She's so ridiculously giddy, she nearly drops her burger. I hate her so much right now. "Alright," she leans in. "So how did it happen? And don't skip the details, I want to know it all, line by line, play by play, and lay by lay."

I fill Mackenzie in on how Nicholas texted me and took me out for dinner at the fancifully cheap sushi buffet. I also tell her about our little detour to the park, and how he had a bad experience with his dad, but I insist that it's not my business to say any more than that. I'm not sure that Nicholas would appreciate me spreading around that his dad got another woman pregnant and took his room away for the baby. Details like that feel too personal to share. Still, I do feel a little guilty, because it's really difficult giving someone all of the details without giving up all the details. I really have to pick and choose what's worth telling Mackenzie, and what's okay to tell her, without actually knowing what's okay to tell her.

One thing I do mention — which I probably shouldn't — is the fact that Nicholas almost hooked up with his ex-girlfriend. Mackenzie cocks her head like she doesn't quite know what to make of this information. I go on to tell her about how Nicholas forced me to go swimming with him, how he kissed me in the pool, and how he brought me to his place where we had sex, but her expression doesn't change.

"Did he say why he met up with his ex-girlfriend?" Mackenzie asks, her brow now furrowing.

"Umm… he said he was feeling lonely. Why?" I reply. Of all the details I gave her, the ex-girlfriend is the one detail Mackenzie hooks herself into. It kinda has me worried. What is she thinking?

"Hmm… I don't know, Erik. I'm in two minds about this one."

"What do you mean?"

"Well, on one hand, it seems pretty clear that Nick likes you, but on the other hand it also sounds like he might be pulling an Andrew."

"No, Nicholas would never," I say coming to Nicholas' defense, despite that thought having already crossed my mind. I don't believe that he'd use me for sex. He's my friend. He's my best friend. But… then again, I don't know, because he's not even gay. Ugh, this whole situation is so confusing.

"Let's be real, Erik," Mackenzie begins. I really don't like the sound of her tone right now. "As good of friends as we've become with Nick, we've only really known him for, like, a month. Plus, this thing between you two has been kinda whirl-windy, don't you think? I mean, if it didn't actually happen to you, I would think you were pulling the plot out of some sorta fairytale." I don't want to admit it, but Mackenzie does have a point. It feels like I've known Nicholas forever, but I haven't. And this whole thing did come out of the blue, and it did happen really fast. Maybe that's why it doesn't feel real. I might just be tired from my lack of sleep, but last night with Nicholas feels like a dream. A weird and incredibly vivid sex dream, but a dream nonetheless. It also doesn't help that he's not here to confirm that it wasn't a dream, so I really don't know what to make of it. And by the looks of it, neither does Mackenzie.

I check my phone before heading over to fifth period. Nothing. Nicholas hasn't texted back yet, and it worries me. I know I shouldn't be thinking this way — he's probably just taking a nap or something — but I can't help wondering if he's avoiding me because of what we did together. Yeah, he initiated and yeah, it looked like he enjoyed it, but we didn't exactly bring it all to a conclusion. We just left it there at a cliffhanger.

You know, things are different in the light of day. You see things clearer. There's no magic of the night sky or dancing in the moonlight. Everything is laid out in plain view, in plain sight. Maybe his view is the same as mine. Maybe he sees that what we did was a mistake. As much as it kills me, I know that's what it was. Because, like my mom said, "It's not right." I mean, maybe Nicholas leaving me hanging is a sign. There is such a thing as divine intervention, and what if this is it?

Fifth period is a nice distraction. It's Choir, my second elective of the day, so I'm able to turn my brain off for a little while. We're currently learning "Danny Boy," which I think is really pretty, but a lot of other kids in class think it's slow and boring. I think they're just bitter because our choir teacher won't let them do their fancy R&B trills and melismas, which is really for the better because it sounds terrible when they do. It always ends up clashing. Now, I'm not really a great singer, but even I know when the music says, "Unison," we're all supposed to sing the same thing.

Our teacher lets us have the last bit of class to ourselves after we've done a "stumble-through" of the three songs she has us learning. We're not supposed to have our phones out in class, but I sneak a glance at mine. Being in choir reminds me of Nicholas and that time he sang along to that one song on the radio when we hung out for the first time. God, his singing voice was so bad, but it was really cute how much he got into it. I want him to talk to me. I want to know that our friendship is okay. I want to know that we're okay. I look at my phone, and nothing. This is so depressing.

I'm staring at my phone the whole way to sixth period. At this point, I don't even care about getting caught with it out. I just want to hear from him. I know I'm obsessed, but this isn't like Nicholas. I could understand if he was one of those people that's never on their phone, or if he had a habit of reading messages and not responding, but he's not and he doesn't. Unless he's at school — which he's obviously not — he's always really prompt about replying to his messages, usually texting back within a couple minutes or so. Maybe he's avoiding me.

I get to sixth period and walk over to my assigned seat. Andrew's already here, his head resting in his hand as he flips through the pages of his textbook. I don't really pay him any mind anymore. Ever since Nicholas told him he's been painted into a villain and to leave us alone, Andrew doesn't talk to me. He seems to have gotten over it, since he doesn't try to hinder me anymore when we get paired up either. Our only communication now is when classwork calls for it. Other than that, we mind our own business, which is why it throws me when I notice he's staring at me as I take my seat.

"Hey," Andrew says. There's a glimmer in his eye that makes me nervous, like he knows something…

"Hey," I reply, suspicious. It almost sounds more like a question.

"So I overheard you and your friend talking this morning." Holy shit! He *does* know something. "You might want to be more careful with what you talk about in public. Some people might not like what you're saying." I can feel myself tensing up.

"I don't know what you're talking about," I defend, though my voice comes out so flimsy, making it obvious I'm lying.

"Yeah, you do. You don't gotta lie to me, Erik."

"Why does that sound like a threat?"

"You're the one taking it that way," Andrew says smoothly. He's so cold and stoic about it, I can't get a read on him. What is he thinking? Should I be scared? "Painted me a villain, remember?" Yeah, I think I should be scared.

Andrew doesn't say much more to me, but the whole exchange with him has me on edge. I feel like he's watching me, but every time I look over, he's minding his own business. Ugh, I'm so paranoid, I hate it. I still can't decide if he was actually threatening me or if it was all in my head. I don't know what he's capable of, and that's kinda terrifying. See, this is why I'll never understand why people argue that being homosexual is a choice. Why would anyone choose this for themselves? If there is any choice involved, it's whether or not you're gonna act on it, and I've already done that, so… I don't know, I just feel so uneasy. Knowing that people know what I did makes everything seem like it could fall apart if someone decided to talk, and I can't exactly trust Andrew to keep his mouth shut. I mean, I don't *think* he's a vindictive person, but then I also don't have a great track record when it comes to reading him, so there's that.

After sixth period lets out, I text Mackenzie to see if she'd be willing to give me a ride home. We live in opposite directions from school, so I try not to ask her for rides too often. I usually just take public transportation but today, I don't know if I'll make the whole bus ride home without falling asleep, and falling asleep on the bus can be tricky. What if you miss your stop? What if someone steals your bag or something? My school should really provide school buses. I mean, they probably do, but I've never actually seen them used outside of field trips and stuff, so… I dunno. Plus, I don't imagine falling asleep on a bus full of my peers would be any safer. Luckily, Mackenzie agrees to give me a ride — she always pulls through for me — and we meet up in the parking lot after I make a quick stop at my locker.

"You look sad. I take it Nick never texted you back?" Mackenzie says, as we're pulling out of the parking lot. I shake my head. After my run in with Andrew, the situation with Nicholas feels a little less dire. "I'm sure he'll come around. This is Nick we're talking about."

"Actually, right now I'm more worried about Andrew," I explain. Mackenzie perks up, surprised. "He said he overheard us talking this morning and that I should be careful because people might not like it."

"Bullshit," Mackenzie interjects. "He's not worried about you. If anything, that was a threat."

"That's what I thought too. You don't think he'd spread it around, do you?"

"Oh, like wildfire." She says this so confidently, like it's a definite certainty that Andrew would. "He didn't get what he wanted from you and now he finds out that you got what he wanted from Nick. I wouldn't put it past him to be a little bitch about it. But then again, he is a complete closet case, so you might be safe. At the very least, you've got a weapon against him."

I don't say much the rest of the drive home. The thought of this getting out has me scared straight. If only I could be scared straight, maybe then I wouldn't have to deal with this. I keep thinking about what my mom said, "You don't know how cruel and difficult the world can be." This must've been what she was talking about.

When I get home, I climb up to my bedroom, drop my bag, and crawl into bed. Today's been such a heavy day of emotions, all I want to do is sleep. Forget about homework. Forget about Andrew. Forget about even Nicholas. I just want to sleep and get away from myself and all of these things that are weighing so heavily on me. But I can't, because everything that's weighing down on me is what's causing me to sink further and further into the abyss.

A chime comes from my phone and I wake up with a start. I'd fallen asleep and, again, had that same dream of drowning that's been haunting me night, after night, after night. My phone chimes again. It's a quarter past nine when I check it. My eyes are still coming into focus, but I can see I've got a couple of text messages. They're from Nicholas. My heart skips a beat when I realize it. I'm not sure what I'm expecting the messages to say. Is he scared? Is he confused? Or, maybe, he's even mad. I don't know how to prepare myself, so I just tap the messages open before I can hesitate and hope for the best.

"Hey you," the first message reads.

"Sorry. Phone on airplane mode. Totally forgot about it," the second message reads. So that's why he wasn't texting me back. I breathe a sigh of relief and start to type something. I want to make sure we're cool, but as I'm typing, another message comes in.

"We need to talk," it says. I delete what I was typing and just stare at the message for a little while. "We need to talk." That's what people say when they're about to let you down, or when they're about to break your heart. "We need to talk" is never followed by good news. If he's gonna tell me something disappointing like, "We shouldn't have done what we've done," then I don't want to hear it — or in this case, read it. Not tonight. I don't want to give up the hope that, maybe, we could be something. It's not likely, I know, but as long as there's hope, there's something to hold onto: possibility. And I don't want to let go of that because, if I do, I'll be admitting to myself that I gave everything I had to someone who doesn't care. And that would kill me.

I decide the best thing for now is to leave it where it is. I exit out of the text box, open my settings, and put my phone on airplane mode, just as he did with his. I'll deal with it when I absolutely have to. Tonight, I just want to forget about it. I put my phone aside and lie in bed, just staring up at the ceiling, waiting patiently for the crashing waves of sleep to eventually engulf me for the rest of the night.

The fuck?

Erik's not answering. It's been like an hour since I texted him. What could he be doing that's keeping him so busy on a Monday night? Homework? If he is doing homework, can't that wait? I mean, we've got a lot to talk about. I need to make sure that we're okay and that things don't get awkward between us. I also need to make sure that he understands that what we did last night was… I don't want to call it a mistake, but it doesn't mean that I have feelings for him. Not romantically.

Don't get me wrong, I care about Erik deeply, but last night was just sex. It was us riding a high and trying something new. It wasn't a declaration of love or

320

anything like that. In fact, I don't know what it was, because I'm not even gay. At least, I don't think I am.

I spent most of the day mulling it over. I asked myself all the questions a straight person might ask a gay person: Have you been attracted to anyone of the same sex before? No, not that I can recall. Do you still like the opposite sex? Yeah, I think so. Is there a difference between kissing a guy versus kissing a girl? Physically, no. But if I had to pick between two people — say between Brenda and Erik — honestly, as suspect as it might sound, I'd pick Erik every time. His mouth is more receptive. His form is less aggressive. He just seems to enjoy kissing me more and that makes me want to kiss him more. If making out with Erik is a dance, then I'd liken making out with Brenda to a championship wrestling match. Both are awesome in their own right, but so far, I've never ended a make out session with Erik feeling battered and bruised, but I digress. Kissing really has nothing to do with their genders. All of my self-reflection came down to one major question. The question that I'm sure all gay people have been asked at least once in their life: How do you know that you're gay? My answer is… I don't.

I like girls, but I went and had sex with Erik, and I liked it. I like girls, but I got it up for Erik when I couldn't get it up for Brenda. I like girls, but the one person on my mind right now is Erik. I could understand it if I found other guys sexually attractive, but I don't. Or at least, I don't think I do. So far, it's just Erik. But Erik's not answering me right now. I keep trying to call him, but it keeps going straight to voicemail. I don't even think his phone is on. Why isn't his phone on? Is he avoiding me? I mean, he did say he wasn't allowed to like boys. Maybe us having sex freaked him out. I don't know… I guess I'll just talk to him tomorrow. If he is avoiding me because of religion or whatever, there's no way for him to keep avoiding me when I'm standing right in front of him.

Tuesday. November 5th.

I wake up feeling really anxious. I don't know what I'm gonna say to Erik. I don't know what I want to say to him. All I know is that I wanna know that we're okay, and that he hasn't gotten the wrong impression. We're friends. We are just friends. Nothing more and nothing less. I shower, get dressed, and scarf down two bowls of cereal and a banana before driving to school.

The walk to Erik's locker from the parking lot feels way longer than it ever did before. I can feel the nerves building up inside me. My anxiety is building, boiling over like a hot soup. My hands shake and my breathing shortens. I don't think I've ever felt this nervous about anything. Even my visit with my dad didn't make me *this* nervous. I don't know why I'm freaking out. It's just Erik. There's nothing scary about sweet little

Erik, right? I have to remind myself of that as I enter the main campus building. It's just Erik. It's just Erik. There's nothing to be worried about. But then, as I'm approaching Erik's locker, I see he's not there and I breathe a momentary sigh of relief. Mackenzie's not here either though. Huh, I wonder where they could be? I pull out my phone and shoot them both a text.

"Hey, where you at?" I send to both of them in a group text. If Erik doesn't respond, Mackenzie will for sure. A minute or two pass and nothing. No response. I plop myself down, my back against the lockers, and stare at my phone. I keep scrolling to refresh the text box, hoping a new message will load, but nothing ever comes. I'm sitting here in the middle of the hallway looking like a complete loner. What gives? Did I really mess up that bad? Did losing myself and having sex with Erik scare him away and, in turn, drive Mackenzie away with him? Did I just lose my only two friends because I couldn't keep my dick in my pants? No. They wouldn't ditch me like that. Would they?

The first bell rings and I still haven't gotten a response from either Mackenzie or Erik. I wanna cry, but I refuse to break down at school, so I put on my angry face to fight back the tears and head over to first period.

When I get to Ms. Maple's class, I see Erik sitting alone in the corner. He looks up at me with wide eyes, like he didn't expect for me to show. I want to be upset, but funny enough, seeing him in front of me makes me feel… I dunno, good? I hadn't realized how much I was missing him even after only a day. I forget everything that I want to talk to him about. I just want to be near him. So I force myself to give him at least a half-smile before I walk over to take the seat next to him.

"Hey," I say. God, I'm so nervous I feel like I sound like a total scrub.

"Hi," Erik says back. His voice is soft and timid. I sense he's as nervous as I am. I want to say more. I want to talk to him, but before I can, Tim Martinelli takes the empty seat in front of him, which is odd since Tim is one of those nerdy kids who likes to sit right up front with the teacher.

"Hey, Erik," Tim says. "I was told to give this to you." Tim pulls out a folded sheet of paper and offers it to Erik. Erik takes it, unfolds it, and reads. The expression on his face drops, and he immediately crumples up the sheet of paper, leaving it on the corner of his desk.

"What is it?" I ask, swiping the crumpled paper away before Erik can stop me.

"Nicholas, no," he pleads, but I'm ignoring him. What's on this paper that's got him looking so upset? I have to know and when I do, I almost wish I didn't. The paper reads:

Stupid faggot. Kill yourself.

It's scribbled in permanent marker and in handwriting so scratchy it could pass for a joke font. I hate to be sexist, but it seems obvious to me that it was written by a dude. But who would hate Erik that much to send Tim to deliver him this note?

"Tim, who gave this to you?" I demand.

"I'm not supposed to say," he tells me.

"Tim, I'm not playing. Who gave this to you?" I'm fighting the urge not to punch him in his buck toothed, pimpled face. He better freakin' tell me.

"I can't say. They threatened to beat me up."

"TIM, IF YOU DON'T FUCKING TELL—"

"Nicholas!" Erik scolds in a harsh whisper.

"What is going on back there?!" I hear Ms. Maple shout. The whole class is staring at me. I've clearly made a big scene of myself.

"Nothing. Sorry," I say. Ms. Maple eyes me like I'm about to be a problem child before she goes about starting her lesson plan for the day. I crumple the paper back up and squeeze it hard. I'm so pissed off someone would dare send this to Erik, I can feel myself shaking in my anger. Suddenly, my phone vibrates in my pocket and I double check to see that Ms. Maple isn't looking so I can pull it out. I've got a text from Erik.

"Chill. Pretty sure I know who did it," Erik's message reads.

"Who?" I type and send my reply.

"Andrew," Erik texts back. I almost don't believe him. Andrew has been a non-factor for a while now. I haven't seen or heard anything from or about him since I told him to just leave us alone and now, suddenly, he's back in the picture? What? I look over at Erik to see if I can get anything from his expression, but he looks as serious as he did when he read the note. He's fully convinced it was from Andrew. Well, shit. It looks like I might have my work cut out for me.

"Nicholas, where are you going?" Erik asks, struggling to keep up with me. As soon as first period let out, I bolted from class and started out of the English building. I don't have any classes with that butt chinned asshole, but I'm pretty sure he and I cross paths between classes at some point. Where is he? "Nicholas, this is totally not the right way to our second period."

"Erik, do you happen to know what Andrew's second class is?"

"Why would I know that?"

"Come on, you guys have class together. You were lab partners. He never mentioned his schedule to you at all?"

"He did but…"

"But?"

"You're acting weird. I'm afraid to tell you," Erik explains.

"Erik, come on, I'm trying to be a good friend here," I say, as delicately as I possibly can. I can't make it obvious that I want to kick Andrew's ass. Erik would never allow that, so I've got no choice but to bullshit him. "Just tell me where his next class is. I promise, I just want to talk to him." Erik stares at me. He doesn't look one hundred percent convinced, so I pull out all the stops and hit him with one of my sad pouty faces. It does the trick.

"I'm pretty sure he has Algebra II," Erik mumbles sadly in surrender. I flash Erik a satisfied smirk and head over to the main campus building, where all the Math classes are held. Erik follows me, reluctantly. He doesn't have to come with me, but I'm glad he does so I can show him I got his back, and that I'm looking out for him. Erik, though not entirely a push over, is a little meek. He'll speak up for himself, sure, but he's the type that people don't often take very seriously. The quintessential target for a basic ass bully. I suspect that's one of the reasons he hangs out with Mackenzie. He can rely on her to stand up for him, and I want him to know that he can rely on me too.

We get to the main campus building and I spot Andrew walking halfway down the hall, flanked on either side by the two neanderthal looking goons I had a run in with on my first day. Oh, this is gonna be fun… I'm not looking forward to getting jumped, but I ain't no bitch. I sigh, then walk over to them, picking up my stride as I approach.

"Yo, Andrew!" I yell, gaining on him. He turns to me, and I immediately grab him by the shirt collar and forcefully pin him against the lockers.

"What the hell, man?" Andrew yells. I pull out the note that Erik got from Tim in first period and hold it up to his face.

"Did you write this?" I demand.

"I don't even know what that is."

"'Stupid faggot. Kill yourself.' Did you write this?" Andrew stares at me silently. I don't doubt that he's the kind of guy who rarely gets confronted, because he doesn't seem to know how to react. I can't tell if he's scared or what, but either way I don't give a fuck. He had it coming. "Look me in the eye and tell me you didn't write this," I demand again. Andrew stays quiet, but the look in his eyes is that of a guy who has just been caught. It's pretty obvious to me that Erik was right. Andrew was behind the note. His lack of an answer is answer enough. "I thought so. Stay the fuck away from my friend." With that, I let Andrew go, despite the fact that I *really* want to beat his ass right now. I turn around to see his two neanderthal looking friends staring at me, puffing out their chests like they wanna do something. I feign a lunge toward them, and they back up. Couple of scared ass bitches...

"Faggot!" I hear one of them yell as I start to walk away.

"Yo, come say that to my face!" I yell back, turning to face them.

"Guys, quit," Andrew says to his lackeys before they can hurl any more insults.

"You just gonna let him punk you like that, Drew?" they reply.

"I'm not gonna fuckin' fight him, bro. Just let it go." Andrew then walks away from his two dumbass friends, surprisingly. I was bracing myself for a three-on-one brawl, which truth be told, I'd probably get my ass beat. It's not exactly a fair fight, you know? At least one of them has some sense, thankfully. I head over to Erik who's wearing a kind of concerned look. "You okay?" I say, checking in. He nods.

"I'm fine," Erik says. "It's just... that whole thing kinda scared me."

"Oh, I didn't mean to scare you. I'm sorry."

"It's okay. I just never knew you could get like that. It's surprising is all." Huh... I was so gung-ho about standing up for Erik, it didn't even occur to me that he would react to it with fear. I might've just shot myself in the foot here. The last thing I want is for Erik to be scared of me. I gotta make it up to him somehow.

"Hey, do you wanna say fuck it to the rest of the school day?" I ask, trying to sound as gentle and harmless as a puppy. "I wanna hang out with you." Erik considers for a moment. Say yes, Erik. Just say yes.

"Okay," he says, with a slight smile. I'm suddenly feeling really good about everything again. Because I take it as if he's saying we're okay. And so is our friendship.

I decide to take us out for some frozen yogurt. The satisfaction I got from thinking Erik and I were okay has now dissipated. You see, it's one thing to say or — in this case — imply that things are okay, but it's another thing to act like it. Erik isn't saying much during the drive over. I want to talk to him, but I don't know what to say. It's turning out to be just what I was afraid of. I was scared of things getting awkward between us, and now that's exactly how things are. We sit in silence for most of the drive. I don't even put on the radio. Music feels inappropriate right now. I don't think I'd enjoy it anyway, so what would be the point?

"So… Andrew's a dick, huh?" I offer, making a sad attempt at small talk. It's not good small talk, but it's talk.

"Yeah," Erik mutters back. We go silent again. I let a few minutes pass before I make another attempt.

"Hey, so how'd you know it was Andrew that sent the note?"

"He overheard me and Mackenzie talking, and he didn't like it. He sorta threatened me about it."

"He threatened you?" Andrew is quickly climbing higher and higher on my shit list. And just as I was thinking I should probably give him a little bit of credit for walking away.

"Well, not exactly, but it sounded like he was."

"What were you and Mackenzie talking about?" Erik goes silent again. "Erik," I say insistently. He turns away from me and looks out the passenger window. "Erik, come on. Tell me… please?" Erik doesn't budge. He just keeps staring out the window. I'm thinking, there's no way he's gonna tell me. He won't even look at me. But to my surprise, he does.

"You," he mumbles, still refusing to turn to me. "You and me." He raises his hand to his face to wipe his eyes. I can't see for sure, but I think he might be crying. I don't say anymore. It's probably best to back off for now.

We pull into the parking lot of the Frozen Yogurt place. I turn off the car's ignition and lay my head back against the headrest. I notice Erik reaching for his door handle, but I'm not ready to go in yet. There's too much left unsaid between us that I doubt either of us will enjoy our frozen yogurt unless we deal with it.

"Wait," I say. Erik stops and finally looks over at me. His eyes are red, and he looks so incredibly sad. It's killing me to see him like this. "I think we should talk." He bites his lower lip, like he's trying to keep himself from crying, and the sight of it is breaking my heart. I wanted to protect him. I wanted to stand up for him, but it looks like I'm the reason he's so upset. There's so much I need to discuss with him, like: What are we doing? What does he want out of this? And will we be okay if it turns out that I can't give him what he wants? All of these questions are racing through my mind. Say something, Nick. Say something, anything. But I don't. Instead, I find myself lunging toward him and pressing my lips onto his. My heart is racing like a mile a minute. My tongue slips into his mouth, his tongue slips into mine, and our dance begins. And I can't do a thing to stop it. And frankly, I don't want to.

"Do you really want yogurt?" I breathe. The question sounds super random, but we did come all this way. Erik shakes his head. His eyes are locked into mine, and he's wearing a really dreamy expression. "Do you wanna go somewhere more private?" Erik nods. I kiss him again before turning the key to the ignition. I'm breathing hard, and so is he. When I glance over, he looks like he might be a little bit in shock, like he can't believe this is happening. *I* can't believe this is happening. I can't believe I'm doing this, but here we are. I reach over and take his hand, lacing our fingers together so they're completely intertwined. His palm is soft and warm. He squeezes his grip, as if to make sure this is real. Yes, Erik, it is real.

I drive us through neighborhoods I'm not familiar with at all, keeping my eyes peeled for anywhere that looks like it might be secluded enough for us to do whatever we're gonna do. I would drive us back to my uncle's, but I don't want my mom to catch me skipping school. Erik's house is also off limits since his mom's work schedule is totally unpredictable. Scouting the neighborhoods seems to be our only option.

We drive for what feels like forever. Everything always takes forever when you're anxiously waiting on something. Eventually, we find this park, nestled behind a small apartment complex. It's not exactly out of the way, but there are only a couple of other cars here and the lot is pretty big, so we can park far enough away from them that they won't be able to see into ours. I park us under a tree, as far away from the actual park as I can, then I get out and climb into the back seat. Erik does the same. We're sitting here, staring at one another. Erik looks about as uncertain as I feel. Are we really gonna do this again?

Yeah.

Yeah, we are.

My lips are on his before I even have a moment to second guess it. I rip off his sweater. He gently takes off mine. I then pull him onto my lap, never once letting our mouths separate. I slide my hands into the back of his khakis and give him a light squeeze. He smiles and I can't help but smile back. I'm hard as a rock now. I didn't realize how much I wanted this until it started happening. Erik. Sweet, little Erik.

"Do you have protection?" he asks, and my heart just about stops. I don't… Shit! I didn't think to bring some. Why would I? I didn't foresee this happening again.

"Uhh…" is all I can manage to say.

"Should we go get some?"

"Uh huh…" I nod. I can't even speak. I'm so mad at myself for being completely unprepared for this situation. Still, I want this to happen. My body wants this to happen. Every bit of me wants this to happen. Without getting out of the car, I climb into the driver's seat and start the car up once again. My whole body is shaking with anticipation. How long am I gonna have to wait?

"I think there's a gas station not far from here," Erik offers as I'm pulling out of the parking lot. He gives me directions and I'm driving like a freakin' maniac, just trying to keep my libido at bay. "Slow down, Nicholas."

"Sorry."

The drive to the gas station is less than five minutes. I pull into an empty spot in front of the gas station shop and let myself out of the car.

"Stay here, I'll be right back," I tell Erik. I think it would be a bit awkward for two boys to walk up to a counter asking for condoms. I don't think that's something that Erik would be up for, and he doesn't fight me about it.

I walk into the gas station shop and take a quick look around. I can't seem to find them in any of the aisles. I'm about to give up when I spot them hanging behind the cashier. Shit...

I've never had to buy condoms before. I don't know if I need to be of a certain age or what. My whole stash came from free clinics, so this is something entirely new for me. I take a deep breath. I figure as long as I look like I know what I'm doing, then the cashier won't question a thing. I walk up to the counter and pretend to look around, all discreet like. I even grab a candy bar, thinking it might make things a little less awkward. You know, like, "I'll take this candy bar... oh, and five of those Ribbed For Her Pleasures."

"That all for you?" The cashier asks. He doesn't look much older than me, but the bored expression on his face reads like he's already ready for life to be over.

"Yeah," I answer. "Oh, and can I get a couple of those Ribbed For Her Pleasures?" The cashier stares at me unflinching.

"How many you want?"

"Umm… I dunno. Five?" I shrug. Is five too much? Maybe five's too much. Eh, whatever. The cashier turns, grabs what I ask for, and shoves it all into a little brown paper bag. I pay him with some of the cash I got from Tio on my birthday and leave the store, all cool and smooth like. Deep down, I'm freaking out. I can't believe I just bought condoms for the first time, and I'm actually about to use them. I hop into my car, toss Erik the candy bar, and speed back to the park.

I don't know how much longer I can wait. As soon as we're back in the spot under the tree, I climb into the back seat, unzip my jeans, and pull Erik into a fierce kiss. His hands are all over me, and I'm loving every second of it. I slide off his khakis, pull him onto my lap, and wrap myself up. It takes a little while for him to accept me, but when he finally does… God, how could I possibly go on without this? Erik, sweet, little Erik. He has no idea how much power he holds over me right now.

I lasted a little longer this time — you know, counting from the moment I was fully inside — and I'm feeling really good about myself because I got him to finish before me. I don't know how I did it, but I did, and I'm claiming that as my own personal victory. We're sitting in the backseat, trying to catch our breath. I hand Erik my shirt to wipe himself off. My tank and sweater will do fine for the rest of the day. He looks tired. I must've really done a number on him. I know he did one on me. I'm watching him, Erik — this strange and curious creature that has me doing all sorts of out of character things — and I can't figure it out. What is it about him that has me losing all sense of myself?

As I'm watching Erik, I notice his eyes are glistening. He's got tears pooling in them. He tries to wipe them with the back of his hand, but it's too late, I've already seen.

"Hey," I say gently as I lean in. "What's wrong?" He smiles a weak smile that I wouldn't buy for even a penny.

"Nothing," he shakes his head.

"Erik." He wants to tell me, I can see it, but he's hesitating.

"Really, it's nothing. I'm just feeling... I dunno, loose?" I can't help but chuckle. He really just said that.

"You're funny."

"Oh, geez, I just realized how that sounded," he says, and we're both cracking up over the stupid innuendo. I'm pretty sure what he meant to say was that he was feeling easy. That's the last thing I want to make him feel, but I don't know how I wanna go about tackling the subject. I mean, should I apologize? Should I suggest we not do this again? Because, if I'm being honest, I fail to see how stopping this would be beneficial for either of us. I know he wants me, and for more than just sex, but I also know that I don't know if I can give him more than that. Not yet. I need time to really figure this out. Could I be with Erik? Am I even gay? How do I define myself given the circumstance? If I keep exploring this, maybe it'll all become clear. I can give Erik as much of myself as I'm able — that's the win for him — while I continue to explore my own sexuality in the process — that's the win for me. If I just keep letting this happen, there's no way for either of us to outright lose, you know? We both win… sort of.

Maybe?

I hope.

"Hey, you wanna go get some food?" I ask, trying to lighten the mood. He nods, and I steal one more kiss from him before climbing into the front seat. "Consider me your chauffeur for the day, good sir." Erik laughs. This is good. He's happy now. That's all I want for him. "Where do you wanna go? My treat."

"I dunno. Wherever," Erik shrugs.

"How about we head to the good mall? If I'm not mistaken, I thought I saw they were opening a new crepe place when we were last there," I suggest. I see Erik nod in the rearview. I also see that he's holding the candy bar I bought him when I picked up the condoms. "Give me that candy bar, you'll ruin your appetite." Erik rolls his eyes before handing it over. I take it, tear the wrapper open with my teeth, and take a bite.

"Hey!" Erik whines.

"What? I said you'll ruin *your* appetite. I didn't say anything about mine." I hear Erik gasp and chuckle in the backseat. Then, as I'm pulling out of the parking lot, I feel something touch me. It's Erik, resting his chin on my shoulder. I smile to myself and give him a quick peck on the cheek. I don't know how I feel when it comes to the subject of my sexuality, but at this moment, maybe, just maybe, I could get used to this.

chapter twenty-one

erik

I'm resting my head on Nicholas' shoulder.

I love the way he smells right now. It's the familiar scent of ocean breeze, mixed with the heavy aroma of his sweat, and just a little bit of me sprinkled in. It's hard to believe we had sex again. After all that worrying about us not being okay, we did it *again*. Admittedly, it hurt a bit more this time around — we didn't have that sexy time liquid-y goo to make things slipperier — but just being with Nicholas was more than enough to make up for it.

I'm having a hard time accepting this is real. I'm inhaling his scent so that I can store it away among my favorite memories, the way someone might store away the smell of their mother's cooking. If there was any doubt before that I might be in love with this guy, I don't think there's any doubt now. But as much as I want to enjoy the moment and not think about anything, I can't. There's this looming feeling that this might not last very much longer. That Nicholas might come to his senses and realize that what he's doing is *not* what he wants to be doing. We haven't even discussed it yet, so there's nothing that I can be sure of. On top of that, I feel really guilty. Dirty even. On so many levels, it feels wrong to be doing this, like I'm defying the word of God. I don't know. I don't wanna think about it right now. There's no point in thinking about it now. It'll only put a downer on the rest of the day, and it's barely even noon.

When we get to the mall, Nicholas insists he saw a crepe place opening up, but I don't recall seeing anything like that. Then again, I'm finding that when I'm around him, I'm not entirely aware of my surroundings. He tends to take up a lot of my attention. He doesn't mean to, but it's hard for me not to be enamored by him.

"I'm pretty sure the crepe place is on this side of the mall. You don't remember, do you?" Nicholas asks.

"Honestly, I didn't even know they were opening up a crepe place," I reply.

"Oh? Were you too busy staring at me the last time we were here?" He turns to flash me that signature smile of his before climbing out of the driver's seat.

"No," I blush. I'm such a bold-faced liar, it's no wonder I feel so guilty. I'll be punished for this too. I climb out of the backseat and Nicholas comes around the car to meet me. He grabs me by the hand, lacing our fingers together like he did outside the yogurt place, and it freaks me out a little bit. My eyes dart around to see if anyone's looking. "Nicholas, what are you doing?"

"I'm holding your hand, what does it look like?" He says this so cool and casually, as if this is a normal and acceptable way for gay people to behave… and maybe it is. Straight people do this all the time, right? But then again, straight people don't get ridiculed, and bullied, and damned into the fires of Hell for being straight so… maybe that's the difference.

"People will see," I warn him.

"So? Let them. Who cares?"

"I care." I let myself loose from his grip. I regret letting go of him, but I don't think I'm ready to handle being so out in the open about being gay, which I know sounds funny, considering I smell of sex. "I'm just not comfortable yet."

"Okay," Nicholas responds. He seems almost disappointed. He shoves his hands into his pockets and gives me a closed mouth half-smile, the kind you give to someone when you feel things have taken a turn for the awkward. I wonder what he's thinking. Why does he want to hold my hand? And in public. We're not even in a relationship.

. . .

Wait. Are we?

If we are in a relationship, maybe I *should* hold his hand. It's too late now though, he's already walking towards the mall entrance. I simply let out a sigh, then follow.

Nicholas and I are walking up towards a mall directory when I hear my phone start to ring. I pull it out and my heart drops. It's Mackenzie. Oh, no, I never texted her that I went off campus, and it's about time for our lunch period. I'm suddenly in a panic, and it shows.

"Hey, what's up?" Nicholas asks, raising one of his perfectly shaped eyebrows.

"It's Mackenzie," I say. "You didn't tell her that we left campus, did you?"

"No, should I have?"

"Oh, no, she's gonna be mad. What do I do?"

"Answer it." I tap the answer button on my phone and brace myself for what could be Hurricane Mackenzie. Since we really only hang out with each other, she doesn't like it when I leave her out of the loop on anything. This could be bad.

"Hey, where you at?" Mackenzie's voice comes through to my ear. As soon as I hear her, I hold my phone as far away as my arm will stretch and cover the speaker with my other hand.

"She's asking where we are," I say in hushed tones to Nicholas. He just smirks in amusement. This really isn't funny.

"Here, lemme talk to her," he offers, taking my phone and bringing it to his ear. "Hey, Mackenzie, what up?" Nicholas sounds so straight, and it's weird to hear him talk like this. I mean, I've heard him talk like this before, but not after being intimate with him. How does he do it? And so convincingly. "We went off campus… Sorry, it was sort of a last minute thing. We left right after first period. Andrew was being a dick, so I thought I'd cheer him up… He sent Erik a really fucked up note. It's cool though, I dealt with it… Anyway, you're cool that I took Erik out, right? He thought you might be mad… We just drove around…" I notice he leaves out the part about us having sex again. I'm not sure if it occurred to him that I told Mackenzie and that she already knows we've done it before. But then again, I don't know if that would change anything. I mean, he seems so un-burdened by this whole thing. "Actually, we're about to pick up lunch. I'm taking Erik to try out this new crepe place at the mall." Wait. What did he just say? Did he just tell her… ugh! I smack my face with my hand. Nicholas looks at me all confused, not realizing what he just said and how pissed Mackenzie's gonna be because of it. "Hey, we're gonna go. Talk later?" Nicholas hands back my phone and in return, I give him my deadliest of Filipino death stares.

"Why would you tell her that?" I scold. "You know how she feels about crepes!"

"I'm sorry, I forgot," Nicholas shrugs innocently. "No offense, but Mackenzie isn't exactly in the front of my mind right now." I narrow my eyes. He then leans in and taps me lightly on the nose. "Boop."

Ugh! It's not fair. I want to be mad at him, but it's really hard to be when he's being so cute. And the whole undershirt and sweater look he's got going on right now isn't making it any easier on me. God, why can't he just zip that thing up?

We get to the crepe place, which is nestled right in the center of the food court. It's one of those vendors that's sorta like a pop-up that you can walk around on all sides. It's cool. You can see everything they're doing, all the ingredients and stuff. The menu though is a little overwhelming.

"What should we get?" I ask Nicholas as we queue up in line.

"Whatever you want," he answers with his signature crooked smile. God, I love it so much! We end up ordering three crepes to share: one spinach and goat cheese, one ham and cheddar, and one peanut butter and chocolate with banana slices. Nicholas leads us to a table in the corner and we sit down to eat. He starts to dig into the spinach and goat cheese before I'm even settled into my seat. Watching him eat is cute. He enjoys food so much it's a wonder he's able to maintain his washboard abs. Meanwhile, I'm here gaining five pounds from drinking a glass of skim milk. Like, what is that? It's supposed to be skim.

"It's funny," I smile to myself. Nicholas stops. He looks up at me, and his cheeks are so full of crepes that he looks like a hamster. "You were so against crepes when we went to the city. What changed?"

"I think a lot has changed," he answers, after swallowing the bites in his mouth. I stare at him for a moment. This seems like the perfect time to figure things out between us. I want to define this. I don't want our relationship to become this thing where we don't acknowledge having given ourselves to one another. I don't want to tiptoe around that fact like we're afraid of setting off a landmine, because I have a strong feeling that today won't be the last time — I don't want it to be — but I don't want to feel like a slut every time it happens. It's just not me. It's not who I am. At least, I don't think it is.

"You look like you want to say something," Nicholas says. And he's right, I *do* want to say something. I just don't know what. He looks down at my hand resting on the table. Then he looks up at me, and I see a vulnerability in his eyes that makes me think he wants me to see into his soul. And it's the most beautiful thing I've ever seen. "Can I ask you a favor?" he asks softly, almost at a whisper. I raise my brow in curiosity. "Can I hold your hand?" It surprises me. That's what he wants? Why? Why is he so fixated on holding my hand? What does he get out of it?

"Okay," I answer reluctantly. I'm increasingly more aware of my surroundings now. I think it's because I know what I've done, so the paranoid part of me thinks that the world knows too. There's not a lot of people here, but there *are* people. I even notice a few of them giving us suspicious glances from time to time. I don't know if it's because it's clear that Nicholas and I are skipping school, or if it's the fact that we're two boys sharing crepes — which sounds gay enough on its own — but I notice people looking. And if they aren't, I'm convinced they are.

Nicholas reaches over and grabs my hand. I'm nervous now. I feel like a spotlight has been put on us. My heart is racing in my discomfort.

"Hmm. I like this," Nicholas mumbles, smiling to himself. His eyes lock into mine, and suddenly everything around me seems to fade. His eyes are the only thing I can focus on. They're like two copper moons, shining out at me through his perpetual pensive squint. It's a look that unbuckles me from all my restraints and relieves me from my sense of fear. I see Nicholas leaning forward, almost in slow motion, and I suddenly feel like I'm losing my breath. He kisses me softly on the mouth, as if to breathe life back into me. He makes no movements. He doesn't slip in any tongue. This one, he keeps plain and simple. It's a definite assurance: I'm in love with Nicholas.

"Hey," a woman's voice cuts through, abruptly ending the moment. I'm immediately brought back to reality. Nicholas and I look over to see a woman staring at us at a nearby table. She wasn't there when we sat down, I don't think. She must've arrived when Nicholas and I were transfixed on each other. She's got a baby on her lap and a small boy — I assume her son — sitting in the seat next to her. I'm expecting her to say something rude and I squeeze Nicholas' hand, thinking I might be forced to hold his temper back if she does. But she doesn't.

"You two are cute together," the woman says with a smile. Nicholas and I look at each other and laugh. It's a huge relief, really, though I'll admit it *does* feel a little bit awkward receiving a compliment like that. I mean,

we're not together, so… yeah, awkward. But you know…
it's awkward in a good way.

nicholas

I'm feeling really lethargic. I'm sitting in third period Algebra II, losing myself in a daydream, completely ignoring whatever the hell our teacher's talking about. The day is dragging on, and on, and on. We've got a week and a half left of school before Thanksgiving break, which is annoying because they're making us come to school next Monday and Tuesday. It's really dumb. Like, why not just give us the whole week off? Once I realized how close we were getting to the holidays, I sorta mentally checked out. I've got a lot on my mind.

This is the first year that I'll experience Thanksgiving, Christmas, New Year's without my dad in the picture and it's actually pretty depressing. Don't get me wrong, I'm still mad at him, but he *is* my dad. It's weird, every now and then I think about calling him and possibly forgiving him — or at the very least, giving him a chance to explain his side or whatever — but whenever the thought comes up, I just want to punch him in the face.

"Hey, you okay?" I hear Erik say. His voice brings me back to reality.

"Yeah, I'm just spacing out," I explain.

"Talk about it at lunch?"

I nod.

Erik and I have been hanging out a lot lately. He and Mackenzie aren't exactly on good terms at the moment so it's just been the two of us for the most part. Neither of us hang with anyone else. I feel kinda guilty that he and Mackenzie are on the outs because I know I'm partly responsible. You see, the day after Erik and I went to get crepes, I went over to Erik's locker to meet him and Mackenzie for lunch. Erik was apologizing repeatedly for getting crepes without her. Mackenzie shrugged it off like it was no big deal, but it clearly was. She kept making these snide comments about how Erik and I are gonna ditch her now that we're having sex, which I know she might've meant as a joke, but it's really none of her business. I tried to let her comments slide, but Mackenzie was relentless. The comments kept coming for a couple of days after and, eventually, I couldn't keep ignoring it. I got so annoyed, I straight up yelled at her when she brought up the crepe thing for what felt like the thousandth time.

"They're just flat pancakes! Get over it!" I told her in my sharpest tone. She just stared at me with narrowed eyes, as if I had no right to speak to her like that. Erik got really upset with me about it, claiming that that's just how Mackenzie is and that we just need to laugh it off. But sometimes, you gotta teach people how to treat you, and she was being a bitch. It's not my fault she has this unhealthy obsession with crepes, but she can't ban us from going to get them when she's not around. That's stupid. I dunno. Maybe I just don't know how to have friends, but to me, that's stupid. Anyway, I had to convince Erik to let me drive him home that day, so I could make it up to him. We ended up going back to my place and having sex. Third time's a charm.

I really like spending time with Erik. And not just because of the sex, as satisfying as it may be. I like spending time with him because, despite our intimate encounters, we're friends first. Actually, that's why I've been so fixated on wanting to hold his hand, and cuddle, and do all the things that I would normally do with a girl. I want to see if I could be with him the way I would be with a girl, and I had hoped that the answer would've become clear on its own. But it hasn't. After two weeks of hugging, kissing, holding hands, and sex stuff, I don't feel any more gay than I did the first time we did anything like that. I don't know if the answer will ever become clear, but I'm hoping that it does because life would be far less confusing with definite answers. I guess that's why people insist on putting labels on everything.

Erik and I meet up at his locker at lunch and we head over to the cafeteria to pick up some food. We don't wait up for Mackenzie. She's been avoiding us ever since I yelled at her and yeah, I feel bad, but if that's how she's gonna be, let her be. Erik leads me around the outside of the football field and behind the bleachers. Apparently, this is where he and Mackenzie would go to have private chats, and low and behold, here she is sitting against one of the support beams, reading a cheesy romance novel and smoking a joint. The smell makes my eye twitch. There aren't a lot of things that my mom forbids me to do, but pot is one of them. Not because she wants me to "Say no to drugs" or anything, but because she finds the smell disgusting. Plus, it gets all in your clothes and shit.

"Oh, God, you're here?" Mackenzie says as we approach.

"Since when do you take pot?" Erik asks, genuinely surprised.

"Since the eighth grade. Just never around you. I know how you are. And we've been over this. You don't 'take pot,' Erik."

"Oh… well, are we still fighting?"

"*We're* not. Me and your boyfriend are though," Mackenzie explains to Erik as she casts daggers at me with her side glance. "Call me when you get your dog on a leash." She drops the joint and steps on it before sauntering off.

"What a bitch," I murmur under my breath.

"I wish you'd stop fighting with her," Erik says.

"She's the one being a bitch!" To me it seems like Erik's taking her side, which really pisses me off. I'm not the one who's wrong here. I want to say more about it and defend myself, but I know I can't without upsetting Erik, so I drop it. "So, how's your class with Andrew been? Is it still super awkward?"

"Yeah," Erik sighs. "He refuses to speak to me. Doesn't even acknowledge my existence, which is fine. I don't care. It's just inconvenient when we have to do class work together."

Apparently, Andrew was pretty raw about me confronting him over the note he sent to Erik. The day after, when Erik showed up to class, Andrew was all, "Nice sickin' your boyfriend on me. You should learn to fight your own battles," to which Erik responded, "And you should probably stop sending anonymous notes to people telling them to kill themselves." It was nice to hear Erik standing up for himself. Of course, Andrew denied it.

"You can't prove that I sent it," he told Erik.

"Can you prove that you didn't?" Erik asked, and he didn't have a thing to say. It's funny how silence can speak volumes. Anyway, I've just been making sure to check in on the situation from time to time, because I don't like it when a bigger dude like Andrew messes with a smaller kid like Erik. If we ever had to scrap one-on-one, no doubt, I'd wipe the floor with him. And I'm not saying that just to be cocky either. Based on our last encounter, the guy's all for show. He may be built, but he's a passive aggressive bitch. Plus, Erik's my buddy. I *gotta* stand up for him.

"I'm hoping I won't have to deal with him for much longer though," Erik says. "We should be due for a new seating arrangement soon. There are only so many times you can pair the same people together." I nod in agreement as I start to unwrap one of my cafeteria burgers. Erik pops a potato chip into his mouth. "So what were you spacing out about in third? Your dad again?"

"Is it that obvious?" I ask.

"Well, that's all you've been talking about the last couple days. I'd be surprised if it were anything else."

"I'm sorry. You're probably tired of hearing about it." Erik shrugs and pops another chip into his mouth.

"I don't mind. I like listening. Except you do repeat yourself a lot."

"Yeah… I do that sometimes when I can't get over something." I'm feeling pretty guilty right now. At this point, Erik must've heard me talk about the same thing at least a hundred times already. He's been helping me through my issues with my dad since all these feelings came up. I've talked his ear off so much about it, he probably has my every thought memorized when it comes to the subject. Despite this, Erik's never once asked me to stop talking about it, and he's never made it seem like he was tired of hearing it, even though I know he is. He *has* to be.

"You're just trying to be heard," Erik offers, crunching on his chips. "I figure that's why you repeat yourself so much."

"Probably," I agree, taking a bite from my burger. It's an interesting take. I never thought about it that way before.

"That, or you're just really narcissistic."

"Me? Narcissistic? Never." Erik smiles and shrugs me off. I chuckle, knowing full well I might just be that narcissistic. Erik and I finish our food while we talk about nothing for the rest of the lunch period. When it's time to go, I swoop in on Erik and give him a peck on the lips before we come out from behind the bleachers. He's still not entirely comfortable with PDA at school, and understandably so, especially after getting that note from Andrew. Then, we walk back towards the campus buildings together until we have to go our separate ways.

There's this girl in our third period class, Mariana Ramos. She's a shorty — shorter than Erik — but she's got a lot of curves to her and she's actually super pretty. Despite this, I never paid much attention to her. I always sit next to Erik in all the classes we have together, so I never really took the time to meet or get to know our other classmates. I never felt the need to. I kinda wish I did though, because as I'm taking my usual seat next to Erik in Algebra II, Mariana approaches me. I don't think I've said more than two words or a passing hello to her the whole time I've been in this class, but here she comes.

"Hey, Nick," Mariana greets me.

"Hey, Mariana," I say. "What's up?"

"I was wondering if you're any good at Math?"

"I'm okay."

"Well, we have that quiz coming up on Monday and I could really use a study buddy. I was wondering if you'd want to, maybe, help me study for it?" She says this with a coy smile, and I'm not really thinking very much about it. She needs help studying, I don't have a reason to decline.

"Sure," I shrug, offering her a genuine smile.

"Great," she replies. "Let me give you my number and you can text me." She pulls out a permanent marker from her bag and proceeds to write her digits on my hand. "Maybe we can meet up tomorrow night?"

"Yeah, tomorrow works." Mariana smiles and tucks a loose curl behind her ear. She then walks over to sit down with her friends a few rows in front of us. As she's walking away, my eyes drift down her butt and I can't help but get a little excited. I think I just got a date.

"Nicholas," I hear Erik say beside me. I turn to him, and he's got this funny sort of expression on his face, like he's confused, but hurt, yet also angry. "I thought we were going to the movies tomorrow night?"

"Oh, shit," I say. I completely forgot I had made plans with Erik. We've been hanging out so much, I don't even think about him when it comes to my schedule since we'd always just get together without really planning anything. "I'm sorry. Well, maybe we can push the movie to Saturday?" He looks at me super annoyed, the way Mackenzie might look at me in this situation. Either they've got more in common than I thought, or she's rubbed off on him throughout the years. Regardless, I'm not sure how I can make this better right now. "Look, I just told Mariana I'd help her. I don't want to bail on her."

"You're bailing on me," Erik says, all matter-of-fact like.

"I'm not bailing on you. I'm just trying to make everything work. Besides, you and I hang out all the time. What's one night?"

"It's fine. Whatever." The word "whatever" is probably the worst response you can give to someone. It means that you care about something, but not enough to fight for it. Like the outcome doesn't matter anymore. Hearing Erik say that word to me, in *that* way, pisses me off.

"Don't 'whatever' me, Erik," I say.

"*Whatever*, Nicholas," he responds. And I absolutely hate him for it.

At lunch, I meet up with Mariana. I don't want to be around Erik right now, not when he's being so petty, so I texted Mariana during fourth. She thinks the food in our cafeteria is gross, so I'm driving her over to the nearby coffee shop for a sandwich and one of those blended ice drinks.

"Thanks for driving," Mariana says. "Usually, my friends and I walk, and it takes up the whole lunch period so I'm always late to fifth."

"Oh, yeah?" I say, doing my best to humor her. "That sucks." If I'm being honest, I'm not really interested in what she's talking about. It's all just stuff about how school sucks, social media, and who her friends are dating. My mind is too preoccupied with Erik. I feel bad because I ditched him and I keep thinking, what if he's sitting in the quad or the cafeteria alone, or worse? What if he's hanging out with Mackenzie, and she's poisoning his mind against me?

"You all there, Nick?" Mariana asks.

"Yeah," I say, coming to. I need to stop thinking about Erik. He's being a butt, and I don't like it. It's not fair that he's taking up all this space in my mind when I'm with other people. I need to be present and focused on the person in front of me. Especially when that person is someone like Mariana, who's pretty but in an approachable way, with her curly hair cascading down from her center part, framing her delicate heart shaped face.

"¿De qué estás pensando?" Mariana says.

"Umm… what?" I reply. Her speaking Spanish to me catches me by surprise. By now, everyone's probably learned my last name is Santiago and figured I'm Latino, but it's still weird being spoken to like this by anyone other than my family.

"¿No hablas español?"

"Uhh…." Mariana laughs girlishly.

"I'm sorry. Your name's Santiago. I thought you were Hispanic."

"I am."

"But you don't speak Spanish?"

"Nah. My parents didn't teach me. Pretty sure they wanted to be able to talk shit about me in front of me."

"Sounds about right," Mariana giggles. "Did they claim it was so you didn't get confused learning two languages at once?"

"Yes!" I say excitedly, finally getting into the conversation.

I pull into the drive thru and we place our order. After, Mariana and I talk about everything and nothing at the same time. It's cool and easy. Talking with her is nice. There are no judgements or expectations. We're just two people chatting over ridiculously overpriced paninis and blended iced pumpkin spiced coffee drinks. So what if we're basic?

Friday. November 22nd.

The next morning, I oversleep a little but still manage to get to school on time. I make it to Ms. Maple's class just as the final bell rings and I see Erik sitting there, in our usual spot. I figure he's probably mad at me for ditching him at lunch yesterday and is probably still mad about me rescheduling our plans. I really don't want to deal, but I know that if I don't sit next to him, it's probably gonna turn into a bigger deal than it is. I take a breath and brace myself for impact.

"Hey," Erik says timidly, as I'm taking the seat next to him. I don't say anything. Whatever, Erik, remember? I can be just as petty as him when I want to be. I'm already mentally preparing myself to ignore him for the stretch of our three shared classes when he slides a plastic container onto my desk. I look up at him. "Truce?" he asks. I open the container to find a pile of homemade cookies. They're all sad and misshapen. It looks like a child baked them.

"Did you make these?" I say. It's not really a question, I already know the answer. Erik nods.

"I tried to. I salted them with my tears," he replies. I suddenly burst out laughing. "Salted them with my tears," the fuck? Ha!

"Alright, settle down everyone," Ms. Maple says from the front of the class, eyeing me as she says it.

"Sorry," I reply, trying to gain control of my laughter. When I do, I turn to Erik and whisper, "Thank you."

Second period goes by pretty quick. Our teacher's just as checked out as we are. He simply assigns us a chapter to read then leaves us to our own devices. Erik and I spend much of the period sharing the cookies he made me. Aside from having a hint of salty bitterness to them, they're pretty good. I mean, cookies aren't meant to be salty or bitter, but he tried…

"I think I used too much baking soda," Erik mumbles.

"Nah, these are great," I encourage him. It's the thought that counts.

I like that Erik and I are back to normal. It really sucks when you're fighting with your best friend, even if it is for only a day. I'm so relieved by our reconciliation it doesn't even occur to me that we might run into an issue again in third period until we get there.

Mariana is seated just one row in front of where Erik and I usually sit. She's smiling expectantly, as if she were waiting for me. Erik and I take our usual seats behind her and I can already feel myself starting to tense up.

"Hey, Nick," Mariana greets me. "Do you wanna go to the coffee shop again for lunch today?" I quickly glance over at Erik and he's clearly waiting to hear my response.

"Um, actually my buddy, Erik, and I already made plans," I explain. I'm not an idiot. "Maybe we can go after school?"

"Yeah, I'd love to." Thankfully, Mariana seems satisfied with this. And so does Erik.

The rest of the school day is a boring trudge. It always is on a Friday, but today is especially so since it's the last Friday before Thanksgiving break. Aside from my lunch period with Erik, which Mackenzie surprisingly decides to join us for — I guess she and Erik reconnected when I left with Mariana yesterday — everything is going by so slowly. The boredom of my last two classes is so exhausting I almost forget I'm supposed to meet up with Mariana so we can study after school.

"Where do you wanna meet?" she texts me as my sixth period is about to end.

"Parking lot," I text back.

Mariana and I stop at the coffee shop and queue up at the drive thru. Apparently, a lot of our peers had the same idea, because I see a couple groups of them pass by as they head into the shop. I can only assume that's why the line at the drive thru, which is bleeding out onto the street, is so long. We sit and chat while we wait, and the conversation is as easy as it was the day before. That is until...

"Can I ask you a personal question?" she says.

"Sure," I respond, wondering what's up.

"You and Erik..." Mariana hesitates for a moment, and I'm starting to get a little wary. I have a feeling I know where this is going. "You're not, like, a thing, are you? I mean, you're not into guys, right?" I frown at this. "I'm sorry, you don't have to answer if you don't want to."

"No, I'm not into guys," I say, almost immediately. And it's true. I'm *not* into guys. I'm only into one specific guy. That's not the same thing, I don't think. At least, I don't count it as the same thing.

"Oh, good," she breathes a sigh of relief.

"Why do you ask?"

"Well, you guys are always together, and everyone seems to think that Erik's gay. I mean, I dunno if he is, but I guess I was worried he might be into you. I mean, who wouldn't be? You're gorgeous." Suddenly, it seems like the world stops. What's happening right now?

"Wait, are you into me?" I ask. The words sound almost stupid coming out of my mouth. How could I have missed it? How could I have been so blind?

"Maybe," she smiles coyly. I'm feeling a lot of mixed emotions right now. I should be happy knowing that a beautiful girl like Mariana Ramos is into me, but I'm not. In fact, I'm honestly a bit confused.

After we get our blended iced pumpkin spice coffee drinks, Mariana directs me to her place. When we get there, no one else is home. According to Mariana, her parents are both at work, her older brother is probably off playing gangbanger, and her little sister has dance practice, so we've got the place to ourselves. She suggests we post up in her bedroom so that no one disturbs us if someone comes home, but I don't want to put myself in any sort of precarious situations, so I insist the table in the kitchen will do fine.

Mariana and I pull out our textbooks and we start to go over our notes. I have to explain the process of how to graph a polynomial to her over, and over, and over again, because she doesn't seem to be listening. She's just staring at me all dreamy like, and it's making me really uncomfortable. It's weird. I've never been this uncomfortable around a girl before — not one that I had no interest in romantically anyway — I have no idea why. I want to leave, but I don't want to just dip out on her after I said I would help her study. I decide to just muscle through it for an hour or so. After that, I can say something like, "My mom's expecting me home soon," and go without leaving any hard feelings.

At around six, I decide I've been here long enough. We aren't getting any work done. Mariana has no interest in math-ing, and she keeps trying to flirt with me. Every time I try to direct her back to the functions and variables, she finds something else to talk about like: "Oh, Nick, your hair's so pretty," or, "Oh, Nick, your beauty mark is so cute," or, "Oh, Nick, your arms are so big," or, "Oh, my god, you wear a size eleven shoe?" I know exactly what she's suggesting, but I can't bring myself to want to do anything with her, and believe me,

I could do anything with her. She's making it so easy, but I just… I can't. And I'm running out of patience.

"I should get going. My mom's expecting me home soon," I say, giving her my preconceived excuse.

"Oh, but we were having so much fun," she whines. No, we were not.

"Yeah, maybe we'll do this again sometime." No, we will not.

I put my notebook and textbook into my bag and scoot my chair back to get up from the table. But before I can actually get up, Mariana reaches over and pulls me towards her, planting a fat kiss on my lips. I want to stop this. I really do, but I don't. I follow up her kiss with my own and within seconds, we're in a full on make out session. Suddenly, as I'm feeling around the inside of her mouth with my tongue, I get a picture of Erik in my head and everything stops: the euphoria, the excitement, the passion, the adrenaline. It's all gone. Our lips separate.

"I… can't," I breathe.

"Why?" Mariana asks, still catching her own breath.

"I just… I can't." She lets go of me. The look on her face is that of disappointment and I feel so bad for her. If this had happened a month ago, maybe this would've ended differently. Maybe she would've been my girl. But now, I just can't.

"Is it me?" she asks pitifully.

"No," I say. I know I probably shouldn't because it's not her business, but I get the vibe that I can trust her, so I do. "I lied to you before. I'm not into guys, I don't think. But there *is* something going on between me and Erik. I just haven't figured it out yet." Mariana smiles gently. She looks at me in a way that says she understands, and I'm thankful for that. "Look, maybe we can be friends?"

"Yeah, sure," she nods. "I'd like that."

Mariana walks me to the front door and, as I'm about to leave, I stop and I turn to her.

"Would you mind keeping all of this between us?" I ask. "I don't think Erik would like it if he knew people knew our business." Mariana nods and offers up her pinky. I wrap my own pinky around hers and we shake on it. That's how we end the night.

As much as I appreciate Mariana being cool and understanding about everything, I have to wonder, did she really need help with Math? Because if this was all just some elaborate plan to get into my pants, she put way too much effort into it. Honestly, if she had just walked up to me one day and said, "Nick, can I suck your dick?" she might've had a better chance. I might've actually considered it, you know, if it wasn't for Erik.

It's around noon. Nicholas will be here any minute and I hate everything in my closet. It feels like everything I put on is either too big or too small, so I either look really frumpy or really fat. After trying on several different outfits, I remind myself that we're only going to the movies, and throw on a plain white tee, some jeans, and layer up in my favorite hoodie and simple black bomber. I check my phone to make sure I didn't miss his "I'm outside" text. Nothing yet, so I go over to the bathroom to see if there's any way I can mat down my stubborn cowlick. No luck.

I don't know what it is about knowing a boy is going to pick me up that makes me so nervous, and excited, and giddy. Nicholas and I have hung out dozens of times before, but knowing he's coming always has this effect on me. It has yet to go away and I hope it never does. Even though I *am* still mildly upset with him for bailing on me yesterday to hang out with Mariana. Ugh, I don't even want to think about them together. Nicholas may have been being all "boyfriend-y" with me, but I know Nicholas. I know he's a big flirt, so I imagine he'd like being with a girl who buys into that, and Mariana was practically throwing herself at him. The only thing that could potentially stop them from… fornicating… is if he were already committed to me, and I'm not sure that he is. He's never mentioned anything about being committed to me and he *did* just ditch me for Mariana, which is why I don't want to think about that right now.

My parents are out for the day — Mom's got an open house she's hosting and Dad's visiting with his old college buddies — so I've got at least half the day to myself without having to worry about them calling me home. I just want to enjoy today, and I can't do that if I have Nicholas and Mariana on my mind. No, today is my day. Today belongs to Erik and Nicholas. Nobody else.

I'm sprawled out on the couch repeatedly scrolling up on Nicholas' text box, hoping that it might refresh and load something new, when his message comes in.

"Outside," it says.

"Coming," I text back, then take one last look in the mirror — stupid cowlick — before heading out.

I see Nicholas through his windshield and he's looking handsome as ever in his maroon hoodie and leather jacket. It gives him a sort of bad boy image that's working so hard for him. I can see he's fiddling with his phone when I approach. He notices me and flashes me his signature smirk just as I'm reaching his passenger door.

"Hey, you," he greets.

"Hi," I say, in a rather excited tone. "Did you decide what movie we're seeing? Ooo, can it be that scary one with the ballet dancing witches? Please?"

"Erik, you know how I feel about scary movies."

"I know, but they're so much fun!"

"Fine. How about we just go and catch the first show of whatever's playing next?"

"Deal." I'm expecting him to pull out of the driveway so we can get going, but he doesn't. He takes one more look at his phone and then shoves it into his coat pocket. Then, he sighs and turns in his seat towards me. He seems nervous and it's unsettling, because this is Nicholas. He's rarely ever nervous. I know immediately that I should be bracing myself for some bad news.

"So, there's actually something I need to talk to you about before we go," Nicholas begins. I stare at him, waiting to hear more. "You know how I went to help Mariana study for our Math quiz?" Again, I don't say anything. I'm getting this sinking feeling that I know where this story is going. "Well, she didn't actually want to study…" he trails off. This anticipation is torturous, and I'm losing my patience.

"What? Did you guys, like, end up having sex?" I say, almost as a joke. I figure if I laugh it off now, it might buffer the shock of it if it turns out to be true.

"No! God, Erik, I'm not that easy!" he defends. He seems surprised that my mind would even jump to that conclusion. "But we *did* make out." And there it is. The shot he was loading up. At first, I don't say anything. I want to be mad, but I know that I can't be without looking crazy. I mean, I have no claim here. He's not my boyfriend, clearly. He's not my anything, really.

"Erik?" Nicholas asks, treading lightly.

"Okay," I say, mustering up whatever strength I have to look him in the face. I have to look at him, because if I don't, it'll be obvious to him that I'm upset.

"Okay?"

"Yeah. I mean, it's not like we're together, right?" It absolutely kills me to say this, and I don't know why I do. I guess I'm just fishing. You know, hoping that he'll tell me something better than what I just said. Sorta like when someone says that they're ugly and everyone around is like, "You're not ugly," regardless of whether the person is actually ugly or not. Unfortunately, Nicholas doesn't take the bait.

"Ah, that's a relief," he breathes, letting out a huge sigh. It may be a relief for him, but it's not for me. "I was afraid you'd be mad." I shake my head.

"Why would I be mad?" I'm not mad. I'm heartbroken.

"Well, I was afraid that — you know, with your feelings and everything — that you'd think this," he explains, gesturing to the two of us, "was something more than what it is."

"And what is this?" I say without thinking. I'm not sure I want to know what he would label this, but then again, I don't see how it could get much worse.

"You know, we're friends. I mean, we're just hanging out."

"Right," I smile. I'm not a good liar. How he doesn't see through my facade is beyond me. Or maybe he does see through it but is refusing to acknowledge my hurt to spare his own feelings. I'm Catholic, I know what guilt feels like. I'm sure he does too.

Nicholas drives us to the movie theater and the whole time he's talking about a whole lot of nothing. It's "Mariana this" and "Mariana that" and "We should start hanging out with Mariana." Since when is Mariana Ramos so cool? I mean, she's always been cool, but, like, since when is she so cool to him? Since yesterday? Why? Because they made out? I bet he took his shirt off when they were doing that. I bet he let her play with his little happy trail while they were tongue wrestling and all that gross stuff. I bet they *did* have sex and Nicholas is just trying to spare my feelings. I didn't want to think about him with Mariana, but it seems like she's all he can talk about. By the time we get to the theater, I've learned that Mariana is from Mexico City, her mom's a home caregiver, her dad's the manager of a burger place, and she thinks that the cafeteria food at our school is disgusting, which it is, but no one is too good to eat it. I just wish Nicholas would shut up about her. As if being around him right now isn't hard enough already.

"Looks like the next thing showing is that new romantic comedy," Nicholas says, nudging my arm with his elbow as we stand in front of the box office. "You down for it?"

"Yeah, that's fine," I shrug. At this point, I really don't care. I don't want to see the romantic comedy movie, or any movie for that matter. I just want to go home and be away from him, but I can't without starting something that will surely snowball into a fight, so whatever movie I have to sit through is what I'm gonna sit through. Nicholas cocks his head at me, his brow furrowed questioningly.

"You sure? I know how much you wanted to see the scary dancing witch movie," Nicholas says. "The next showing is in an hour. I don't mind waiting."

"You don't like scary movies. Let's just see the rom-com." I'm about to step up to the box office, but Nicholas stops me.

"No," he says. "You wanna see the scary one, let's see the scary one. I'll sit through it. I won't like it, but I'll sit through it. Why don't we grab lunch in the meantime?" Ugh, I hate this. He's being so considerate. It's annoying. How am I supposed to stay upset now? I already know what's gonna happen: We're gonna have lunch, he's gonna do that hamster thing he does with the food in his cheeks, he's gonna say something cute, and I'm gonna swoon over him, completely forgetting the fact that I've just confirmed I'm nothing more than his sexy time play thing. It's not fair. But what Nicholas wants, Nicholas gets.

The movie theater is situated at the end of a large shopping plaza with a bunch of different food places and department stores. Nicholas and I walk across the parking lot and make our way over to one of the fast food joints nearby. I haven't had lunch yet, so I order a full chicken sandwich meal with fries and a drink, and I'm intending to pay for myself, but Nicholas pokes his head past my shoulder, adds his order to the check and slips the cashier a twenty before I can protest. We then take a seat in one of the booths and wait for our food.

"You didn't have to do that, you know," I tell him. "I can pay for myself."

"Well, I don't want you to," Nicholas shrugs, like it's not a big deal.

"Why? Mackenzie doesn't even pay for me."

"I dunno. I like taking care of you." There it is! It's just as I predicted. I knew he'd say something cute. Granted it came before the hamster cheeks with the food thing, but I totally called it. When we get our food, we dig in and I start watching him to see if he's gonna do the hamster cheeks and he does! It's both annoying and endearing, so I'm simultaneously loving and hating every second of it. I've figured out his move set. He's like a video game character. He only has so many tricks up his sleeves and I know them all! This is how he wins. Every. Single. Time. Because I'm weak to it. I'm weak to him.

After we have lunch, Nicholas and I walk back to the theater and buy two tickets at the box office. Again, he doesn't let me pay. We head in and stop by the concession stand where Nicholas gets us a big tub of popcorn and a massive sized soda to share. How he has any more room in his stomach is completely beyond me.

"What?" He asks when he notices me eyeing him about it. "You can't go to the movies without a big tub of popcorn. It's a part of the experience!"

"I didn't say anything," I defend myself innocently. I *didn't* say anything… not out loud anyway.

Nicholas and I get into the theater just as the first trailers are starting. On screen, there's a girl running as several unseen characters give story exposition. Nicholas and I pick out a couple of seats in the third row, right up front — seats that most people avoid because they're "too close," but I like being right up front where you can really immerse yourself in it. The mangled body of a girl is revealed on screen, followed by talks of exorcism.

"Do we have to sit this close?" Nicholas asks, sinking into his seat. He's already ducking behind the popcorn tub as soon as a montage of the dead girl walking around a morgue facility begins. "Nope. Nope. Nope. I'm getting real Catholic with this one right now." Nicholas is so freaked out, it's hilarious. Especially since the movie hasn't even started yet. These are just the trailers. I turn around and find that we're the only two in this showing. I guess no one wanted to see the scary dancing witch movie today but me. Oh well, empty theaters always make scary movies scarier. There's something more thrilling about it when there's no one else there. I wonder if I should point it out to Nicholas but, judging by his reaction to the trailers, I doubt it would make any difference to him.

The movie starts and immediately Nicholas huddles closer to me, chomping on his popcorn nervously. He's watching the screen with wide eyes in anticipation of anything that might pop up and go "boo!" It's actually more entertaining for me to watch his reactions than it is to watch the actual movie. He's so hyper focused in his fear and because of this, he jumps at every little thing.

"Why do you like these movies?" he whispers. I look over at him and somehow, in his curled up position, he looks smaller than me. I should keep my distance from him. You know, keep him at arm's length. But I can't help myself. He just looks so scared. I thread my arm under his and snuggle up close to him. I don't even think he notices — he's so caught up in the film — but that's okay. Every time he jumps or starts to get tense, he moves closer to me. I can smell the ocean breeze scent on his skin and the artificial butter on his breath, and even though he's sitting right here, I feel as if I miss him. I hate this. I hate having to hold myself back. I don't want to.

If only he were mine…

"Ugh, I hated that movie!" Nicholas exclaims once we exit the theater. "I mean, objectively speaking, it was good, but…" He shivers. "Anyway, what do you wanna do now? I freed up my whole day just for you. You wanna go mini golfing? Or bowling? Nah, I'm terrible at that. Ooo, maybe laser tag?" Sure. Yeah, why not? I'd love to do all those things with him today. I'd love to, but I can't. I can't stop thinking about the fact that he made out with Mariana and that we're just "hanging out." He said it himself. It's not like I'm making this up because I feel sorry for myself. These are his words. I'm just repeating them. In my head. Over, and over, and over again.

"Actually, I should probably get home," I say regrettably.

"Aw, nooooooo…"

"Yeah, I left without telling my parents. They're probably home now wondering where I am." I don't want to end the day with Nicholas, I really don't. But I should. I can't keep letting myself fall deeper and deeper into my feelings for him. It would be stupid of me to. Not to mention self-sabotaging. I mean, come on, falling for a straight guy is bad enough, but falling for a straight guy who has sex with boys is just… ugh! Going home now is the best option, but seeing the look of disappointment on his face tempts me. His squinted eyes are beckoning me to stay with him. How am I supposed to say no to that? "Come on, you can't just text them that we're hanging out?"

"I guess I could…" Don't do it, Erik. Don't do this to yourself. You know better.

"Come on, Erik. We can do whatever you want. I'm yours for the day."

Did he just say he's mine for the day?

Don't do it, Erik.

But he's mine.

Don't.

I wish I would start listening to myself…

But I don't.

"Can we hang out at your place?" I ask timidly. I know I shouldn't feel nervous asking him this because he's sure to say yes. We've hung out at his place lots of times, but this time feels different for me. This time it feels like I'm asking him for so much more, and I think he can feel it too.

"You want to go to my place?" He says. I nod. I can see it on his face that this was probably the last thing that he was expecting me to say. There's a twinkle in his eye and he licks his lips. I'm almost sure he's having the same ideas I'm having. I want to be close to him. I want to feel him against me and be so intertwined that we can't tell where one ends and the other begins. I want to be so connected to him physically that I can make believe that we're together. If this is the only way I can have him, it's better than not, right?

Nicholas drives us back to his place and lets us in through the garage door, directly to his bedroom. I take a quick look around at all the things I've grown so familiar with: the pictures taped to the walls, the cups of water left scattered about, the line of high tops in the corner that are so well taken care of they're in near perfect condition. Nicholas clicks the garage door shut, turns on the heating tower, and slips out of his leather jacket. While he gets settled, I wander over to his desk and take a quick look at all the papers he's got strewn about. On them are hand drawn cartoons and comics, and they're actually pretty good. I'm surprised. I had no idea that Nicholas could draw, or even liked to.

"Don't look at those!" Nicholas exclaims. "They're not finished yet!"

"Did you do these?" I ask. "I didn't know you could draw."

"Well, I can't really. I've just been doodling. Since I don't have a TV in here, I gotta find some way to keep myself entertained, you know?"

"How long have you been doing this for?"

"What? Drawing? Not long. Couple weeks, I guess. I kinda wanted to surprise you." Nicholas walks over to me and picks up a couple of the pages. He flips through them until he comes to a drawing of two boys standing side by side: one shorter one with glasses, and one taller one with thick cartoon-ish eyebrows. "See? It's supposed to be us."

"You made me into a cartoon character?"

"I mean, if you don't mind. You say a lot of really funny things, I thought I'd draw you into a cartoon, make a little comic book or something." I'm flattered. I really am. No one's ever thought about me enough to make me into a cartoon. Finding this makes me want him more and more, and it's getting harder and harder to talk myself out of doing something stupid. Stupid, as in unzipping his hoodie. Stupid, as in peeling off his tank top. Stupid, as in tracing the curves of his body with my fingertips. Stupid, as in letting him take me to his bed so he can have his way with me.

We proceed to have sex for the umpteenth time — at this point, I've honestly lost count — and we do everything we've done before and more. Despite all previous experiences, I treat Nicholas' body as delicately as if it were the first time. There's still so much uncertainty here. Is what I'm doing good for him? Does it feel okay? I never really know, but I take his lack of breath and heavy sighs as a form of positive reinforcement. His moans egg me on, practically begging for me to let him in, and when I do, he touches me deep, bringing with him this overwhelming feeling of ecstasy, I almost can't handle it. What am I doing to myself?

Once we're finished, he lets me lie in his arms, my head resting on his chest. I'm contemplating my actions. How could I have such a lack of resolve as to allow myself to be in this position time and time again, knowing full well that at this point, we're just "hanging out?" The guilt washes over me. I'm covered in sweat and drenched in us, and I feel completely disgusted with myself. Nicholas gets up and reaches for a glass of water. He then goes over to his laundry bin and tosses me a pair of his boxers to clean myself up with. If I have any dignity left, it's getting wiped away with a pair of underwear.

Nicholas looks at me with a twinkle in his eye and a smile on his mouth. His expression reads as if he's just had the best day of his life. It's funny, his best day will be one of my worst.

I check my phone. I've got several missed calls from my parents, as well as a few text messages and a voicemail. I had forgotten to text them letting them know where I am. My clock reads a quarter to eight. I've missed dinner and I'm probably in trouble. Hopefully, they're not too upset.

"I should get going," I tell Nicholas. "My parents have been blowing up my phone."

"Why? Did you forget to text them?" Nicholas asks. I nod guiltily. He lets out an exasperated sigh and rolls his eyes. I try to smile it off all innocent like.

When Nicholas drops me off, I rush into my house without so much as a goodbye. When my parents have called enough times to feel compelled to leave a voicemail, you know they've lost their patience with me. They only ever leave voicemails for business or emergencies, so I'm expecting the worst when I walk in. No time for dilly-dallying with Nicholas. I enter the house as quietly as I can and head straight for the stairs.

"Where have you been?" I hear my mom call out. Immediately, I freeze and turn to face her. She's standing at the threshold leading into the living room with my dad standing close behind her. Both are wearing sour expressions. I'm in trouble now. "We've been calling you for hours. Why didn't you pick up your phone?"

"I'm sorry. I lost track of time," I try to explain. Though it's rather difficult keeping my composure under the watchful eye of my mother's Filipino death glare.

"Lost track of time, ano ka ba?"

"Appa!" I call to my dad, searching for help.

"Oh, no. Don't try to 'Appa' me," he replies. "Answer your mom's question."

"I went to a movie. My phone was on silent, I didn't even realize you called until I was on my way back." Only half of this is a lie. I mean, I'm not about to tell my parents the truth and that I was naked in a boy's bed when I saw that they called. They don't need to know all that. I don't think they'd want to know.

"Who'd you go to the movie with?" Mom asks. Shit. She's been getting more and more suspicious of me. Before Nicholas, I never went out, and now I'm gone more than I'm home. There have been several times where she's connected the dots and figured out that I was with the "handsome boy who reads poetry" but I've always either denied it or avoided her assumptions all together. My mom's no fool though, I know she sees through me. Every answer I don't give her is an answer enough for her. Yes, I was with Nicholas. It's always been with Nicholas. Obviously, I can't say that though. She'd never let me hear the end of it.

"Just a friend," I respond. Mom narrows her eyes.

"O sige, Erik, grounded ka na," Mom says, before making a swift turn and disappearing into the living room.

"What? Grounded? For how long?"

"Erik," Dad steps forward.

"Dad, why is she so mad? Because I didn't answer my phone?" My dad places his hands on my shoulders and leans in to whisper something to me.

"I think you should take a bath. You don't look like you just came from the movies." I look up at him. He knows. I know he knows or he wouldn't have said anything. Is it really that obvious? I nod and turn to climb the stairs.

"Dad? How long am I grounded for?"

"Let's say a week."

"Dad, you know he's just a friend, right?" I say, keeping my voice low and my eyes toward the threshold. Dad shrugs and offers me a pitying smile. I must not be very convincing.

I'm soaking in the tub now, quietly contemplating my actions. I keep playing and replaying the events of the day in my head, hoping to find something that would help me justify my bad decisions. Why don't I listen to myself? Why can't I stop myself from giving too much of me? I've given Nicholas everything… and for what? The more that I think about it, the more that I fear I've become someone I don't recognize. I've become like those people who treat sex like a simple hedonistic pleasure instead of what it could be. Instead of what I believe it *should* be: an act of love. There's no love here. How can there be when we're just "hanging out?"

After my bath, I wipe the fog off the mirror and stare at my reflection for a minute. I look like I always have, but somehow I barely recognize myself. A change has occurred, and I don't know when it did. I don't know if the change happened the moment I realized I like boys or the moment I actually did something about it, but the guy staring back at me… I don't like him. He carries a shame with him so heavy that he can't even bring himself to look at me. He's nothing more than a sad and desperate toy, a play thing, to be used and donated to the next person who shows even a passing interest. It's sad really. And pathetic. I don't want to be that guy.

Growing up in the church, I've always been taught that prayer was the answer to everything. Whenever you're in need of something — forgiveness, strength, serenity, whatever you need — you pray. So, once I'm dressed in my PJs, I hole myself up in my room, pull out the Rosary from my nightstand drawer, and I begin to recite the words and prayers I've come to learn by heart:

Our father, who art in heaven, hallowed be thy name…
Hail Mary, full of grace, the Lord is with thee…
Glory be to the Father, and to the Son, and to the Holy Spirit…

I go through the entire Rosary, praying for forgiveness for what I've done, praying for the strength I so desperately lack, and praying for serenity so I can learn to accept this cross I've been given to bear. I pray that these feelings I have for Nicholas will go away. I pray that I don't see him as this beautiful and attractive creature that I can't resist. I pray that I can rid him from my mind so that he doesn't occupy my every waking thought. I pray, and I pray, and I pray, and when all is said and done, I'm right back where I started: sitting alone in my room with a stomach full of shame and a heart full of regret.

I wish that things could be different. At the very least, I wish I didn't need him the way that I do. Because it's not fair that I do.

But I do.

nicholas

It's Thanksgiving week and we have a quiz tomorrow... Ugh, why!? I swear, some teachers are masochists. They're only creating more work for themselves. I mean, think about it: the more work they give us to do, the more they have to take home and grade. Don't they have lives? Whatever, luckily, it's only Math, which happens to be one of my better subjects. I like the way that there's always a definite answer, you know? Nothing is left to interpretation. $1 + 1$ will always equal 2. $2 + 2$ will always equal 4. It's as simple as it can be complicated, but there's always a definite answer and there's always a way to find it. The same can't be said for some other aspects of my life, but right now, everything's good.

Erik and I hung out yesterday and he seemed to understand what's going on between us. We're just two friends hanging out. Nothing more, nothing less. It was a chill time. Though he did get pretty weird about me paying for him, but I felt bad for changing up the plan on him to hang with Mariana on Friday. I wanted to make it up to him. I didn't think it'd be a big deal, but he seemed to not like it. He got over it pretty quick though considering he got real cuddly with me at the movie theater, which was fine since I was not enjoying that dancing witch movie whatsoever. There was this part in it where this girl's body gets mangled during this whole dance routine, and then they drag her off with hooks, and it was just… not something I ever wanted to see. Having Erik so close to me made the movie a little bit more bearable, because at least I had something to hold on to, but it was still… ugh.

After that horrifyingly disturbing movie, Erik wanted to come over, so I took him back here where he discovered the drawings I had been working on. I was planning on keeping those a secret because I wanted to bind them all together and make them into a comic book to give to him as a Christmas gift. When Erik gave me that poem he wrote for my birthday, I knew I had to come up with something that could match it when the time comes for me to give him a gift. I never considered myself to be much of a creative type. In fact, I didn't even know I could draw until I had absentmindedly made Erik into a cartoon. It was during my fourth period Physics class. I was so unbelievably bored, I started doodling in the margins of my notebook. The doodles were pretty trash, but I kept on drawing them just to pass the time. Eventually, my doodles turned into something resembling Erik. That's when I thought I might have something that could match the value of his poem. But once he saw the drawings, I couldn't keep the idea a secret anymore. Surprise!

We ended up having sex after that. It was some good sex too.

I wonder what Erik's doing today. It's a little past eleven. I know his family usually catches the early mass so they should be out by now. I grab my phone and shoot him a text.

"Hey you," I send.

"Hi," his response comes in minutes later.

"What you doing later? Wanna study for the Math quiz together?"

"Can't. Grounded."

"What for?"

"Parents freaked yesterday when I didn't answer my phone." Shit, his parents went hardcore with their parenting. I can't imagine my mom — or, actually, even my dad — being that strict with me. I mean, it's not like we were out late or anything. It was like eight o' clock. It's no wonder Erik got so nervous about it yesterday. "Sorry. They're telling me to put my phone away. Bye." Well, this sucks. I guess I'm on my own today. To be honest though, it's probably for the best. I doubt we'd get much studying done if Erik *were* to come over, if you know what I mean...

It's right around lunchtime and I am starving. I slept in today, so I missed breakfast. I head into the kitchen where I find Tio Roger sitting at the table with a sketchbook and a cup of coffee. As I get closer, I see that he seems to be working on some sort of building plan. I'd never been all that curious about my uncle's work, but now that I'm starting to explore my own artistic side, I figure I'd give his stuff a once over.

"Nick, it's not exactly the most comfortable thing having you watch over my shoulder," Tio says, pausing mid pencil stroke.

"I'm just looking," I tell him. "Is this for work?"

"No, I'm just sketching out some ideas. I'm trying to design an affordable housing building that uses sustainable energy to keep itself powered."

"Yeah... that's really boring. Cool drawing though." Tio Roger chuckles. I head over to the fridge to see what I can scrounge up. I'm hoping to find something to microwave, or some raw sandwich materials, or something. No such luck. Someone should probably do some grocery shopping.

"You don't have any plans with your boyfriend today?" Tio asks, and I immediately stop. I pull my head out of the fridge and look over at him questioningly.

"Boyfriend?" I respond. "What are you talking about?"

"That Erik kid."

"Erik? Erik's not my boyfriend. I'm not even gay." My uncle looks at me about as confused as I feel.

"I thought you two were... you know, having... relations?" Well, this is embarrassing. You know, I never understood why adults avoid using the word "sex" when talking about sex to teenagers. It's not like we haven't heard it all before. And honestly, avoiding the word "sex" when talking about sex makes talking about sex one hundred percent more awkward. It's a three-letter word, what's the big deal?

"Yeah, we are," I say, responding to my uncle's question, as awkward as it may be. "But it doesn't mean anything. We're just hanging out."

"And you're *not* gay?" Tio asks.

"I mean, I still like girls, so no?" He doesn't look like he quite understands. And frankly, neither do I. I've been trying to figure it out myself for weeks. Since there's nothing at all in the fridge I can eat, I join my uncle at the table empty handed.

"So what are you? Bi?"

"Why do we have to put a label on everything, Tio? There's not always, like, a definite answer. It's not like a Math problem. It's not that simple."

"Maybe it is, and you're just not considering all the variables." I narrow my eyes. Seriously, what is he getting at? If I wasn't so hungry, I'd press him for more on the matter, but right now I can't be bothered. I'm starving.

"Can we order a pizza? You've got, like, nothing in your fridge," I say.

"Sure," he chuckles, completely amused with himself. I don't see why; he's not being amusing. Whatever. He's buying me a pizza. I shouldn't complain.

Just then, Ma comes in wearing her two sizes too small black cocktail dress, a blazer, and her hair pulled back into a ponytail. Uncle Roger and I both look up. Ma's all dressed up and looking fancy. What's going on?

"Do you think this is too much for a diner?" Ma asks.

"Depends. What's the occasion?" Tio replies. Then it occurs to me. Could Ma be going out to see someone? Is she, like, dating again? I mean, the thought has crossed my mind before, but I don't really know how I'd actually feel about it. I suppose I'd be happy for her.

It's just so weird. It's hard to picture Ma with anyone other than Dad, but then again, it was hard to picture Dad with anyone other than Ma and look how that turned out. Plus, it has been a couple months since they split, so I guess it wouldn't be that crazy.

"Ma, are you going on a date?" I ask. Her face wrinkles with disgust.

"God, no. I'm not ready for that," she explains. "I got a job interview."

"Ooooooooooooooooh…" Tio Roger and I say simultaneously.

"So is it too much?"

"A little bit," I answer. "I'd go with something a little less… form fitting."

"That's why I put on the blazer."

"Yeah… but…"

"Rosie, he's saying you look like a high-class hooker," Tio Roger interjects. Ma's jaw drops. I burst out laughing, I can't help myself.

"Oh, my God. I'll wear something else then. Nicky, you don't have plans with your boyfriend, do you?" Ma asks. "Because I'm gonna need the car today."

"Rosie, he and Erik aren't dating. They're just 'hanging out'" Tio annoyingly interjects. Ma looks at me all sideways as she crosses the kitchen to pour herself a cup of coffee.

"Hanging out? Is that what they're calling it nowadays? You know, Nicky, 'hanging out' is how you were made."

"Ma, don't you have an interview to change for?" She shrugs, stirring the milk and sugar she's added to her coffee all condescendingly.

"I've got time. So, you and Erik are just 'hanging out?' Does Erik know that?"

"Yeah." Ma stares at me, her eyebrows raised in disbelief. I notice Tio's looking at me in the same way. What is everyone's problem?

"Why are you guys looking at me like that?" I demand.

"Nothing," Ma says. "It's just that Erik doesn't seem like the type to do the friends with benefits thing."

"To be fair, the nerdy quiet types can go either way." Tio Roger chimes in. "In college, I went out with this really quiet girl, who—"

"Why is this anyone's business but my own?" I say, cutting him off, my voice coming out a little louder than I intended. I'm just getting so frustrated that they have so many questions about it. Can't they just keep their questions to themselves and accept whatever information I decide to give them? The way they're looking at me feels very accusatory, but it's not like I'm doing anything wrong. You see, this is why people keep their relationships a secret. My face must be looking pretty sour because Ma softens her expression.

"Listen, mijo," she says. "You're right. It's nobody's business but your's and Erik's. I just want you to be careful."

"I know, Ma. But you said it yourself, 'never commit yourself to someone unless you're going to commit yourself to someone.'"

"Okay. Yes, but mijo, you can't leave things so up in the air." Ma keeps on talking, giving me advice that I didn't ask for, with Tio Roger chiming in every now and then, but I'm doing my best to tune them out. Everything they're saying sounds like they ripped it straight out of a cheap greeting card or a thirteen-year-old girl's Pinterest page: "Don't be just a lover, be a friend too." "What goes up must come down, but you decide where it lands." "If you're gonna have your cake and eat it too, you might as well be the one to pick the flavor." What does that even mean?!

What do they know about the situation and my relationship with Erik? They can only see it through an outside perspective, and it's easy to come up with things to say when you're not in the thick of it. The more that my mom and uncle talk, the more I'm starting to get pissed off. It's feeling like what they want me to do is put a label on everything, and I can't do that. Not yet. There's still too much I'm unsure of, and I'm not about to break the promise I made about commitment just because I'm being pressured to. I need to be sure of my feelings before I can give anymore of myself to Erik than what I'm already giving him. It wouldn't be fair otherwise. I just don't know how to find certainty in the situation when I can't even find certainty in myself.

Am I bisexual? Should I just label myself as bisexual for the sake of simplicity? For me, that feels dishonest, because Erik is the one anomaly among a sea of women. How can I define myself as someone who's attracted to both guys *and* girls when I've only ever been attracted to girls, and Erik seems to be the one exception? But then again, am I even attracted to girls? It's hard to say because I can't seem to "perform" for them. And how can you tell the difference between an attraction and an appreciation? It's all so mind numbingly confusing. That being said, I can't stop thinking about what Tio Roger said about me not considering all the variables. What did he mean by that? What variables was he referring to? If I could figure it out, maybe it would be simple. Until then, Erik and I are just friends. And we're just hanging out. Erik knows that. He gets it. He understands. In fact, he agreed. So then, why do I suddenly feel so shitty about everything?

Ugh, why does love have to be so complicated?

I need to eat something.

Where's my fucking pizza?

chapter
twenty-five
erik

Being grounded is the worst. I can have my phone, but I'm not allowed to be home alone unless my parents both have something to do that I can't tag along for. Dad made plans with some of his college buddies, so I'm stuck with Mom as she goes grocery shopping for stuff she'll need to make desserts for our family Thanksgiving party. Every year for Thanksgiving we have these big family potlucks at my well-off uncle's house — it's the kind of house that's needlessly big and is outfitted with a full bar — where our massive clan of Filipinos gather to binge eat, drink, and sing karaoke. Dad, being the only non-Filipino Asian in the room — his side of the family is minuscule compared to my Mom's —

usually posts up in a corner catching up with our two white-through-marriage family members, while I typically hole up in my cousin's room and play video games all day.

I'll be honest, aside from the buffet of food, I don't really look forward to, or particularly enjoy, gatherings with my extended family. I dunno why, but I've always felt a little uncomfortable and out of place around them. Maybe it's because I don't feel I really know these people beyond the fact that we're related in some way. We're not the kind of family that sits down and talks about ourselves or our lives in a real meaningful way, and if we do, I'm never a part of those conversations. To me, these people are more or less friendly acquaintances who I bear a little bit of a resemblance to. I don't really have much in common with them. I'm too young to be considered an adult and I'm too old to be considered a child, so I never felt I really fit in anywhere. If it wasn't for my cousin, who's barely in his teens, having a fat collection of gaming consoles, I'd probably be bored out of my mind during those parties.

Mom's leading me through the Oriental food aisle of the grocery store and is complaining that everything here is overpriced.

"It's so expensive here," she mutters to herself. "So much cheaper at the Asian Market." Except the Asian Market is all the way over by the good mall and Mom didn't feel like making the drive today, so here we are. I'm starting to get really bored because my Mom's being extra finicky with her price checking today. I decide to wander away, and at this point, Mom's too busy comparing the prices of two different brands of coconut milk — there's literally only a ten cent difference — to notice.

I'm slowly meandering up and down the aisles while scrolling through Nicholas' Instagram feed. He texted me earlier asking if I wanted to study for our Math quiz tomorrow, but being that I'm grounded, I had to decline. It's probably for the best. I've been feeling really weird about the situation with him today. Basically, I feel like his slut and I hate myself for it. But it's complicated, because I really like him, and I think he really likes me, but we're just "hanging out." Except my definition of "hanging out" doesn't involve us having sex and his apparently does. It's all very confusing and it's made even more confusing when I take into account how he acts like such a boyfriend in so many ways: paying for my food and movie ticket, holding my hand, kissing, cuddling, and loving on me, all of the things you don't do with a friend who you're just "hanging out" with.

The fact that Nicholas refuses to call what we're doing together anything other than us "hanging out" is concerning. It makes me feel like he doesn't care, like he doesn't feel anything for me. I mean, he knows how I feel about him. He's already goaded me into admitting it and yet, he's still leaving me in the dark about everything. I may as well have been a geisha and he just happened to be the guy who placed the winning bet on my virginity. Then again, being a geisha sounds like it might come with a little bit of dignity, but this… well, this is just sad.

I'm really fighting the urge to text him right now. The best thing for both Nicholas and I is for us to keep our distance. At least, until we can come to an agreement about what's really going on between us, because it is not "hanging out." I refuse to accept that it's just us "hanging out." He's either my boyfriend, or he's simply using me. There can't be an in between. Of course, as I'm saying all of this to myself inside my head, I scroll past a shirtless photo of him on his Instagram and I go weak. Why does he have this effect on me? Why? I hate it!

A text message comes in from my mom.

"Where are you?" she asks. Getting bored and simply wandering away would not be a good enough excuse for my mom, so I quickly look around to see if I can find anything of use. I'm currently in the cereal aisle. Perfect! I'll just say I went to get some cereal. I grab the nearest box and then make my way back.

"Can we get these?" I say, when I get back to my mom in the Oriental food aisle. She eyes me suspiciously. Why? What did I grab? … Plain cracked wheaties! No wonder she's looking at me funny. The only people who buy this kind of cereal are old people, people with health conditions, and hipsters, so this must be looking really out of character for me right now.

"Erik?" I hear the familiar voice of a woman come from behind me. I turn to see who it is, and my face immediately drops. It's Mrs. Santiago, Nicholas' mom. She's staring at me with a pleasant smile, looking very business professional in her cardigan and button up. She has no idea what her presence here could do. My first reaction is to disappear as quickly as humanly possible, and to do that, as stupid and nonsensical as it may be, I bring the box of wheaties up to my face and duck behind it, as if that would do anything at all. "Erik, what are you—" Mrs. Santiago begins, but I cut her off.

"Nope. No Erik here," I say quickly.

"Erik, what's going on?" Mom asks. Crap. "Who is this?"

"It's okay, Mom, I'll go ahead and put the cereal back." I'm feeling myself starting to panic. They *cannot* talk. If they talk, this could be bad. Very, very bad.

"Mom? So you're Erik's mother?" Mrs. Santiago asks, and my heart just about explodes. This cannot be happening right now.

"Yes, and you are?" Mom responds.

"Rosalie, Nick's mom. It seems our boys have been spending a lot of time together." Mom cocks her head at me questioningly.

"Have they now?"

"Yes! We've… uh, been working on a project together," I offer, quickly cutting in. "For class." My mom doesn't look convinced.

"Oh? What class?" Having my mom staring at me with narrowed eyes is enough to instill the fear of God right back into me. I go silent, completely at a loss for words. The moment seems to last forever. I can feel it. The world's gonna come crashing down on me. My mom's gonna find out what I've been doing with Nicholas and there will be hell to pay, I just know it.

"Drama, right?" Mrs. Santiago says suddenly. I turn to her in surprise. "That's what you boys said, right? You're working on a scene for Drama?"

"Drama?" Mom asks, not totally convinced. "Erik, you don't take Drama."

"I'm in drama now," I reply innocently. Mom eyes me curiously. She's not buying it, I can tell. She's not believing a word of this.

"Well… it was nice to meet you, Rosalie," Mom says. "I've still got some more shopping to do for Thanksgiving. If you'll excuse me." I'm nervous about my mom's reaction because there wasn't much of one. I know her though, and I know that something is festering. How much she's figured out on her own is a mystery, but there's no way she doesn't know that I'm seeing a boy, and that the woman she just met is that boy's mother. My mom pushes her cart down the aisle and disappears around the corner.

"I take it you're not... you know..." Mrs. Santiago begins to ask once we're alone.

"Oh, I am," I explain. "It's just not something we talk about, because... you know, religion. We're very Catholic." Mrs. Santiago nods.

"Ah, I see," she says. "Well, if you ever need someone to talk to, our door's always open for you. And of course, you've got Nick." Mrs. Santiago pats me on my shoulder and then heads off down the aisle. Her words strike a chord with me. "You've got Nick," she said. But do I? Do I really? I wonder. After all, she *is* his mother, so Nicholas is likely to tell her things that he doesn't tell me, especially things about me. Then again, it's entirely possible that she's as much in the dark about the situation as I am, and that she was just saying "You've got Nick" to be friendly and reassuring. I don't know. I just don't know. I'm thinking now, maybe I should call him. Maybe I should just ask him flat out: What are we, Nicholas? Are we boyfriends, or am I just... the object of a mizuage? I'm not sure I want to know because I suspect I already know the answer, and I'm not feeling great about it. Still, the longer I let this thing between us go undefined, the more painful it'll be for me in the long run. I decide to bite the bullet and call him. I'd text, but I'm not sure I can handle waiting on a response.

"Hey, you," Nicholas answers on the second ring. "Still grounded?"

"Yeah," I say, the butterflies in my stomach starting to flutter.

"Damn."

"Hey, are you busy right now?"

"Super busy. Procrastinating from studying. You know how it goes. What are you up to?"

"Grocery shopping with my mom."

"Fun."

"Actually, we ran into your mom." Nicholas goes silent for a moment. He knows as well as I do how badly that could've easily gone.

"My mom didn't say anything about us, did she?" I can hear the panic coming from his voice. His concern is reassuring. Regardless of what we are, at the very least, he cares. That much is clear.

"She did, actually," I explain. I hear him groan on the other end and I quickly continue before he has a chance to freak out. "Oh, no, it was nothing bad. It just got me thinking. I… uh, actually wanted to talk to you about something." Nicholas breathes a sigh of relief.

"I'm listening," he says. This is it. This is the time. I have to get him to put a label on this, once and for all. There's no backing out now. I have to, no matter how much it might scare me.

"Nicholas," I begin, my voice quivering with a nervous anticipation. I take a quick glance up and down the aisle to make sure I'm alone. The last thing I need right now is for my mom to come back and overhear everything. Nicholas is waiting, silently, patiently. I take a breath. "Nicholas, are we... um..." Just say it, Erik. Say it. But I can't. The word won't leave my lips, no matter how many times I tell myself to just say it. I can't bring myself to say the word: boyfriends. Of course we're not boyfriends. We're just "hanging out." There's almost no use in saying it, so I don't.

"Are we... what?" Nicholas asks. My heart sinks. I've cornered myself and I'm panicking. How do I get out of this?

"I... uh... don't really know how to say this word," I stammer.

"What word?" My eyes dart around, searching for something, anything, that might be helpful. I just need an idea, a word, something to say to fill in the blank I've left with my stupidity. I then look down at the box of plain cracked wheaties I've been holding onto for dear life, and the word leaves me so absentmindedly I'm not even entirely sure what I said.

"Boy-fren-lavin."

"What?" Nicholas says, his tone filled with a mixture of genuine surprise and confusion. Obviously, I have no idea what I'm saying, but staring at the cereal box gives me an idea of how I can possibly explain myself without looking like a completely desperate fool.

"Sorry, I'm just reading the ingredients on this cereal box and I never realized how many things go into cereal. It's like... wheat, grain, riboflavin, boy-fren-lavin, all this complicated stuff I can't even pronounce."

"Dude, you're so weird," I hear him laugh. If he's caught on, I really can't tell. As long as he's humoring me, I think I'm safe. I don't want to dance around the subject because I need an answer, but now that I'm here trying to get one, I don't know if I'm brave enough to. At least, not head on. Nicholas scares me, but in the best possible way. I love him. I owe it to both of us to get an answer for this, so if I have to dance around the subject to get it, I'm gonna do it.

"Nicholas," I begin, pressing on. "What would you say if I said you're like the milk to my cereal?"

"I'd say that's cute," he replies. I can hear it in his voice that he's smiling. He's flattered, I can tell. "That's pretty sweet."

"Well, these aren't. These are like wheaties. And they're not even the frosted kind." I'm chickening out, I know. Every step forward gets more and more nerve-racking for me. I just need to suck it up.

"Oooooooh noooooo..." he adds, dramatically. "You gotta get the frosted kind." Ugh, he's being so cute and playful, it's hard to think he's taking me seriously right now. I've gotta regain control of this conversation.

"Nicholas, would you say that cereal is good without milk?"

"I mean, cereal is cereal." Well, that's not the most encouraging answer.

"Do you like cereal?"

"Of course," Nicholas answers. Alright, now we're getting somewhere. "Don't you?"

"Yeah, but I like it better with milk."

"Well, yeah. It's better that way. You can't have cereal without milk. That's, like, barbaric." He chuckles. I notice a slight shift in his tone when he starts to speak again. "But then, it is *just* cereal," he says, sounding a little more serious. I suddenly feel naked and vulnerable, like he's seen right through my nervous little diversion. He must know that we're talking about so much more than cereal. Otherwise, why would he insist that it's *just* cereal? "It is what it is," Nicholas adds after a brief pause.

I don't understand. What does that mean, "It is what it is?" What is it? If this was a game of wits, I've lost it completely. Somehow, he managed to turn my sidestepping into a way for him to sidestep out of the whole thing. He's avoiding the subject way better than I am approaching it, and he's doing it so smoothly and confidently I don't even realize he's doing it until it's already been done. At this rate, I might never get a definition for this that's better than us "hanging out." Us "hanging out" isn't a definition, it isn't a label, of course it's not. The more that I think about it, the more I'm starting to wonder if this is his cop out. If it is, it would make so much sense. The reason he hasn't given us a proper label would be because he doesn't *want* to. I'm suspicious that he might want to play without commitment. To have his cake and eat it too. Because why wouldn't you?

I'm such an idiot to think that it was anything more than that.

"Hey, I'm gonna let you go, alright?" Nicholas says. "I should probably actually start studying. Talk to you tomorrow?"

"Sure."

I hear Nicholas hang up the phone and I do the same. What do you do when you're in love with your best friend, but for whatever reason, he won't claim you himself? What do you do? I honestly have no idea. I hug the box of cracked wheaties close to me. I need comfort from somewhere. Though my mom's not gonna be happy about having to buy these, we're going to have to, since I know the cereal box too intimately now to leave it behind.

Two days until we go on Thanksgiving break. All I have to do is last two days — that's twelve classes and two lunch periods — with Nicholas, and then I'll have five full days away from him. I'm at a point where I feel like I need to be without him for a while so that I can somehow find a way to get over him. I have no idea how I'm gonna get over him, but the time apart should help. These two days are going to be difficult though. I know I need to keep my distance, and I know I need to not let his cuteness get the better of me. But it seems like it's gonna be impossible to do that without things getting weird between us. If I'm too closed off, he'll know something is up, but if I'm not closed off enough, I'll likely find myself making the same mistakes with him over, and over, and over again, and I just can't do that to myself anymore. It's not healthy.

In fact, it's downright sinful.

When I get to my locker, I see Mackenzie, and to my relief, she's alone. Mackenzie and Nicholas don't interact much anymore. Ever since he yelled at her that one time, things have been strained between the two of them, and Mackenzie's not one to let things go. She thrives in the pettiness, so their relationship has devolved into little more than the snide, sharp comments they throw at one another every now and then. These days, they only really talk when I'm there to mitigate. I'd say they're still friends, but not friendly.

"Ugh, is it me or do these two days of school feel like a complete waste of time?" Mackenzie complains as I approach.

"It's not just you," I agree. I know I shouldn't be asking about Nicholas, but he's never not here in the morning unless he's just not at school. My curiosity gets the better of me. "You wouldn't have happened to see Nicholas at all yet, have you?"

"Actually, I thought I spotted him in the quad with some Hispanic chick, what's her name... Maria?"

"Mariana?"

"I dunno. Probably," Mackenzie shrugs. "You'd know better than I would. I don't keep tabs on that boy." I feel a pang of jealousy in my stomach. I knew he and Mariana started hanging out, but when did he start showing up to school and meeting up with her first thing in the morning instead of meeting up with me? Relax, Erik. This might be a good thing, like a blessing in disguise. I need to get over Nicholas, and if he's busy latching himself onto other people, maybe it'll be easier for me to do just that.

I'm sitting in Ms. Maple's class when Nicholas walks in seconds before the final bell and takes the seat next to me, as per usual. Allegedly, he was hanging out with Mariana, and because of Mariana, he was nearly late, but more importantly, he wasn't with me.

. . .

No. Let it go, Erik. Let it go.

"Hey, you showed up," I say, feigning happiness. I'm doing my best to not go against my better judgement. "I didn't think you'd be here since you weren't at my locker earlier."

"Yeah, I was hanging out with Mariana," he replies, all nonchalantly. I should just drop it right here before I say something stupid and end up digging myself into a hole.

"So what's going on between you two?" Stop it, Erik. Listen to yourself. But I can't. The green eyed monster has come to play and it's in no mood to be pulling any punches.

"Nothing. She's a friend. Why? Are you jealous?" Nicholas' tone is uncharacteristically serious. He doesn't seem like himself. No, he seems closed off and cautious. Not playful at all like I know him.

"No. Why would I be jealous? We're just 'hanging out.'" I don't know what set me off, but I can hear the disdain in my voice as I say those last two words. Nicholas has certainly heard it too. His eyes narrow. It's clear my tone is putting him off.

"Exactly," Nicholas says. He then turns away from me and goes silent. This is the moment that things become awkward between us. We don't talk for the remainder of English and throughout the entirety of History. Then, when third period rolls around, he does something so petty, I almost don't believe it. He sits next to Mariana, leaving me to sit here alone. Why? Did the implication of my jealousy really have such a profound effect on him? Did it scare him away or something? Because he never seemed to have a problem with my feelings for him before. What gives?

Nicholas doesn't show up for lunch and I'm so ticked off that I don't bother to text him. He's probably with Mariana doing God knows what. Mackenzie and I spend our lunch period behind the bleachers, and I complain about Nicholas this and Nicholas that, it's like every other word that comes out of my mouth is his name.

"Can we drop it now, Erik?" Mackenzie asks, visibly annoyed. "You've been talking about him non-stop. It's starting to get old."

"Wow, thanks for your support," I reply, my voice dripping with sarcasm.

"Sorry, but you are obsessed."

"You know, that's funny coming from you. Weren't you the one who was obsessed with trying to get us together?"

"Yeah, and now you're together."

"We're not together!" My voice comes out louder than expected.

"Then why are you so mad!?" Mackenzie shoots back. Her voice is sharp and piercing, it startles me. I take a second to regain my composure.

"You're being a really bad friend right now," I say, almost pitifully. Mackenzie scoffs at this.

"*I'm* being a bad friend?" she replies. "You have not once asked me how I'm doing today. And if I remember right, you ditched me — not once, not twice, but, like, a whole bunch of times — just so you could ride that dick, and *I'm* the one being a bad friend?"

"That's not fair, Mackenzie."

"No, Erik, this isn't fair," she says. She pulls out a cigarette, lights it, and takes a puff. She then blows the smoke in my face as she starts to walk away. "Call me when you're done playing the victim in all this. I'm over it."

What Mackenzie says pisses me off, but the more that I think about it, the more that I start to wonder about my role in all this. I keep blaming Nicholas for everything, but Nicholas didn't just have sex with himself. And it's not like it wasn't consensual on my part. I wanted him as badly as I felt he wanted me, knowing full well that the likelihood of us being together in the end was slim to none. Knowing that, I can't help but wonder if I'm a bad person. Because, if I'm to share the blame, it means I've given up on myself and my morals. As dirty as I may feel, I let myself be used. I was already wondering if there's a place for me in Heaven because of this whole gay thing, but now…

I don't know. Maybe I'm overthinking it. Maybe it's my Catholic guilt coming out to play. Sometimes it feels like God is playing a cruel joke on me. Like, maybe this was all a test.

And I'm failing it miserably.

Tuesday. November 26th.

The waves come crashing down on me violently. I'm struggling to reach the surface, but to no avail. I'm sinking, slipping deeper and deeper into the abyss. Everything around me is dark. I can't see. I can't breathe. My lungs are constricting, holding onto their last bit of breath. It hurts.

I'm drowning.

It feels like I'm gonna die.

This dream is getting old, but it's not getting any easier.

Today is playing out more or less like yesterday with Nicholas. He doesn't show up at my locker again, which is disheartening since neither does Mackenzie, but that doesn't surprise me. He shows up to class just seconds before the final bell and takes the seat next to me once again, as per usual.

"Hey," Nicholas says. That's pretty much all he says. He's being cordial, but not friendly. We don't say much to each other throughout first or second period, and when third period comes around and he goes to sit next to Mariana, I want to cry. He's only sitting a few rows up, but he seems so far away from me now. I had planned to keep my distance, but it looks like he's taking care of that for me. Maybe it's for the best.

At lunch, I decide to forego grabbing food — I don't have much of an appetite today — and hole myself up in the library. It's been a long time since I last spent my lunch period alone. I haven't had to do it since before Mackenzie was a part of my life. It's not fun, especially now when I'm feeling down. Being alone without someone to talk to, or even just to sit by you to occupy the same space, can be difficult. I'm left to wrestle with my thoughts and feelings without the comfort of knowing someone cares enough to listen. It's a sad day when you're counting down the minutes till the end of lunch. I mean, no one ever really wants to go to class, but at least that would be better than having to sit in silence, alone with my thoughts.

...

The bell finally rings, and I head off to fifth period. Only two more classes and then I'm free. I can wallow in my sorrows at home for five days and hopefully that's all I'll need to feel better about everything.

Oh, who am I kidding? I'm probably going to be freaking out about this for as long as I know Nicholas. It's not fair. But the five days away from him — so long as I can resist contacting him — will surely be a relief.

Fifth period is a nice break from my thoughts. Our teacher has already mentally checked out for the holiday, putting on a movie musical and leaving the class to their own devices. The movie is one of those old musicals from the fifties where all the actors are super hammy, and there's a whole lot of tap dancing. I actually kind of love it. It's so happy and colorful, I'm kind of sad that I probably won't get to see the rest of it. Note to self: must look up this movie so I can see what happens to the man with the rubbery legs, who dances while singing about making people laugh.

The bell rings, and fifth period lets out. Only one more class to go now. I head over to Bio and take my seat next to Andrew, thinking nothing of it. We haven't said much to each other in a long while and I don't expect that to change, but my expectations with him seem to never be on the mark so…

"I noticed you and Nick weren't hanging out today," Andrew begins without warning. "Or yesterday." Why is it his business? What does he want? I wonder…

"I don't know what you're talking about," I deny. I'd rather not be discussing my personal matters with someone like Andrew. I mean, it's *Andrew*. Why would I want to discuss anything with him unless I had to?

"I saw him hanging out with that cute Hispanic chick."

"I really don't want to talk about this. Not here. And definitely not with you." The bite has come out of me. I'm not in a very agreeable state. My relationship with my non-boyfriend, Nicholas, is completely up in the air, and my friendship with Mackenzie is currently on a time out, so forgive me if I'm lacking in my usual mild-mannered temperament. I'm not in the mood to be messed with.

Andrew takes a second to consider something. He glances around and then leans in towards me. It's making me rather nervous if I'm being honest.

"Look, I'm sorry," he offers in a whispered tone. It takes me by surprise, but not enough for me to let my guard down.

"It's fine," I say quickly.

"No, I mean, I'm sorry for everything." I'm not sure I believe what's coming out of his mouth. It seems so random and out of the blue, but I suppose I shouldn't be too suspicious of someone trying to apologize. "I'm sorry I said what I said to you and I'm sorry that it felt like I was just trying to take advantage." He seems earnest, so much so that his voice starts to crescendo ever so slightly, as if he'd forgotten where we are. My eyes dart around the room nervously, hoping that no one is listening in. Thankfully, it doesn't look like anyone is. Andrew's staring at me now, his eyes locked into mine to ensure that I'm receiving his apology. "I'm especially sorry about that note. It honestly wasn't even my idea. My buddies are assholes and thought it'd be hilarious, but it was a shitty thing to do and I'm a shitty person for going along with it."

"Can you keep your voice down, Andrew?" I say, shushing him. I'm in total disbelief, not sure what to make of this. I mean, an apology — like, an actual sincere apology — from Andrew was not exactly on the top of my list of things to expect on this Tuesday afternoon. In fact, it wasn't on my list of things to expect at all. I just assumed that we'd mind our business, eventually end the school year, and then never speak to each other again. That's what I was prepared to do.

"Sorry. It's just… I look at you and you seem to be okay with yourself. Like, you don't care how people perceive you."

"Actually, I care a lot."

"Yeah, but not like me. You don't walk around trying to impress anybody. You just keep to yourself and mind your business. And because of that, you got what I wanted. At least, it looked like you got what I wanted."

"Thanks... I guess?"

Andrew nods and turns to face the front of the class. I pull out my notebook and stare absentmindedly as our teacher explains the stupid over-the-holiday assignment we're being given. Homework over Thanksgiving? So much for being thankful... Anyway, I spend the rest of the class period reading over the assignment packet and taking notes whenever our teacher says something vaguely important sounding. When the bell finally rings, I'm home free.

"Have a happy holiday, everyone," my Bio teacher calls out as I, along with the rest of the class, file out of the classroom to our five day weekend. It could not have come any sooner.

Wednesday. November 27th.

Peaceful waves.
Sandy shores.
Oarless boat.
Crashing storm.
Sinking deeper and deeper. This dream has become all too familiar. It's been months and it's still my one recurring nightmare. Some days, I try to stay asleep

longer just to see how it will play out in the end, but there's never anything but a dark abyss and an awful constricting feeling in my lungs. When I can't hold my breath any longer, the dream forces me awake. It's almost unfair. Today's no different.

It's around noon when I look over at the clock on my nightstand. Curious, I reach for my phone to see if I've gotten any messages. Nothing. There's a consistent tapping sound on my window. It's raining, and it's coming down pretty hard. It's the perfect kind of day to sit around and play video games. I mean, it's not like I had any other plans. Plus, I'm kind of exhausted.

I had a hard time sleeping last night. This whole thing with Nicholas was really bothering me that I spent much of the evening moping around all depressed like. When I went up to my room after dinner, I found myself staring at my phone, repeatedly scrolling up to refresh his text box just hoping that, by some miracle, he would've texted. He did not.

You know, I thought that the time away from him would be good for me, but given how things have been between us the last couple days, being away from him last night only made me miss him more. I really wanted to talk to him, but I couldn't bring myself to just say, "Hello." What if he didn't want to hear from me? What if everything was over between us? Did I mess up? Did I want too much from him? All these thoughts came racing through my mind that I almost felt like I was going crazy. Why couldn't I stop thinking about him? I mean, is this really how love is supposed to feel? Is love supposed to hurt this much?

I needed a distraction, so much so I even voluntarily did some chores. I picked up my room, started a load of laundry, got a head start on my homework, but nothing could get my mind off of Nicholas. No matter what I did, he was there. I kept seeing his signature crooked smile and his sweet maple eyes in my mind, and all I wanted to do was to be with him. I wanted to lay in his arms and stroke his cheek with that perfectly placed beauty mark beside his right eye. I wanted to listen to his heartbeat while I laid my head against his chest. I wanted to smell his scent of that familiar ocean breeze. I wanted… him. I just wanted him.

I needed to gather and get my thoughts out somehow. Since I couldn't bring myself to talk to him, I figured maybe the next best thing would be to write to him. So I pulled out a notebook and that's what I did...

Dear Nicholas,

You're probably gonna think this is stupid and pointless since we talk everyday — or we used to anyway... I like you. You know I like you. You've already gotten me to admit it. What you don't know is that I think I'm in deeper than like with you, and I don't know how to handle it. I always knew that we'd probably never be anything more than friends, but then you kissed me, and we had sex, and I'm, like, really enamored with your happy trail and... I don't know what I'm talking about. That's gross.

Anyway, the more that things kept happening between us, the more I wanted to believe that you felt something too. I could actually picture us being together like a couple. But then, when you said that we're just "hanging out," it made me question things. Like, was I stupid to think that we could be together? Those thoughts kind of haunted me, because I know being with a guy is wrong. But when I'm with you, it feels like it's okay, and I just hoped that maybe we could be something. You know, I'm not supposed to feel this way about a guy. Because if I did, it would be really bad.

I want to ask you to put a label on what we've been doing together, because I can't keep doing things with you if I don't know what we are, or what I am to you. But then again, I suppose this is a two-way street. So, if I had to pick a label for what we've been doing, if I had to call it anything, it would be something that I've felt for a while. I think I started to realize it on the day that we went to the city, even before we ever did anything. It's been so overwhelming that it scares me to put it into actual words. It's silly and I feel stupid, because I'm nervous sitting here, even just writing this. So I'll just say

The letter took a long time to write, and when I finished, I couldn't help but laugh. It was so pitiful. I mean, how could I send this? I would never. That's the beauty of writing letters. You're not obligated to send them, so no one ever has to see. It can just stay in my notebook forever. The saddest part though, is that even after writing the letter, I still couldn't get Nicholas off of my mind, so I ended up staying up playing video games to try to keep myself occupied. I had gotten myself lost in one of those throwback turn-based JRPGS and before I knew it, it was 3:00am. I wouldn't consider myself a huge video game nerd, but it's hard not to get wrapped up in it when your characters are steadily leveling up, and you're unlocking all these different job classes for them to switch into. I'm sure I'm not the only one out there who plots out my party's job class combination before actually gaining access to those jobs, but I digress.

Before I settle in for a day of gaming, I decide to head downstairs and grab some food. Currently, I'm eating through the box of plain cracked wheaties that my mom was forced to buy on Sunday. It's not the worst cereal in the world, but it does take a few spoonfuls of sugar in order to make it edible.

I go into the kitchen and find my mom sitting at the table reading from a notebook. It must be the recipe to her family's famous ube dessert or something. She is making it for Thanksgiving tomorrow and — strangely enough — she doesn't seem too happy about it. Whatever. I know it's probably difficult and all, but it's not like anyone's forcing her to make it.

"Morning," I greet her, to which I get no response. I shrug it off and walk straight over to the pantry where I grab my box of wheaties and the canister of sugar. I place the two items on the table then make a beeline to the fridge for the milk, and then to the dishwasher where I grab a bowl and a spoon. As I come back to the table for the cereal and sugar, I notice my mom's staring at me. Her eyes are glassy, wet with restrained tears. "Is something wrong, Mom?" She takes a breath, then pushes the notebook towards me. I glance down at it, and it takes less than a second for me to realize that my mom wasn't reading an old dessert recipe. No, she was reading the letter I wrote to Nicholas. My heart sinks. "Why do you have that?"

"I went to ask you to get your laundry. I needed the dryer," Mom explains stoically, though her eyes are pooling with tears. "You just left it right there on your nightstand." She pauses, staring at me as if waiting for me to explain myself, but the words never come. I'm frozen in silence. "Do you want to read to me what that letter says?"

"No," I respond, nervously swallowing my words. Mom's staring daggers at me, though somehow she manages to keep her voice soft, calm, and even, which is actually way more unsettling than it might sound.

"Nicholas is the boy that came over and read poetry to you, isn't he? You know, I had my suspicions. And then, when we ran into his mother at the grocery store, I knew for sure something was going on. I knew you were hiding something. I knew you liked him." Mom takes another pause. Her anger is building, I can see it in the way her shoulders are tensing up and how she's refusing to break eye contact with me. I want to run away. I don't want to have to defend myself against her, because I know there's no way for me to win, but I can't move. It's like her piercing gaze has severed my ability to walk. I'm frozen in fear, like a little baboy about to be made into lechon. "You listen to me, Erik, this is not going to go anywhere. It can never go anywhere, kasi there is no love between two men. Not in the eyes of God. I want you to stop this. I want you to stop seeing him. Whatever's going on, it needs to stop. Okay? I want you to stop it." With that, Mom gets up from the table and moves to exit. At that moment, I feel a tear start to roll down my cheek and words finally escape me.

"I love him," I say, without thought or hesitation. Mom stops and turns to me.

"Erik, tigas ng ulo mo," she scoffs. "Have you not been listening? This is not love. It is a sin! It is a sin and you will go to Hell for it! Please, you have to break it off."

"Mom, that's not fair."

"Not fair? Ano ka ba? Life isn't fair. Why don't you understand that I only want what's best for you?"

"What about what *I* want?" Mom recoils and begins to collect herself. Her expression darkens.

"Commandment Number Five, Erik," she says, now sounding devoid of all empathy. "What does it say?"

"That's not fair," I respond pitifully.

"'Honor thy father and mother.'"

"No, that's not fair! You can't use God's words against me, because they're not fair! They're not real!" I can hear myself screaming now, yelling at the top of my lungs. My mom's face drops. Through my peripheral, I see Dad enter through the threshold, but it's too late. I've gone off into the deep end. Even if I wanted to stop, I can't. "I have tried to pray, and I have tried to ask God to make these feelings stop, but they never stop. They just get stronger and stronger until I can't control myself anymore. I have tried, Mom, but he doesn't answer! God never answers!" Suddenly, the world goes silent, and this split second of time, this moment, seems to last forever.

"Get out of my house," I eventually hear my mom say. She doesn't sound mad or angry. She sounds… I don't know, dead? It's like I've killed her somehow with my words. "I taught my son better than this. You are not my son."

"Chris," Dad tries to interject, but Mom's not listening.

"I said, 'Get out of my house!' GET OOOOOOOOOUT!!!!" Mom suddenly lunges forward, snatches my notebook from the table, and hurls it at me with as much force as she can muster. In reaction, I back into the fridge and watch in horror as my dad grabs my mom from behind and holds her back. Mom flails about in his arms, screaming and crying, the tears leaving her eyes like rain from a cloud during a hurricane. This is all happening so fast, but somehow I'm experiencing it in slow motion.

"Erik, go!" I hear Dad yell over Mom's cries. "Just go!" So I do. I run past my parents, keeping as much distance between myself and my mother as possible, racing out of the kitchen, and towards the front door. I don't stop to grab anything but a pair of sneakers from the shoe rack — not even a sweater — before heading out into the storm.

chapter twenty-six
nicholas

Finally off! Man, these last two days at school were killer but, like, in a slow and torturous way. Half of my teachers didn't want to be there as much as I didn't want to be there, which was fine but super boring. The other half were being real extra, trying to cram in some last minute bits of learning with their pop quizzes and assigning work over the holidays. Why? I don't get it! I mean, it's only two days. Take a break and let us have one too. It's Thanksgiving for fuck's sake. Whatever. It's over. Now that I'm on vacation, I'm just gonna relax, turn my brain off, and just get away from everything. I think that would be best.

These next five days, I really want to focus on myself and just spend some time with me. Mariana suggested that I should. She said that I should take the time off to do some soul-searching and figure out what I want out of my life and my relationship with Erik, without any sort of outside influence. It's just hard though, because it seems like everyone wants me to define things and put a label on everything. Even Erik, which doesn't help his case at all.

On Sunday, he called me to talk about cereal, of all things, but it was all just a thinly veiled analogy for what he really wanted. I'm not dumb. I know he wants to be with me, and for a while, I even thought maybe I was okay with that idea. In fact, I might've even wanted it. That is, until he started asking about it. I don't know. It's hard to explain. It's like… you know how when you like something — let's say soccer — and it's cool, and it's fun, and whatever, but then people see that you like it and suddenly everyone wants you to play and join a team or something? Suddenly, soccer doesn't sound so fun. And even though you might enjoy it, you don't want to play anymore. It's like that.

After Erik's call on Sunday, I couldn't stop thinking that maybe things are getting a little too close between us. I've always told him that what's happening between us is just two friends hanging out and he always accepted it, so it kinda freaked me out when he used the word "boyfriend." Well, actually he used the word "boy-fren-lavin," claiming to be reading the back of a cereal box, but Erik's never been a very good liar. It'd actually be pretty hilarious if it wasn't so concerning.

I guess my main issue is that I wanted more time. I need more time. How do you go from being one thing all your life to finding out you're something completely different without feeling like the world is suddenly spinning in the opposite direction? I thought if anyone would understand, it'd be Erik. He went through the change not too long ago, so surely, he couldn't have already forgotten how confusing and complicated it is to have to redefine yourself, could he? It feels almost unfair that he's asking about a relationship when he knows that this is an entirely new thing for me. Doesn't he know this isn't easy? Doesn't he know how scary it is to have to declare yourself something you never knew you were? I don't know… Maybe it's different for me than it was for him. Maybe he didn't have to redefine himself. Maybe he always knew deep down that he likes what he likes. Who would've thought that between the two of us, Erik would be the one to have things seemingly all figured out? That's why I went to Mariana.

Mariana and I have been hanging out the last two days and she's been helping me work through my issues, letting me vent about my feelings. With everyone putting pressure on me about the Erik situation, it was nice to have someone who would be an ear, and who would give me advice on how to make things better for *me*. Everyone else seems to be more concerned about how I can make things better for Erik, and that's great and all, but what the fuck am I supposed to do with advice like: "You can't leave it up in the air." Like, duh! I know that. It's the whole reason I'm so troubled by it. Everyone is so focused on Erik and how *he* must feel, but what about *me*? What about how *I* feel?

As far as Erik goes, I don't even know if he's on my side anymore. He's clearly jealous about me spending time with Mariana, and the fact that he's jealous makes it harder for me to be around him. His jealousy makes me feel like he thinks he might have some ownership and — don't get me wrong — he does. We've been having sex. He has every right to be jealous, but the fact that he *is* makes me feel like I owe him something. Like I don't have a real say in the matter just because we boned. That's why I'm keeping my distance. Five days. So long as I don't answer his calls or read any of his messages — I should really just put my phone in airplane mode — I'll have five whole days to make sense of everything. Hopefully, after that, I'll have a little more clarity.

Oh, who am I kidding? I've been racking my brain about it for a month. Five days isn't gonna do anything. Whatever, a break from the world will be nice regardless.

It's really loud in my room today. There's an incessant tapping against the garage door. I don't need to look through a window to know that it's raining, I can just tell from the sound. And it's pretty hard too. I can barely hear myself think. I grab my phone, find a pair of earbuds to put on some music, and get to work on drawing my cartoons and making my comic book. Erik may be putting me off, but the comic book is for him, and I've put in a lot of work already. I'm not just gonna scrap it because things are rocky. It'd be a total waste.

Mariana texts a little while after I've gotten into a groove.

"Hey love! How you holding up?" her message reads. I reply with a thumbs up emoji and flip my phone over so that I can't see the screen. Now that I'm in the middle of creative work mode, I can't be bothered to talk about my feelings. Right now, I'm good. But I appreciate the concern. Mariana's a good friend.

The drawing I'm working on is shaping up pretty good. Basically, it's Cartoon Erik holding a bowl of cereal, complaining that his wheaties are dry, and Cartoon Me offering him some milk. It's a lot cuter than it sounds. I think the baby anime-like style — I think it's called *chibi* or something — that I'm doing is what really makes the drawing. I dunno. It's endearing.

I've been drawing for maybe an hour when my mom barges into my room.

"¿Por qué no me contestastes?" she exclaims angrily. I throw off my earbuds. Honestly, I didn't even hear her knocking over my music. She takes me by surprise. She's never been the type of mother to just come in. She's always respected my space for the most part. I guess she must've been knocking for a while to come in this upset. That's when I notice someone standing behind her. It's Erik. He's dressed in his pajama bottoms and a plain t-shirt, and he's soaked from head to toe. What's going on?

"Erik? What are you doing here?" I ask as Ma leads him into my bedroom.

"I didn't have… anywhere to go," he starts to explain. He's whimpering, gasping for breath between each word, and he's shivering like crazy. It's really worrying me. "My mom kicked me out… She was really mad… She said I'm… I'm not her son." His face scrunches up into a full on ugly cry. He's trying so hard to be strong, trying to stifle his sobs with the back of his hand, but it's just not working. He's got no strength left. This is a guy who's been completely broken. I can't stand to see him like this. I can't. It absolutely destroys me. Without thinking, I walk over to Erik and pull him into a tight embrace, enveloping him completely. He wraps his arms around me and begins to cry into my shoulder uncontrollably.

"Mijo, when he calms down, I'm gonna need his parents' number," Ma says gently, watching from the sidelines.

"I'll get it," I say. Ma nods and quietly leaves the room. I hold Erik tighter and wait for him to catch his breath. He's soaked. I'm soaked now too. The moisture sends a chill through me, but it's the least of my concerns. All I care about now is how I need to take care of him. "Come on, let's get you out of these wet clothes." Erik nods and I proceed to peel his shirt off of him. I go over to my dresser, grab a couple towels, and help him dry himself off. "I hate to make this awkward, but you're gonna need to take your pants off." I smile with the feeble hope of lightening the mood, but Erik's not all here. He's in complete shock, so I go ahead and do it for him. I remove his pajamas and boxers and dry him off myself. If we hadn't done what we'd done together, I don't know that I could've helped him the way I am, so we're lucky for that.

Once Erik's dry, I dress him in a pair of my sweatpants, a V-neck, and a gray cardigan. Surprisingly, everything kinda fits. Even though he's a bit on the pudgy side, we're miraculously not too far apart in size. I guess he's really that much smaller than me. Erik takes a seat on my futon bed and curls himself up into a little ball. Meanwhile, I change out of my wet shirt and boxers and into a fresh set. I then move my heating tower a little closer to the bed and sit down next to him.

"You okay?" I ask. Erik seems to be lost in his own world.

"I like this sweater," he says sadly, fiddling with the sleeves. "It reminds me of the city. You were wearing it then."

"Yeah, I guess I was." His memory is impressive. It's a bit odd, if I'm being honest, knowing that someone can recount the little details of your life better than you can. I can't say I'm not flattered though, but there are more pressing matters at hand. "So what's going on with your mom?"

"I'm so stupid. I'm so, so stupid. I guess she came into my room when I was asleep and she found my notebook… I didn't put it away. I'm so stupid. I should've put it away…"

"Wait. What's so bad about her finding your notebook?" I ask, not really sure what to make of what he's saying. What was in the notebook that was so bad that it would lead to this? I'm curious, Erik. What did you do?

"I wrote a letter in it… It was a letter to you." My breathing gets heavy. I have suspicions. At this point, I'm hoping that it wasn't what I think it was. But before I could even hold on to that little bit of hope, he drops the bomb. "It was a love letter." My heart sinks when he says it. All this time we spent hiding the fact that we were doing what we were doing from his parents — particularly his mom — and it's suddenly all undone by something he wrote… to me. I feel guilty, like all of this is my fault. That's when Erik says something that just freaks me the fuck out. "Tell me you love me." I turn to look at him, my ears perked in disbelief. Is this really happening right now?

"I… uh…" I'm opening my mouth to say something, but nothing comes out. My voice is just a jumble of incoherent sounds. I can't seem to form any words.

"I love you," Erik says. I'm panicking. This has gone way further than I ever meant for it to. I knew he liked me and everything, but I thought we had an understanding, and the minute that it felt like we didn't, I backed off. That's why I stopped being so friendly with him these last two days. That's why I ran to Mariana. That's why I wanted to be away from him for a little while, but I guess it was too late. I didn't want this to happen. I didn't want to have to break his heart, but now I don't really have a choice. I can feel my lips quivering, searching for something to say. I have to say something to stop this.

"Erik, this was a mistake," I finally manage. There, I said it. I didn't want to, because it's not true, but what else could I say? Erik's staring at me with widened eyes. The world stops for a moment, and I'm forced to watch as Erik begins to crumble right in front of me. Tears start pouring from him like waterfalls. He starts to hyperventilate. He's shaking. He looks around the room, for what, I don't know. Then, he suddenly gets up and heads for the door. The next thing I know, I'm running through my uncle's house, chasing him down. He's almost to the front door when I reach him.

"Erik, wait!" I yell, grabbing him by the arm and pulling him so that he turns to face me. I see the saddest look upon his face. It absolutely kills me.

"Don't touch me!" he screams. He's on the defensive, and I can't blame him. I would be too. I notice Ma coming over to us from my peripheral, but I don't care. Right now, it's about me and Erik.

"Let me just… try to explain," I'm stammering. I have no idea what I want to say, what I *need* to say to make things better. I have absolutely no idea what I'm doing, or what I hope will come out of the next few seconds, but I just… I can't let him go. He's my best friend, and I love him, and I can't just let him go. Not like this. "Erik… please… just give me a second to…"

"Get away from me! Let go!" Erik cries, his glassy, heartbroken eyes flooding his face with tears. With his free hand, he grabs the handle to the door, but I can't let him go. I just can't. I immediately reach for his other arm and try to pull him away from the door, but he continues to fight against me. Suddenly, I feel something strike me across the face. It takes me a second to realize... Erik slapped me. It catches me by such surprise that I can't help but let him go.

"Erik!" I hear Ma yell, but Erik's already out the door. I'm frozen in complete shock. I feel like I'd been struck by lightning. And I may as well have been. Erik hit me with such force, it was as if his life depended on it. And, I don't know, maybe it does... considering everything that's happened.

Because, clearly, I'm no good for him.

chapter
twenty-seven
erik

I don't know what to do.

I don't know where to go. Mackenzie lives clear across town and the rain is coming down harder than before. It'd take me hours to get there.

What do I do?

What am I supposed to do?

Please, God, give me a sign. Something. Anything.

. . .

It's useless. Why do I turn to him when he never seems to answer me? Why do I need him the way that I do? I want to *not* care. I want to chalk things up to pointless happenstance, but to think everything occurs randomly and without reason is such a foreign and tragic concept to me, I could never accept it.

I'm running as fast as my tired legs are willing. I run and run until I can't run anymore. Then I trudge along, soaking, ankle deep in every puddle I walk through. I don't know where I'm going. I don't know what I'm doing. I'm just moving aimlessly, straight ahead to nowhere. How did I get here? Alone… and in the rain with no one to turn to? Somewhere, I messed up. I *had* to have messed up. It would be the only explanation for such a cruel punishment. That's what this is. Then again, maybe this isn't a punishment. God never answers me. How am I to know that he's even real? Maybe the stars just aligned in a way that would be unfortunate for me. Maybe this is just completely random, and I was the unlucky fool to come out with a raw deal. Who knows?

As the weather beats down on me, I begin to play everything back from the very beginning when this all started. I think about Andrew and how he propositioned me. I think about how I was nothing more to him than a potentially easy score. I think about the priest, who — rather than help me — pretty much turned me away because "God has spoken." I think about my mom and her reaction to the whole gay thing. She tried to be supportive and sweep it under the rug like we're supposed to, and I went and threw her beliefs in her face because things aren't how they're supposed to be. *I'm* not how I'm supposed to be.

Then I think about Nicholas…

I want to be mad at him.

I want to cast blame on him.

I want to hate him.

. . .

But I don't. I can't. As angry and as worthless as he may have made me feel, I know that it's my fault. And I know how pathetic that sounds, but it's true. What idiot falls in love with someone who… they're just "hanging out" with? Only a fool does that.

The rain is getting really heavy, so much so that I can't see through my glasses. I decide to take them off and everything immediately goes out of focus. I see the world as if it were a blurry watercolor painting. Trees are just splotches of greenish brown. The road is a messy black mass, melting and dancing in the puddles I sink into. The sky is a canvas covered with erratic brushstrokes of gray and white. Then, in the distance, something — a place — comes into view. Without my glasses, I don't recognize it one bit. I carefully begin to make my way over to it. Wherever it is, maybe I'll get lucky and find somewhere to wait out the storm. I won't hold my breath though.

As I approach the place I can't quite make out, I'm greeted by blurred lines forming diamond shapes in front of me. What is this? A fence? Where am I? I look around for a moment to see if I can recognize anything, but the world around me is literally a blur. I take my glasses and wipe the lenses off with my fingers. It won't be long before they're covered in rain again, but at the very least I'll catch a glimpse of where I'm at. As it turns out, I'm at the community pool.

Staring at the pool, with the rain causing it to crash and form waves, I'm reminded of something: my dream. The dream that's been haunting me for the past few months. I'm entranced by it. Hypnotized by the way the water and the rain has changed this pool into the violent sea of my nightmare. Then, I'm hit with a sudden impulse. The next thing I know, I'm climbing down the other side of the fence and walking toward the edge of the pool. Replace the chain link with a palm tree and the cement with a sandy shore, and I'd swear I'm back on that island staring out at my inevitable fate. This can't be happening right now...

Why am I here?

Do you ever have those moments where you feel like it's the culmination of everything that's happened prior? Like how a birthday party, for example, is the culmination of planning, cooking, buying gifts, inviting people, whatever. This feels like that. I've been having the same dream of drowning night after night for months now, and no matter how hard I try to see it through to the end, I can never seem to stay asleep long enough to see what happens next. It's almost as if my dreams have been teasing and taunting me. Now, suddenly, I'm here, standing on the edge of what would be a vast ocean, roaring and crashing in the middle of a violent storm.

I keep my eyes fixated on the pool, looking, searching for some clarity in all this, as if the chlorine filled waves somehow hold the meaning to my recurring dream. I draw out every detail in my mind: the island, the palm tree, the rowboat, the sea. All of it leads to my demise. My drowning. My death. I scoff. This is silly. No, it's crazy. I don't want to hurt myself. I don't want to die. I slowly start to back away from the pool, but as I turn to face the fence, I feel a powerful gust of wind smack me in the face, and I have to stop to hold my footing.

The trees beyond the fence are swaying towards me. The rain is falling at an angle against me. The wind is making it difficult to move forward. It's as if I'm being pushed back toward the pool. Then — and it's very possible that my mind is playing tricks on me — I hear a voice in the distance calling my name.

"Erik!" It seems to echo, breaking through the overbearing symphony of the storm. "Erik!" It calls again, and I can't decipher whether it's the voice of a man, or a woman, or both. It's a voice calling from a far-off distance… Could it be?

"What do you want?" I mutter to myself before crying out at the top of my lungs. "WHAT DO YOU WANT FROM ME?!"

…

Nothing.

The whole world seems to fall silent despite the chaos around me. Did I really expect an answer? Suddenly, the strangest thing happens. The clouds part and, for only the briefest moment, the rain stops falling on the pool, leaving the waters to ripple and dance calmly. It happens so quickly I'm almost fully convinced I'm hallucinating. How bad is it out here for my mind to paint such vivid pictures?

I start to feel a strange knotting sensation in my gut. It's weird. The wind, the rain, the instant flash of a peaceful sight, all of it seems to be pointing toward the water, and my gut is telling me… to jump. I'm freaking out. I have no idea what's going on in my head anymore, and here, something is telling me to jump in the pool. Why would I ever do that? I can't swim. What sense would there be in that? I look up at the sky, hoping to find an answer and still, there's nothing. So I start to pray, silently to myself. My prayers are a jumbled incoherent mess. I go from one script to another without completing the one I've started before. They feel less like prayers and

more like ramblings from someone who's at a complete
loss, but I keep on praying. What else is there to do?
Our father, who art in Heaven, hallowed be thy name…
Jump. My gut twists with a pang.
Hail, Mary, full of grace…
Jump. They say that your gut is never wrong.
You just have to trust it.
The Lord is with thee…
Jump.

chapter twenty-eight
nicholas

Where is he?

Where would he have gone?

Mom and Tio Roger went together to search around the neighborhood. They told me to check anywhere that I thought Erik might've gone to, but the only place I could come up with was Mackenzie's house, so I'm heading there now. I'm not holding my breath though since she lives across town, and it's unlikely Erik would go all that way on foot. Not in this rain. But where else would he go?

Water beats down against the windshield as I'm pulling into Mackenzie's driveway. She lives in an older neighborhood, in a little one story bungalow complete with a tiny porch, with just enough space to fit a bench and a few potted plants. The rain's coming down really hard now, and I'm regretting not bringing an umbrella. I'm especially regretting the pajama bottoms I threw on before I left the house. I'm about to get drenched. I step out of my mom's car and quickly jog up the steps to Mackenzie's front door where I ring the doorbell about four or five times, just for good measure. After a minute or so, the door swings open and Mackenzie's standing in front of me, dressed in an oversized t-shirt, and sweatpants, looking completely annoyed.

"Are you fucking kidding me right now?" she scolds from behind her screen door. "Once is enough, Nick. Asshole." If Erik's not here, I'll take pissing her off as a minor consolation. "What do you want?"

"Is Erik here?" I say, cutting straight to the point.

"No. Why would he be?"

"He came by earlier, freaking out. He said his mom kicked him out and that he had nowhere to go."

"Seriously? Holy shit," Mackenzie mutters, mostly to herself.

"Yeah, and then he ran off," I sigh. Mackenzie cocks her head, like she doesn't quite understand.

"Wait. Why would he do that?" she asks. I stare at her blankly, trying to look as dumbfounded and innocent as I possibly can. She doesn't need to know the details. Mackenzie narrows her eyes, suspicious, and I start to tense up. "What did you do?" I shrug, shaking my head in denial. I don't have to answer to her. "Nick?" But women are scary when they get determined. Especially when it's so painfully obvious that you're holding out on them.

"I didn't do anything!" I say, practically yelling. Mackenzie raises her eyebrows in cynical disbelief and crosses her arms, waiting for me to continue. "I didn't! He came over, was freaking out about his mom, and then he told me to tell him that I love him."

"And what did you say?"

"I said it was a mistake." God, hearing myself say it again makes it sound so much worse than when I said it the first time. Guilt rushes through me like a current into a storm drain as I'm realizing… I'm a huge asshole. Mackenzie pushes open her screen door and steps out onto the porch with me. She then positions herself directly in front of me, and without warning, smacks me across the face. "WHAT WAS THAT FOR?!" I scream in response.

"Wouldn't you slap yourself?" she replies, all finger-wagging and matter-of-fact like. "God, how stupid can you be? No wonder he ran off."

"What was I supposed to say?" I ask defensively.

"You're supposed to say that you love him, duh!"

"I'm not obligated to say that. I mean, what if I don't? What if I'm not even gay?" Mackenzie's face drops and her expression immediately goes to a blank sarcastic stare that is wholly unamused.

"Are you serious?" she begins. "Look, I don't have the patience for all this self-hating denial — or whatever — bullshit you're trying to pull right now. You're gay, your hair's gay, your dick's gay, and the pattern on those pajamas you're wearing right now is *very* gay." Seriously? What in the actual fuck? What is it with people and wanting — no, *insisting* on labeling me? What's that about? I'm not gay. I'm not straight. I'm not sure what I am! Why can't people just back off about it?

"Real talk, Mackenzie. This whole thing was just a big experiment between friends, okay? We were just exploring. I like girls. I'm the freakin' top!"

"Oh, you're the top? Well, I'm sorry. That makes you even gayer!" She's really starting to piss me off now.

"How does that make me gayer?"

"You're the one who has to get it up!" She exclaims. In a reflex, I open my mouth to rebut her, but...

. . .

Yeah, I got nothing. What can I say? That makes a lot of sense. She has me beat in that respect. I let out a defeated sigh and take a seat on the bench. I'm an idiot. I messed up. Big time.

"Look, we were just hanging out," I start to explain. "I told him we were just hanging out and he always agreed with me. I mean, I knew he had feelings, but that's why I always insisted that there was nothing more to it."

"*Is* there nothing more to it?"

"I don't know. The last thing I wanted to do was hurt him. When I kissed him for the first time… things felt right. It felt good. I guess I just wanted to explore that a little more. And, like I said, I told him what it was. We were just hanging out. I didn't think his feelings would get involved."

"Okay, but this is Erik we're talking about," Mackenzie says, taking things more seriously now. She takes a seat next to me. "How could you think that his feelings *wouldn't* get involved?" I shrug, shaking my head. "So, you were just using him then?"

"No! I just… I don't know…" I let my voice trail off. I wasn't using him, was I? I try to go over it all in my head to make sense of everything, but no matter what train of thought I go with, all roads seem to lead to yes. Yes, I was using him. If there's an award for being the biggest douchebag, there's no doubt in my mind that I would make the shortlist.

"God, and to think we thought gay men were different. Turns out *all* men are stupid," Mackenzie says, more to herself than to me. I let out a small chuckle. "You know, it's funny. You never seemed to have a problem with any of the gay stuff. At least, not until today."

"He told me he loves me," I explain.

"Exactly," Mackenzie replies. I sigh and then bury my face into my hands. The level of shitty-ness that I feel in this moment is almost unbearable.

"God, why does love have to be so complicated?" I mumble pathetically to myself.

"What did you say?" Mackenzie asks.

"Why does love have to be so complicated?" I repeat, not really knowing what she's getting at. She narrows her eyes as a smile starts to form on her lip. It's kinda freaking me out. "What?"

"What's complicated, Nick?" she says. I think for a moment and...

. . .

. . .

. . .

Holy shit.

HOLY SHIT!

As soon as I realize, the whole world stops. My eyes widen, my heart starts to race, and my breathing gets heavy. I'm... in love. Is this what love's supposed to feel like? Because it's kinda terrifying. I'm in love with Erik. How did I miss that? How could I have let something so huge slip past me? I finally understand all those songs that talk about love taking the singer by surprise. It definitely took me by surprise. For a minute, I'm in shock. I'm frozen here on the bench, just trying to get a grasp on the sudden realization that I'm in love with a dude. But it's not even about that. Who cares if he's a dude? I'm… in love. What the hell do I do?

"I gotta go," I say, when I finally come back to myself. "I gotta find Erik. I gotta figure this out." I get up to leave when suddenly, my phone starts to ring. I pull it out and glance at the screen. It's my mom.

"Nicky, mijo, we found him," my mom's voice comes through my phone. She sounds winded and she's talking fast, like she's panicking. "We found Erik!" Something's up. Ma's not exactly sounding happy or relieved to have found Erik, so I don't really know how I should be reacting at this moment.

"That's great," I say.

"No," Ma responds quickly. "We're at the community pool. He jumped in." My heart sinks and I go back into shock. I'd drop my phone if I didn't need it to hear more. "The ambulance should be on its way."

"Ma, is he okay?" I somehow manage.

"He's got a pulse, but he's out cold."

"Is he okay?!"

"No sé, mijo. I gotta go, your tio needs help."

"Ma, is he okay!?" But she's already hung up. Panic starts to set in. I can feel myself start to shake.

"Nick, what is it?" I hear Mackenzie ask. I'd almost forgotten she was here. I turn to her, tears in my eyes. "What's wrong?"

"My mom. She found Erik."

"That's good, right? Is he okay?" I shake my head.

"They're at the community pool. He jumped." Mackenzie's face goes white. Her expression goes from concern, to worry, to dread in a matter of milliseconds. I don't have time to console her right now. I got to get to Erik. "I gotta go," I say.

"Wait, I'm coming with you," Mackenzie tells me, before running back into her house to grab a coat and a pair of boots.

Mackenzie's driving us. When we got into my mom's car, I was too shaken to even get the key in the ignition, so we switched at Mackenzie's demand. She's at the wheel while I correspond with my mom via text message. Ma tells us to meet her at the nearest hospital, which is roughly a thirty minute drive from Mackenzie's place. It's the longest thirty minutes of my life. We seem to be getting held up, either by a series of red lights or behind an asshole who can't drive in the rain. I have no idea what I'm gonna do when I get to the hospital. I don't know if there is anything for me to do when I get there. All I know is that I need to be there. I need to be close to Erik.

When we arrive at the hospital, I begin texting my mom frantically, one text message after another without giving her a chance to respond. It feels like forever that we're wandering around the halls before she finally responds with where to go. Mackenzie and I take the elevator up, and all the while, I'm shaking. Mackenzie's rubbing my back trying to calm me down. How she's keeping it together the way she is is baffling to me. Once we exit the elevator, we quickly head down the hall to a small waiting area where we find Ma and Tio Roger sitting nervously.

"Ma! How is he? Is he okay?" I say, jogging up to my mom.

"We don't know yet, mijo," she replies. "They haven't told us anything." I breathe an exasperated sigh. I wish it were one of relief, but sadly, no. Waiting around for an update is gonna be torture but, really, what else can we do?

About an hour goes by when I notice a familiar couple — a small Filipino woman and a Korean man who bears a striking resemblance to Erik — come into the waiting area. Are those Erik's parents? I've only really met them once so I'm not entirely sure, but that man looks so much like Erik it's hard to deny it. I want to go up to them, maybe talk to them, and possibly even get to the bottom of what set this whole thing into motion, but I don't. I just sit here and watch as they approach the check-in counter, and the nurse directs them to have a seat. That's when Erik's mom notices me staring at her. She comes over, looking like she's been carrying the weight of the world on her shoulders. I feel sorry for her. She and her kid had a fight, and then just a few hours later, she finds out her kid's in the hospital. And I thought *I* was broken up about it. I can't imagine how she must be feeling.

"Mackenzie," Erik's mom says when she approaches us. Mackenzie, who's sitting next to me, gets up. "Have you heard anything?"

"Not yet," Mackenzie replies without her usual sarcasm.

"What happened?"

"I don't know. Nick's mom and uncle found him." Erik's mom turns to my mom, who stands up as well.

"Um… Rose, right?" Erik's mom asks.

"Basically. It's Rosalie," Ma answers, wearing a weak smile. "You know, I don't think I ever got your name."

"Christine." Erik's mom and my mom shake hands. It's as awkward as it is somber.

"You know my son, Nick, right?" Ma gestures over to me. I get up as Erik's mom turns to me. The look in her eyes comes as a surprise. It's a look of sadness, but there's a bit of gentleness in there that I wasn't at all expecting. Not with the way Erik talks about her. She nods at me with a slight smile, a simple pleasantry. I'm not sure if I should say something or just keep my mouth shut.

"Hi," Erik's mom says. I offer her my hand. We shake and she doesn't let go. She keeps my hand in hers and locks her eyes into mine. It's actually really uncomfortable. I can see her searching, as if trying to look into my soul or something. I don't really know. But I'm taken aback when she finally speaks. "Tell me, Nick, are you dating my son?" The question throws me for a loop. At this point, what does it matter? I'm not sure how to proceed, so I decide on sticking to the truth.

"No," I say. Hearing the word breaks me. I bite down on my back teeth in an effort to hold in my tears. "No, but I should've been," is my full answer, but I can't bring myself to say it. Erik's mother gives me a soft smile while a tear rolls down her cheek. She lets go of my hand and quickly wipes the tear away.

"You know, he really likes you," she says, before her voice dissolves into a whimper. Within seconds, she's sobbing. Ma and Mackenzie both offer her support, while I fall back into my seat and begin to cry into my hands.

I don't know how long it's been. After a while, I resolved to not look at the clock. Counting the minutes was excruciating, I couldn't do it anymore. Waiting is the absolute worst. The whole time I keep thinking, maybe the reason no one's come to talk to us is because Erik's gone. Erik's gone and they don't know how they're gonna break the news. Erik's gone and the last thing I can remember saying to him is, "This was a mistake." It wasn't a mistake. I chose it. I chose him. I'd choose him every time, but I was too scared, stupid, and self-involved to realize it before. I need another shot. It can't end like this. It can't.

Finally, after what feels like an eternity, a doctor comes into the waiting area through a set of double doors just to the side of the check-in counter.

"Mr. and Mrs. Park?" the doctor calls out, reading from a clipboard. Erik's parents get up and approach the doctor, meanwhile the rest of us sit and watch, waiting, hoping for some good news. The doctor talks and talks but I can't hear a word of it. What are they saying? Is Erik okay? Less than a minute goes by before Erik's father goes through the double doors with the doctor, leaving Erik's mom behind in the waiting room. What happened? My leg is bouncing up and down, going a mile a minute with anticipation. Then, Erik's mom comes over to us.

"Erik's fine," she begins to explain. Myself, along with the rest of our group, breathe a collective sigh of relief. Thank God. "He's awake, but the doctors want to keep him overnight to make sure there aren't any complications, since he was unconscious for so long. They said it was a miracle."

"Can we see him?" I say eagerly. I can't help myself. After everything that's happened today, I can't wait to see him. I *have* to see him.

"Give them a minute, will you, mijo?" Ma tries to tell me, but I don't care to listen.

"It's okay," Erik's mom says. "Come on, we'll go together." She goes through the double doors and I start to follow, but stop momentarily to look back at Mackenzie. I'm surprised to see that she's not following me.

"You're not coming?" I ask.

"You go," Mackenzie says. "I'll see him in a bit." At first, there's a part of me that thinks she's being ridiculous, but then she nods, nudging me to go on ahead, and I get it. I know what she's doing, and I owe her a massive "thank you" for it.

When we get to the room, Erik's mom and I stand just outside the threshold. I can see Erik's dad standing beside the bed. My stomach is in knots. I feel this crazy sensation in my gut, like a million butterflies are dancing in a whirlwind. I don't think I've ever been this nervous in my life. Not for anyone. Until now. Erik's mom goes into the room and joins Erik's dad at the bedside. I decide to take my mom's advice and wait, so

Erik and his family can have a moment together. I'm trying to think of what to say, mentally rehearsing for the dialogue I'm about to have. Should I just lead with "I'm sorry. I love you?" Is that too much? Is that even appropriate considering how we got here in the first place? God, I'm such a mess.

"You alright?" Erik's dad asks when he steps out of the room a little while later.

"No," I reply, shaking my head. Really, I should be the one asking *him* that question, but he seems to be holding it together pretty well all things considered. Erik's dad nods understandingly. He places a firm hand on my shoulder and looks me right in the eye. Even though he's, maybe, four inches shorter than me, I'm finding it rather intimidating. I guess that's an ability you gain when you level up to Dad Status.

"You're the one that Erik wrote the letter to, right? Nicholas?"

"Yeah." I nod. He nods. I'm not sure where this is going or what Erik's dad's thinking, but this exchange is making me increasingly uncomfortable.

"So, how do you feel about him?" he says. The way he delivers the question is neither angry nor accusatory, but gentle and curious, as if he actually cares to know. My emotions overwhelm me, and I feel a tear escape. I have to bite my bottom lip just to keep myself from breaking down again. Erik's dad wipes the tear from my cheek and offers a warm smile. "Why don't you tell him?" I nod. He then leads me into the room, where I can see Erik lying in the bed. He looks small and pale, worn from everything he's been through. When he looks up at me, he seems surprised. I guess I can't blame him. "Chris, let's give the boys a minute, yeah?" Erik's mom turns to us. She seems to consider something before nodding and leaving Erik's bedside. "Go on," Erik's dad urges me, and then I'm alone… with Erik. He's staring at me with a blank expression and it's making it difficult for me to return his gaze.

"Hey," I manage, overcoming my hesitation.

"Hey," Erik responds with a small voice.

"I, uh… I'm glad you're okay."

"Thanks. The doctors want me to stick around to make sure I don't start acting funny, you know?"

"Makes sense. Kinda puts a damper on Thanksgiving though," I say, forcing a chuckle. God, I'm so awkward. Erik shrugs. It's weird. He seems so far away from me, so closed off, I worry that there might be no coming back from this. I messed up. I hurt him, so much so that he went and jumped in a pool knowing full well he can't swim. I'm responsible for that. "I'm sorry," I say, deciding to bite the bullet. "I didn't mean what I said before. This wasn't a mistake, you and me. When you told me you loved me, I… freaked out. I… I panicked and…

I said the first stupid thing that came into my head, but I didn't mean it. I got scared, you know?"

"Scared of what?" Erik asks.

"Everything," I reply. I pause for a moment, considering what to say next. I mean, I want to be honest and tell him that I think I'm in love with him, but I can't get past the fact that he nearly died. I can't even begin to fathom how he must've felt to resort to doing what he did, no matter how heartbroken he must've been. "How could you do that, Erik? How could you jump in the pool like that?" At this point, I'm full on crying. I can't keep the tears from falling despite my best efforts. Meanwhile, Erik lays there seemingly unaffected. I make my way over to his bedside and grab onto the railings of the hospital bed. All of these feelings got me weak in the knees, I need to hold on to something just to keep myself steady.

"It's not what you think," he begins to explain. "I wasn't trying to hurt myself... and I didn't wanna die."

"Then what was it?" Erik takes a moment then lets out a deep sigh.

"You know that dream I've been having? Being at the pool reminded me of it; the raging water, the crashing storm, all of it. It all felt like... this is it. This is my dream and — I know this is gonna sound stupid — but I've been wanting to see it through to the end. Something was telling me that I had to, you know, jump in the pool. If I jumped in the pool and I had a little bit of faith, everything would be okay. Somehow everything would make sense. I don't know, it's hard to explain. But as soon as I hit the water, I felt like… everything *would* be okay. Like *I* would be okay."

"Luckily, you are okay," I tell him.

"But I'm not," he says. This is the moment when Erik cracks. Gone is his unaffected facade. Tears start to form in his eyes and his voice breaks as he continues to speak. "I'm not okay. Look at me, I'm a mess. I'm a broken down, sad, pathetic mess, who couldn't even save himself, and I hate that. I hate that I needed someone to rescue me. I hate that I need people so much."

"It's okay for you to need people, Erik."

"No, it's not. Because that's not fair. It's not fair."

"What isn't fair?" I ask him.

"This," Erik answers. "The way that I am. The way that we are. People like us aren't supposed to fall in love. Because, if we did…" He lets his voice trail off for a moment. Then, rather than finishing his previous thought, he says, "It's not fair, because I did." Damn… He beat me to the punch. Again.

"So did I," I say, leaning in. Erik gazes at me with a look of uncertainty. Our eyes lock together, his searching for some sort of confirmation and mine attempting to offer it. "I'm in love with you, Erik. I'm in love with the way that you always look so nervous and concerned about everything. I'm in love with the way that you wear your heart on your sleeve, and how bad you are at lying. I'm in love with how gentle, innocent, and careful you are when it comes to… everything, basically. I fell for all of your little quirks. I fell for all of it. I fell for you." Erik stares at me with wide eyes full of disbelief.

"Are you just saying that because I jumped in the pool and almost drowned?" he asks, wearing a cautious expression. I shake my head.

"No. I mean it. I was just too stupid to realize it before," I insist. Erik looks so delicate just lying there staring up at me. I want to hold him. I want to protect him. I want to be the guy that comes to his rescue. I want to be the person that he needs. I want him. I want Erik. "I really want to kiss you right now, but I'm scared I'll take your breath away," I say.

"So cheesy," Erik replies, completely killing the mood. I can't help but laugh.

"You did almost drown." At this, Erik smiles, albeit weakly.

"Nicholas, I want to believe you when you say that you love me, but… I don't know if I do. It just seems really convenient if I'm being honest." Clearly, Erik is not entirely convinced and frankly, if I were him, I wouldn't be either. I mean, he's right. The timing is super convenient, and after keeping everything up in the air for a month, I fully understand that I'm not exactly the guy that you'd feel most comfortable getting into a relationship with. That being said, now that I know how I feel, I have not a single doubt in my mind that I, Nicholas Ray Santiago, am in love with Erik Alan Tolentino Park and, damn it, I need another shot.

"Look, Erik, I'm sorry," I say, taking his hand in mine and lacing our fingers together. "I can't promise that I won't hurt you again, but I'm gonna do my best not to. Because whether you need people or not, I need you. I want you. All I ask is that you let me try again, but for real this time."

"Not just hanging out?" Erik asks warily.

"Not just hanging out." He considers this for a few moments. I can see he's hesitating, which actually makes me really nervous to hear what his answer is gonna be. I wait anxiously whilst he has me suspended in Limbo for what feels like eternity. He thinks, and thinks, and thinks. Finally, Erik opens his mouth and begins the words that will put me out of my misery.

"Okay," he says, and it's official. We're gonna give this thing another go.

This time, with feeling.

epilogue *erik*

Merry Christmas Eve!

It's been about a month since the whole pool incident and, thankfully, I haven't experienced any complications. Not physically anyway. For the first week or so, it felt like everyone who knew about my near-death experience was walking on eggshells around me, which was really uncomfortable. I guess I can't blame them. It was just difficult because I felt like I was constantly defending myself, having to explain over and over again that I wasn't trying to hurt myself. Though it's not exactly the easiest thing to explain given my actions. To be honest, I think the reason I've had such a hard time getting people to understand why I did what I did is because, some days, I'm not even sure I understand why I did what I did. All I know is that when I was standing at the edge of the pool, I heard something. There was a voice telling me that everything was gonna be okay. All I had to do was trust that it would be.

I don't know. Maybe I'm just a drama queen. Maybe I just enjoy the theatrics of it all. Like, look at this brave soul who overcame this tremendous obstacle. What a terrible way to think. It's crazy really, because the whole situation, in a way, sort of restored my faith. Is that crazy? I don't know. Maybe *I'm* crazy. Maybe I'm just blindly optimistic. But I like to think that the voices in my head were a divine intervention. Corny, right?

Anyway, after everyone settled down with their worries, life started to get better. Mackenzie and I made up, as we always do. She and I had a long heart-to-heart where she explained to me that she felt I was replacing her as my best friend. And, in a way, I was, but that doesn't mean she's any less important. It just means that our friendship has to adapt to all the changes in our lives. Mom agreed to start lightening up about the whole religion thing. She even started asking me if I'd *like* to go to church, rather than just flat out telling me to go, which gives the illusion of choice. Though I know she'd be disappointed if I ever declined. And Dad's… Dad. He's probably been the cause for the least amount of conflict since the whole gay thing came up, but that's what I love about him. He's reliable. As for me and Nicholas, well...

"Knock, knock," my *boyfriend* says, with a duffel bag slung over his shoulder, standing at the threshold of my bedroom. He's a sight to behold, dressed in a pair of slim fitted khakis, a pink button up, and a navy blazer.

"Oh, you look nice," I tell him. "Very well put together." I stand up from my desk as Nicholas enters my room. I notice something different about him. "You pierced your ears."

"I did. Got it done this morning. It was something I've been wanting to do for a while, but I never did. You know, macho insecurities."

"Ah, well, I like it."

"Oh, yeah?" Nicholas flashes his perfectly crooked smile and pulls me close to him, his hands resting dangerously low beneath the small of my back. Then he kisses me softly. "So, where can I shove my bag?"

"Anywhere is fine," I say. "Make yourself comfortable."

"You know, I still can't believe your parents agreed to let me spend the night," Nicholas explains, setting his duffle bag down beside my bed.

"Truth be told, I had to do some bargaining. I told them this could be my Christmas gift." Nicholas raises his eyebrows flirtatiously. "Except, we gotta keep the door open." His expression falls and he nods, playfully disappointed.

"Damn," he replies, taking a seat on my bed. "So, I was thinking, would you want to go for a quick drive with me? I want a little bit of time alone with you before all your relatives get here for the party."

My family celebrates the Christmas holiday on Christmas Eve. It's usually a dinner potluck that goes on till midnight when we open all the gifts. Then everyone either slowly starts to leave or falls asleep wherever they can find a space. Much to the dismay of my wealthy uncle with the fully stocked bar, my parents insisted that we have the celebration at our house this year. I mentioned in passing how much I didn't look forward to family gatherings, and since we were still in the midst of my parents walking on eggshells with me, I guess they took it as a hint. A really big hint at that. I'm just thankful that they agreed to keep our extended family in the dark about the pool incident. My parents and I agreed to tell everyone that I had been stricken with a serious bout of pneumonia, which was why we didn't show up for Thanksgiving. I know it's a complete lie, but it was easier than giving up the truth. My mom was surprisingly okay with that explanation when my dad suggested it. It's better this way, I think. They can't be shamed for their parenting, and I wouldn't want them to be.

"Yeah, sure," I say, to answer Nicholas' question. I pull on the gray cardigan he put on me the day I jumped, which he let me keep — it's since become my new favorite sweater — and we head downstairs. Dad is busy setting up some chairs and a fold out table while Mom arranges and rearranges her dessert display with an assortment of homemade desserts including ube, leche flan, and puto. Nicholas got a kick out of it when he found out what puto was, since it's one of the few words he knows in Spanish. Dad and I got a good laugh out of it too when Nicholas explained it. Mom was a little less amused, but at least she's been welcoming to him.

"Where are you two going?" Mom asks when she notices us heading for the door.

"Just taking a quick drive," I explain.

"We'll only be gone a few minutes. Promise," Nicholas assures.

"Oh, let them go, Chris," Dad interjects. "It's not like either one of them is gonna come back pregnant."

"Ay, bastos!" Mom scolds Dad who simply rolls his eyes, shaking his head. "Nicholas, are your Mom and uncle coming tonight?"

"My uncle might stop by, but Ma's gotta work."

"How's the diner treating her?" Dad asks.

"She complains about her feet a lot, but I think she likes it. She's making her own money now, which she's really proud of."

"That's good." Dad nods.

After the pleasantries with my parents, which took way longer than they should have, Nicholas and I hop into his car and he proceeds to drive us somewhere. He won't tell me where though.

"Where are we going?" I ask.

"You'll see," he responds. "Somewhere special."

We pull into the parking lot of the park with the community pool. I hadn't been back here since the day I almost drowned. What are we doing here, I wonder? Nicholas climbs out of the driver's seat and runs around the car to grab something from the trunk. I let myself out and he takes me by the hand, boyfriend style with our fingers all laced together, leading me across the parking lot up to the paved path.

"Nicholas, what are we doing here?"

"You know, you're the only person that calls me Nicholas," he says, completely ignoring my question. "Everyone else calls me Nick. Even my mom calls me by a *Nick*name."

"But Nick's not your name."

"You got me there."

"Do you want me to call you Nick?" I ask, as we come to a stop beside the fence surrounding the pool.

"I want you to call me whatever you want to call me," he replies, all smooth and sexy-like. "Babe, Love,

Boy-fren-lavin." I narrow my eyes and give him a playful backhanded smack on his shoulder.

"You're making fun of me!" He just laughs. It's obnoxious, but I enjoy it. When the moment settles, he reaches into the gift bag — the thing he retrieved from the trunk — and hands me a stack of paper, all hole punched and tied together neatly with a bit of yarn.

"Merry Christmas."

"Your drawings!" I exclaim, my mouth dropping in awe. "You actually made them into a comic book?"

"Yeah. Do you like it?" He says, wearing a somewhat nervous smirk.

"I do, but… are you sure you don't want to keep it?"

"Well, I made it for you so…" Wow, I'm so surprised by this, I don't even know what to say. It's the best gift anyone's ever given me, I can't help but thank him with a kiss. I haven't exactly gotten comfortable with PDA, but at the moment, I don't care. There's no one else around anyway. "I got something else for you too," Nicholas goes on. He then reaches into the gift bag and hands me a padlock, on which he's written E&N 11/27 in permanent marker.

"What's this?"

"Our initials, plus the date we became official."

"I got that, but why the padlock?"

"Well, remember when we went to the city? I remember seeing all these padlocks on the fences and stuff, and I got curious. So I did some research and, apparently, people use these as a symbol of their love, lock them onto something like a bridge or whatever, and then throw the keys away in the ocean. That's why we're at the pool. This is where everything happened for us." I can feel the tears welling in my eyes. Nicholas put so much thought into this and I'm in absolute awe. It's hard to believe that this guy, this thoughtful, loving, and beautiful guy is… mine. Where did I go right in all this? "Shit, you're crying. You hate it," Nicholas says in a panic. I shake my head.

"No, I love it. I just… I'm a mess." I laugh. He laughs. We laugh together.

"Come on, let's find a place for this. Somewhere where they won't cut it down."

Nicholas and I settle on a spot on the fence behind a bush. I want this padlock to be here forever, so I suggest we avoid putting it in plain view. It could be our special thing. Something that only he and I know. Something that only he and I would be able to find. Once the padlock's secured, Nicholas gestures for us to climb the fence.

We stand at the edge of the pool, hand in hand, side by side, looking over the water. After what happened, I never imagined I'd be looking at this place with such fondness. But the bad memories get drowned out when I think about who I'm standing with and how we shared our first kiss here. Nicholas offers me the key to the padlock and smiles. I hold it tightly in my hands, thinking back on everything that's happened. It's crazy to think that only a few months ago, I was a different person. It's crazy to think how much I went through and how much we've been through together in this short period. But I believe that, with a little bit of faith, you could come out better for it. I did. And I drop the key into the pool, never to be seen again.

At night, I wake up with a start. I had the dream again. The island, the boat, the storm, and the seas. I revisited all of it for the first time since I nearly drowned and, though all of it was more or less the same, one thing was different.

"Nicholas, are you awake?" I whisper. He's lying in my bed next to me. I can only somewhat make out his features from the little bit of moonlight seeping in through my bedroom window, but he's here. I can see as much.

"Hmm?" he groans, his eyes still shut. I scoot in closer to him so that the tip of his nose touches mine.

"I had the dream again." This is when he opens his eyes, albeit groggily and unfocused. He blinks a few times and squints, searching for me in the darkness.

"What happened?" He manages to say.

"That dream where I'm drowning. I had it again."

"I thought that was done with?"

"Me too. But it was different this time."

"Oh?"

"Yeah, I finally saw it through to the end."

"And how'd it turn out?"

I search his eyes for some assurance that this too isn't just a dream, but I'm not fully convinced. I pull my hand out from under my covers and place it gently on Nicholas' cheek. He's here. I can feel him. I can touch him. If he were to kiss me right now, I could taste him. This isn't a dream. This is real. And it's hard for me to believe it.

I take in a deep breath, preparing to tell Nicholas how my dream ended, but I'm only able to come up with two words. Nicholas is staring at me, patiently waiting for my response, which comes out in a whisper.

"I survived."

acknowledgements

I have tried to tell this story in many different ways over the years. It started as a screenplay. I adapted it into a musical. I drew comics of it that I posted onto Instagram. And now I'm here, having novelized the whole thing. I want to thank everybody who has made any contribution, big or small, to any iteration of this story. These characters and this story have become such a big part of my life that I'm just grateful to anyone who's helped in shaping them. That being said, I want to give particular thanks to…

… my husband, Richard. Without you I couldn't do half the things that I do or pursue half the things that I pursue. Thank you for supporting me in every way possible.

… Carla De Leon Zeitoune, you've been instrumental during the whole editing process. You keep my comma usage in check. Even though I'd keep adding and subtracting more every time I'd read through this.

… Nina Gosiengfiao, you've supported me every step of the way with this ever since I dug up the original screenplay and began working on this story again.

… the members of The Garage Theatre Group, all the actors who indulged me when I was pushing this story as a musical, to Director Robert Allan Ackerman for expressing interest and telling me that I have a voice.

… everyone who read earlier drafts of this manuscript or even earlier iterations of this story, including the comics I posted on Instagram. Unfortunately, I can't name everyone since there were so many whom I don't know personally, who simply found this story online through social media, Wattpad, or other manuscript sharing sites. All of the comments and feedback I received were incredibly helpful and encouraging.

… you, the reader. It's been quite a long road to get to this point. I've poured a lot of myself into these characters and into this story over the years; I just want to be able to share it with as many people as possible. Thank you for being a part of that. It really means the world to me.

about the author

Daryl Leonardo is a first time author. Born in the Philippines and raised in the San Francisco Bay Area, he began writing in order to create roles for himself whilst pursuing a career as an actor. He now resides in Los Angeles, California with his husband and two dogs, where he continues to take roles in independent projects and local theatre.

www.ingramcontent.com/pod-product-compliance
Lightning Source LLC
Chambersburg PA
CBHW031045110726
47900CB00003B/814